W9-ANB-891

The Winter List

Also by S. G. MacLean

THE ALEXANDER SEATON SERIES

The Redemption of Alexander Seaton
A Game of Sorrows
Crucible of Secrets
The Devil's Recruit

THE CAPTAIN DAMIAN SEEKER SERIES

The Seeker
The Black Friar
Destroying Angel
The Bear Pit
The House of Lamentations

STANDALONE
The Bookseller of Inverness

S. G. MACLEAN

The
Winter
List

QUERCUS

First published in Great Britain in 2023 by

QUERCUS
Quercus Editions Ltd
Carmelite House
50 Victoria Embankment
London EC4Y 0DZ

An Hachette UK company

Copyright © 2023 S. G. MacLean
Map © 2023 Nicola Howell Hawley

The moral right of S. G. MacLean to be
identified as the author of this work has been
asserted in accordance with the Copyright,
Designs and Patents Act, 1988.

All rights reserved. No part of this publication
may be reproduced or transmitted in any form
or by any means, electronic or mechanical,
including photocopy, recording, or any
information storage and retrieval system,
without permission in writing from the publisher.

A CIP catalogue record for this book is available
from the British Library

HB ISBN 978 1 5294 1 422 6
TPB ISBN 978 1 5294 1 423 3
EBOOK ISBN 978 1 5294 1 424 0

This book is a work of fiction. Names, characters,
businesses, organizations, places and events are
either the product of the author's imagination
or used fictitiously. Any resemblance to
actual persons, living or dead, events or
locales is entirely coincidental.

10 9 8 7 6 5 4 3

Typeset by CC Book Production
Printed and bound in Great Britain by Clays Ltd, Elcograf S.p.A.

Papers used by Quercus are from well-managed forests and other responsible sources.

To Eveline

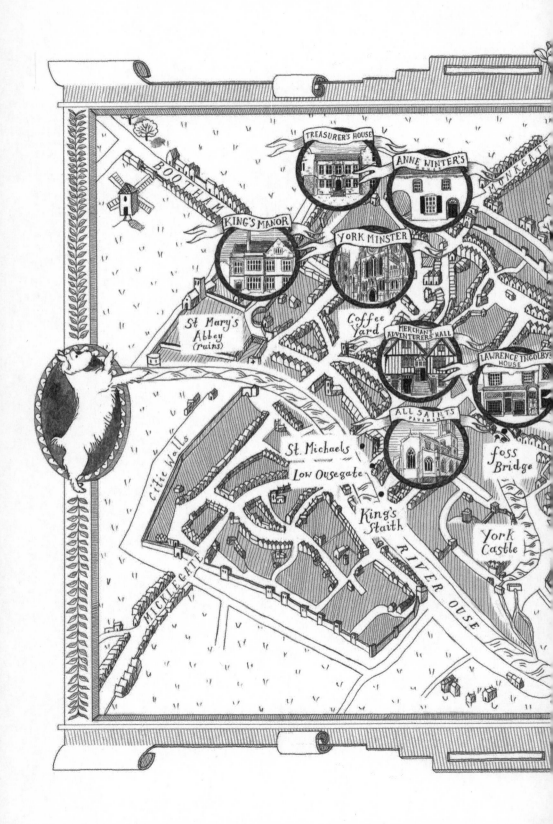

TREASURER'S HOUSE

ANNE WINTER'S HOUSE

KING'S MANOR

YORK MINSTER

BOOTHAM

MONKGATE

St Mary's Abbey (ruins)

Coffee Yard

MERCHANT ADVENTURER'S HALL

LAWRENCE INGOLBY'S HOUSE

ALL SAINTS PAVEMENT

City Walls

St. Michaels

Low Ousegate

King's Staith

Foss Bridge

York Castle

MICKLEGATE

RIVER OUSE

PROLOGUE

London

The pages yellowed then browned, smoke creeping along their undersides until the corners began to curl in on themselves. Letter by letter, words – that no one was in any case close enough to read – were consumed. Lawrence, though, like so many others in the crowd, did not need to see the print to know what they said – words written over eleven years since, to justify the killing of a king:

> . . . for their sakes who through custom, simplicitie or want of better teaching, have not more seriously considerd Kings, then in the gaudy name of Majesty, and admire them and thir doings as if they breath'd not the same breath with other mortal men . . .

At last the pages took light and John Milton's words flamed high into the summer's afternoon.

As the books burned, the city's executioner read out

Parliament's proclamation against the blind poet and his work, allowing for little doubt that should the authorities have been able to find the author of such sedition, they would happily have set him atop the pyre with his books.

'Where is he?' asked Lawrence Ingolby, under his breath.

'Safe,' said the man beside him, 'for now.' Andrew Marvell kept his voice low. 'But the Council of State is at this very minute busied with drawing up a list of those to be exempted from His Majesty's mercy.' The Act of Free and General Pardon, Indemnity and Oblivion that had been put before Parliament within days of Charles Stuart's agreement to return to England as King, enshrined within it his promise of clemency to his and his late father's enemies. Or at least it enshrined a promise of clemency to some of them, for the young King had astutely, almost casually, allowed that some of those enemies should be excepted from his mercy, although 'only such persons as shall hereafter be excepted by Parliament'. Major General Thomas Harrison had been the first to be excepted from that mercy, to be followed the next day by six of his former comrades, the most notorious of the regicides who had had the King's father's sacred head severed from its neck. More than forty names had been added the day after that.

The numbers grew and the parameters shifted beyond those individuals known to have tried and ordered the execution of the King. Next was ordered the search for the executioners. John Thurloe, who had held all in his hands under Cromwell, was arrested, and put in the Tower, his blood called for. It seemed, though, that somehow he would avoid the rope, the disembowelling hook, the flames and the axe. Perhaps John Thurloe knew too much about the innocence or otherwise of those now in power. At first, some men believing the King's promise of clemency had handed themselves in, only to be swiftly disabused of that notion. Others, seeing their fate or having guessed it in advance, fled to the continent or even the Americas. Almost daily, it seemed, the definition of guilt shifted, the list of those to be excepted from the royal mercy grew.

'John Milton's name's never on it?' In his surprise, Lawrence had forgotten that it was not entirely advisable for he and Marvell to be seen talking together.

Marvell grimaced. 'I have worked night and day to persuade them to take it off. I think His Majesty, thank God, is of a mind to be gracious to those that did not have an actual hand in his father's murder.'

Ingolby raised his eyebrows. The apparent ease with which Marvell had managed to pirouette from staunch Cromwellian and firm upholder of the Commonwealth to ardent Royalist still rendered him almost speechless. It had been the work of days, hours perhaps, or even a moment for his friend to amend his language and keep his job, and perhaps, for all either of them knew, his head. The clamour for revenge from the Royalists returned to Parliament grew louder by the day and neither Lawrence nor any of his acquaintance knew where it might stop.

Marvell flushed and raised his chin, avoiding Lawrence's eye. 'We all have a living to earn.'

'True enough,' said Lawrence, turning away from the spectacle and readying himself to go back to his own employment, which lay waiting for him in half-written depositions, indentures, articles of agreement and much else that was piled upon the desk and floor of his small chambers in Clifford's Inn. 'We can hope it's only the ones that put the old King on trial that have to worry . . .'

Marvell said nothing, merely shook his head.

The fire crackled and spat and all around them was laughter and jeering as the pyre of forbidden books went up in flames, but something in Marvell's look chilled Lawrence's very stomach.

Marvell affected to inspect a piece of ash that had landed on his collar as a woman selling peaches amongst the crowd passed close by them. He leaned a little closer to Lawrence and murmured, 'You should leave London, now.'

'Me?' Lawrence spluttered. 'What have I done? I wasn't twenty years old, still at home in Yorkshire, when the King was put on trial.'

'I know that,' said Marvel, still inspecting his collar. 'But there's another list.'

Lawrence looked at his friend as if he were mad. 'The Council of State's never going to bother themselves about me, Andrew.'

'You're not listening,' Marvell muttered, looking around

him a moment before leaning in closer. 'There's *another* list, that the King and the Council of State know nothing about.'

'What?' Lawrence's mockery gave way to apprehension. 'What kind of list?'

'One drawn up by an individual impatient that King and Parliament will not dig deep enough, and hell-bent upon his own revenge.'

Lawrence's eyes were wide. 'Who?'

Marvell shook his head again.

'But you're saying my name's on it?'

Marvell lowered his voice even further. 'No. But Damian Seeker's is. You must go back to Yorkshire, and you must take the captain's daughter with you.'

The peach seller watched Andrew Marvell go off in one direction while Lawrence Ingolby went in the other. Ingolby would be returning, no doubt, to his chambers at Clifford's Inn. It was too early in the day for the lawyer to repair to the Black Fox on Broad Street, where he had lodged for the last four years and where his young wife had been in the employ and protection of the landlady since first she had arrived in London. Marvell looked constantly to his left and right. Well, many nowadays had especial cause to look about them, lest they come under the scrutiny of those not quite convinced by their protestations of loyalty to the restored King. Marvell did right to take care.

Without shifting her gaze, the peach seller suddenly grabbed at the wrist of a young thief whose hand had darted into her basket. She turned it firmly before placing two plump fruits into the upturned palm and telling the child to be gone. As the boy ran off with his booty, she left Lawrence Ingolby to his business, for now, and set her course after Andrew Marvell. The peach seller was not entirely fooled by the Whitehall under-secretary's volte-face of loyalty, but then she had never been entirely convinced of his commitment to the Republican cause, either. As she went after him she was forced to concede that he was getting better at this, at moving discreetly without drawing undue attention to himself. Everyone learns, when their life is at stake. Even so, she had been at this business for longer than he and was not so easily shaken off. He was going to see Milton, she was sure of it. She followed at a distance as he walked unhurriedly away from the crowd around Old Bailey and out through Newgate. She quickened her step in time with his when he turned up Giltspur Street. Smithfield. There had been rumours already that Milton was holed up somewhere in Smithfield. The blind poet had certainly been hiding himself somewhere since May, when it had become clear even to him that the Republic could not hold and that the Stuarts must return. She wondered if he could smell the smoke of his own burning books over the reek and fear of the animals at market.

Marvell was almost at Pye Corner when she saw him suddenly pull up short, hesitate and then turn back down towards Holborn. Beyond him, coming down the street towards her, were two officers of the King's Regiment of

Guards. She arranged her hood better around her face as she approached them with her basket. The nearer of the two – she recalled him from Brussels – waved her away, and she continued up the street. She glanced down in time to see Marvell disappear around the corner of St Sepulchre's, whose bell was ringing the half hour, reminding her she had an appointment of her own and must leave the poet to his wanderings.

Roger L'Estrange sat in his cabinet in the little house that backed onto Palace Yard. It wasn't much, but it would suit his purposes, for now. There was such a clamour for places at Whitehall that he had been lucky to make good a claim to anything at all. The little house was convenient, after all, for the chamber of the Commons, and the MPs over whom his pamphlets and arguments were increasingly bringing him influence. He was not yet quite as successful as he would like to be in persuading others to his views, but then, as his grandmother had been wont to say, there was more than one way to skin a cat. Here, L'Estrange was close enough to the royal presence to make himself familiar, whilst being far enough away from the noise of court life to get on with his business unimpeded. The King's heart was too soft for his own good, and too inclined to forgiveness. Parliament, which had no heart at all, was too taken up with its own interests. Many who had profited from and enabled Cromwell's regime would be let off the hook, for no better reason than that they had the right friends. And some, that ought even now to be languishing in the Tower of London awaiting trial for their treason, had fled altogether. This didn't trouble L'Estrange as much as it might have done – they would be apprehended and dealt with by the proper authorities, in time. His own interest, though, was another thing altogether. *His* interest went beyond that of the established authorities. *His* interest went beyond dealing with those who had sat in judgement on the King and signed their names to his death warrant. *His* interest was in the others, in those who had not been amongst the men of power, and so believed their deeds to have been unremarked or forgotten. Roger L'Estrange was determined to find them and to lay bare their secrets.

He glanced up from his list, his pen paused a little above the paper so that a drip of ink fell upon it without his noticing. He was sure he could detect the slightest hint, just a ribbon, of smoke in the air. Not the smoke of sea coals and a hundred Whitehall fires, but of pages curling and burning, calfskin bindings crackling in the flames. It gave him satisfaction to think of that smoke curling under the doors of those who fancied they might hide themselves from retribution. The moment was broken by the tentative knock of his clerk on the door.

'A woman wishes to see you, sir.'

'What kind of woman?'

'A peach seller.'

In any other gentleman's house, a woman selling peaches would not have got beyond the kitchen at best, but L'Estrange's servants knew that this was another sort of house. A moment later the peach seller had been shown into his cabinet and the door closed behind her.

He didn't invite her to sit. 'Well?'

She made her report. There had been a significant crowd there at Old Bailey, at the first burning of Milton's books. One or two printers and booksellers amongst them, in fact, had been keen to show their support for the new regime by handing over any of the condemned works that might be lying about their stores or presses.

'Hmmph.' L'Estrange knew that the most obdurate amongst the Republican printers would not have been there. They would be dealt with, come time. Roger's patron, Henry Bennet, had promised him the post of Surveyor of the Press, perhaps more. In the meantime, there was other business to be attended to. 'And who amongst his friends was there? Marvell? Davenant?' The latter had been loud, the former persistent, in their pleas on the blind poet's behalf. In Cromwell's time, Milton had used his influence to save Davenant from the executioner, and the playwright, now in his pomp, was determined to repay the debt. As for Marvell, what he did not owe to Milton he owed to Cromwell. L'Estrange was unconvinced by the turn in Marvell's loyalties.

'Marvell was there,' his informant told him.

Roger felt a little jolt of satisfaction.

'Alone?'

'No, he was talking to a lawyer friend of his. Lawrence Ingolby.'

'The name means nothing to me. Should it?'

The woman appeared to be considering. He found her irritating, but most of the female intelligencers he knew had abandoned their trade, now that the King was back, and there was not a large pool to choose from. 'I don't believe so. He's a lawyer at Clifford's Inn, and was pupil to a man named Ellingworth, who was radical in his views. Ellingworth left for Massachusetts shortly after Cromwell's death, but Ingolby seems to have shown no inclination to go with him. A coming man, they say.'

'"A coming man."' L'Estrange smiled. 'The best kind — not inclined to offer trouble to the prevailing authority. And what did they speak of, Marvell and this Ingolby?'

'Of John Milton,' she said.

'And?'

'Marvell knows where he is but didn't tell Ingolby. Just that he was safe, and that he was fighting to get him off the list of names excepted from the King's mercy.'

'Did they speak of anything else?'

There was the slightest pause before she said, 'No.'

He regarded her closely. 'You're certain?'

'Nothing within my hearing.' He would have pressed her more closely on that but now she was telling him how she had followed Marvell and where he had gone.

'Smithfield?'

She nodded. 'He turned back quite suddenly when he saw two of the King's Guard approaching. I'm all but certain he was on his way to see Milton.'

'Hmm,' L'Estrange mused. 'I'll have a search party sent to Smithfield.'

She picked up her basket and made to leave, but he held up a hand. 'Not quite yet, if you please.'

She stopped. 'I have nothing more to tell you.'

'But I have something to tell you, or to give you. Sit down, please.'

The woman's expression was wary, but she sat.

'I believe you were still on the Continent when Richard Cromwell was brought down by the grandees of his own army?'

'I was,' she said. 'But the news was not long in reaching me.'

'Nor me,' he said. The news of the collapse of the Protectorate had been a golden moment in L'Estrange's life.

'And were you aware that John Thurloe was removed from his post as director of the usurping regime's espionage at the same time?'

'To be replaced by the regicide Thomas Scott, I understand.'

She was well informed. Good – it would save time.

'Thurloe,' he continued, 'remains in the Tower. I and others have made efforts to have him excluded from the King's mercy, but our pleas appear to have fallen upon deaf ears, and he is unlike to be tried for his life.'

Her views on the likely fate of John Thurloe were impossible to gauge. He continued to his point. 'Thomas Scott is also in the Tower.'

Some surprise flitted across her face. 'I thought he had fled England,' she said, 'got himself abroad.'

'Yes, he had. As far as Brussels, where he became acquainted with how greatly the affairs of the world have turned.' Scott, who had bragged of his part in the murder of the King, had been taken in the Spanish Netherlands. There he had misconceived, or been encouraged to misconceive, the meaning of the King's language in the Act of Oblivion. L'Estrange's voice hardened. 'Thomas Scott was "persuaded" to return home. They'll all be caught in the end, one way or the other.'

'And what will happen to him?'

L'Estrange sniffed, as if he were being asked about the fate of a kitchen boy who had not come up to the mark. 'Thomas Scott's name is on the King's death warrant, whereas John Thurloe's is not. Scott seeks to bargain for his life. He thinks to obtain mercy in exchange for information, but he has spoken too often of his pride in his part in the murder of God's anointed. His information will not save him.'

'And yet?'

'And yet,' he said, 'what has been extracted from him is of use to us.' He indicated the paper in front of him. 'This is a list of names of those who were in His Majesty's circle in exile and whom Scott asserts spied for the Protectorate. *Traitors*, in other words.'

She glanced towards the paper but he had made sure to shield it with his arm. 'Other than those we already knew of?' she asked.

'Some of those whom we already knew of were dealt with as their names were discovered. Others that were turned once have been turned again, and now spy for us. They are the fortunate ones. The names on *this* list, however, Thomas Scott's list, are of those he claims have got away with their treachery to His Majesty and who have sought to blend back into a retired life, or even one of influence, now that His Majesty has returned.'

She frowned. 'Scott may well have made it up, this list of names. Out of spite, or to gain himself time, or mercy.'

He nodded. She really was quite intelligent. 'That is my concern. I have no desire that the innocent should be punished because of one man's malice. I am too closely associated with powerful men to be able to go where I would need to or ask the requisite questions to establish the truth or otherwise of what Thomas Scott has said.'

He saw that she understood.

'But I am not,' she said.

'Precisely.'

She put out her hand, clearly expecting him to give her the list, but he held it back from her. 'I think it's best that you focus your attentions on one subject at the time. You are less likely to raise suspicions that way.' He wrote one name and a set of dates on a small piece of paper and handed it to her, along with a purse. 'Find out where this individual was between these dates, what he was doing, who he was in contact with. Write to me when you have done so – not here, but to the safe house I have indicated.

That being done, I will send you further funds, and the next name, and the location of the next safe postal drop. You do not need to come here again.'

She took the paper in one hand, glanced at it a moment then handed it back to him with a nod. The purse she put in the small bag hanging from her own girdle. She picked up her basket and went to the door. 'Goodbye, Mr L'Estrange,' she said.

He blew sand across the words he had just written at the top of the paper.

The Winter List

'Farewell, Lady Anne,' he said.

Roger L'Estrange was still looking at the list of names, wondering how long it would take her to work through it, establish the truth or otherwise of what Thomas Scott had said, when his clerk again knocked on his door.

'What now?' he said, with some impatience.

'Godric Purvis is here, sir.'

'Purvis?' Roger inspected the clock on the wall. He had spent longer talking with Anne Winter than he had intended to. 'Let him in.'

Purvis came in, wiping his mouth on his sleeve, a ripe peach dripping juice onto the fingers of his right hand. L'Estrange felt his annoyance kindle.

'Where did you get that?'

Purvis glanced at the fruit in his hand. 'There was a woman, as I was coming through the yard . . .'

L'Estrange wondered if he had misjudged Purvis. He preferred that his agents knew nothing of each other. Clearly, Purvis had had no suspicions of Anne Winter, but he was not confident that she would have had none of him. No matter. 'Come in,' he said. 'And close the door behind you. I don't need half of Whitehall knowing my business.'

A glint of interest appeared in Purvis's eyes.

L'Estrange explained to Godric Purvis what was to be expected, any day now, from the King's Act of Indemnity and Oblivion, of the debate raging in the corridors of Whitehall over whose names should be on the condemned list and therefore excepted from King Charles's unfathomable mercy. The paltry seven names on the list to begin with had been an insult to the martyred King's memory. But the list was growing, and if L'Estrange had any say in matters, it would continue to grow. Purvis nodded. Everyone in England knew who the most notorious regicides were.

L'Estrange took out his pipe. He did not offer one to Purvis. 'But there were two involved,' he continued, 'that had a very hand indeed in the murder of the King but whose names are not known.' He watched Purvis for a moment and saw a spark of understanding then a smile creep across the lips. He had it.

'The executioners,' said Purvis.

'Exactly. Or more precisely, one of them – the one who wielded the axe.'

Purvis nodded, then started to voice his ideas. Ideas straight from the coffee houses, from the draughty alleyways around the Inns of Court and Chancery. But L'Estrange had his own idea about who had been the heavily disguised man who had swung the axe before an astonished crowd on that freezing cold January day in 1649 and severed the head of England's anointed King from his body. He knew who it had been, he was certain of it. He told Purvis.

Purvis narrowed his brows and frowned. 'Are you sure? Is he even still alive? I've heard of him all right – but no one has seen him for years.'

'Oh, Damian Seeker is alive all right.' He could feel it. His hatred of the man crawled beneath his skin, the years, the defeats, the humiliations, the plans he had laid so carefully that Seeker had found out. Roger would have been much further advanced in his career, stood much higher in the King's counsels – where for the moment he did not stand at all – had it not been for Damian Seeker. 'Others might be fooled but I am not. And wherever on God's earth he might be, I will have him found and I will have him brought to justice.'

ONE

Whitehall, London

Two years later. October 1662

Samuel Pepys was strolling down King Street, musing on a ditty he had heard that morning from one of Lord Sandwich's clerks. He would sing it to his wife tonight, when they were alone. He was considering whether he should cut down to the right and take a boat downriver, to enjoy his dinner at home as he had said he would, when a dunt on the shoulder jolted him out of his reverie and almost into the path of an oncoming butcher's boy.

'Good Lord!' he said, stepping swiftly one way as the butcher's boy deftly stepped the other and a well-set man with a close-cropped brown beard and a ruddy complexion mumbled something that might have been an apology. Pepys was still brushing at the shoulder of his jacket when something in the other fellow's gait caught his eye. 'William?'

The man stopped.

'William Briar!'

Now the fellow turned and after a moment's puzzlement,

a look of recognition dawned on his face, to be followed by a smile.

'Sam Pepys? Surely not! When in the world did you grow so fine?'

'Or you so clumsy?' said Sam, embracing his old friend before taking him by the arm. 'But we are a mere step from the Dog – come, let us get a bit of dinner there and you can tell me all your news. What on earth has brought you back down to London? I thought we had quite lost you to the north.'

'Would that you had,' said Briar, and then in response to Sam's look of astonishment he tapped the flap of the leather satchel that was slung across his body. 'Business,' he said. And then, his voice lowered, 'With the Duke of Buckingham.'

Sam had not expected this. News touching the interests of the Duke of Buckingham was not the sort of thing a prudent man would bandy about anywhere in London, still less within the very gates of Whitehall itself. He too lowered his voice. 'With Buckingham?' he said, sending an involuntary glance to William's satchel.

'Some plans he has had me draw up, pertinent to his forthcoming duties as His Majesty's lord lieutenant in the north,' said Briar. His tone suggested that further talk of the duke and his business would be unwelcome.

Sam did not need a second hint and it was with some relief that he led the way through the door of the Dog. 'But it is quite marvellous to see you again, William,' he said, when they had secured a table in the snug. 'I had all but given you up for dead.'

'I have been in York little more than a year, Sam.'

'Indeed. Which is a year longer than I could stomach it, I am sure.'

William took a moment to send a glance from Sam's fashionably shod feet to the lately purchased hat on his head. 'I don't doubt it. You appear to have become a man of fashion.'

'Oh, hardly that,' said Sam, colouring, 'but one must take care to secure one's position, and much depends on the face one presents to the world.' Then pausing a moment to take in the sober brown suit of his companion, he coughed. 'In London, at least. For my actual self, I am as I ever was.'

'I'm glad to hear it,' said William, great warmth in his brown eyes.

They were a good hour and a half in the Dog, washing down their dishes of bacon and beans with first one and then another bottle of sack. Sam relayed which plays he had been to see lately and warned William most strenuously against *A Midsummer Night's Dream*. 'Do not even consider wasting your time on it – not two lines of sense together in the whole thing.'

William interjected that he had no interest in the theatre, and was determined to be on a boat for Hull the very minute his appointments in London were finished. Sam shook his head in dismay, then prattled on, of his service for my Lord Sandwich, of his prospects at the Navy Office, of his happiness and tribulations with his wife. And then he stopped.

'Oh, my dear fellow, I am so sorry. I have let my tongue run on so, where I should not.'

Briar smiled. 'It does me good to hear of your happiness, Sam.'

'And yet, it was thoughtless of me, and I hope it will never be said of me that I would cause pain to a friend.'

William shook his head. 'Never.' He pushed a solitary bean around his now empty wooden platter. 'I see you have heard my history, though. I suppose it has been round all the offices.'

Sam did not attempt to deny it. William Briar's betrothal to the pretty daughter of a York cooper and then her jilting of him at the altar in favour of another man had been news amongst the offices of Whitehall for a day, two even, until new and better wonders had taken its place.

'And she did marry this other fellow, I suppose?' ventured Sam.

William nodded.

'Then may she long rue her folly.'

William gave a tight smile. 'Don't say that, Sam. All in all, he's a decent enough sort that she has married. Honest. A stonemason.'

Sam pushed out his lip. 'You're a better man than I, William. I would have had her up for breach of promise.'

'Oh, I thought of it, at first. Threatened all sorts, but my lawyer persuaded me that none would benefit from such a course but him, and so I thought better of it.'

'An honest lawyer?' said Sam. 'Then I would counsel you to stay in York, for you will find precious few of the sort in London! Ah, wait. Of course – Lawrence Ingolby.'

William smiled. 'I have lost a wife but found a friend, and over time I think I may have done better by the bargain.'

'But he is in town just now too – I took my dinner with him only the other day.'

'I know. I had hoped to travel back up with him, but His Grace's business made me miss other appointments, and now I must wait an extra day to make them up before I can return to York.'

William's other appointments being at Custom House quay, at the eastern end of the city and not far from the Navy Office, Pepys suggested they might take a boat together from Scotland Dock. They had got perhaps halfway across Scotland Yard when a figure emerged from the back door of the small house Sam knew to be occupied by Roger L'Estrange. He felt his mouth contort at the very thought of the man and was about to express his views on the journalist to William Briar when he realised that William had stopped and was staring after the figure who'd come out of L'Estrange's house.

William called after the person now going quickly down the passageway towards the gate leading back out onto Whitehall, but aside from a momentary glance and a brief hesitation in the step of the other, his calls appeared to go unheard. He called again, but this time there could be no doubt that he was positively ignored.

'What's the matter?' Sam asked of William who was now in a state of some consternation.

'That fellow, I know him from York, but he's ignoring me.'

'So it appears,' said Sam. 'Perhaps he owes you money?'

William made no reply, and looked to be on the point of following after the other when another acquaintance came upon them and assured William that whoever it was he thought he might have seen, the man's name was Godric Purvis, and certainly not that which William had been calling.

TWO

Northumbria

Anne Winter sat by the turret window of the house high on the cliffs. Below her, the cottages and inn clustered about the harbour braced themselves against the malevolent storm. The wind rattled the panes in the windows, hurling bullets of hail against them with such venom that it was a wonder to her they didn't splinter in her face. Far beneath, grey waves crashed against rock, breaking, only to fall back and come again.

Anne's fingers were cold, a bloodless white to their tips. If Grizel came in, she would chide her and ask what point there was in her having set and lit the fire if Anne would not sit by it? The discarded core of an apple lay browning on the small console table by her empty armchair and the letter arrived in the night from London lay open on the hearth where she had left it. She took a long drink of her wine and set the glass down again to watch its red surge and fade in the crystal where the candlelight caught it.

In her mind, she went over again the words of L'Estrange's letter. He had opened with a commendation of the report she had lately sent him from Edinburgh and his sat-isfaction with the outcome of her investigations there. Anne took no pleasure in his praise – the more pleased he was with her information, the worse it would be for someone else. The icy tentacles of his interest found their way to the far reaches of His Majesty's kingdoms. Edinburgh had not been far enough away for his targets to escape him, just as Northumbria was not far enough away, and still less was York, and to York she must now go. There, on the hearth, appended to his paragraph of praise, was the name of the next man L'Estrange would have her investigate. Anne had known this name would be added to her list, eventually. She had had her own suspicions, long before now, but she had stashed them away, and hoped she would never have to confront them. Thomas Faithly.

York, England, some nights later

The flames of the fire Lawrence had made amongst the ancient broken tombs gave off a good warmth, but as dark-ness had fallen the sky had begun to dot with stars that signalled a hard frost. On the last few miles of his journey northwards, he had increasingly detected the smell of snow in the air. He tightened his arm around his wife's shoulders.

'You sure you're warm enough?' he asked.

She lowered the pewter cup of burned wine from her lips and laughed. 'That is the fourth time you have asked me.'

'I know,' he said, 'but if you should catch cold or take

a fever . . .' He gestured towards the swell of her stomach, visible beneath her heavy wrappings.

'I will not,' she said. 'This is a Yorkshire child, through and through. Were you and I not both raised on the moors? The cold is its birthright. Just think – there is no child heartier than our Lizzie.'

'That's true,' he said, 'but Lizzie was a summer bairn.'

She put up a hand to stroke his face. 'This winter child will be even stronger. I know it. Besides, these furs you have brought me from London would keep me warm on the top of Mickle Fell.'

He grinned. 'They're good, aren't they? London is awash with furs since the Russians came to town. Sam Pepys is full of talk of the great spectacle they made.'

She laughed. 'Sam is always full of talk, about everything.'

Lawrence was silent a moment and she gave his hand a squeeze. 'Do you miss London, your friends?'

He shook his head. 'Nah. This is the place for me. I'm in London plenty, anyway, though I hope to be there a good deal less once Thomas's case is done with. And I have friends enough to do me here – Thomas, William Briar . . .'

'I thought William might have travelled back from London with you.'

'He'd hoped to, but there's that much building going on at Whitehall it was taking him much longer than he'd planned to see the people he needed to see. He was as keen as me to get home, but Buckingham's business held him up. He was planning to get the next boat for Hull.'

'And what about Jed Penmore – did he truly like the town?'

'Oh, aye. No worries there. Knows what an opportunity looks like, that one. He'll make his mark. Took to the place like a native.'

'And you think he'll do well at Clifford's?'

Lawrence thought about his clerk. 'He's a bright enough lad, just needs a bit of polish. If he really thinks to get taken on by Sir Thomas, he needs to be at the Inns for a while. I'll send him back down to Clifford's in January and if all goes well, Thomas'll be in possession of his estate and looking for help with the management of it by the time Jed's finished down there.' He heaved a sigh. 'And for me, well, I'd be better with a younger lad that I can train from the start. It's time Jed was off – twenty's a good bit older than most lads are when they arrive at the Inns.'

'You were older when you first went.'

He squeezed her and nuzzled into her neck. 'Special case. I had a fortune to make for myself, so I could marry you.'

She smiled to herself as she poked a stick into the embers. 'You had not a groat in your pocket when you asked me.'

'No, I didn't,' he said. 'But you said "Yes" all the same, didn't you?'

The moon was up now, bright in the dark sky and lighting the long sweep of frosting grass that stretched down before them to the black cold waters of the Ouse. Around their feet, where in springtime a carpet of green would be studded with yellows and purples pushing up to meet the sunshine, all was crisp and bare. Above them the ruins of St Mary's Abbey spoke of an old magnificence. 'If I can make my mark at the quarter sessions, and show my face down in Westminster Hall from time to time, well, one of these days, when they're appointing new justices . . .'

'Lawrence,' she breathed, 'the assizes. You aim to be a judge?'

'Why not?'

'Why not indeed? You will make a success in this.'

'With you beside me I will.'

She laced the fingers of her gloved hand into his and he pulled her up, to start for home. 'You would have made a success of your life whoever you'd chosen.'

He'd said she was mad, when she'd declared they should celebrate his homecoming from his six weeks in London with a moonlight supper in the abbey grounds, but there had been magic, not madness, when he'd looked in her eyes. Manon was naive about so much of the world, but in the matter of him and her, he had come to learn that she was always right.

Their house was towards the top end of Fossgate, elevated from the waters of the Foss and on the other side from the hall of the Merchant Adventurers. He'd given a great deal of thought, when first they had come to York over two years ago, at the height of the hangings and beheadings of the regicides, to exactly where they should set up their home and he his practice. 'Most of my clients will be merchants, and the thing that makes merchants more nervous than anything else is the thought of losing money. Supposing he gets bad news down at King's Staith, then what does he do? He runs up to the Merchant Adventurers' Hall with his bad news, thinking to get help from his friends. And as they tighten their grip on their purses, his friends will tell him to get himself a lawyer, and to lose no time. So off he'll run, out into the street again, and what will he see?'

Manon had smiled. 'He'll see the house of Lawrence Ingolby, lawyer, on Fossgate.'

Some might have wondered how it was that a young lawyer of no family had the means to buy such a property, and Lawrence did nothing to disabuse those who voiced their assumption that it had been his patron, Matthew Pullan, who'd provided the funds. Matthew had helped, of course, with furnishings and draperies not needed at Faithly Hall, but the actual money had been waiting for them with the Liverpool agent of Manon's father. All through the years of the Protectorate, Damian Seeker had stashed away most of his income against the possibility that one day the Stuarts might return. As it became clear to him that that was what was happening, he had taken what he needed of it to make a new start, far across the Atlantic ocean, and the rest he had left for his daughter. There had been enough for Lawrence and Manon to take the house on Fossgate, with two full storeys and an attic. 'We'll need the attic, for the servants,' Lawrence had said.

'You've thought it all out, Lawrence,' she'd said.

Lawrence's face had become very still then. 'I've thought everything out, Manon, my whole life. It's the only way to do it.'

They were making a good life in that house on Fossgate, with its door the colour of ferns in summer. She loved that door, and so did he: their own front door, to their own house. Now, Lawrence reached out a hand to lift the brass bear's head knocker that he wasn't quite so keen on, but that she had insisted upon the minute she'd seen it. Before he had rapped a second time, the door opened to reveal his clerk, Jed Penmore, waiting for him.

'Let us by, Jed – we're like to freeze to death out here.'

Jed stepped back and pointed to the door of Lawrence's business room. 'You have a visitor, a client,' he mouthed.

'What, tonight? We're only just back from London.'

'That's what I told him, but he insisted you would see him. In your office.'

Manon gave him a peck on the cheek as she took the basket and headed towards the kitchen. 'Who is he then, that can't wait till morning?' he asked Jed.

But Jed was bundled aside before he could reply.

'Just off a Dutch boat at King's Staith! Foreigner – at this time of night!' The portly woman of indeterminate age who'd presented herself a few inches from Lawrence's face was aglow with disapproval.

Lawrence uttered an oath under his breath, and leaned towards her. 'Madge, if I've told you once, I've told you a thousand times: you steer clear of my clients, and you mind your *own* business, there.' He pointed down towards the kitchen.

'Hmmph,' Madge muttered as Jed turned her by the shoulders back in the direction of her proper domain. 'You see if I'm not right.'

Lawrence glared at Jed, who mumbled his apologies for his grandmother. How it was that, not a fortnight after taking on the young man to train for his clerk, he had somehow also found himself saddled with Jedediah Penmore's harridan of a grandmother remained a mystery to Lawrence, but saddled he was. Manon, within the space of an afternoon, had become inexplicably devoted to the woman and there was no getting rid of her. At least she could cook, that was something.

When Jed returned from the kitchen, Lawrence handed him his hat and muffler. Now he lowered his voice. '*Is* he foreign, this new client?'

Jed shook his head. 'English. Says his name's Horace Appleton.'

Lawrence paused for a moment in the act of hanging up his cloak.

'Right, well, you get up to the parlour and see to it that the mistress has enough coals for the fire, then you can get off out to the Golden Lion or somewhere, give you peace from your grandmother a while.'

'Will you not need me to make a note?' asked Jed.

Lawrence shook his head as he handed the young man some coins from his pouch. 'I know this Appleton,' he said.

'It'll be something and nothing. You get yourself on out for the evening. Tell your friends all about London.'

Jed didn't need telling again. Once his clerk had disappeared Lawrence went to open the door to his office. A man, heavily wrapped in winter travelling clothes and with his back towards the door, was bent over the fire, rubbing his hands. Lawrence stepped into the room and closed the door behind him. 'Well,' he said. '"Horace Appleton". And I thought you were still in Holland.'

Andrew Marvell turned around, unravelling a heavy black muffler from about his neck. 'I *am*,' he said.

Lawrence Ingolby knew for certain that he was looking at a man of flesh and bone and not a spectre. 'Are you indeed? Then what's brought you here tonight, to York?'

Marvell paused in the midst of divesting himself of his outer garments. He looked at Lawrence, then at the door, then back at Lawrence. His voice was very low. 'The old business,' he said.

It was a short time later, the fire blazing and the key turned in the lock, that Andrew Marvell was warmed up enough and ready to tell his tale. He poured himself a second glass of wine from the jug Lawrence had gone himself to fetch.

'You know I have been abroad these past several months?'

'What I know is the Corporation of Hull's none too happy their commissioner isn't at Westminster, representing *their* interests.'

Marvell manifested a touch of injured pride. 'The town

of Hull might do well to remember that there are higher interests than its own.'

Lawrence was tempted to remark that the town of Hull paid Andrew's wages, but he held his tongue. Instead he said, 'They might be more understanding if they knew what those higher interests were.'

Marvell gave him one of his direct, meaningful looks. 'That's what I'm here about. I was sent to the Low Countries several months ago, to conduct certain matters on behalf of his lordship the Earl of Carlisle.'

Lawrence waited.

'I journeyed first to the Hague where, as you know, George Downing is in residence and conducts our relations with the Dutch on His Majesty's behalf.'

'Oh yes,' said Lawrence, 'the unimpeachable Mr Downing.'

Marvell coloured. Downing, like himself, owed his early advancement to the patronage of great figures in Cromwell's Protectorate. Unlike Marvell, Downing had begun the process of saving his own skin long before the Republic had gasped its last, and had commenced his betrayal of his former cause and comrades as soon as it became clear that the Stuarts would regain their throne.

'I do not claim to *like* the man,' said Marvell by way of defence, 'but "he must needs go, that the Devil drives".'

'Aye, well, if anyone's the Devil, it's George Downing,' said Lawrence.

Marvell bit his lower lip. 'I fear he may prove to be.'

'Out with it, Andrew.'

'Well, as you know, many of the regicides excepted from the King's mercy and his Act of Oblivion are suspected to have fled abroad.'

Lawrence said nothing and so Marvell hurried on. 'With some few exceptions, most notably Thomas Scott, early attempts to track down or entrap them down proved unsuccessful.'

Lawrence lowered his voice and measured his words carefully. 'These are not nothing, these men you seek, Andrew. These are not nobodies. By their very nature, those that the King will not forgive for their role in his father's death are able men.'

Marvell swallowed. 'I know that, Lawrence, and I . . . I do not . . .'

Lawrence wondered if Marvell was going to claim he did not seek them, but his visitor moved on. 'They are not nobodies, and that is why it was resolved last year that it should fall to George Downing to find them.'

'Aye, and he did, didn't he? He found them and betrayed them. Shipped them back to England to be put to death without a trial.'

Marvell was now looking at the floor. 'I believe there was a trial, though . . .'

But Lawrence wasn't having it. 'That wasn't a trial. All they did was confirm it was them, before they executed them,' he said in disgust.

Marvell was a little hoarse. 'I do not claim that there is any honour in what he does, but in my position . . .'

Lawrence relented. 'I know, Andrew. It's not safe for you to go against him.'

All Marvell's accustomed pomp was gone from him. 'I am under instruction to travel the Netherlands on our nation's business, and I am to listen in taverns and coffee shops, ingratiate myself in places where our English exiles are known to be.'

'And you pass on to Downing what you hear, and Downing hires mercenaries . . .' said Lawrence.

Marvell gave one slow shake of his head. 'There was a *rumour* that Downing suggested assassination of any regicide they came across but he was told that the King would not countenance it. Even I trust Downing little more than you do and I only pass on to him information that might tend to our nation's economic interest, or that hints at a threat to His Majesty's person. As I go about the King's legitimate business, I watch for strangers on market days in small Dutch towns, I observe who comes and goes at certain inns. And in the town of Vianen I heard something that caused me to leave that very night and come here.'

Lawrence waited, feeling his breathing grow heavier, becoming more conscious of the silence in the air between them, the crackling fire, the happy noises from the floor above them.

'It concerned,' another glance at the door, another lowering of the voice, 'it concerned your wife's father.'

Any tiny flutter of hope that might have begun to stir in Lawrence died. Seated on a stool facing Marvell, hands planted on his knees, he drew a heavy breath and summoned what resilience he could. His wife's father, Captain Damian Seeker, feared intelligence handler and army captain in the service of Oliver Cromwell. He had left England not for the continent but for the Americas shortly after the Protector's death. 'What's he done?'

Marvell stared at him. 'Done? My dear fellow, I have no idea what he might lately have done and, with all due respect to your lovely wife, I have absolutely *no* wish to find out.'

'I don't understand then.'

Marvell put down his glass and leaned closer to Ingolby. 'As far as I am aware, only two people in England know where Damian Seeker is.' He raised his glance briefly to the ceiling. 'One of them is upstairs,' he lowered his gaze to meet Lawrence's eye, 'and I am looking at the other one.'

Lawrence shook his head. 'I love you like a brother, Andrew, but I'm not telling you where he is.'

'And I'm not asking you to. But something came to my ears in Vianen that you need to know. Someone's looking for him.'

Lawrence relaxed. 'Still?'

Marvell nodded. 'There are men in positions of power now who will not let go their grievances, and one of them nurses a grievance against Damian Seeker.'

Lawrence puffed out his lips. 'I daresay there's more than one – I mean, he didn't exactly go out of his way to make friends, did he?'

'Ahem, no. I believe that circle was fairly small.'

'More like a dot,' observed Lawrence. 'Anyway, you're always welcome here, Andrew, but none of this is news, and certainly not worth your slipping over here from Holland, in disguise, to tell us.'

'I haven't finished.' Marvell looked aggrieved. 'There is a man in London, a writer and stirrer of controversies, called Roger L'Estrange. Did you ever come across him?'

'Not in person, but I've come across his pamphlets. "No Blind Guides", against Milton – that was him, wasn't it? Nasty stuff.'

Marvell nodded. 'I've had dealings with him myself on occasion, over his attacks on Milton and others. He is determined upon the office of Surveyor of the Press. He is not a pleasant man.'

'And what's his interest in the captain?' So few people knew of their true relationship that Ingolby never had occasion to use the phrase 'Manon's father,' and so could not quite get it over his tongue now.

'I don't know what lies behind it, but L'Estrange has a particular and very personal dislike for Damian Seeker. He has, it seems, spent the last year and a half seeding the idea that your father-in-law was the late King's executioner.'

Lawrence laughed. 'What? And anyone's listening to him? The size of Damian Seeker? If it had been him, folk would have known straight off. L'Estrange will never prove that.'

'Won't need to,' said Marvell. 'People who think they saw one thing can be persuaded they saw something else, if told it often enough. L'Estrange aims at controlling the presses — there's word of him bringing out a new news-sheet. By the time he manages to get his hands on the captain, he'll have managed to convince half the country that Damian Seeker was the man who swung the axe over the late King's neck.'

'He'll never find him.'

Marvell looked him directly in the eye. 'He's utterly determined, Lawrence. Henry Bennet has just been named Secretary of State and has dismissed Joseph Williamson from his office. Williamson had charge of intelligence matters up to now and it's doubtful that Bennet will be able to run the office without him, but L'Estrange is rumoured to have his eye on Williamson's place. To produce the late King's executioner would give him exactly the credentials he needs.'

'He'll never find him,' repeated Lawrence.

Marvell continued to look at him from beneath heavy brows. 'I'm afraid that what I discovered in an inn three nights ago in Vianen suggests he has been making progress. It seems that L'Estrange has at some point learned of the connection between yourself and the captain and has sent someone to York to look into it.'

'Who?'

'I don't know. All I know is that they may well be already here.' Marvell looked again towards the floor above, from which sounds of childish laughter were drifting to them. 'You must take great care, Ingolby.'

Lawrence sat perfectly still, digesting what his friend had said. Perhaps they had been foolish to think the danger of those past times was gone, that old resentments had died with the last cry of the first butchered regicide. After some moments of silence, he stood up and placed his hands on the mantelshelf, his back to Marvell. He was damned if he would let anyone damage the life they'd made here and would be damned for all eternity if he was going to let any harm come to his family. 'I will, Andrew,' he said at last. 'I will take care. Thank you for coming to warn me.'

Marvell got up and began swathing himself once more in his outer garments.

Lawrence looked at him. 'You're not going now, are you?'

'I leave from King's Staith before dawn. I plan to be back in Vianen before I am missed enough for word of it to reach George Downing in the Hague. And . . .' he looked regretful, 'it would not be good for either of us if I were to be found here.'

Lawrence understood, but he made an effort to lighten things between them, arranging his face into the more carefree demeanour Marvell was familiar with. 'But you can stay a half-hour, can't you? My clerk won't be back till well after nine, and the old termagant in the kitchen goes to bed early. I'll be skinned alive and fed to the neighbour's cat if I let you go without getting you upstairs to show you to Manon. You always were a favourite with her.' He grinned. 'Though goodness knows why. And besides, you haven't seen our treasure yet, have you?'

'Your treasure?' stammered Marvel, a little put off by the sudden change of tone.

Lawrence was beaming. 'Our little Elizabeth, Lizzie. Sixteen months old and the cleverest little thing you ever saw.' He opened the door and, with a brief look towards the kitchen, waved a hand for Marvell to follow him up the stairs. Marvell did, after hastily gathering up his wet hat and cloak.

'She – ahem – doesn't take after her grandfather, does she?'

Lawrence stopped and turned around, horrified. 'What? Not a bit of it! Not a hair on her head like him. But come, come on.' He bounded up the remaining stairs and threw open the door into a warm and homely parlour. 'Look who's come to see us, love, and to meet our little princess. She's not sleeping, is she?'

Marvell stepped tentatively into the room, then saw Manon Ingolby and felt his own face broaden into a smile. In the glow from fire and candlelight, Manon was the very image of the blooming seven months expectant mother, her face suffused with good health and happiness in place of what had always been a pale and wary beauty. She crossed the room to embrace him, kissing him on both cheeks and then, for all she was a good deal younger than him, stood back to appraise him in the manner of an indulgent aunt surveying a favourite nephew. 'Oh my, Andrew, but you look well, and I am so pleased to see you here!'

'And I you, and so healthy and flourishing. Another happy event is expected, I take it?'

Manon grinned and put a hand to her stomach as Lawrence put a protective arm around her shoulders.

'This woman, Andrew, this woman is every blessing a man could ever want, and the best mother a child ever had. And wait till you see our Lizzie.'

Ingolby then crouched down to speak to something that appeared to be hiding behind its mother's skirts. 'Come on, love, I know you're not shy. Come and meet your uncle Andrew who's come from away over the sea just to see you.' He bent down and lifted up the child, turning with a triumphant beam to present her to Marvell.

'Our Lizzie. Have you ever seen such an angel?'

Marvell looked, speechless, from one besotted parent to the other, then back upon the plainest child he had ever set eyes on. A small, pointy face, wisps of hair of an indeterminate brown, her father's dun-coloured eyes as opposed to her mother's sapphire blue, and none of the comfortable fat to be expected of a sixteen-month-old baby. All in all, she had none of her mother, and all of her father. She was a woodland thing, the small image of Lawrence Ingolby. That was, until she caught him in her look, and it was a look that went straight to Andrew Marvell's marrow, because he had last seen it more than six years ago, in the visage of the child's grandfather, Damian Seeker.

THREE

A Rude Awakening

The clattering from the kitchen below told Lawrence that Madge was up and attacking the day at her usual ungodly hour. It had started in the back yard, with the breaking of ice in the water butt, and continued, with many imprecations from herself and the chickens in their coop, into the kitchen where coals were raked and the poker banged against the chimney as a precursor to the clashing of pots. Lawrence had given up trying to persuade Madge to make less noise and had given up, for now, suggesting that they really needed a housemaid in to help her. Every such suggestion had provoked mortal offence. He was determined, nonetheless, that before Christmas the said maid should be in place, on the grounds of Manon being so near her time. It would be his first victory over the housekeeper, and the thought of it warmed Lawrence's heart.

On almost any other morning, Lawrence would have rolled over, clasping his pillow about his ears as he cursed the day that had brought Madge Penmore to them, but this morning he was glad of the intimation that the world was at last up and about, that he might be too. He had lain awake all through the long night, thinking of the news brought by Andrew Marvell, as the bells of St Saviour's and All Saints Pavement had tolled the hours back and forth to one another.

Beside him, Manon slept soundly, as did Lizzie in her cot. Lawrence had told his wife nothing of the true reason for Marvell's visit, and he'd sworn Marvell to say nothing of it to her either. The one blight on their happiness, for her at least, was the absence of her father. The only blight on his was that he couldn't fill for her the void the man had left. Now, Lawrence gently brushed back some of the blonde hair that had fallen over her face and touched his lips to her cheek. She smiled and murmured contentedly, but did not wake. He pulled back the bed drapes on his side and swung his feet to the floor, feeling the hit of the cold air on his bare skin as he did so. It was still dark, darts of moonlight slicing through the shutters helping him see his way around the bed. He crossed to the hearth and carefully brought life to the embers of the previous night's fire, dressed as silently as he could, and went downstairs.

Madge was peering into a pot that hung over the hearth, and stirring. Without turning around she said, 'Didn't think to see you up so early, with your visitor leaving so late.'

Lawrence walked over to the dresser and got down his favourite pewter mug from its hook. He pointed a finger at her. 'You don't know when my visitor left. You were sound asleep. We'd a job to conduct our business at all over the noise of your snoring.'

She brandished her ladle, scarlet and indignant. 'I never . . . !'

'Ah, save it for your cronies.' He looked into the pot and sniffed. 'What you got for us this morning then?'

'Well,' she said, taking his cup and dipping her ladle into the spiced, milky concoction, 'it's really for the mistress, to keep her strength up. And babby likes it too, of course, but I *suppose* you might have some.'

Lawrence beamed at her. 'You're a treasure, Madge. Just a treasure. You ask Manon — I'm always saying it.' Then he pointed towards the bowl of batter and slices of apple waiting ready on the scrubbed board of the table. 'Don't suppose there's any chance of you doing me a couple of them apple fritters before I go?'

The hot fritters in their napkin warmed his hands as he set himself against the snow being blown down onto York from the moors. Few doorways had their lanterns lit at this hour, but his way was lighted by the great lantern of All Saints, shining through the darkness to guide hardy travellers across Knavesmire, safe to the gates of York. For a time, Lawrence followed where he knew the footprints of Andrew Marvell must have been, a few hours earlier, leading away from the Ingolbys' green door to make his way by streets and lanes and snickets down to the dock of King's Staith. Those footprints had long been covered by a soft white powder. Lawrence mouthed a silent prayer for

his friend's safe passage back to Holland, and turned his
own footsteps in the direction of the Castlegate. There was
only one man in this entire city with whom he might talk
freely about the worries now occupying his mind.

The air grew colder and the breeze strengthened as Lawrence crossed the bridge over the moat to the northern
gatehouse of the castle. It seemed the wind came at him
one way from the Ouse and the other from the Foss. He
was glad to recognise faces he knew amongst those of the
guards who were stamping their feet and warming their
hands round the braziers at the gatehouse entry. Used to
Lawrence coming and going on business, they didn't detain
him long before opening the gate to him. 'You know where
to find him?' asked one.

'I know, all right,' replied Lawrence. 'Safe and sound in
his bed.'

'Unless he's in someone else's,' the guard laughed.

Lawrence grinned and went on his way across the inner
bailey courtyard.

Seven years ago, the man he had come to see had been
bound and shackled in the dungeon of this castle, awaiting
transportation to the Tower of London. Sir Thomas Faithly,
then lately returned, incognito, from the King's court in
exile, had been captured by Damian Seeker in the very act
of trying to raise a rebellion against Cromwell's authority,
in the name of Charles Stuart. That, at least, was the story
that had been given out to the world, and with which the
world had appeared satisfied. But Lawrence knew different.

He knew that, tired and demoralised with his life in exile, Thomas had returned home to give himself up, in the hope that he might live freely in England once more. He had thought to bargain with information brought over from the King's court, but the bargain that had been struck hadn't been the one that Thomas had hoped for. He would be allowed to stay in England, but only on condition that he turned spy upon his fellow Royalists. Sent from York Castle dungeon to the Tower of London, for the sake of appearances, Thomas had not long been out of the Tower when he had repented of his bargain, and not much longer still before he had gone back on it and fled, once again, to the Stuart court in exile.

But those things were never spoken of between Thomas and Lawrence – they were treated as though forgotten, or as if they had never been. The world had turned, and if Sir Thomas Faithly were found in the castle dungeons now, it would be because he was holding the keys and doing the questioning. Across the yard Lawrence went, unimpeded, through a low doorway and up well-worn stone stairs to arrive eventually at Thomas's lodging and the door to the small suite of apartments occupied by his friend.

'Come on, Thomas,' he called as he rapped at the door. 'Time you were up and about.'

At the third round of rapping a bleary-eyed page appeared at the door, his face only unscrewing itself slightly as he recognised Lawrence. 'He's still asleep,' the boy said.

'Excellent,' said Lawrence, stepping past him. 'All the better for the surprise.'

He stopped once inside the outer office and frowned at the chests and packing cases distributed around the floor. 'What's all this? Is he going somewhere?'

'King's Manor,' replied the page. 'Major Scott has arrived to take care of the arsenal in the tower here, and Sir Thomas is needed at King's Manor, in preparation for His Grace's arrival.'

'Hmm,' said Lawrence. The prospect of the Duke of Buckingham taking up his post as lord lieutenant was not one that filled him with pleasure. He doubted that Thomas would much relish this new role as Buckingham's administrative dogsbody either. 'With any luck we'll hardly see him.'

'Sir Thomas?'

'Sir Thomas?' repeated Lawrence. 'No. Buckingham, of course.'

The young boy's eyes widened in shock to hear anyone speak in such a manner about the duke, but he said nothing. Then Lawrence's eye fell upon the bucket of coals by the hearth of the outer office, and he reached down to take hold of it. 'Better take this. You know how soft he is about the cold an' all.' Without waiting for the boy to announce him, Lawrence strode into Sir Thomas's room and started rattling the fire dogs. 'Wakey, wakey, slugabed. Time you were up and doing.'

Sir Thomas Faithly, who had sprung upwards and taken hold of his sword, now sank back against his pillows and uttered a stream of expletives.

'Thomas! Mind your language with the lad there. You're not at some play at the Cockpit now, you know.'

His eyes closed, Thomas dropped his sword with a clatter to the stone flags. 'Ingolby,' he groaned. 'What in God's name are you doing here at this hour?'

Lawrence affected surprise. 'I'm back from London and come to discuss your case, of course.'

Sir Thomas rubbed his eyes with the heel of a hand. 'My case has been rotting in Chancery for over two years. I hardly think I need to be woken before dawn on a frozen November morning to hear of it. Unless,' he said, reopening an eye, 'you are come to tell me that the old woman is dead?'

'What? Oh no. For which you should give thanks, for if she were to die, you can be sure a ragbag of heirs would pop up from every corner.' The Puritan widow in possession of the small estate left to Sir Thomas by his grandmother, and decreed forfeit in the later years of the Protectorate, was showing a great disinclination to see it handed back to him without a fight. The King, on his return, had left the vexed matter of the restitution of estates to the wisdom of Parliament. Parliament had soon made it clear that those who had had their estates sequestered during those dark days should have them returned. Which was all very well, Lawrence had explained to Thomas, but there was the small matter of the law to be considered. When Thomas had protested that surely the Parliament of England made the law, Lawrence had smiled at him and shaken his head. 'The common law of England, Thomas, is your greatest protection and friend, and it is most certainly not to be dispensed with on the whim of parliaments. Oh no.'

Now he said, 'You get yourself dressed whilst that lad of yours fetches you your morning draught, and I'll tell you all about it.'

After Lawrence had summarised the details of Thomas's case as they had been prior to his latest visit to London, Thomas mumbled, 'Who would have thought an old widow would be so tenacious?'

'Tenacious?' replied Lawrence. 'I haven't met a widow yet that didn't know her rights, but now that I've tracked down all the contracts and bonds on the Langton estate, I can finish my deposition for the court on your behalf.'

'Ah,' said Thomas, 'The never-ending deposition. How many pages does it run to now?'

'There's not a thing can be left out, Thomas,' he told him sharply. 'All must be laid out before the court, but never you worry,' he tapped his skull, 'it's all in here as well as down on paper and it's a thing of beauty. The judges'll weep to hear of the injustice and tribulations you've been put to, the scoundrels that have stood between you and your inheritance. This time next year you'll be master of Langton and you'll have forgotten you were ever anything else.'

Sir Thomas's page was not long in returning with a steaming cup and a hunk of bread with cold beef on a platter which he set down on a small table. Lawrence helped himself to some of the bread then waved the boy away. 'Good work, lad. Now, you get yourself off back to your bed for another hour, Sir Thomas won't be needing you awhile.'

Once the boy had left and closed the door behind him, Thomas went to the mantelshelf and picked up a pipe. He offered one to Ingolby, but the lawyer shook his head.

'What is it, Lawrence?' he said. 'Why have you really come to me at this hour?'

Lawrence took a long breath and Thomas saw now in the dawning light that the lawyer's face was even paler than usual, and that dark circles framed the eyes from which the usual good humour was all but gone.

'What is it, Ingolby? What's wrong?'

Lawrence settled on the floor with his back against the wall of the hearth and seemed to take a moment to pick his words. 'I need you to tell me what you know about a man named L'Estrange.'

Thomas was surprised. 'You mean Roger L'Estrange, the pamphleteer?'

'If he's the same one that writes the pamphlets attacking Milton and has his eye on the censor's office, then yes, Roger L'Estrange, the pamphleteer.'

'Well,' said Thomas, 'he came out for the King at the very beginning of it all. Parliament more or less had his head in a noose in '44, but he won a last-minute reprieve from the Lords. He spent time in gaol, was in and out of exile, found himself under sentence of death again during the Protectorate but somehow made enough of an accommodation with Cromwell to be allowed back into England in the fifties without being marched straight to Tyburn.'

'Did he now?' said Lawrence.

Thomas nodded. 'There were some questions about him, in the King's circles, over the years and he's determined to deflect from those by finding fault with everyone else. Presbyterians, sectaries, Republican sympathisers of any sort, all have cause to fear the pen and the bile of Roger L'Estrange. His voice was amongst the loudest pressing to extend the list of exemptions from the Act of Oblivion. Not a man you'd want to be on the wrong side of – he has a blood lust for revenge. Why do you ask?'

'Because I'm here to find out why this L'Estrange is hell-bent on finding Damian Seeker.'

Lawrence hadn't moved, but Thomas felt as if the lawyer had just punched him in the stomach. He took a moment to recover from the shock. His voice was hoarse. 'Lawrence, we don't talk about . . .'

'Oh, I know, Thomas. If there's one thing we don't talk about, it's Damian Seeker, but we're going to have to start.'

Thomas went to sit in the walnut side-chair by the window. For almost twenty years, since he'd ridden out as a lad of eighteen to the King's standard at Nottingham, his life had been lived in the eye of the Stuarts' storm. He had shared in the tribulations, the exile, the poverty and the humiliations of the prince who was now King. The tale of King Charles II was as a memory palace down the corridors of which Thomas could wander at will, and without a guide. But there were murky corners in the architecture of his own life that he did not want others to know of and that, in fact, he didn't wish to remember himself. Things that he had tried to close the door upon. And he'd told himself that he had managed to do that. He had begun to feel safe. But here now was Lawrence Ingolby, his closest friend, stepping out from behind the door he thought he had closed and telling him he had managed no such thing.

Footsteps hurried by in the corridor, with complaints against the cold. The world around them had awoken and was getting on with its day: boys were running around lighting fires, guards changing, dogs barking, the water fowl on the Knavesmire and the King's Pool raising a cacophony as they set about their mornings. In the castle yard a party on horseback made slushy tracks to the gates to take orders out through the Ridings. But in this room, in Thomas's chamber, there were just the two of them and the knowledge of Thomas's betrayal six years ago of the King's cause, when he had spied for a time for Damian Seeker. It had been a short time, a kind of madness, Thomas thought, but it had happened: he had betrayed his King to spy on behalf of Oliver Cromwell, and Lawrence Ingolby knew it.

Thomas felt the knowledge of it like a weight of lead in his stomach. 'All right,' he said at last, 'all right. I'll tell you about Seeker and L'Estrange, for all the good it might do you. You remember, some years ago, when you and I encountered one another in London, and Seeker set us to work for him on the business involving one of the animals left over from the closing of the Bear Garden. We went in search of the hounds . . .'

'Oh, I remember all right,' said Lawrence. 'It was almost exactly six years ago, and the reason I remember the business so well, if *you* recall, is that it nearly killed me.'

'Yes,' said Thomas, looking away for a moment. He remembered. The party that had 'liberated' him had left Lawrence Ingolby for dead on Lambeth Marsh. 'I recall it often, and with shame. But to your question about L'Estrange – you will recall our business for Seeker was to aid him in the frustrating of a plot to assassinate Cromwell?'

Lawrence nodded. 'I do. Go on.'

'Seeker's intervention was the ruin of a series of attempts against the Lord Protector at that time, and it led to the capture of those involved.'

'Of all but one,' said Lawrence. 'A Mr Boyes, wasn't it?'

Thomas leaned towards him. 'I would counsel you in the strongest terms to forget you ever heard that name and to focus on Roger L'Estrange.'

'Oh?' said Lawrence.

Thomas shook his head. 'More than my life's worth, Lawrence. But to L'Estrange – although he was nowhere near London when the attempts were being carried out, he had been deeply involved in the planning and promotion of the whole debacle. Its failure – the repeated failures – caused him a great deal of humiliation and loss of standing, as well as money. And it seems that he holds Captain Seeker directly responsible.'

'I see,' said Lawrence.

'But how does this affect you? I am certain L'Estrange cannot know of our part in helping Seeker that time.' A slight sense of foreboding began to creep up Thomas's arm. 'Or have you had any intimation that he does?'

Lawrence was clenching his fists. 'I've had word, through Andrew Marvell, that L'Estrange has discovered Seeker is Manon's father, and has sent someone to York to try to discover, through her, where he is.'

'Who?' said Thomas.

Lawrence shook his head. 'He doesn't know.' Then he stood up. 'But never worry, Thomas. I'll deal with it.'

'Oh no,' replied Thomas. 'If L'Estrange's interest in Seeker touches on you, on Manon, on Lizzie, it touches on me.'

He could see emotion in his friend's eyes that the lawyer rarely allowed himself to show.

'Thank you,' said Lawrence simply. Then he adopted his more usual brisk manner and clapped him on the shoulder. 'Right then, keep your eyes open. Time I was off, though.'

'Me too,' said Thomas, reaching beyond Lawrence for his own hat.

'Oh? Where are you off to?'

'King's Manor. I've been working between and betwixt here and there for weeks. I'd rather remain here at the castle, amongst the soldiers, but most of my belongings are being taken up to King's Manor and I must settle myself there now, to oversee preparations for His Grace's arrival, and make a start on all the paperwork the duke has no interest in.'

'Hmmph. Buckingham.' Lawrence grimaced. 'Lord, Thomas, you do hang about with some murky folk.'

'Yes,' said Thomas, casting an eye over the lawyer's dull clothing and mud-spattered boots as they set out into York to the sound of the city's bells, 'I do.'

Griselda Duncan had arrived in York only the night before but, as in all her travels in the service of Anne Winter, she had wasted little time in setting about her part of their business. Anne had her own enquiries to make this morning and by the time they were both returned to the house her mistress had taken on the corner of Ogleforth and Chapter House Street, their investigations on behalf of Roger Lestrange would be firmly begun. Grizel had never been in York before, but as she headed for the knot of streets at the city's heart, she told herself it would not be so different from all those other towns and cities where she had set out upon her business. Town to town, street to street, church to church, this was always the beginning. In York, as in Brussels, Cologne, London, Edinburgh, the dead lay silent, folded under grass and flowers or iron-hard frost, oblivious to her passing through their churchyards. But the living could not keep silent, no matter how hard they tried, and they told Grizel things, even when they did not realise they were doing so.

L'Estrange always chose a church as the safe house from which his communications might be collected. Today, she passed by Holy Trinity Goodramgate with its graveyard, then St Andrew's and St Saviour's with theirs, giving them scarcely a glance. Her feet, the snow seeping into her boots as it turned from pure white to a browning slush, were taking her to All Saints Pavement, and there, she knew, she would pick up the end of the yarn with which someone had woven their life and she would begin to unravel it.

Rising high above the bustle of the Pavement market, All Saints appeared to have more on its mind than the souls of the citizens who thronged the streets around it. They had seen the lantern tower last night, she and Anne Winter, as they had approached York, a beacon for those trying to find their way. This morning the doors were closed. She tried the handle on the one then the other, but neither budged. She tried the brass knocker, its thuds dull against the thick, damp wood. In return, nevertheless, came a call to wait and then the sound of shuffling feet and a key turning in the lock. The door was opened a few inches and a round face bearing little hint of welcome looked out at her. 'Well?'

'Why is the church locked?'

The man snorted. 'Vagrants, beggars, thieves.'

'Souls in the image of God to perish out in the streets on a night such as last night was.'

The verger shrugged, unabashed. 'Vicar says it would be unseemly. There's to be no unseemliness at All Saints.'

Grizel sniffed. 'And should I stand out here all day, the blood freezing in my veins, all over the heads of unseemliness?' she asked.

The verger's eyes narrowed. 'Depends what you want. It's hours yet till evensong.'

She might have told him she was as unlikely to participate in his evensong as he was to sign the Covenant. 'I'm not here for that.'

'What are you here for then?'

She leaned her head forward a little and looked him very close in the eye. 'I am here,' she said, '*to buy a blackbird.*' A blackbird, a coded letter sent from Roger L'Estrange in Whitehall, that Grizel's mistress Anne Winter would make sing.

FOUR

At King's Manor

Surrounded by the packing cases and chests that had been brought up for him to King's Manor from the castle, Thomas Faithly was tempted to have them all loaded once more on the cart and taken away again. He preferred the company of soldiers – the directness, the issuing and obeying of orders – to the politics and subtleties of the officials at King's Manor. The garrison at York Castle might guarantee the King's control over his northern territories and cow any who thought to threaten it, but it was the endless work of officials with pen and ink, dictating, scrawling away, drawing up accounts and awarding contracts, that would raise the taxes and oversee the running of those territories on His Majesty's behalf. What Whitehall was to the kingdom, King's Manor was to its northern outposts. Where the King might reign from London, Buckingham would maintain that rule on his behalf from York. Buckingham, or those he chose to deputise for him. It was Thomas's great misfortune that Buckingham's eye had, for now, fallen upon him. Will, Thomas's page, was busied at unpacking coats, hose and doublets in his bedchamber, whilst Francis, the somewhat unsatisfactory clerk appointed to his office, was moving piles of correspondence from one surface to another, picking up the occasional letter only to lay it down again in a desultory manner. Thomas could hardly blame him — for himself, he was not sure he cared for any of it, but until such time as Lawrence might win back for him his inheritance, he was in no position to refuse the patronage of the Duke of Buckingham.

Somehow, nonetheless, the latest correspondence had been found, and dates and appointments were being written into an already cramped ledger. Francis had a habit, at first annoying but now, Thomas had come to feel, useful, of reading aloud much of what he wrote. This morning, though, with Lawrence Ingolby's revelations fresh in his mind and disorder all around him, Thomas could well have done without the intonation of the endless round of mundane duties that lay in wait for him. He gritted his teeth and tried to ignore the commentary, but then looked up from the crate he was examining. 'What did you say, Frank?'

Francis consulted his ledger once more. '"Expected, second week of November, in advance of an audience with His Grace the Duke of Buckingham, Major David Ogilvie . . ."'

Thomas left off what he was doing and stepped over to his clerk's desk, pulling the ledger towards him. 'Are you sure, Frank, that it definitely says, "David . . ."'

'"Ogilvie,"' a low voice from the doorway finished for him.

Thomas felt first incomprehension and then a surge of happiness as he looked up to see a tall, dark-haired man of around his own age, in mud-spattered riding boots and sodden travelling clothes. 'Ogilvie! Truly, it is you!'

The man standing there pulled off and examined a hat from which all the snow had yet to melt and gave a brief smile. 'I am inclined to believe it is, my friend.'

Thomas strode across the room to grasp him by the arm. 'By God, Ogilvie, it is good to see you!'

'And you too, Thomas. It's been a long time.'

'It has indeed. Worcester.'

'Aye,' said Ogilvie, his Scots voice soft, and rumbling into Thomas's ears like stones in a river, just as he remembered it. 'I went northwards, home, and you followed the King into a second exile.'

Thomas sighed. 'Eleven years.' Then he clapped Ogilvie once more round the shoulder. 'But now the Devil Cromwell is dead and his bones dug up and buried beneath the gallows, and the King is in exile no more.' He beamed at his friend then shook his head. 'And it has taken you two years to come to see me!'

Ogilvie cast an eye around the disordered office. 'We cannot all be gentlemen at leisure, shuffling pieces of paper.' He picked up a cushion from the window seat. 'I've had a burned-out tower-house to make habitable again and ravished lands to return to husbandry, while you have been lying on velvet cushions, no doubt eating sugared plums.'

Thomas laughed. 'And how is that old ruckle of stones,

as you were wont to call it? Not yet fallen into the sea?'
He had once spent a terrifying night in Ogilvie's family
seat, a small and ancient castle barely clinging to its perch
on a cliff above the Moray Firth, and was astonished to
learn that after the ravages of the war in that part of the
country, there could be anything left of it.

'Not fallen into the sea quite yet,' said Ogilvie. 'My
mother was not inclined to allow it.'

'I am glad to hear it,' said Thomas. 'But tell me, whatever
brings you to York at so unseasonable a time of the year?'

'What takes any of us anywhere, these days?' answered
Ogilvie. 'I have been down in London, chasing debts long-
owed and pensions long-promised.'

'Dear Lord,' said Thomas. 'I think I have been better off
sitting on cushions eating plums.'

'Indeed,' laughed Ogilvie, 'but my mission was not
without success. There remains one bond to be realised, the
funds owing being in the name of our dear friend, George,
Duke of Buckingham, who assured me that should I attend
him in York, he would certainly be able to present me with
my money when he arrives to take up his duties. And so
here I am. And glad to find you here, if not yet him. I was
afraid the good duke had dandled your presence here as an
enticement to win a few extra days from me.'

Thomas gave a grim nod. 'That would be within his
capabilities, certainly, but whatever has brought you here,
I'm glad of it.' He led Ogilvie into his private chamber,
telling Will to leave off his unpacking and build up the fire

for his weary guest. 'And fetch us some wine, and some food for Major Ogilvie. He has had a long journey and we have much to talk about.' Once Will had gone to fetch the wine Thomas added, 'And who knows how long we shall have to talk of it? For once Buckingham is arrived, there will be no one can talk but him.'

They spoke a little of Worcester and how they had each got away, but Thomas understood that Ogilvie, no more than he, wished to relive those long, hard years. They spoke of mutual acquaintance, and where they were now, of Ogilvie's family and of Thomas's hopes for the future. At length, Ogilvie stood up. 'I must go and see that my horse has been well stabled and show my face at my lodging.'

'But surely you will stay here,' protested Thomas.

Ogilvie grimaced and clapped his friend on the shoulder. 'When I am not confined in that ruckle of stones, I prefer to be in the heart of a town.' He went to the window on one side of Thomas's chamber, which looked across to Bootham Bar and, rising above the walls of York, the twin-towered western face of the minster.

'You will not have the like of that in your homeland,' said Thomas, coming up behind him.

'Oh, we have kirks enough for our purposes,' murmured Ogilvie, turning from the window.

Thomas continued to look out, though, and then an, 'Oh,' escaped him. Ogilvie turned back.

Beneath the archway of the Bar, a fine dappled grey horse had emerged from the town, its steps sure in the falling snow. Its rider wore a mantle and hood of deep green velvet, trimmed with sable, and the fat snowflakes fell upon it as if seeking out moss in the forest. Long tendrils of dark chestnut hair escaped from the hood, and an elegant gloved hand came up to push them back a little.

'Like the Queen of Winter,' Ogilvie said. 'Cloaking all around her in ice and snow.'

'You know,' said Thomas, never taking his eyes from horse and rider as they crossed the white ground between the walls of the city and the outer precinct of King's Manor, 'you speak more truth than you know, David. She *is* Winter, and she is no ordinary woman.'

Ogilvie looked at him, curious.

'Her name is Lady Anne Winter,' said Thomas. 'Widow of a Cromwellian officer, but a faithful servant to the King. She lost much and ventured much in His Majesty's cause. I have not seen her since a night four years ago in Flanders, when I had to fight for my life.' He shivered and then caught the look on Ogilvie's face. 'What is it?'

'I have heard that name, and that for all her beauty her heart is made of ice. I hope you are not of a mind to get cut by its shards, Thomas.'

The soft fall of the snow to the ground made the people all around her move, it seemed, with a better grace and lent a quietness to the air. Sharpness, harshness, were muted, edges blurred, hardness covered. As she'd passed the masons' yard of the minster, even the clang of the hammers and chisels, iron on stone, had been dulled. Footprints, hoof-prints, cart tracks had their moment and then were lost, but even those remained in Anne's mind's eye. She had learned over these last ten years that things that were lost could be found again. The sight of vicars and choristers, clutching their music as they hurried in their surplices to the minster, where only a few years ago the New Model Army had stabled its horses, told her so. And just as things that were lost could be found again, things that had been hidden could be uncovered, brought once more into view, like cobbles through the snow.

She passed with ease through the main entranceway to the grounds of King's Manor. Her friend Lady Fairfax's pass was as a key which opened any door in the north. Few would gainsay Lord Fairfax, but none were likely to forget the courage of his wife, who had cried out her contempt for the court that had condemned the old King, even as the Republic's guards shook their halberds in her face. The very sight of her seal gained Anne the access she required without the letter being further looked at. Few people were as cautious now as once they had been, and some were not nearly as cautious as they should be. Such carelessness since the King's return had filled cells in the great dungeons of England and given work to the builders of scaffolds.

Anne had played her part in sending some of the guilty there. Grizel had asked her, once, why she did what she did, why she hunted down men of their own side, Cavaliers, who in the time of the Republic had betrayed the King's cause for Cromwell. Anne's father and brother had died in the King's cause, and with them had gone everything she had understood about what her life should be. She had not hesitated in her reply. 'I hunt them because what they did cost more honourable men their lives.' Men who had been brave enough to plot to restore the King when Oliver held sway had been caught, taken, tried, executed, all because of the treachery of those they had thought their friends and brothers. When she had asked Grizel why she, in turn, did what *she* did, the Scotswoman's reply had been, 'Because I must do something.'

And now they were in York because of the latest name sent to them by Roger L'Estrange, and as she contemplated what she and Grizel must do, she could not help feeling a coldness in her stomach that had little to do with the snow and ice all about her.

She was turning the horse towards the stables when two men emerged from a doorway just ahead of her. Their eyes were fixed on her and she brought her mount to a halt. She could not have told whether it was the man in blue velvet or the one in dun browns and greys who looked at her more intently. No matter, the first stage of her quest was completed – Faithly was indeed here.

'Lady Anne! I thought a moment that my eyes did deceive me when I looked out from my window and saw such a vision emerge from the cold stone walls of York.' Sir Thomas Faithly's eyes were as blue as the velvet of his doublet, and his open smile as engaging as ever it had been.

She could not help returning it with one of her own. To the side she saw that his companion, his clothes telling the story of a hard journey and recent arrival in York, was ill at ease. She turned her head a little to him and Faithly said, 'Oh, your ladyship, you must excuse me. This is my very good, very old friend, Major David Ogilvie, on his way home to Scotland.'

She inclined her head towards the man and he made a brisk and somewhat reluctant-seeming bow.

'You travel a long distance at an ill season, I think,' she said.

Ogilvie said nothing but Thomas Faithly was ready to fill the silence. 'And your ladyship,' he replied, 'have you travelled far? I have not seen you for so long – Damme, I believe it was?'

'It was,' she agreed. They might have been talking of a day at the races, not a night of darkness and desperation in a small Flemish town. 'But I have not come here from as far away as that, only from Northumbria, where I have made my home. The people of the coast told me we are to expect a harsh winter, and I thought York would be a more convivial place to spend it.'

Faithly looked delighted. 'We will endeavour to make it so!' She couldn't help but glance again at his companion. 'Oh,' said Thomas, following the direction of her glance. 'Pay no mind to Ogilvie, one learns to live with his misery. But are you to lodge here or at the Treasurer's House?'

'Neither.' Had her friend Lady Fairfax been in residence,

she would indeed have had to stay as her guest in the Treasurer's House, the large mansion in the eastern shadow of the minster, but the Fairfaxes' absence gave her much greater freedom of movement. 'Lady Fairfax and his lordship are gone to Nun Appleton for the winter, and I do not wish to get in the way of His Grace the lord lieutenant's business here at King's Manor, so the dean has been kind enough to grant me use of a small house on the corner of Chapter House Street and Ogleforth.'

'Indeed?' Thomas raised his eyebrows. 'Such benevolence is not like him.'

She smiled and patted the pocket in which Lady Fairfax's letter nestled. 'Her ladyship's recommendation casts a spell wherever I produce it. But I am afraid most of the grooms have gone to Nun Appleton with the Fairfaxes, and I am anxious about the care of my horse while I'm here.'

Thomas Faithly couldn't hide the delight in his eyes. He always had had an excellent eye for a horse, as she had remembered. 'But nothing is simpler, your ladyship. If you would consent to stable this beautiful animal here at King's Manor, my own groom will look after him and I will see that he has the best of attention. I'm on my way to the stables at this very minute.'

Anne could see from the look on his companion's face that Thomas Faithly had not been in the act of going anywhere near the stables, but if the Scotsman did not like this new development, that was his lookout. And if, as was also clear from his face, he did not like Thomas Faithly's offer to hand her down from the horse, or her acceptance of it, that too was not her concern. The bridle once in his hand, Faithly looked into the horse's eyes as deeply as he had into her own.

'Might I leave you to arrange for his stabling, Sir Thomas, and return later to look in on him?'

'Nothing simpler,' repeated Faithly, smoothing a hand down the horse's neck.

'Excellent,' she said. 'Then I am of a mind to go and have a look at the minster before I return to Ogleforth to see how my maid has been getting on this morning.'

Thomas Faithly turned towards her now. 'If you care to wait a short while, I can accompany you.' Closer up now, she saw that his eyes sparkled still, bluer now, it seemed, than in those hard days of exile. There was hardly any silver to be seen in his long blond locks, and his jaw was still firm. She wondered what he saw when he looked at her.

'That's kind of you, Sir Thomas, but I only wanted a glance for now. I will leave you to your friend.' She extended a hand and he kissed it, then she inclined her head towards the other man. Faithly's companion made a very slight bow in return There *was* grey to be seen in his hair, shafts of granite through the black. He might have been around the same age as Sir Thomas, but the lines around his mouth and the furrow between his dark brows was deeper. Whereas Faithly's features might have been painted, this man's had the look of being hewn. His eyes did not sparkle as Thomas's did, but glistened like mica behind long, black lashes.

It was now that the man spoke. 'If your ladyship has no objection, I will escort you there myself. I have a mind to see something of this wonder that Thomas tells me so outdoes our simple kirks.'

Anne had no choice but to accept.

Lawrence's mind was whirling. His conversation with Thomas had done nothing to assuage the concerns brought from Holland last night by Andrew Marvell. Someone had been sent to York to dig deeper into the connections between his family and Damian Seeker, deep enough to enable them to track down the captain to where he was now. Lawrence wasn't indifferent to his father-in-law's fate, but as Seeker would have been the first to say, he could take care of himself. Lawrence's concerns were for his wife, for the child she was carrying and the child they already had, the life they had. The butchery that had driven them from London to York that stinking, blood-soaked London autumn of 1660 was not over and done with, but waited, ready to be unleashed again at the behest of some malign will. Even on his latest trip to London there had been talk of more trials and executions. Worse, whenever he had gone to the courts at Westminster Hall, Lawrence had been forced to pass beneath the impaled head of the regicide lawyer John Cooke, its eyes long picked away by rooks. Cooke had been a lawyer's lawyer, and Lawrence felt those eyes on him even now. By the time he reached York's grand Guildhall, where he had business to conduct, Lawrence was clear that he must get Manon and Lizzie away to a place of safety.

It was almost dinnertime by the time he arrived back at his house on Fossgate. Enticing smells of a rich stew greeted him as he stepped over the threshold out of the sleet, one compensation for having to put up with Madge Penmore. He could hear Lizzie's laughter from the kitchen, and Manon's soft tones. Hastily removing his wet cloak, he took a quick look into his office, but no one being there, he went down to the kitchen to join his family.

Lizzie came toddling to him and he tossed her up in the air, catching her as she squealed for him to do it again. As ever, Madge's terrier was barking in protest at his arrival. Lawrence, who had seldom in his life encountered a dog he could not control, bared his teeth and growled at it so that it took refuge under its mistress's skirts.

'Lawrence!' chided Manon, as Madge prepared her accustomed outrage.

'"Lawrence," nothing,' he said. 'If that glorified ferret wasn't such a good ratter, he'd be out on his tail. And *her* with him,' he added under his breath.

Manon shook her head and took Lizzie from him to set in her high chair. The aromas coming from the pot hanging over the hearth were mesmerising. 'What is it?' asked Lawrence, leaning in that direction.

Madge rapped him on the hand with her wooden spoon. 'Venison stew. Best meat.'

'Oh aye?' said Lawrence, 'I suppose that means I paid over the odds for it then.'

Madge now pointed her spoon at him. 'No butcher has ever got the better of Madge Penmore, no, not for a groat.'

'Hmm,' said Lawrence, taking his seat at the end of the table. 'So where's Jed then? He's not in the office.'

Manon had opened her mouth to speak, but Madge got there before her. 'Off out into town, in search of you. And in such weather!'

Lawrence looked from one woman to the other. 'What was he looking for me for?'

Manon leaned forwards. 'William Briar,' she began.

'Him that was jilted,' added Madge, to a swift glare from Lawrence.

'So, William *is* back from London then?'

'First thing this morning, it seems. He arrived at the door not long after you'd left. He was very anxious to see you.'

Lawrence frowned. Whatever had brought William, only just arrived from London, straight to their door was unlikely to be anything good. 'What did he want to see me about?'

Manon shook her head. 'I don't know. I was occupied with Lizzie, and by the time I came down the stairs to see what the commotion was, he was gone.'

'Aye,' interjected Madge, dropping a good ladleful of stew from the pot into Lawrence's bowl. 'Such a racket that if the bairn hadn't already been awake, it would have wakened her. If Jedediah hadn't been here to send him on his way, I daresay the watch would have to have been called.'

Lawrence now gave his full attention to his housekeeper. 'What exactly did he want?'

'Oh,' the old woman turned away to give the pot another stir, 'something to do with the jilting, no doubt.'

'The jilting? Don't be daft, woman. That was all past seven months since, and Juliet Venn married these five.' He'd have to wait till Jed got back to hear anything sensible about the visit of William Briar.

Lawrence was on his second bowl of stew when they heard Jed come in by the back way and curse as he stepped on his grandmother's dog. There was a great deal of squealing from the animal and muttering from Jed before the clerk eventually appeared, the tails of his shirt dirty and sodden and his feet bare.

'Jedediah Penmore!' exclaimed his grandmother. 'Where in the world are your stockings?'

Jed turned a dripping head in the direction of the back yard. 'Hung up out in the laundry shed, soaked through with everything else. Got splattered by a dung cart, heading up from the Shambles. Have you dry stockings for me?'

A few minutes of bustling and fussing later, and Jed was seated close to the stove, dry stockings on his feet and a dish of stew on his lap. He had hardly got a second spoonful of food to his mouth when his grandmother pounced again. 'Jedediah! Your good cuff, trailing in the gravy!' And she was busied again with an old damp cloth, that only seemed to make matters worse.

'Leave the lad be,' said Lawrence. He got up and went

to crouch in front of his clerk, who looked truly miserable. 'Right, Jed. So what's all this about William Briar this morning then?'

Jed wiped his stained cuff across his mouth, heedless of his grandmother's complaints. 'Couldn't make head nor tale of him, but,' and here he lowered his voice, glancing towards Manon, 'after what you said this morning about being careful who I let in the house . . .'

Lawrence nodded.

'Well, I thought it was best to get him out quick smart. He left to look for you, he were in a state, and I thought I'd be best to come and warn you.'

'Raving at our Jed, he was,' interjected Madge.

Lawrence shushed her and focused on his clerk. 'Well, you didn't – warn me, did you?'

Jed coloured. 'I went up to King's Manor, as you'd said you'd be going to see Sir Thomas, but they hadn't seen you, so I thought you must have been at the castle, and by the time I got down there they said you were gone. Then I tried a few other places . . .'

'But I told you I was going to the Guildhall after I'd seen Sir Thomas.'

Jed put his head in his hands. 'I know. I'm sorry – I drank a bit much up at the Three Tuns last night. By this morning I felt as if I'd been at sea a week.' His cheeks were crimson. 'I wasn't listening properly to what you said.'

Lawrence felt irritation rising in him, then felt Manon's hand on his arm. 'Jed isn't used to strong drink,' she said.

'Like his father and grandfather before him,' chimed in Madge; Jed, his father and his grandfather being the three great saints of her Trinity.

Lawrence let out a sigh. It was his own fault. It wasn't like Jed not to listen properly, but he'd given his clerk too much money to go to the tavern the night before to keep him out of the way, and this was the result.

Madge wasn't finished. 'And just look at the lad! Half dead of the cold after trailing all over York looking for you. And I don't suppose that Briar fellow found you either, did he?'

'No,' said Lawrence, in a clipped voice.

'Well, then,' said Madge, her arms folded across her apron, and the argument won.

Lawrence focused his attention on Jed. 'I take it you didn't come upon William again either?' he said.

Jed shook his head.

'Right,' said Lawrence, standing up. 'Well, you get yourself tidied up once you've finished that and get on with filing them papers we brought back up from London. Whatever it is he wanted, I daresay he'll be back.'

After David Ogilvie had left her, Anne sat in the darkened chapel, a small sanctuary amidst the busyness and noise of the minster. Choristers were at practice in the quire, their voices rising like larks, only to be cut down before they could reach their height by the lacerating tongue of their master. She had walked up the north aisle behind some canons passing to the Chapter House, snatches of intrigue or petty concerns coming her way, complaints about the cold, the damp, the fatter prebend handed to a rival. The cathedral was its own city, a city of men.

But this small chapel was a place of silence. The colours of the window glass were muted by the grey of the sky outside, shadows of flakes darkening them further as they passed downwards. The candle Anne had lit gave a memory of warmth and a promise of life amongst the dead grey stones, and a reminder that there were women here too. Everywhere in the minster, in fact, there were women: the Madonna with child, the Assumption, shining from golden bosses in the ceiling, the Queen of Heaven gazing beatifically from leaded windows. The Mother of Christ wept at the foot of the cross, as virgins and martyred saints saw out the centuries in coloured glass. The minster was filled with the voices of men, but sit still long enough, and the sound of them was drowned out by the silences of women.

Anne listened carefully to the silence, and put the other noises of the minster to the edges of her mind. The light outside grew greyer. She became aware, at some point, that the choristers were gone from the quire. In this space she had created for herself, she considered the words of David Ogilvie as they had walked through the snow from King's Manor to the minster. He had wasted little time in pleasantries.

'You last encountered Sir Thomas in Flanders – Damme, in fact?'

'Yes,' she said. 'Do you know it?'

He shook his head. 'I have never been there, but I have heard of the place, and what happened there. A traitor to the King was exposed, a man killed, Thomas had to fight for his life and somehow, in the midst of it all, there was you, and there was Damian Seeker, who made his escape.'

She felt her body tense at the words and hoped he would not have felt it too through the hold he had on her arm as they walked. 'If you know of Damian Seeker, there can be little else in that tale that surprises you,' she said.

'Little enough. Other than what you might have been doing there.'

'That's hardly a mystery. Under the Protectorate, my choice was exile overseas or incarceration here at Cromwell's pleasure. Unlike yourself, I had no home to return to, and chose Flanders, as did many others loyal to His Majesty.'

'That hardly explains what you were doing in Damme, on that night.'

Some excuse would have provided itself easily enough, but Anne was not disposed to humour this man's questions. 'I am astonished you think it your business to know that, Major Ogilvie,' she said.

He had been silent then for a few minutes as they'd passed through Bootham Bar and gone along High Petergate. As they cleared the bustle of the street and came within the precincts of the west door of the cathedral he began to speak again. 'I heard word of you lately having been in Edinburgh, Lady Anne, and before that, from time to time in other places. It seems you don't settle anywhere for long.'

'The years of my exile gave me a taste for the peripatetic life that I have found difficult to shed. But I am curious as to your interest in my movements, Major.'

They had now passed through the great west door to be confronted by the immensity and cold beauty of the nave. Anne could see her breath in front of her. Ogilvie had seemed momentarily transfixed by what they saw but then his hand had dropped from beneath her arm and he'd turned his back on the vista, to face her instead. 'Only that you are a woman who trails mystery behind her, and Thomas Faithly trusts too much. He is my friend, and a man to whose courage in battle I owe my life. If you seek to meddle with him in some way, I would counsel you to think again.'

Then he had given a curt bow before striding up the south aisle, away from her and, eventually, out of her vision.

FIVE

William Briar

The two stonemasons' labourers were well accustomed to the cold, but neither had ever felt quite the chill they did on entering the east crypt of York Minster that day. The older of the two shivered as they descended the steps.

'Don't know what he thinks we'll find down here — nothing but old rubble.'

'Dean wants it checked. Says someone thought they heard noises earlier.'

'Noises?' The older of the pair scoffed. 'When are there not noises in the minster? Rats, or stray cats, like as not. No one's been down here in a hundred years. Nothing but a fool's errand. Now you hold up that lantern before I break my neck on these old steps!'

The young man did as he was told, but then almost dropped his light. To his left, a hideous scene of death and depravity had emerged from the darkness. Ghoulish, empty-eyed faces leered out at him from a large stone slab as men, women and beasts tumbled into Hell around them. His companion followed his gaze and let out a low

exclamation. 'The Doomstone.' He shuddered. 'My grandfather spoke of it and he was told of it by his. Who would
come down here with that thing guarding the entrance?
Some places are best let be.'

They moved closer together and continued nonetheless down into the crypt. As they lifted their lanterns, the
younger man drew in his breath. Massive carved pillars
held up the vaulted stone roof, and above that, which was
insanity even to think of, was the whole edifice of the
minster. 'Sweet Jesus,' he said in a low voice.

'Hmmph. I doubt Jesus takes much to do with this place,'
said the older man. 'And I'm damned if I'm staying here
waiting for the whole lot to fall on my head. You swing
your lantern over that way, and I'll swing mine over this,
and then we'll be off back out of here, our duty done, before
we're bones and dust, too.

'Bones and dust,' he repeated, lifting his lamp in a careful
arc to content himself that there was nothing there that
shouldn't be.

He was about to suggest their work was done when the
younger man, his voice almost a croak said, 'And blood.'

'Don't be daft,' he began, 'the dead don't—'

And then he saw what his companion was looking at,
and it was he who dropped his lantern, scarcely aware of
the noise as it smashed on the stone floor and its light went
out. Dimly illuminated now in the bowels of the vault, and
draped over the remains of a column that looked much
more aged than those holding up the roof, was the body

of a man. He was face down, as if slung there, his neck twisted horribly and a dark sticky mess that had issued from his throat stained the stone, and the chisel, beneath him.

'Good God,' breathed the older man.

When he could command his voice again, the younger said, 'You see who it is?'

'Yes,' he answered, before stooping to pick up the chisel, 'I do.'

It was Madge who brought the news. Lawrence was busy at his desk with drafting what he hoped would be the final arguments of his deposition in favour of Thomas Faithly's claim to his late grandmother's estate of Langton. He was putting off till supper the more difficult business of persuading Manon of the necessity of his escorting her and Lizzie up to Faithly Moor, until such time as the person Roger L'Estrange had sent to York on the trail of her father could be dealt with. Jed, now dressed in clean, dry clothes and his Sunday boots, was occupied in the careful cataloguing and filing of all the papers they'd brought back with them from London. Lawrence's own notes of his conversations over many evenings back at Clifford's with his old colleagues and new students were set aside for taking to the bookbinder. 'It's how the law grows,' he'd told Jed, as the line of his special green-bound notebooks had begun to creep along the shelf above his desk. 'The common law of England breathes there.' At the sound of the housekeeper's distinctive bustle coming along the corridor, Lawrence braced himself for the interruption. The knock at the door, however, when it came, was uncharacteristically tentative.

Lawrence glanced at Jed who went to the door.

'Grandmother, you know you are not to— Grandmother, what is it?'

Lawrence looked up again and saw the look on the woman's face. He put down his pen. 'What is it, Madge?'

She looked from him to her grandson and back again, her mouth hanging open as if she'd forgotten how to speak.

She swallowed. 'It's that William Briar – him that was jilted. He's dead,' she blurted. 'Murdered.'

Lawrence had been pacing the floor of the anteroom to Faithly's apartments in King's Manor for over an hour, and the sky outside was already darkening, when Thomas finally appeared.

'Is it true? he said, as soon as he saw Thomas in the doorway. 'I can get nothing out of him.' He glanced in the direction of Thomas's clerk.

'Francis has been instructed to say nothing, to anyone, about this.' Thomas opened the door to his own office, to the side of which lay his private bedchamber.

'Well?' insisted Lawrence once the door had been shut behind them. 'Is it true? Is it him?'

Thomas let out a long breath. 'I'm afraid so.'

'*Murdered?*' said Lawrence. 'Who the hell would want to murder William?' He could scarcely believe that his client and friend, William Briar, who had been so anxious to see him that very morning, was dead.

Thomas sat down behind his desk and put his head in his hands. 'I don't know, Lawrence. I can't even begin to imagine.'

Lawrence's mind had been scurrying around possibilities ever since Madge had brought the dreadful news, but each possibility dissolved before his eyes almost as quickly as he could conceive of it. 'I mean,' he was pacing now in Thomas's office just as he had been in the clerk's anteroom, 'who in the world? I mean . . . who found him? What happened?'

Thomas stretched out a hand for the jug of claret on his desk and poured a large goblet-full for himself and one for Lawrence. 'One of the canons had reported noises from the east crypt. When he reported it to the dean, the dean had the master mason send two of his men down there.'

'Why all the palaver? Why didn't the canon just go down there and look for himself?'

'It seems none of the clergy had entered the crypt for years, centuries, possibly, not since the west crypt was filled in to shore up the foundations. The east crypt was opened up then but filled with a great deal of rubble. There was no certainty that it was safe – no one but stonemasons or surveyors ever went down there.'

'So why did William go down there? He was only back in York this morning. Did he go down alone?'

'That's what I've been trying to find out. I haven't been able to get into the minster – the dean isn't much disposed to let the lay authorities assume jurisdiction until he's had a good poke around in the matter himself—'

'Not much disposed?' interrupted Lawrence. 'Well the dean needs to be told that the law—'

Thomas held up a hand. 'I know, Lawrence, but this is *York*, and the authorities of the minster must be accorded their place. I have at least been able to ask some questions here, in King's Manor.'

'And?'

'And it seems a message arrived here this morning for William asking that he, specifically, go to the east crypt. His colleagues in the surveyors' office were surprised, for it was the first they had heard of anything being required to do with the vaults, and they weren't even aware that William had arrived back from London. It was almost mid-morning that he appeared, still in his travelling clothes with his satchel over his shoulder and his portmanteau in his hand. He was in a state of some agitation, apparently.'

'I know,' said Lawrence. 'He'd been down at my house looking for me first thing.'

Thomas looked at Lawrence in some surprise. 'You didn't tell me.'

'I'm telling you now.'

'What did he want?'

'Well, I don't know, do I? I was with you. Anyway, what happened when he got this note?'

'He left again almost immediately. His colleague says

he offered to go to the minster in his stead, but William wouldn't hear of it. He never came back.'

Lawrence let out a sigh of frustration. 'And this message?'

Thomas shook his head. 'Nowhere to be found. He must have taken it with him.'

'So, it'll still be on him.'

'We can hope. If the men in black ever let us near him. The dean is not inclined to accommodate our questions until such time he has satisfied himself that William's death doesn't fall within the Church's jurisdiction.'

'It doesn't. Murder is a capital crime, as the dean and the archdeacon and the archbishop himself know full well.'

'I did run into one visiting prebend who was more garrulous than the dean would have him be, though.'

'Oh?' said Lawrence, his face alert.

'The wound in William's neck was deep, and gaped almost an inch long where the weapon had entered. No weapon was found, though.'

Lawrence walked over to the window and leaned against the sill, looking out into the gathering darkness. He closed his eyes and forced himself to think. 'And it was stonemasons that found him?'

Thomas nodded.

'Come on then.'

'What? Where?'

'The stonemasons' yard. The dean might have got his clerics all under lock and key, but I bet he hasn't set foot in the masons' yard.'

'They'll be finished for the night. It's almost dark out there.'

'Right,' said Lawrence. 'You're right.' He drummed his fingers on the sill a moment. 'But what would you do at the end of your working day if you'd happened to have found the body of a murdered man in a crypt?'

Thomas thought for a minute. 'I suspect I'd be in need of a drink.'

They found them in the third tavern they tried, a gaggle of masons and labourers in the taproom of the Golden Slipper, and two of their number, a ruddy-faced older man and a young fellow, white as death, the focus of their comrades' attention. Lawrence murmured to Thomas to go and sit somewhere within earshot, but to steer clear of him and the masons.

'Why?'

'Well, even if you weren't in the service of the lord lieutenant, you scream gentry, that's why.' He looked Thomas briefly up and down. 'You've even started walking like the rest of them that's in authority. They'll not say a word in front of you.'

Thoroughly offended, Thomas nonetheless did as he was told and found himself a place near the window in a better part of the tavern from which to observe events.

'All right, lads?' said Lawrence, approaching the workmen.

A burly fellow with a nasty scar across his nose flexed his arms. 'Who's asking?'

Lawrence took out his purse and signalled to the tavern-keeper. He indicated the group of stoneworkers then held up his purse. The tavern-keeper understood and began to fill up more flagons of ale.

'Name's Ingolby,' said Lawrence. 'I hear it was some of you men here that found my friend in the minster this morning. William Briar.'

The head of the red-faced man at the foot of the table shot up at the name.

Lawrence whipped his head round. 'You, was it? That found him?'

The man jerked a thumb towards his pale-faced companion. 'Me and him.'

Lawrence was about to address the young man when a voice behind him said, 'What *kind* of friend?'

It was the burly interrogator again.

'What?'

'What *kind* of friend were you to him they found?' the man said.

Lawrence turned slightly and leaned in a little closer, bringing himself eye to eye with the huge stonemason. 'I was his lawyer.'

The man seemed to shrink back a little and most of the other stoneworkers did likewise. Somehow, the way opened for Lawrence to the two men seated at the bottom of the table. Those closest to them moved up to clear a space for him. He settled himself and waited till the landlord had finished setting out the fresh jugs of ale.

'Right,' he said, when the man was gone. 'I won't beat

about the bush. I need you to tell me everything you saw, and everything you heard, when you were down there.'

The younger man, utterly miserable and quite sick-looking, turned to his workmate who nodded. 'All right. That all right with you, Hugh?'

'S'pose so,' mumbled the younger man. 'But we never heard anything, did we?'

Lawrence looked to the older man who dipped his chin in confirmation. 'Not a thing.'

'All right then. Tell me what you saw.'

Lawrence listened, and felt his frustration grow. There had been no one else in the crypt, not while they'd been in there, at least, no one but them and William Briar's body. He had definitely been dead when they'd come upon him, but the blood had still been sticky on the stones. They didn't know if he'd been warm or cold – they'd never touched him. Yes, the floor of the crypt must have been dusty, but they didn't know if there had been other footprints or signs of struggle – it had been dark and besides, they hadn't thought to look.

Lawrence took a long draught of his own ale then a deep breath, summoning his patience. Out of the corner of his eye he could see Thomas's glance travelling from himself to the door, ever watchful. The Protectorate years on the run had left their mark.

The more they drank and the longer they spoke, the more relaxed the two stoneworkers became. Their companions had turned their attention to a game of dice. Lawrence drew a little closer to the pale boy. 'And it was you that spotted him first then, Hugh?'

Hugh nodded. 'Saw his feet first. Then his body, draped over the stub of the column as if he'd landed there drunk. And the mess at his neck . . .'

Lawrence looked from one labourer to the other. 'He'd definitely been stabbed?'

'Oh yes,' said Hugh.

'Aye,' concurred the one called Dick, 'definitely.'

'What with?' said Lawrence.

The younger man flushed and the older looked resolutely at the table top.

'Well?' said Lawrence.

Dick continued to stare at the table, but Hugh's evident panic grew. 'It wasn't ours!' he said.

Dick cursed and glowered at the young man.

'What wasn't?' said Lawrence.

At last Dick raised his eyes to meet Lawrence's stare. 'The chisel,' he said.

Lawrence didn't shift his own gaze. 'But there was no chisel down there by the time the alarm was raised.'

'Course there wasn't!' said Dick. 'Do you take us for fools? Anyone comes down there and finds William Briar stabbed in the neck and a bloody chisel lying on the floor is going to think we did it.' He took a long draught of his ale and looked away. 'We took it away.'

Lawrence looked up and down the bench to where the other labourers and stonemasons sat. He frowned. There was someone missing that he would have expected to see there. 'Where's Ralph Plowman today?'

Hugh shot a glance at Dick who said, 'Never came in today.'

'Right,' said Lawrence, 'and this chisel you found – Ralph's, was it?'

Neither man spoke and their silence hung in the air like a promise of thunder.

'Right,' said Lawrence again, standing up. He looked round to where Thomas was sitting and jerked his head towards the door.

'So?' said Thomas, striding along the middle of the icy street to keep pace with Lawrence. 'What have you learned?'

'That William was stabbed with a chisel, and that those two found the chisel and took it away with them in case the churchmen came down and found it there and blamed them.'

'And you don't think it was them?'

Lawrence shook his head. 'When I looked around that table, I saw that one of their number was missing.'

'You know *all* the stonemasons of York?'

Lawrence grimaced. 'No, but I know one of them. Ralph Plowman. And the reason I know Ralph Plowman is he's the man Juliet Venn married after she jilted William Briar, and *that's* what first brought William to my door. Ralph Plowman wasn't in the Golden Slipper with his workmates tonight, and they tell me he never showed his face in the masons' yard today either.'

'And the chisel used to murder William . . .'

'Exactly. Now come on.'

SIX

A House on Oglethorpe

Anne lit another candle. It had been cold as death in the house when she had returned earlier in the day. Grizel refused to have a fire anywhere but the kitchen if they were to be out, and they had both been out much of the morning. Her housemaid's abhorrence of waste did not always allow Anne's life to be as comfortable as it otherwise might be, but the fire was lit now, and the crackle of its flames drove away the silence that, until the Scotswoman returned with their supper, would only be interspersed by the sound of bells.

Anne liked the bells.

'Vanities,' Grizel had muttered when she'd said it earlier. 'All vanities to the ear of the Lord.'

Anne had opened her eyes. 'And to the ear of Grizel, I think.'

'Hmmph.' Her maid had shaken out a linen sheet and commenced the process of making up Anne's bed. 'As if Grizel should have time for contemplating vanities.'

The house on the corner of Ogleforth and Chapter House

Street was as a doll's house compared to the forbidding stone tower in Northumberland that she had chosen for their home, but they were adept at settling themselves wherever their business required them to be. Anne sometimes wondered if she and the strict Presbyterian maidservant might be two sides of the one coin. They had met four years ago in a small town in the Spanish Netherlands, two widows in exile while the British state convulsed itself again and again, neither certain where she would go next. They were both somewhere around thirty-five years of age now, and each of them might have married again, had she wished to. But neither had wished to. Anne could not recall, precisely, how or when the decision had been arrived at that they would travel together, but when they had encountered one another in that small town somewhere on the road between Bruges and Brussels, each had recognised in the other a will to survive, and that had been enough.

That, Grizel had informed her more than once, was where their similarities ended. Grizel had been born to work, Anne to be an ornament on some rich man's arm. Grizel knew the truth of the Word, freely preached by the godly ministers of the Kirk of Scotland, whereas Anne, as she was wont to remind her, was near enough a heathen and her English homeland now returned to the very margins of idolatry. The King had been restored to his rightful throne, and they might each have gone home to their own countries and their former lives, had it not been that whatever their former lives had been no longer existed. So, their irreconcilable differences notwithstanding, they had made a different life for themselves, and Anne would no more have thought of travelling about on her business without Grizel than she would have gone out without shoes. And Grizel, for her part, would not have let her.

Sometimes, Anne felt she knew little more about her companion than she had done on that first day. There was something of herself that Grizel kept locked away, even from her. Over time, Grizel had allowed small pieces of information about her past to fall from her careful lips, and Anne had gradually been able to piece them together in a way that would have defeated anyone not privy to them all. Grizel had given Anne to understand that she was also a widow. Unlike Anne's, Grizel's husband had not been a good man. There had been violence in their marriage and none to listen to her or help her. His death had been a release not simply from the marriage, but from the whole life and place it had bound her to. 'I can't go back,' Grizel had told her once, 'I will never go back.' Sometimes, Anne wondered whether Grizel's husband was dead at all.

Tonight, it was the mundanities of life that had sent the housemaid out into the icy darkness. For all the Scotswoman's many talents, there was only a handful of things beyond her staples of porridge and broth that she would consent to cook. Her view that such a diet offered sustenance enough for any Christian body might be true, but Anne's early life and her subsequent travels had taught her to expect more than oats, beans and kale. 'A spot of meat, Grizel, that isn't mutton or the carcass of an old hen, a bit of fruit that is not a berry – surely these cannot be offensive, even to you?'

Grizel's response, when Anne had finally voiced this long-suppressed plea, had been that it wasn't a question of offence, but of necessity. If Anne wished to squander her money on fripperies, so be it, but she need not think that Grizel would squander her time on cooking them. So tonight, at the end of their first full day in York, Anne had sent her maid out to get something for their supper from the nearest decent inn or tavern that she could find. In a dish in the middle of the table she'd put some of the oranges and nuts they'd bought not long since in Berwick. She'd set the table with the delftware ready provided in this house on Oglethorpe. The scenes painted on the bowls and plates as she laid them down put her in mind of places they'd been in the Netherlands, while waiting for the King to be called home. On the dresser were bottles of claret and white burgundy sent that afternoon from the archdeacon's own cellar, along with assurances that Lady Anne was only to ask for more if she should need it.

Anne didn't know if she would need it. She didn't know how long they might be here, whether the spring would see them back in her tower house in Northumberland. Much depended on the accuracy of the contents of the letter from Roger L'Estrange that Grizel had collected that morning from the safe house of All Saints Pavement. Anne had spent the earlier part of the afternoon decoding L'Estrange's blackbird, making it sing. She understood the reasons behind the enormous levels of caution exercised by L'Estrange, the safe houses, the coded letters: some of those about whom he harboured suspicions were powerful people with some degree of standing or influence with the King, and should they discover that he had sent agents looking into their past, the tables might well be turned and he find himself ascending the scaffold.

This letter had told her that Thomas Faithly was suspected of having been a double agent, in the employ of Cromwell's intelligence service, for a period of several months in the autumn and winter of the year sixteen hundred and fifty-six. Six years ago. L'Estrange believed Thomas Faithly might have been instrumental in betraying details of a plot aimed at the assassination of Oliver Cromwell to Damian Seeker. Anne remembered. The plotters had been captured or killed, and it had only been by the Grace of God that Prince Rupert of the Rhine, who was thought to have led the plotters under the name of 'Mr Boyes', had avoided capture.

'They'd never have held him, though,' Anne had asserted as she'd filled in the background to L'Estrange's letter for Grizel.

Grizel had disagreed. 'They would have put everything they had into holding him, they would have tried him in shorter order than they did the King, and then they'd have hung him from the buttresses of St Paul's.' She'd gestured towards the letter. 'But you have spoken well of this Thomas Faithly before. Do you believe it's true, that he was in Cromwell's pay?'

Anne had considered as she'd consigned the sheets of paper to the flames of the kitchen fire. 'I would be sorry if it did prove to be true, but I don't in all honesty know enough of him to discount it. What I do remember from that time is that he was much in the company of a lawyer named Lawrence Ingolby who I understand is also now in York. If we are to discover what there is to be known, I think we must get you into Ingolby's orbit while I work upon Sir Thomas.'

And so the beginnings of their plan of action were laid, and Anne had sent Grizel out into York to fetch their supper. The turning of the key in the lock followed by a stamping of feet and some imprecations in her native Scots announced the return of the housemaid. Grizel was soon at the top of the stairs, a lidded pot hanging from her hand. Anne hastened to take it from her so her friend could divest herself of her damp outer clothes.

'It's still snowing then?'

'As if till doomsday,' said Grizel.

Anne lifted the lid of the pot with a napkin. 'What have you found us?'

'Pigeon stew with dumplings,' muttered Grizel, ushering Anne aside so she could ladle the food out into the bowls.

'What's wrong, Griz? You seem distracted.'

Grizel sat down. 'I passed one or two places that were none too salubrious, but they seemed to keep a decent enough house at the sign of the Golden Slipper, a good bit down Goodramgate, so I went in there.'

'And?'

'There was some rumpus amongst stonemasons, and I did not like the tenor of it.'

'Rumpus? What about?' Anne was about to lift her spoon, but at the look in the housemaid's eye, she left it. A short grace was said, redolent of their gratitude and unworthiness. Anne was glad when the grace ended and she could finally begin to eat. 'So?' she said as she spooned the first mouthful.

Grizel took up her napkin. 'As I waited in the Golden Slipper for our supper, I was close to a table at which were seated perhaps a dozen stonemasons. I wasn't paying them as much heed as I should, but I heard the gist of what they were talking of. Today, as the noonday bells were ringing, a canon of York Minster was telling the archdeacon of troubling noises he had just heard coming from the east crypt of that place, and when two stonemasons were sent down later to check on matters, they came upon the body, not yet cold, of a lately murdered man.'

Anne found that she had suddenly lost her appetite. 'What time did you say this was, Griz?'

Grizel chewed a mouthful of her own stew before replying. 'Noon. That was when the strange sounds were said to have been heard. The body was found later.' Then she narrowed her eyes as she looked at Anne. 'Why, what is it?'

'As the noon day bells were ringing, I was seated there, in York Minster, in a side chapel.'

Grizel put down her spoon. 'And you heard nothing else?'

'Nothing,' said Anne. 'But, Griz, I had been talking with a man there, and he had not long left me.'

Grizel's brow wrinkled. 'A man? What man?'

Anne was trying to make sense of it herself. 'It was a friend of Thomas Faithly's that I had met when I engineered my encounter with Sir Thomas just outside King's Manor. He crossed with me into the minster. We spoke below the west window − it's quite beautiful, you know, there's a heart in it. Anyway, he seemed to have some suspicion of me, and was keen to warn me off too close an association with Sir Thomas. He said his piece then stalked off down one of the aisles and out of my sight and I sought out my sanctuary in a chapel. I would have mentioned it earlier, but my mind was taken up by the matter of L'Estrange's letter. I had set all thought of him aside until I could think of some reasonable suggestion as to what he might mean by his warning.'

'But who was he? Have you ever come across him before?'

'He is a Major David Ogilvie, and comes from somewhere in the north − Scotland, by the sound of it. He is a friend of Sir Thomas's who fought alongside him in the late wars of these kingdoms and . . .'

Anne broke off, because it seemed to her that Grizel was not listening. 'Griz? Griselda?'

Grizel was standing. 'Are you sure? That he is a Scotsman and his name is David Ogilvie?'

'Certain. His speech was not unlike your own, in fact. What is it, Griz? Do you know this man?'

Grizel merely shook her head. 'No, but I'm tired. It has been another long day. I bid your ladyship goodnight.' And she left, not even closing the parlour door behind her, the food in her bowl all but untouched.

SEVEN

Juliet Venn

'You're certain he'll be there?' said Thomas as they hurried along St Andrewgate on their way to Ralph Plowman's home off Spen Lane.

'He'd better be,' said Lawrence grimly.

The cottage was in a small courtyard at the bottom of a short snicket. It was of two storeys, and squashed somehow between two larger properties. A lantern was lit at the entrance to the courtyard, affording all the light there was, save the tiny chinks coming through shutters closed against the night. There was no knocker, so Lawrence rapped hard with his knuckles. A dog barked somewhere, and a baby cried somewhere else. There was a slow creak as the door in front of Lawrence was opened. Lawrence recognised the man in the doorway — Juliet Venn's father — and he saw that Venn had recognised him too.

'Mr Venn,' said Lawrence.

'Mr Ingolby,' said the man, wary. 'It's a strange hour for a visit. On such a night.' He peered beyond to where

Sir Thomas stood, but it was clearly Lawrence that he was more worried about.

Lawrence didn't bother with niceties – his foot was already over the threshold. 'Your son-in-law at home, is he?'

The man squared up a little in front of him. 'Ah, now then, Mr Ingolby. That business was sorted long ago. I trust William Briar's not threatening to drag my daughter up to court over it again, is he?'

'It's not your daughter that's in danger of being dragged to court, Mr Venn. Now is he in?'

'Yes, my husband is here.' From somewhere behind the householder, a young woman had appeared. Juliet Plowman, that had been Juliet Venn. *Juliet*. 'What were her parents thinking of, calling her that?' Madge, a great devotee of the playhouses in her youth, had said. 'Asking for trouble.' And on that point, Lawrence was inclined to agree with his housekeeper. Looking at her now, six months on from her marriage, he saw little to make him change that view. Juliet Venn was far too pretty for a poor girl in a poor courtyard at the end of a narrow snicket in York. She was too finely made to be a labourer's daughter. That she would have taken the attention of a man of a higher station in life had been inevitable. And it had been William Briar's fate that it had been his attention she'd taken. Juliet's parents had hardly been able to believe their good fortune, her good fortune, that a man with such prospects had wanted to marry their daughter. And Juliet had for a while been taken up in the excitement of the whole affair. That was until she had set eyes on Ralph Plowman, stonemason, and he on her. A man with a respectable trade, a good man closer to her own world – in all ways a more sensible match. But there had been more to it than that. Again, as Madge had said, Ralph Plowman had 'turned her head, that stonemason. A good-looking, well-built fellow. A girl likes a bit of muscle.' Whatever the reason for Juliet Venn's attraction to Ralph Plowman, poor William Briar had not been able to compete with it.

'Where's your husband, Mistress Plowman?' Lawrence asked the frightened-looking woman.

'Where else? In his sickbed,' she replied, her dark blue eyes huge in the dim light.

'Oh aye,' said Lawrence, suspicious and trying to see past her into the murky interior of the house. 'What's wrong with him, then?'

Juliet Plowman took a step back. 'See for yourself, but you must close the door to keep the cold out.'

The room they entered served both as kitchen and parlour. A fire roared in the hearth, and a simmering pot suspended over it gave off a hint of chamomile amongst fumes of cloves that caught in Lawrence's throat. A lamp hung over a scrubbed pine table in the centre, and here Juliet's father now sat, packing his pipe and watching them carefully.

There was no light anywhere else in the room, and it took Lawrence a moment to see where Juliet was. Soft sounds of her voice made him look to his left and he saw her now, seated on a small stool, at the dark edges of the room. Wooden steps led upwards to the floor above, and beneath them was a trestle bed. Juliet was seated beside this, talking in quiet tones to the man, swathed in many blankets, laid out on it. Ralph Plowman.

She might be talking, but Lawrence didn't think Ralph was listening. His eyes wandered somewhat hopelessly, and on his pale, almost green face was the sheen of a fever. As Lawrence stared at the afflicted stonemason he had come to question, Thomas went past him to the man's bedside.

'How long has you husband been like this, Mistress Plowman?'

'Since last night. Well, it began to come on like this at dawn, but it started last night.'

'How did it start?'

She lifted the uppermost of the blankets. The right sleeve of his nightshirt had been cut to the elbow, and as they leaned closer, they saw why. Plowman's forearm was dark and swollen, his wrist twisted so that the bone almost protruded through the skin. It was clearly broken, and Lawrence noted that there was a deep gash running down the right side of the man's face.

Thomas asked. 'Who did this, Mistress Plowman?'

She was shaking her head and just as Lawrence was wondering what on earth could have possessed William Briar to do something like this, now, to the stonemason, she said, 'No one. No one did it to him. No one but himself. And me. He had gone out to the woodshed to fetch our fuel in

last night. I opened the door to call after him not to forget
to make sure the pig was secure. He turned too quickly at
my voice and went over on the ice. It was so icy last night.'

'Yes,' said Thomas, 'it was.'

'The wood was under his left arm and he put out the
right one to try to stop his fall, but instead his own full
weight came down upon it. Father and I got him inside and
Father went out for a surgeon straight away.'

'Did the surgeon come?'

Juliet nodded. 'But Ralph said he wasn't having a butcher
anywhere near his arm and it would set itself fine by
morning.' She began to weep. 'And this is the result.'

'Juliet,' said Lawrence, his voice as gentle as he could
make it, 'I think you must fetch a physician for your husband, and soon.'

She swallowed. 'I fetched one this morning, and he looked
at Ralph's arm and said he must submit to the surgeon there
and then or lose more than his arm.'

'And your husband still would not allow it?' Thomas
was incredulous.

'It's his livelihood, Thomas,' Lawrence murmured to him.

Juliet was stroking her husband's face. 'The fever had
already begun to creep on him by then, and his understanding was . . . I gave him the powders the physician
prescribed, from the apothecary, but they have done him
no good.' Lawrence glanced over to the pot in which she
was now throwing together whatever remedy she could
think of in the hope that it might somehow help.

'He has been here since last night then,' Sir Thomas said, a statement rather than a question.

She nodded.

Lawrence put his hand on his friend's arm and said, 'Come on, Thomas. Let's leave them in peace.'

As he passed the table where Juliet's father was still sitting, pipe unlit, he leaned down and placed some coins in front of the older man. 'Send for the surgeon, now.'

The older man nodded and stood up.

They were almost out of the door when Thomas murmured to Lawrence, 'Just to be sure,' then turned to Juliet's father, who was tying on his cloak. 'The physician who came this morning, what was his name?'

It was not a half-hour later that they were leaving the physician's house.

'So, that's it confirmed,' said Thomas. 'It cannot have been Ralph Plowman who murdered William Briar.'

Lawrence's face was grim. 'No. By the time William was at my house this morning shouting to see me, Ralph Plowman was already too ill to stir from his own bed. But whoever *did* kill William went to some lengths to make it look like Ralph Plowman had done it.'

Lawrence brushed aside all questions when he arrived home and summoned Jed into his office. 'Close that door behind you and sit down.'

Looking apprehensive, Jed followed him into the room and made to take his usual seat at his own small table by the door but Lawrence said, 'No, not there, there,' and pointed at one of the two armchairs positioned by the hearth. The padding on one arm still appeared a little damp from the melted snow that had dripped from Andrew Marvell's cloak the night before.

'Right,' said Lawrence once his clerk had settled, 'I need you to tell me *exactly* what William Briar said when he was down here this morning.'

Jed shook his head. 'I don't know,' he said at last, his fore-head screwed up as if the effort to remember was hurting his head. 'He were shouting and ranting and I thought he might do all sorts, after what you said about keeping strangers out of the house . . .'

'I know, I know,' said Lawrence. 'But this is really import-ant. And William Briar wasn't a stranger.'

'But the way he were shouting . . .'

'I know he was shouting,' said Lawrence, studying to keep his calm. Jed was rarely troubled by anything, but he could see the young man was genuinely anxious now. 'But you must remember something of what he said.'

Jed's fingers flexed, the knuckles white as he rubbed his fists on his knees. 'He was demanding to see you.'

'He must have said something of what it was about, though?'

Jed furrowed his brow as he thought, evidently desperate to come up with something he might tell his master.

'I mean, did he mention Ralph Plowman at all? Juliet Venn's husband?'

Lawrence saw Jed swallow again and colour as he bit his lip.

'Jed? You'd best tell me now, because the longer you don't, the worse it'll go for you.'

The clerk took a deep breath and lifted his eyes to look Lawrence in the face at last. 'I think that was the name he was saying, something about the stonemason, but I couldn't really make out what he meant.'

Lawrence stood up. 'Why on earth didn't you tell me this before?'

Jed held up his hands. 'I wasn't sure, and you know how angry you get any time Mr Briar's name comes up and my grandmother goes on about him being jilted. I thought you'd say she was just putting ideas in my head. And maybe she was, because he was going on so, and my head was still too full of ale from the night before.'

Lawrence muttered an oath then went to lean against the mantelshelf, running his hands through his hair. It wasn't like Jed to be so stupid, but then it wasn't like him to be hung-over either and it was Lawrence that had given him the money to do it. 'All right,' he said at last. 'Get off to your bed.' Jed got up with alacrity and made for the door, but before he'd turned the handle, Lawrence stopped him and said, 'But if anything like that ever happens again, you tell me *everything*, whether you think it'll make me angry or not. Understand?'

'Yes,' said Jed, breathing a sigh of relief, obviously glad to be getting out of the room, 'I understand.'

Lawrence sat by the fire in his study for a good while afterwards, nursing a goblet of wine and trying to make sense of what Jed had told him in light of the events of the day and what he and Thomas Faithly had discovered at Ralph Plowman's house that evening, but Jed's admission only muddied things rather than clarifying them. Then, as he stared over the top of his glass, the slight discolouration of the pink velvet on the arm of the chair opposite him caught his eye. He could picture Andrew Marvell sitting there, warning him that someone had been sent to York to try to track down Damian Seeker through him, through Manon. Lawrence closed his eyes and put his head back against his own chair. Maybe that was what William Briar had come here to tell him too. Browbeating Jed into remembering things he might never have heard in the first place would hardly help. William was dead, and Lawrence had to see to the safety of his own family. He covered over the fire and went upstairs to his wife.

EIGHT

Searchers

Anne Winter had woken that morning, as she did every morning, to the sounds of a psalm being sung. She had first heard these psalms in cold Scottish churches with plain windows and bare walls, where black-frocked ministers had seemed to look her in the eye and tell of her damnation. For herself, Anne had little enough faith, but she found reassurance in colour, light, golden thread on surplices, the scent of incense wafted from censers. She preferred a marble altar behind a carved screen, a reredos, the images of the saints, the marvellous polyphony of organ and choir to the starkness of a Presbyterian pulpit. Should God look down upon an Anglican church, there would be far too much else to take his eye among the obfuscation of smoke from censers and the glinting of colours through stained glass for Him to notice Anne Winter. But in Grizel's bleak Scottish churches, there had been nowhere she might hide herself.

She couldn't make out the words or tell which psalm it was this morning. They all sounded alike to her; they all excluded her, dead words of dead men. She pressed her fingers to her temples and closed her eyes before pushing back the bedcovers to set her feet on the cold floor. The day would not deal with itself.

'Tell me more, then, of this Ingolby we are to begin looking for this morning,' said Grizel after she had ladled porridge into their bowls and said the grace.

'Lawrence Ingolby is a lawyer, a Yorkshireman,' said Anne. 'He was a friend to Damian Seeker.'

Grizel paused in the act of lifting her food to her mouth. 'I thought you said that man had no friends?'

Anne wrinkled her nose, considering. 'Not friends, precisely, but people whom he tolerated more than he did others.'

'And what if they did not tolerate him?'

Anne smiled and reached for the honey. 'I don't think that was a question he ever troubled himself much over.'

Grizel made a small noise of approval. 'And I take it this Ingolby also knows Thomas Faithly?'

'From boyhood,' said Anne. 'Sir Thomas's father came across Lawrence Ingolby as a foundling. There was a dissolute mother, I understand, but she was not long in the picture. The boy showed promise from a young age and was fostered by a wealthy Puritan family of the name of Pullan, in Faithly village, up on the moors. The son of that family is now in possession of Sir Thomas's former home. Are you following?'

Grizel nodded. 'So Ingolby is of the Puritan persuasion?'

Anne laughed. 'Ingolby is of the Ingolby persuasion.

Anyway, he was in London six years ago, at around the same time L'Estrange believes Sir Thomas was released from the Tower, possibly into Damian Seeker's employ. Given their connection in Faithly village and that Ingolby is known to have associated with Seeker, it is very likely that he and Sir Thomas spent time in one another's company in London in those days. If anyone knows what Sir Thomas was doing in those few months between his release from the Tower and his flight back to the continent, it's likely to be Lawrence Ingolby.'

'Mmm,' said Grizel, agreeing. 'And by what means do you think we should approach him?'

'We must get you into his household. Specifically, we must make you acquainted with his servants.'

Grizel nodded. They had done this sort of thing before. 'But that may take a little time – to engineer a meeting in the market place, or at their preferred church.'

'No.' Anne picked up their empty bowls and set them down on the dresser. 'That will not be necessary on this occasion. For I know Lawrence Ingolby's wife.'

Manon had waited until Lawrence had left for an early appointment at the coffee house off Stonegate, then she had kissed Lizzie on the forehead and quickly said to Madge, 'I'm just popping out for a little while. I won't be long.'

'Out?' the old lady had said as if she had never heard of such a thing. 'But Master said I was to keep an eye on you and make sure you took your rest. Whatever can you be needing to go out for?'

Manon smiled at Lizzie and put a finger to her lips, then said, 'It's a secret.'

'Secret? Master would not approve of anyone in this house having secrets, specially you!'

'I'll be gone no time. And he'll approve this secret when he discovers it. Remember it's his birthday soon.'

'Ah,' said Madge. 'Not a word will pass my lips.' But as Manon pulled up the fur-trimmed hood of her heavy blue woollen mantle, the housekeeper added, 'But Jedediah must go with you.'

Manon stopped. She did not mind Jed, but she found his company a little dour and oppressive to her spirits, and she'd been looking forward to this small adventure of fetching Lawrence's present for some time. She looked over to where the young man was seated by the hearth, employed in the cleaning of Lawrence's second-best boots and looking no happier at his grandmother's suggestion than she was. 'Jedediah has his own work to attend to,' she said, 'and my husband would not be best pleased if he came back for his dinner and found tasks he had left him not done. I'll hardly be an hour.' And then she was gone before Madge could raise any further objections, out of the front door, across the street and into Cheat's Lane.

Manon preferred to stay away from the main thorough-fares. She was not indifferent to the mess that could be thrown up by passing animals and carts, but neither was she indifferent to Lawrence's warnings of the night before. He'd come back a good while after suppertime having been up to see Thomas at King's Manor when they got the terrible news about William Briar. Manon could hardly believe yet that William was dead – he'd been a quiet, solid sort of person, serious but kind, and she had liked him. She could hardly think that anyone would want to kill him. But as Lawrence had emphasised to her, they should act with caution. Whatever he had discovered while out with Thomas, he had been even more troubled by the time he'd come home than he had been before he'd left, and seemed certain that the murder of William was tied up in some sort of threat to themselves. Manon could hardly see why this should be the case, and Lawrence had flatly refused to tell her, only repeating that she must trust him. Before at last coming to bed, he'd made extra checks on the doors and windows of their home, and this morning he had changed his plan to take Jed with him about his business in town and instead told him to stay at home keeping guard on the house, and to let no stranger in.

As these thoughts wafted about in her head, Manon knew that Madge had been right – Lawrence would not have been happy about her going out into town on her own. She felt that her husband sometimes forgot how she had had to fend for herself for long periods during her childhood with a neglectful mother and malicious stepfather, before her own father had found her at last. But Manon was Damian Seeker's daughter, through and through, and she could look after herself, whatever her husband might think. Besides, no harm could come to her in broad daylight, and no stranger would know their way as she did round the snickets and ginnels between her home and the shop of the silversmith on Coppergate that she had commissioned to make Lawrence's gift.

Picking her way carefully up Cheat's Lane, it wasn't long until she was turning into Bakehouse Yard, where she was known to all the shopkeepers. She had almost stepped out onto Pavement when she was forced to step back to let a man going quickly along the street pass by. He nodded to her as he pressed on, his hand to the brim of his hat, but then the movement seemed to be arrested by what he saw, by herself. He paused for the slightest moment and she thought he was about to speak but instead he bowed his head slightly before looking away again and continuing, more slowly, on his way.

Manon hesitated at the top of the steps until he was lost to view, wondering whether she should turn back and go home. She was near to certain that she'd never seen the man before, but that of course didn't mean he'd never seen her. She told herself not to be foolish and stepped out onto the street of Pavement.

Thomas Faithly rolled the orange in his fingers. He had a flash of memory, of being in Seville, and of reaching up to pluck a fruit from an overhanging bough. He closed his eyes and thought for a moment of the late afternoon sun on his face, the sound of the cicadas' incessant chirruping, the smell of heat rising from honey-coloured walls. But he remembered too that he had plucked the orange from the tree because he had been hungry. The orange, when he had got it, had been bitter and he had longed for nothing more than the taste of a crisp English apple.

That had been the start of it, that bitter Seville orange. It was as if amongst its pips had been the seeds of his discontent with a life in exile. He had travelled France, Spain, Germany, Flanders in the service of the exiled King. No matter what he had tried to do, he hadn't been able to wash that taste of bitterness from his mouth, and the longing for home had grown. It had not been Spain that had been the problem, nor the Low Countries, nor France. It had not been Germany either, but it had been there, one day over six years ago in Cologne, that he had decided he could bear his exile no more and had slipped away from the King's court to make his way up the Rhine to Rotterdam, and at last, in the company of some Flemish sailors, had found a passage home.

He had put his faith in Fate, and Fate had soon manifested itself in the six-foot-four form of Captain Damian Seeker, a fellow Yorkshireman seconded to the service of Cromwell's Major Generals. Thomas was still tormented by the knowledge that he had offered himself up as a spy for Cromwell. His entanglement in Seeker's investigation into a string of conspiracies against the Lord Protector had soon revealed to him that one of the conspirators, living incognito in London as 'Mr Boyes', was Prince Rupert of the Rhine. Thomas's loyalties to Charles Stuart might have been waning, but to Rupert they never would. He'd reported nothing of this to Seeker, and when the plots had failed, he'd fled England, alongside Rupert, back into exile.

He told himself, again and again when he heard of old treacheries being uncovered, that he had given Seeker nothing. But sometimes, in the cold dark of the night, or when he had been alone for too long, Thomas remembered that that was not true. On that first flight from Cologne he had taken with him a list of names of 'well-affected' Royalists in England who'd been in the early stages of planning against Cromwell. Those plans had withered and died as had so many before them and the men named on the list had simply been watched by the Republican authorities, but the knowledge of what his treachery might have cost them sometimes kept Thomas awake at night. It wasn't a thing he could talk of to Lawrence. Lawrence had never compromised himself that way, never hazarded and lost all for a belief, a cause, never risked losing what little he had left by turning his back on it.

After he had finally parted company with Lawrence Ingolby the previous night, Thomas had gone to meet with David Ogilvie and, in his cups, come close to unburdening himself of his guilt. Ogilvie at least knew what it was to fight and risk all in another man's cause. He wasn't sure what had stopped him – a sudden flash of sobriety, of discretion, or perhaps a wish that this old friend who had known him before he turned traitor would not think badly of him.

Or perhaps it was because of what Andrew Marvell had travelled secretly from abroad to tell Ingolby – that someone had come to York on Seeker's trail. Thomas knew that wherever Damian Seeker might be, that trail might lead first of all to himself. As he had lain in his chamber at King's Manor, watching through the night, he had sensed a new and heavy load of snow, travelled down from the north and looming over York. He could smell it and he could feel the weight of the snowbound heaths pressing on this city, hemming them all in. By the time dawn at last started to send a little light beneath his shutters, and the noises from the anteroom next door suggested his young page and clerk were beginning to stir, he was filled with a sense of foreboding. He needed to see Ingolby again, learn whether the hours of the night had given his friend any clarity on how best they might meet this threat.

Thomas swung himself out of bed and, swiftly dressed and breakfasted, he was soon out through the wall in the abbey gardens and into the heart of the town. The folk of York, hunched in on themselves, moved carefully through the streets and no one seemed inclined to impede his progress down to the Ingolbys' house, but as soon as he crossed from the end of Colliergate to turn down Fossgate, he saw that all was not well.

There was some sort of commotion in the street outside the house with the green door. The door stood open, and a gaggle of people were gathered outside. Thomas hurried down and pushed his way through the assembled neighbours and into the house where he followed increasingly audible sounds of female distress to the kitchen.

Lawrence's housekeeper was standing over her grandson and giving the young man a thorough and almost incoherent tongue-lashing. Jed was seated, hands gripping his knees, eyes glaring and mouth pursed as if it was all he could do to keep his composure.

Thomas closed the kitchen door firmly behind him, and both Madge and Jed jumped, shocked to see him there. 'What's going on here?' he demanded. 'Where's Lawrence?'

Madge stared at him, her mouth agape, but it was her grandson who seemed to recover himself first. He stood up, and patted down his hair, which Thomas now noticed was sodden. 'He's out looking,' he said.

'Out looking for what?'

Jed hesitated and a distraught Madge broke in, 'The babby! He's out looking for the babby!' Then she was sinking, howling, into her kitchen chair and wiping eyes and nose with the apron which she had thrown up over her face.

Thomas felt dread like a lump of lead in his stomach.

'Lizzie? Little Elizabeth? Where has she gone?'

The housekeeper blew her nose loudly and rubbed again at red and swollen eyes. 'Well, we don't know, do we?' and then she collapsed into howling again.

Thomas turned back to Jed. 'Tell me what happened.'

The young man took a deep breath and rubbed his hands over his eyes, as if looking for time to find the right words.

Thomas lost his patience. 'Out with it, for God's sake!'

The voice was low and sullen. 'I didn't know she'd followed me.'

'Followed you where?'

'Into the yard, out the back gate when I went to put the waste out for the night-soil men. I didn't see her – she must have toddled out behind me when I wasn't looking and . . .'

'And what?' demanded Thomas.

'I didn't know she'd gone out into the back lane after me. When I came back into the yard, I closed the gate behind me.'

Thomas's sense of dread grew. 'And how long till it was realised she was missing?'

Madge glanced towards the clock hanging on the wall. 'Hardly half an hour,' she said. 'Not much more than a quarter even.'

It was a moment before Thomas could master his anger enough to speak. 'And Lawrence has gone to look for her?'

Madge nodded. 'Jed went for him the minute the mistress came back from being out to the silversmith's and we realised little Lizzie was gone. Stone mad, the master was. He's that distracted this last couple of days, Sir Thomas – I think he'll kill someone.'

Thomas looked about him. 'Manon? Where is she?'

Jed swallowed. 'The master had me fetch a physician. He's with her now.'

Thomas made to head for the stairs, then stopped. 'And you,' he demanded of the clerk. 'Why aren't you out looking too?'

Jed's grandmother answered for him. 'Master said he'd to stay here, protect the household and the mistress.'

It was all Thomas could do not to take the clerk by the scruff of the neck and throw him out on the street. 'Protect the household! The street door was wide open to the world. I walked straight in here,' he waved a hand at his sword, 'armed. I might have been anybody. I might have slit the throats of the lot of you.' He brought his face close to Jed's. 'Get out and help your master find that child, and don't show your face back here till you've got her. You can tell Lawrence that I am here, and that Manon is safe.'

Thomas had hardly finished speaking and Jed was gone. Then Thomas turned his attention to the housekeeper. 'Lock the doors, front and back, and don't let anyone but your master in without my say-so.' The woman had one last blow at her nose and nodded. 'And for pity's sake, will you shut that dog up!' An incessant yapping from Madge's malign terrier ringing in his ears, Thomas went up the stairs to Manon Ingolby.

Madge's bosom was heaving and she could hardly breathe. 'Stop now, Madge, stop,' she said to herself, steadying herself with her hands on the back of a chair. 'Be no good to babby or the poor mistress if you're dead of an apoplexy. And who would keep an eye on Jed then?' She stood and three times took in a deep breath, three times letting the breath out slowly. 'Now then,' she said, bending down as she felt better, 'whatever is wrong with you, my little Prince Hal?'

Prince Hal, seeing that he had her attention, only began to bark the more furiously, jumping up to scrape his claws on the kitchen door. 'Poor thing,' said Madge, 'you're needing out and all forgotten in the middle of everything.' Glancing in the direction of the other door, leading to the hallway and stairs up which she had heard Thomas Faithly bound, she unlatched the back kitchen door for the dog to get out. 'Two minutes, no more,' she admonished the terrier, 'or there'll be no end of it from Sir Thomas if I haven't all the doors and windows locked!'

Still muttering, 'no end of it,' to herself, she shuffled down the hallway to lock the front door. Going back to the kitchen, she realised that Prince Hal, now out in the yard, was barking with even greater vehemence. 'What in the world can the creature want?'

Out across the yard, white against the snow that continued to fall thickly and was already lying, the terrier was now raising his racket at the back gate. Madge hastily pulled on an extra shawl and went out after him. 'Hal! Hal! Is she there, is she home?' Fumbling at the bolt with cold fingers, she pulled it back expectantly. There was nothing except for the empty passageway and not the tiniest of footsteps visible in the snow. As a crestfallen Madge was looking to one end of the lane and then the other, Prince Hal ran out between her skirts and the gatepost and hared off, still barking, up Straker's Passage. Madge clamped her hand over her mouth, tears almost coming again. 'Oh, Hal!' she said, turning and beginning to hurry as quickly back through the gate and across the yard to the house as the ice and slush allowed her, 'Oh, you clever, clever boy!'

Thomas stood helpless. He'd never seen Manon like this, not even in the earliest days of their friendship, when the mysterious, pale young girl had been escorted from York-shire to London in the care of Anne Winter, by those same soldiers who'd been escorting him down to the Tower. He'd tried asking Lawrence, once, about Manon's history, but had swiftly been told it was not his business. In time, though, he had come to understand the astonishing truth that she was Damian Seeker's daughter. What might that man not have done had he been here now?

Manon's eyes were wild as she paced distractedly about her bedchamber, having dismissed the physician and his pleas that she would take a concoction that might calm her to sleep. She had almost lunged at Thomas when he'd come into the room, and it was only his presence and the midwife's dire warnings about the risk to her unborn child that kept her from going out in the snowstorm in search of her daughter.

She clutched his hand. 'Oh God, oh God, where is she, Thomas?'

'Hush,' he said, passing his hand over her brow, 'Law-rence will find her.'

'But what if she has gone down to the wharf, tumbled into the river? What if someone has taken her?'

'The boatmen would have caught her had she got

anywhere near the wharf, or some person crossing the bridge would have seen her. Never fear about that, Manon – she will not have gone into the river.' He said nothing to her fears that someone might have taken the child. The lie that no one would think such a thing would not force itself over his lips. Instead he held her hand more tightly. If what Marvell said was true, and someone had come to York in order to discover from Lawrence the whereabouts of Damian Seeker, taking the Ingolbys' child was the only possible way that Lawrence might be forced to talk. It would do Manon Ingolby no good to think her child was in peril because of her husband's past association with one of Cromwell's agents – her own father.

Thomas had just persuaded Manon to lie down and assured her that yes, Jed had now gone out to join in the search too, when a shrill shrieking of his name shot up the stairs. 'Sir Thomas! Sir Thomas! Oh, you must get after Prince Hal!'

'Damn the woman!' said Thomas, striding to the door with a view to telling her to keep her voice down. But Manon had sat up and was now very determinedly getting out of bed, her face enlivened with new hope.

'Of course.' Going past him to the door and pulling it open she greeted the housekeeper excitedly. 'Prince Hal! Why did I not think of it?'

'Who is Prince Hal?' said Thomas, hastening after her.

The two women looked at him in astonishment. 'The dog, of course,' said Madge.

'Yes,' said Manon, taking Madge's hand as the older woman lighted her down the steps. 'Lizzie loves Hal and Hal Lizzie, and he will not happily be parted from her. We must send out Prince Hal to find her.'

'But he is already gone, my dear,' said Madge. 'That is why I called down Sir Thomas here. He must go after him.'

Manon had turned to him, her eyes alight, 'Oh yes, Thomas, you must. You will, will you not?'

'But I cannot leave you women alone here.'

'Pff.' Madge was contemptuous. 'I will lock the doors after you and should anyone attempt to breach them, they will find me ready.' Thomas saw now that in her left hand she brandished a pistol.

'Where on earth did you get that?'

'It's the master's. He keeps it in the drawer of his study.'

Thomas looked to Manon who did not appear troubled at this development, then back to Madge. 'You know how to use it?'

'Oh, don't you worry yourself about that. Madge Penmore could take down a Spanish buccaneer at forty yards.' She laid a protective hand on Manon's arm. 'No one will get near my mistress. But you must go, sir. Get you after Hal – he could be at the other side of York by now!'

Thomas was far from convinced but he saw refusal would do Manon's state of mind more harm than good. Admonishing Madge once more to let nobody into the house and to discharge her pistol if she had to, he went off in the direction she told him the animal had gone. He followed the pawprints of the small dog all the way up Straker's Passage then onto Black Horse Passage and into the Stonebow where they became lost amongst wheel tracks, hoof and bootprints. He looked distractedly around him. A pair of butcher's boys had set down the pig carcass they were carrying and begun to hurl snowballs at a passing brewer's cart.

'You boys!' he shouted. 'Have you seen a terrier come out this way?'

'Aye,' said one. 'Madge Penmore's tyke came darting out that vennel and went yapping and snapping up Colliergate like its tail were on fire. Must a' been after a rat or something.'

But Thomas was already running, cursing as he slipped in the slush, from the end of the Stonebow across Pavement and onto Colliergate. The street was busy with people hurrying as much as they could in the swirling snow, trying to get in what they needed then get safely home. Carters with wheels sticking cursed at the red-faced children who were hurling balls of snow their way. The snow grew heavier and heavier and it was becoming difficult to see more than a few feet ahead. Thomas shouldered encumbrances aside without apology as he ran, not caring who or what he might bump into in his pursuit of the terrier. Then suddenly he was brought to a halt by a woman's surprised cry as she fell into the road beside him. Thomas spun round, apologising, and reached down a hand to help, only to notice a small red apple that had been tipped from her fallen basket roll an inch or two before coming to rest in the snow at his feet.

He stared a moment at the apple then reached again for the woman. 'Forgive me,' he said, as he pulled her up somewhat roughly, 'but I must get after that dog.' It was only as he'd set her on her feet and was about to run again that he realised, to his horror, that the woman he had knocked over was Anne Winter.

He started to mumble an incoherent apology but was halted by the sardonic voice of the Scotswoman who had evidently been accompanying Lady Anne and who had stooped to pick up more spilled apples. 'Would it be that wee dog over there?'

Thomas followed her gaze. With a jolt he saw Prince Hal disappear down a very narrow snicket. He apologised again and rushed across the street after the animal. He reached the top of the path only to realise that the Scotswoman was at his back.

'What's he after?' she asked.

'A missing child,' he shouted behind him, as he continued in pursuit of the small white dog, who was now barking furiously at the rotting wooden door of a small shack at the far end of the snicket. Thomas was soon at the door, turning the handle, but the door refused to move, a bolt near the top, he now noticed, securing it with a padlock. He reached his dagger up to the padlock in an attempt to prise it off but could not shift it. The terrier was now frantic, and as Thomas looked around for some other implement, the woman behind him exclaimed in exasperation, 'For ony sake, pit yer shooder til it, man!'

'What?' he said.

'Your shoulder! Put your shoulder to it!'

Thomas lost no more time before hurling himself, shoulder first, at the door. It gave at the second assault and swung inwards, away from them, into a dark and windowless coal store in the corner of which Lizzie Ingolby, sobbing and streaked with dirt, clutched a kitten to her chest.

The dog was through the door in an instant, and the woman after it, Thomas following. The woman had crouched down and reached out a hand to the little girl. 'My wee pet, my poor wee pet. All will be well. You're safe now, and all will be well.'

The child's eyes in her soot-streaked face were huge and terrified. Thomas put a gentle hand on the woman's shoulder and said, 'No, let me. She knows me.'

The woman moved aside and Thomas crouched down before the little girl. 'Lizzie. Lizzie, my sweetheart. You needn't be frightened any more. Uncle Thomas is here. I'm going to take you home.'

NINE

At the Ingolbys' House

The reception was tumultuous. As he passed the child over to the exultant housekeeper, Thomas feared for a moment that Lizzie, kitten still in her arms, would be crushed in Madge's embrace. Manon had almost fainted at the sight of her daughter and Thomas only just managed to catch her and help into her hearthside chair. Throughout all, the dog continued to yap and the hairs of the terrified kitten's fur stood on end.

'Thomas.' Manon clutched his hand and let her tears flow. 'Thank God, thank God. You have found her.'

He settled her in the chair before taking the child from Madge and passing her to Manon. The Scotswoman, who had again come in behind him, somehow obtained possession of the kitten.

As Madge bustled off to fetch blankets and clean, dry articles of clothing for Lizzie, Manon covered her daughter with kisses. Running a thumb gently over the smear of coal dust and tears on the little girl's cheek, she looked up at Thomas. 'We will never forget this, as long as we live. And we can never repay you.'

He touched a finger to the one lank brown curl at the nape of Lizzie's neck. 'I did nothing more than any friend would do, Manon. And I was fortunate to have help.' He turned to indicate the Scotswoman, but she was no longer there. The kitten had been placed on the hearth rug at Manon's feet. As Madge came hurrying in from upstairs with a bundle of soft woollen items, the stranger emerged through the door from the back yard. She was carrying a large ewer of water, which she proceeded to pour into a pot she had suspended over the fire. Madge stopped, struck dumb to see a stranger make herself so much at home in her domain. The Scotswoman glanced her way. 'The bairn will need an infusion of ginger and lemons, lest she take cold. Have you lemons?' Giving no further explanation of herself, she set about rifling the spice drawers in Madge's kitchen cabinet. Thomas had never before seen the housekeeper rendered speechless, and had it not been for the circumstances, he might have enjoyed the spectacle. 'I'm sorry, Mistress Penmore,' he said, indicating the stranger. 'In all the urgency of finding Lizzie, there was no time for us to be introduced.'

'Griselda Duncan,' said the woman, without taking her eyes from the pot into which she had begun to stir various items. 'Sir Thomas here cowped my mistress ower in the street, and a thing else fell oot fae there.'

The housekeeper continued nonplussed, and from behind Thomas, the voice of Anne Winter, whom he had forgotten about, drifted towards them. 'You must excuse Grizel, Sir Thomas, Mistress . . . Penmore is it? My maid is prone to slipping into her native tongue, but she is of a very practical bent.' Then she slipped past him, into the heart of the room. 'Manon. Oh, my dearest girl. It has been such a very long time.'

It had been almost six years since Damian Seeker had entrusted Anne Winter with the care of his daughter on her journey from York down to London. For all their past encounters, their battles of wits, the mutual enmity of their causes, nothing in her relationship with the Cromwellian captain had affected her as much as that simple but momentous request. He had not told her that Manon was his daughter, of course, but it was clear he knew she'd guessed it. His request had exposed a humanity in him that she thought few could ever have witnessed, and it had evidenced a greater trust in herself than she'd thought to merit from anyone.

She'd heard, some few years later, of Manon's marriage to Lawrence Ingolby and she'd been pleased. The lawyer had the name of an honest man, and a clever one. Now, as she looked about this trim little house on this prosperous street in York, Lady Anne felt that Seeker's daughter had chosen well. She wondered whether Damian Seeker knew. She hoped so. She hoped too that, wherever he might be, Seeker knew that she, Anne Winter, had never told a living soul who Manon Ingolby really was.

Manon's face broke into a smile, lively with disbelief.

'Lady Anne? Is it you? Really you?' she laughed, the remnants of tears still in her eyes. 'Come like the fairy godmother in a children's tale to bring me back my child!'

Anne laughed a little too, and knelt in front of Manon, resting her hand on her knee. She was careful not to go too close to the child who was regarding her with a look of deep mistrust.

'It was an accident that brought me here.' She raised her eyebrows in Thomas Faithly's direction. 'A happy accident. And it was Grizel there who noticed the dog, and went off after it with Sir Thomas.'

'A terrier wouldna run aff lik yon but guid cause.'

'Grizel,' chided Anne, 'English, please. We are in my country now.' They had found it useful, from time to time, for Grizel to speak in her own Scots tongue. Assumptions were made then about her understanding of English, her intelligence. People were less careful how they spoke in front of her or what they left within her view, when they thought her mind worked in Scots.

The maid breathed in, lips pursed, the very image of affrontedness, but it seemed she had found an unexpected ally in the rotund, frizz-headed housekeeper, who had guessed enough of what she'd said. 'You're right there. My Hal doesn't stir from that yard without my say-so. He knew there was something afoot. Nothing would have kept him from going off after our Lizzie.'

'But where did you find her?' asked Manon, having released the child once more to Madge's care.

And so, with the occasional necessary elaboration from Grizel, Sir Thomas told her.

'But what on earth was she doing there? How did she get there?'

Anne was watching everyone in the warm, lamplit kitchen very carefully, but both Sir Thomas and the house-keeper looked as curious as did Manon Ingolby.

It was Grizel who spoke. 'She'd have gone in after that kitten.'

Like everyone else, Anne turned her eyes to the little creature that had somehow got from Manon's feet to her lap.

'She was holding that kitten for dear life when we got in there, and she wasn't for letting it go.' Grizel addressed Manon. 'Is it your kitten, Mistress Ingolby?'

Manon shook her head. 'We have no cat. Prince Hal would not permit it.'

'Cannot abide cats of any nature, my Hal,' agreed Madge. 'Tom, queen, young, old, ginger, tabby or whatever else, he will not have them! And there's none better than him with a rat or a mouse. No, no need for cats in this house.'

Thomas Faithly cleared his throat. Anne smiled to see him so nervous in the face of the housekeeper. 'Well,' he said, 'it would seem you are in possession of one now.'

Lizzie, freshly dried and dressed, had clambered back up onto her mother's lap and taken the kitten once more firmly in her embrace. The terrier, as if sensing his hegemony was at an end, had slunk to lie at the far side of the hearth, from where he emitted the occasional perfunctory growl.

Thomas leaned over by Manon's chair and put out a hand to stroke the kitten. 'Where did you find the kitten, my pet?'

Lizzie looked from him to Madge then back to him and murmured something in a voice so tiny Anne could not hear it. Neither could Thomas, who leaned a little closer. 'What was that, Lizzie?'

She was a little louder this time, but still quiet and looked reluctant to speak, fearful, Anne thought, that someone might take the cat from her.

'Ah.' Thomas patted her hand and sighed as he straightened up.

'I could not hear her. What did she say?' asked Manon as everyone else waited.

Thomas's look was not hopeful. '"Shed."'

There was a collective, 'oh,' of disappointment around the room.

'She must have followed it in there,' said Manon. 'That must be why she wandered off. Lizzie loves animals, and she is so good with them.'

This idea seemed to content the mother and the old housekeeper, but Anne could tell from the expressions on the faces of Grizel and Sir Thomas that the same thought was passing through their minds as had taken root in hers: even if little Lizzie Ingolby had indeed toddled all the way up to the end of the vennel off Colliergate on the trail of a kitten, then some unknown person had closed and locked the door of that small, grimy shed behind her. Anne spoke to the housekeeper. 'Where is your master, Mistress Penmore?'

The woman, who had already favoured her with one or two glances redolent of a decided disapproval, now looked at her as if she were wanting her wits. 'Well, he's out looking for the babby of course, isn't he?'

'In that case,' said Anne, 'do you not think he ought to be sent for and told the child is safely home?'

The woman Penmore clapped a podgy hand to her mouth. 'Of course! I clean forgot. And Jedediah too!'

'Jedediah?'

'Her grandson,' said Thomas. 'Ingolby's clerk. I sent him out to look for Lizzie too when I got here.' A moment later, Thomas had sent two boys from the street out to find Lawrence Ingolby and his clerk. Anne saw that he himself was intent on staying here to look after Ingolby's small family until the lawyer himself arrived home. Someone in York wished them ill, and the enticing from home and imprisonment of their small daughter might only be the start of it. She found herself, not for the first time, warm to the goodness in Thomas Faithly. It was a complication nonetheless: it hadn't been her intention that he should be present when she made her first essay upon the confidence of Lawrence Ingolby. There was nothing for it but she must come back another day.

'Grizel, if the tonic is ready, I think we must go and leave this family in peace.'

'Very well, your ladyship.' Then Grizel turned to her new friend. 'If you care to let this cool just a little, Mistress Penmore, enough that the bairn can safely drink it, and give her a cupful before her dinner and her supper, it's sure to take good effect and guard against all manner of fevers and inflammations.'

Manon protested that they must stay to take a little warmed wine before they went back out into the snow, but Anne refused. 'Your husband will want to see no one but you and his daughter when he gets home. And of course,' she added, glimpsing the slightly tired blue eyes of Thomas Faithly, 'his good friend, Sir Thomas. He will not want to return after such a morning to find his house filled with strangers.'

Manon touched her fingers to Anne's hand. 'You are not a stranger to me, Lady Anne, nor ever will be. You did me a very great kindness once, and it is not forgotten. I beg you will stay.'

If Anne were being honest, it was a pleasant half-hour, seated there at the Ingolbys' kitchen table, eating an excellent plum tart and drinking warm spiced wine, while Sir Thomas told stories of some of his boyhood escapades on the moors to entertain them all. He had just finished telling a riotous story of a trick he had played on the village grave-digger, which had even Grizel in tears of laughter, when suddenly there was a loud bursting open of the front door. Sir Thomas was on his feet in an instant, his hand drawing his sword, when Lawrence Ingolby came charging into the room. The lawyer looked around a little madly, as if he hadn't seen any of them before, and then found where his wife was seated with their daughter curled up asleep on her lap. He sank to the floor, hands over his face. 'Lizzie. Thank God, thank God.'

It was an hour later, after Anne Winter and her servant had gone and the unfortunate Jed had at last returned from his search, again soaked and near-frozen, that Thomas handed Lawrence a brandy from the cabinet in Lawrence's closet.

'Drink that. It will do no one any good if you should fall ill.'

Lawrence took it and downed it in a single draught. 'Oh, I won't be falling ill, don't you worry. I've no intention of falling ill or anything else until I've found who took her and I've put their head on a pole at Mickelgate Bar.'

There had been no need for Thomas to broach with Lawrence the idea that someone had enticed away and deliberately imprisoned his child. The lawyer had already been convinced of it from the moment he'd heard she was missing. 'It's my own fault. I should never have gone out and left them. I should have had them away from here, Manon and Lizzie, as soon as I had Marvell's warning.'

'It was only a day and a half ago.'

'A day and a half too long. I should have had them off to Faithly that very night, taken them myself . . .' He shook his head. 'It's too late now, though. The roads to the north are blocked and I'd find no carter nor coachman willing to attempt it.' He took a more measured sip from the glass Thomas had refilled. 'Manon's almost too far gone to be travelling as it is.'

Thomas knew that all of this was true. He sought to offer some comfort, but instantly regretted it. 'I suppose we must be thankful that Lizzie came to no harm,' he said.

'What?' said Lawrence, the anger returning. 'Locking a child that's not two alone in a coal shed in this weather and leaving her there is no harm? She might have frozen to death before we found her.' He stood up and began to pace the floor. 'I'll kill them. I swear to God, Thomas, when I find out who it is, I'll kill them with my bare hands.' He'd traversed the room back and forth three times, fists clenched, when he seemed to recall that Thomas was still there with him. 'And I'll tell you something else. *That* woman – Anne Winter – knows more than she's saying.'

It had been awkward at best when, having let go his wife and child after a long and emotional embrace, Lawrence had at last become aware of Anne Winter sitting at his kitchen table. The joy and relief on the lawyer's face had disappeared in an instant. 'What's she doing here?' he'd demanded of Thomas whilst pointing at Lady Anne.

The only person in the room who hadn't seemed taken aback by this had been Lady Anne herself. She had stood up calmly and, assuring a mortified Manon that she would come again soon, gathered up her servant and left, as if Lawrence's reaction to her had been the most natural thing in the world. Manon had still been remonstrating with her husband over his behaviour a good quarter-hour later when Jed had finally slunk into the kitchen to furnish a new target for Lawrence's ire. Only a significant amount of pleading from the young man's grandmother, and of abject apologising from the clerk himself for the carelessness that had led to Lizzie's being out alone in the first place, had saved him his position and the roof over his head. It was only when he had offered to go himself to fetch the horse-whip in order that Lawrence might give him an appropriate lashing that the lawyer had calmed down and told him to get himself dry and to stay out of his sight till suppertime.

But now, in his closet, Jed was forgotten, and Lawrence's mind was back on Anne Winter. 'What was she really doing here, Thomas?'

Thomas stacked his pipe and put light to it. After puffing a few times he said, 'She claims to have come to York to see out the winter in greater comfort than she might have done in Northumbria, which seems reasonable enough to me. I believe she arrived the night before last or early yesterday morning. I encountered her yesterday at King's Manor, where she had come to stable her horse. And then this morning, well . . .'

'What? You don't think it's strange that she just happened to be on the street right at the end of that snicket where you found Lizzie? Or that her servant chose to come running after you – after a dog?'

'They were out buying provisions, and York is not such a big town, you know, that people out and about will not come upon each other several times a day. And after all, it was her servant who noticed the dog, and told me where it had gone. And it was her servant too who told me to shoulder open the gate when we couldn't open the lock. Lady Anne wasn't trying to impede me in finding the child, Lawrence.'

Ingolby looked far from convinced. 'That woman. I recognised her the minute I saw her.' He shook his head. 'Damian Seeker didn't take her lightly, either. She was one he used to warn me to look out for, back in Cromwell's day. Do you know what he once said to me about her?'

Thomas waited.

'"She is an able adversary."'

Thomas shook his head. 'No. I don't believe you. Damian Seeker didn't think anyone was able but himself.'

'He said it,' insisted Lawrence. 'He said it to me in person and he warned me again not long since in a—'

'In a what?' Thomas stared at Lawrence. 'In a letter?'

Lawrence sat with his mouth slightly open a moment, then clamped it shut.

'Seeker has recently written you a letter?' Thomas was too incredulous even to lower his voice. 'You are still in communication with Damian Seeker?'

Lawrence gritted his teeth. 'He's Manon's father. What am I supposed to do?'

'Then someone has intercepted his letters.'

Lawrence gave a short jerk of his head. 'We're careful.'

'But after what Marvell warned you of, that there was someone in York trying to track down Damian Seeker, you must see that Lizzie was taken in an attempt to force you into telling where Damian Seeker is.'

Lawrence's reaction was not what Thomas would have expected. 'Oh, I see all right. You finding her put paid to that for them. They won't get a second chance at her. But if they'd given me the choice, I'd a' told them at the first asking. He would tell me to himself, rather than risk a hair on her head being harmed. Let the bastards take their chances with him if they're ever fool enough to find him.'

Thomas swallowed, gave an involuntary rub to a shoulder Lawrence knew had been the worse for a past altercation with Damian Seeker. 'Yes, let them,' he said.

That night, as they lay in bed, Manon said, 'It was my fault.'

Lawrence sat up. 'Your fault? About Lizzie?'

She nodded and gave a sniff, and he put his arm about her shoulders and pulled her closer to him. 'Never think that. It was none of it your fault.'

'But if I hadn't gone out and left her . . .'

'You left her with Madge and Jed – how could you have thought she'd be in danger? But I would have you go out alone no more, for your own sake, Manon, and for mine.'

'But, Lawrence, no harm can come to me. I have friends everywhere in York.'

He took a breath. 'But not everyone in York is our friend. Until Thomas can get to the bottom of what happened to William Briar, I don't want you going out alone or even with Madge. You must have me or Jed with you. Or Thomas, if he's about. But no one else.'

Manon furrowed her brow. 'I am sorrier than can be

about what has happened to William. But how can that touch on us?'

'Because I think when he was here and missed us, he might have been trying to warn us of something.'

'But surely that was just over some business matter?'

'I don't think so,' said Lawrence, summoning his resolve. 'I hadn't wanted to tell you this. And you must promise me, *promise*, mind, that you will stay calm when I do tell you.'

She heaved herself round. 'Lawrence, what is it?'

'You've to promise . . .'

'All right. I promise I will stay calm. Now what is it?'

He still thought it might be better not to tell her at all, but he was too far gone in now.

'Your father . . .'

She sat up, alarm in her eyes. He'd made a bad beginning.

'No, Manon. It's all right. He's fine, he's fine.' As far as he knew. 'It's just, when Andrew came to see us that night, it wasn't really that he was passing through. He'd come specially. All the way from Holland.'

'My father's not in Holland,' she said.

'No, but in the course of his . . . work . . . there, Andrew has heard some things. There are people on the continent, hunting down the regicides.'

She bristled at this, as he'd known she would. 'My father is not a regicide!'

'I know he's not,' he said. 'But he made enemies then, plenty of enemies, in the course of his work for Cromwell, and some of those folk are now in positions of power and haven't forgotten it. One man in particular who came within your father's orbit and came off worst hasn't forgotten and wants his revenge.' He held up a hand. 'Now, don't ask me the details of what went on between them, because I'm not going to tell you. All right?'

He could tell she knew he was serious. He carried on. 'All right then. This man, Roger L'Estrange, he's nothing to do with the *official* hunt for the regicides, the things the King knows about.' Any talk of the hunt for the regicides was something that he took pains to avoid in front of her or, in fact, within the household at all, and indeed even Madge and Jed seemed to have picked up that this was a subject they must never broach. There were people enough in England, on the continent, in the Americas, living in fear of the retribution that might come their way for acts and allegiances in the recent past, and he'd worked hard to create a world in which such fears couldn't touch his wife. 'It seems that this L'Estrange has a very personal vendetta against your father. What's more, he's ambitious, and believes that if he can track down your father and hand him over to the authorities—'

At this Manon openly laughed, and Lawrence couldn't help but join with her. 'I know, I know, but like I said, he's ambitious. You see, there's one amongst the regicides they haven't been able to identify . . .'

'The executioner.' She said it for him and he nodded.

'Marvell says L'Estrange is giving out that Damian Seeker was the late King's executioner. And if he can make people believe that, he'll have carte blanche to hunt your father down, and well, it seems that L'Estrange has somehow learned of a connection, although maybe not *the* connection, between me and you and Damian Seeker, and that he has sent someone to York to find out more, so that he might use what they find to get to the captain at last.'

She'd become very pale and he stopped. 'Manon, are you all right?'

She was staring ahead of her, her lips trembling. 'There was a man, today.'

'A man? What man? Where was he?'

'When I was going up to Coppergate. I was about to step out of Bakehouse Lane, but I held back to let a man who looked to be in a hurry go by. He tipped his hat to me but then he hesitated, as if he knew me, before going on.'

'Who was he?' said Lawrence. 'One of my clients?'

She shook her head. 'I don't think so. I don't think I've ever seen him before, but I'm almost certain he recognised me.'

'Which way was he going?'

'He was going along Pavement, I—'

'No, Manon. Which way was he going? Was it towards the top of our street or away from it?'

Her voice was almost a whisper. 'Towards the top.'

'And this was shortly before Madge noticed Lizzie had disappeared.'

Manon nodded. 'Oh God, Lawrence, you think it was him?'

'I don't know, love,' he replied. 'I don't know who this person Roger L'Estrange has sent is or how far they might go to get us to reveal where your father is. These people – these "regicide hunters" if you want to call them that, though they're no better than hired assassins – don't operate by some code of honour. Andrew told me something of them last night. They operate through trickery, subterfuge, homing in on the vulnerable that might unwittingly lead them towards their prey. I need you to be vigilant, to be cautious, to be suspicious. Do you understand?'

She nodded.

'And I need you to tell me every single thing you remember about this man.'

TEN

A Visit to a Widow

Madge was hurrying along Goodramgate, hoping no one at home had noticed she'd been gone so long. She had secured the custard tarts that Lizzie was so fond of from the baker's in St Andrew Gate, in the hope that they might tempt Lizzie to eat and build herself up after the trials of the day before. In truth, Manon had wanted to send Jedediah, but Madge would not hear of it, Lawrence having tasked Jed with keeping an eye on the mistress and the babby at all times. Besides, Madge had another venture on hand this morning, that had taken her to Our Lady Row, and the door of Bella Sugden.

'Rosemary?' Bella had said. 'Not like you not to set enough herbs aside to do you the winter, Madge.'

'I've plenty for my usual requirements, Bella. I just need a bit extra from you.'

Bella had raised her eyebrows at just how much extra Madge wanted. 'You burning it, Madge Penmore?'

'Never you mind what I'm doing with it,' said Madge, thrusting coins in payment to the outstretched hand. 'Old witch,' she added as she hurried down the street after Bella had shut the door. She would indeed be burning it, a bunch in every hearth in the house, to ward off devils, for Madge was certain there was a devil on the loose in York, and that he had her master's family in his sights.

As she bustled on through the snow, Madge became aware of the tolling of the bell of Holy Trinity Church. Three times three it had rung – the death knell – and now it was ringing a slow toll for every year of the departed's life. Madge glanced up the narrow entranceway to the churchyard, but all she saw were the footsteps of what must have been a small funeral party. She hesitated. A minute or two more and she would hardly be missed. She pulled her shawl more tightly about her and went quickly up the snowy path.

The gravediggers were far over to her right, near the wall, a mound of brown earth already heaped by a gaping hole in the ground. Lucky it was snow and not frost, thought Madge as she craned her neck past ancient tombs and crooked headstones to get a better view. There was a small party of men with heads bowed, listening to the vicar – working men, she would say – and, with her back to Madge, one weeping woman. Madge edged a few yards to her right, to get a better look and then she gasped. 'Oh no!' she said, almost dropping her basket before turning and hurrying away down the path.

Manon was relieved to see Madge back at last. 'Thank goodness. I was beginning to worry that some accident had befallen you.'

Madge set down her basket and set to unwrapping her many outer layers. 'Oh, not me, but terrible news that the master shall want to hear.'

Manon took delivery of the housekeeper's shawl and hung it over the back of a chair near the fire. 'But the master will not be back till late. Whatever is it, Madge?'

'Juliet Venn,' began Madge. 'Her that jilted William Briar.'

'What about her?' said Manon.

'Her husband's dead.'

It was after dinnertime but well before it would get dark that Manon, escorted by Jed who was carrying a basket laden with food, entered the courtyard in which Madge had told her she would find the house of Juliet Venn, or Plowman as she now was. Madge had wanted to come too, but reminding her that she would be needed to look after Lizzie, Manon had prevailed in persuading her to stay at home. As she was lifting her hand, about to knock at the door, she turned to Lawrence's clerk and said, 'You wait out here while I go in, Jed. I won't be long.'

'But surely I should come in with you? Master said you weren't to be out on your own.'

'You *are* with me, Jed, and you'll be able to keep an eye on comings and goings in the courtyard from here better than you would be if you were to come into the house. And look at it.' She indicated the small cottage at whose door they were standing. 'She won't want to be crowded by strangers.'

'But if—'

Manon shook her head. 'No, Jed. You are to wait here.'

It was Juliet's elderly father who answered the door, a desolate look on his face.

'Mr Venn,' began Manon. 'I am very sorry for your troubles. May I come in a moment and speak with your daughter?'

The man nodded and drew back the door a little, looking enquiringly at Jed.

'My husband's clerk will wait outside,' said Manon, stepping into the small ground-floor room of the cottage.

Juliet looked up from her seat at the table, and began to stand. 'Mistress Ingolby.'

'Please don't get up,' said Manon. Juliet was no younger than herself, and Manon could not get used to the deference Lawrence's growing status afforded her with those she would have thought her equals. 'Do you mind if I sit with you a moment?'

Juliet shook her head and Manon sat. 'I'm so sorry to hear of your husband,' she began. 'I know my husband and Sir Thomas had hopes the surgeon might have been able to save him.'

'Left it too late,' said Juliet's father from the seat he'd returned to by the fire. 'Poison was right through him before the surgeon got near.'

Juliet was staring at the flickering candle in the middle of the table. 'It's my fault.'

Manon reached out and put her own hand lightly on

Juliet's. 'Lawrence told me how the accident came about. Anyone might have fallen on that ice. You cannot blame yourself.'

'But I do,' said Juliet, turning to face her. 'I am being punished, for betraying my promise to William so that I could marry Ralph, and now they are both dead. It's my fault.'

Manon leaned closer towards her. 'You must not think like that, Juliet. It would have been wrong of you to marry William when you knew you loved another, and would have caused misery to you both. And William had forgiven you, you know. He stopped bearing a grudge against you or your husband almost as soon as Lawrence persuaded him to drop his case.'

'That's what I've been telling her,' said her father. 'He bore Ralph and her no grudge. Was telling Ralph only the other week, before he went off to London.'

'Oh?'

'Met him one night in Le Kyrk Lane, one going one way, one the other. Hardly room there for two gnats to pass, still less two well-built men like Ralph and William. So they'd no choice but to stop and let each other pass. And when Ralph was past, William called him back and said he was sorry for any distress he had caused him and Juliet, and Ralph told him likewise, and they talked some more and went their ways.'

Whatever she or Juliet's father said didn't seem to be getting through to the young woman, and unpacking the basket of food onto the table, Manon got up to leave. Juliet's father had just begun to open the door for her when a thought occurred to her, and she paused and turned back. 'I don't suppose your husband and William Briar spoke of anything else?'

Juliet frowned then looked up. 'Their work, I think. Happier common ground for them than me. Although Ralph said William wasn't happy at all with the work he had to go to London about.'

Manon thought of how William had been on his return from London and felt her pulse quicken a little. 'Did he say what the work was?'

But father and daughter both shook their heads.

Jed looked pleased to see her emerge from the house, and Manon felt a little sorry for having kept him so long standing out in the cold of the courtyard. She searched in the pouch she kept hanging from her belt. 'Here,' she said, holding out a coin. 'Go and get yourself a cup of chocolate to warm you up.'

He stepped back from the money as if it would scald him. 'The master would skin me alive if I left you to walk home on your own.'

'Oh yes,' she said, remembering. 'Well, take it anyway so that you might have it for the next time.'

This time he did put out his hand to take the coin. They walked on in silence a moment and then he said, 'How was she, Mistress Plowman?'

'Her grief has disordered her thoughts a little. She blames herself for her husband's death. And for William Briar's.'

'Mmm.' Jed did not commit himself one way or the other as to Juliet's guilt, but then he said, 'She was still talking about him when you were leaving, wasn't she?'

Manon shook her head. 'She wasn't talking about much, but I just asked her what William had said to her husband the last time he'd seen him.'

Jed was surprised. 'They spoke to one another?'

'Just by chance, but they were very civil with one another, her father says, although it seems William was not happy in his work.'

'Oh?'

'Something to do with what he was in London for.'

Jed was suddenly quite animated. 'Ralph Plowman saw him after he came back from London?'

'Before,' said Manon. 'Why?'

Some of the animation went out of Jed. 'Oh, just it might have been helpful. To know why he was killed.'

Any hopes Thomas Faithly had had that the snow might have lost interest in York were dashed when he'd opened his window shutters the next morning. The stuff was piled in drifts against the columns of the ruined aisle of St Mary's Abbey and halfway up the doors of the old St Leonard's hospital. It had stopped falling for now, but the sky was a leaden grey. As he looked out over the city, churches, homes, yards, walls, towers and streets, all were cloaked in a heavy mantle of white. He could only imagine the depth of the drifts out on the moors: roads and tracks long made invisible, cottages half-buried, animals lost. There was no chance that Lawrence Ingolby would get his family out of York now. Only the Ouse offered a means of escape or arrival. Thomas was certain that whoever had enticed away and imprisoned Lawrence Ingolby's little daughter must still be within the walls of York, and that the murderer of William Briar very probably was too.

He'd stayed late at Lawrence's, offering to billet himself there for their further protection if need be, but Lawrence had assured him that he and his clerk were well able to protect the household. He'd made sure to train Jed in the use of a dagger and a pistol, and besides, the lad was fast on his feet.

Thomas's wry comment – that these were important attributes in any lawyer – had received the response that Thomas would be, 'surprised how irate some folk get when the law doesn't go their way'. Then he'd smiled. 'Besides, I need someone to practise with, keep me sharp, now you're so busy sitting behind a desk all day.' He'd pointed to Thomas's stomach, as if there was a paunch there, which there wasn't. 'You want to watch that. It'll be the gout next.'

Thomas had been pleased to see Lawrence attempting some of his wonted humour, but it was nowhere to be seen when Lawrence had arrived unexpectedly at his offices at King's Manor late the next afternoon, demanding to know what William Briar had been working on. The sky was already darkening and Thomas was surprised to see him, commenting that he'd thought Lawrence would have been in a hurry to get home to his wife and daughter.

'I have been home,' said Lawrence. 'That's why I'm up here now.'

Thomas felt a sense of foreboding. 'Oh?'

'You've heard that Ralph Plowman's dead?'

'Yes. The news came up earlier from the stonemasons' yard. I'm sorry for it, but not much surprised after the way he was when we saw him. What has that to do with what William was working on?'

Lawrence leaned against the back of a chair. 'Manon went round to see his widow this afternoon, and it seems William had been talking to her husband before he went off down to London, telling him he wasn't happy about his work.'

Thomas held out a hand to indicate the papers piled up all round his room. 'He was hardly alone in that.'

Lawrence looked around and shook his head in disapproval. 'Whoever thought to put you in charge here . . . But the thing is, it was some particular piece of work he was doing that he wasn't happy about.'

'Did she know what, exactly?'

Lawrence shook his head. 'No, she didn't. But if we get down to the draughtsman's offices before they all go home, we might find out.'

When they arrived there, Thomas dismissed the two apprentices who appeared to be engaged in copying a diagram of some structure or other. The master draughtsman supervising them was the same man Thomas had spoken to just after William's death.

'I have some more enquiries regarding William Briar.'

'Ah,' said the draughtsman. 'The dean of the minster's been here since last I spoke to you, too.'

'Has he, indeed?' said Thomas. 'Nevertheless, I'm empowered by His Grace the Duke of Buckingham to look into and report on the matter on his behalf, and there are some things that have occurred to me since last I was here.' This was true and not true. Thomas was empowered to act on the duke's behalf, but Buckingham wouldn't know yet of the murder of the surveyor, and his interest in it would only extend as far as it might prove inconvenient to himself. But King's Manor was already abuzz with preparations for the new lord lieutenant's visit, and the duke's name tended to have the desired effect, even in the face of the might of the Church.

'Well, you can tell the duke what I told the dean. There was not a thing wrong with the stonework in that crypt – not a crack, nothing, other than that it was stained in William's blood. I got down there and had a good look at it yesterday.'

Thomas nodded. 'It was already fairly certain that William had been lured there deliberately. I have a question for you.'

The draughtsman's face was grim as he returned to his stool and pushed aside pencils and rule. 'What do you need to know?'

Thomas indicated one of the tables beneath the window. The surface of the table was entirely bare. 'What was he last working on?'

The man pointed to the documents on his own worktable. 'Same sort of thing as usual – we've a never-ending list of surveys and demands from the patent-holders for repairs of this bridge, or that wall, or such-and-such a harbour. William was concerned with bridges.'

'He didn't like this work, though, did he?'

The man looked surprised. 'Where did you hear that? William was good at what he did, took a lot of pride in it. Never heard him grumble about it, not once. Not what we did here, anyway.'

'Oh?' asked Thomas. 'What other work do you do?'

'Me, nothing. But William had some other thing he was working on, on the side, so to speak, that I don't think he was very happy about.'

'Like what?' said Lawrence.

The man puffed out his lips. 'Search me. Something that he was "saddled with" a couple of months ago – his words, not mine. He didn't seem keen to talk about it.'

'And you've found nothing unusual amongst the work he left behind?'

'All fairly standard.'

Before Thomas could ask any more, his attention was taken by a rattling sound. Lawrence Ingolby was working at the drawer below William's work table.

'Where's the key for this?'

The man shrugged. 'William would have had it.'

'Right,' said Lawrence. The next minute, he'd produced a knife from somewhere inside his doublet and set to work on the lock.

'What?' he said in response to Thomas's look of surprise. 'After what happened to Lizzie yesterday, you think I'm going to go about York unarmed?' A moment's splintering and the drawer was opened. Lawrence let out a sound of disappointment. 'Tidy fellow, William. Nothing but this.' He held up a small book, which he then handed to Thomas who was about to open it, then glancing at the draughtsman, thought better of it and kept his hand clamped over it. He thanked the man and said, 'If you come upon anything else that William might have been working on, let me know straight away.'

'Will do,' said the draughtsman, but then, as Thomas and Lawrence were going out of the door, he said, 'Wait!'

They stopped.

'His bag. William often carried papers and small sketches of what he was working on in his workbag. Big leather satchel. He had it with him when he left for London and when he called back in here that morning.'

Thomas looked about him. 'Where is it now?'

'He still had it over his shoulder when he left to go to the crypt.'

Lawrence, who'd been almost through the door, came back in and leaned in very close to the draughtsman. 'Did the dean's men mention it or ask you about it?'

The man shook his head. 'Sorry. And I didn't think to ask them about it.'

The young clergyman who opened the door of the house on Precentor's Court to which they'd been directed made a valiant, if short-lived, attempt to stand his ground. Thomas made no effort at all to conceal his impatience and the clergyman soon seemed to understand that he had pushed the Duke of Buckingham's deputy as far as was safe for a cleric to push a veteran of the late wars. When Thomas turned to an equally impatient Lawrence enquiring whether anyone would rid him of 'this troublesome priest', the clergyman went scuttling out of sight into the dimly lit interior of the house and presently returned, thrusting into Thomas's hands a brown and bloodied satchel.

'That is William Briar's work bag, and everything found upon him on that terrible morning in the crypt – his clothing excepted, of course – is in it.'

Thomas took the bag and nodded his thanks to the closing door.

'Right,' said Lawrence, rubbing his hands to warm them in the cold night air. 'I'm for home. I'll leave that with you, and you can tell me what you find tomorrow.'

'It may have to wait a while,' said Thomas. 'I've to have supper with an old friend.'

'Who?' asked Lawrence, looking mildly offended, as he often did when presented with the possibility of some other having a claim on Lawrence's friendship that might supersede his own.

'Oh, a Scotsman I met long ago, on my travels with our wandering King. No one you would know.'

'I see,' said Lawrence, not much pleased. 'Well, see you don't leave that lying about in some tavern.'

Thomas gave an ironic laugh. 'You may be sure that it will be safely under lock and key before I'm anywhere near any tavern.'

ELEVEN

The Other Widows

Grizel got out her key and let herself in from the street. There was no sign of Anne downstairs and Grizel tutted to herself at the wastefulness of her friend, who was no doubt up in the parlour, with an unnecessary fire when she might have sat in the kitchen that was warm from the still-glowing embers in the grate. Grizel didn't pause to take off her outer things, instead lighting a candle from the one in the sconce by the door and going swiftly up the stairs. There was indeed a fire burning in the small parlour, and seated at the table, with a whole candelabra alight and the barrel of a gun levelled at the door, was Anne Winter.

'Hmmph,' said Grizel, nodding towards the item which Anne was in the process of cleaning, 'you should have done that before we left Northumbria.'

'I did,' said Anne, carefully oiling the cloth she was using to clean the different parts of the flintlock pistol she had got years ago in Flanders from the workshop of Guillaume Henoul. The gunsmith himself had inscribed the rose pattern on the barrel, especially for her, he'd said. He had also, he said, been careful to include the thorns.

Anne began to reassemble the weapon. 'I just want to make doubly certain that all is in order. The abduction of Lawrence Ingolby's child troubles me. There is something at work here in York that I don't understand. It may be nothing to do with our investigation into Thomas Faithly, but I want to be prepared, all the same.'

'Of course,' said Grizel. 'But I'd say from what I observed yesterday, that Sir Thomas himself isn't prepared for much. He certainly has no wariness of you.'

'He is too trusting a person, and forgets that others are not like him. That has always been his great failing.'

Grizel handed Anne the cloak she had picked up for her from its peg at the bottom of the stair. 'Well, let us hope that's the case tonight.'

'Oh?' said Anne, standing as she took her cloak.

'I followed him and the lawyer Ingolby from King's Manor to a house in Precentor's Court where they took delivery of a satchel — it was marked with blood. They parted company and Sir Thomas returned to King's Manor with the satchel, to emerge a quarter-hour later without it. He told Ingolby he was going to meet an old friend for supper — probably this Ogilvie you encountered the other day. You must hurry.'

Anne nodded, and made haste in tying on the thick dark woollen cloak before picking up her plain black gloves. 'You don't know which tavern they were going to?'

Grizel shook her head. 'No, but it won't take me long to find them.'

'And his clerk and page?'

'I left a note that they were to make their way down to the castle to attend Sir Thomas there on important business. I added that if he was delayed, they were to wait there for him.'

Anne smiled. It was a trick they had used time and again. It was surprisingly easy to get hold of an example of their target's handwriting and signature, and even easier for Anne to copy it onto multiple pieces of paper which they might have cause to use in their investigations. She had had Thomas Faithly send round a note of receipt for her horse, lest there were any difficulties at King's Manor stables should she wish to take it out and he not be there. She and Grizel had spent a happy morning perfecting the copying of Sir Thomas's cursive hand and exuberant signature.

'So, the clerk and page out of the way, all I need concern myself with is how long Sir Thomas stays out in the tavern, eating and drinking with his friend.'

'I'll find where they are then get back to warn you ahead of them as soon as it looks like they're leaving.'

'Poor Griz,' said Anne. 'You are a marvel.'

Grizel was not fond of compliments. 'I'm a woman who has her health and knows how to have her wits about her. As you know well enough, it is simply a matter of walking a town till you know it.'

'But we have hardly been here three days.'

'And I have spent most of them walking one end of York to the other. I doubt very much that Thomas Faithly in his cups will manage to leave a tavern and wind home to King's Manor before I've found my way there to warn you. But you must make haste if you are to profit by his absence.'

Anne nodded. She had often thought that Grizel must have been born in a nook and grown up in a cranny – there was no town whose topography she could not make herself mistress of. When they had had business in Edinburgh, she had moved through its closes and wynds with the practised deftness of a rat. Anne slid pistol, powder horn, flint and a candle into the special pocket sewn into the lining of her heavy cloak, then followed Grizel down the stairs and out of the door where they went their separate ways.

Grizel's method was simple: she would enter a tavern, a small pot in her hand, and look around to see if that was the one Thomas Faithly and his friend were in. If Faithly was there, and noticed her, she would claim she had come in to get something to take home for Anne's supper. If he was not there, she would claim to be looking for her husband, as a relative from home had unexpectedly arrived at their lodgings. It would not be long, she thought, before she was directed to whichever tavern Thomas Faithly's Scottish friend had last been seen in.

She had begun with those places closest to King's Manor that looked most respectable, and worked her way towards the inner streets of the town. It was in the third place she tried that she struck lucky. 'There was a Scotsman in the

Black Swan, over Peasholme Green, came in just before I left with one of the high-ups from King's Manor. Daresay you'll find him there.'

Grizel thanked the man then went as quickly as she could through the town until she reached Peasholme Green. She paused for a moment beneath the walls of St Anthony's Hall the more closely to study the area, beyond which was only marshland, river and the walls. A little ahead, past the garden of St Anthony's, she could see the parapet of the belfry of St Cuthbert's, and over across the green was the substantial form of the Black Swan, well-placed to greet traders and travellers alighted from barges on the Foss. The snow, which had held off a few hours, began to fall again, and she crossed quickly to the inn.

Nothing but moving shapes and shadows could be seen through the pale ochre glow of the steamed-up window panes of the inn. She stepped inside and began to pass through dark wood-panelled corridors to the main taproom and parlour. She kept to the darker edges of the spaces she moved through, away from lights glowing from wall sconces or on benches. Her head a little lowered, she slid her eyes one way and then the other, taking in the features of the patrons as they moved in and out of candlelight to talk to one another or to lean over tankards.

A quick survey of those huddled close to the ingle fire failed to show any sign of Sir Thomas or his friend, but off to the side a wooden partition, its upper section divided by finely turned columns, caught her eye. Going closer, she was able to see Faithly and a companion, whose back was to her, seated there in a snug area with its own small fire. Grizel ordered a cup of hot spiced wine and settled herself on a stool close to the partition. After the serving boy had brought her drink, she moved closer still, so that she might listen without being seen.

Grizel had hardly been settled in the warmth long enough for the blood to come back to her fingertips when fear began to creep over her. It started as soon as she heard the Scotsman speak and it almost froze her with panic. She'd thought she had got away from all that. She'd thought she was safe. But the voice told her that here indeed was David Ogilvie on the other side of that partition, and she realised she was in more danger now than she had been for years. She should have stayed in the Low Countries, she should never have come back across the German Ocean. Indeed she would not have done, had it not been for Anne. And Anne was depending on her tonight. Grizel swallowed down some of the drink she had ordered, and made herself stay where she was, rather than slipping away into the darkness, to disappear again.

The men spoke of old days in the King's service, of the difficulties they had known under Cromwell's rule, and of when they had first met. Grizel learned that Thomas Faithly had been with the King when he'd landed at Garmouth, not so very far from her own home. The covenanting leaders had offered Scotland's crown to the young, exiled Charles and David Ogilvie had been of the accompanying party that day. It seemed that despite their many differences, the friendship between him, Thomas Faithly and the Duke of Buckingham, of whom they also spoke, dated from then. But these events had taken place long years before the time Faithly had been suspected of spying for Damian Seeker, and Grizel doubted the substance of them could be of much relevance. Her mind began to wander once more to her own concerns, but then, with a jolt, she realised David Ogilvie had just said the name *Damian Seeker*.

Faithly's response had been choked and was lost to Grizel, but what Ogilvie said next was not.

'I tell you, friend, it sent a chill right through me, here on the streets of York.'

What had she missed? Had Seeker been sighted in York?

'You must have been mistaken,' said Thomas Faithly, still shaken-sounding.

'Oh, no doubt about it,' returned Ogilvie. 'I knew it was not him, of course – could scarcely have been further from being him. And yet – the eyes, the look – to see those in the face of a beautiful young woman, it put the fear of God right through me.'

Faithly gave an uncomfortable laugh. 'I see I am not the only one still haunted by past encounters with that man.'

Ogilvie spoke again. 'I see him in my nightmares. I looked into those eyes at Worcester for the smallest moment, and yet it might have been eternity. Had another not shot my horse from under me, Seeker's axe would have split my head in half. The man who fell beside me told me who it had been. To see those eyes in the face of a young woman upon the street – it was like I had glimpsed a river siren, come to land to tell me my doom.'

Faithly was dismissive, though Grizel detected a shade of nervousness in his voice. 'You always were too superstitious, David. Your people have little else in their heads but malign spirits. You've had a long journey with little rest, that's all. Exhaustion can do things to a man's mind. I doubt very much that Seeker has taken on female form in . . . where was it exactly you saw her?'

'She was coming out of an alleyway near to my lodgings on the Coppergate.'

'Then you had been too long in the Three Tuns, I think.'

'Or not long enough,' said Ogilvie, and their conversation moved onto other things, none of which Grizel judged to be of any interest. It must have been an hour later, and Grizel thinking that Anne had had a good long time to search Sir Thomas's apartments, that they spoke of leaving. Grizel hastily put on her own cloak, ready to get out after them, and to go ahead of Sir Thomas to warn Anne.

She waited until the men were halfway across Peasholme Green before stepping out of the doorway of the Black Swan, the hood of her cloak pulled up and a heavy muffler around her neck and covering most of the bottom half of her face. Even should Thomas Faithly turn around and notice the woman walking with her head down some way behind them, he would be hard put to recognise her from their encounter over the missing child, Lizzie Ingolby. The snow had stopped when she'd been in the inn, and the ground gleamed a sparkling pale blue beneath the frosty sky. Not only their footprints, but the men themselves were very clear to her. They were moving quickly against the cold and soon she realised that rather than cutting off at Spen Lane and returning to King's Manor past the minster and out by Bootham Bar, Thomas was intent on seeing his friend, less familiar with York, safe to his lodgings on Coppergate before himself heading home for the night. Grizel breathed a sigh of relief and set off up Spen Lane. If she hurried, she would get back to King's Manor ahead of him.

The skeleton key she carried with her had allowed Anne entry into Thomas's locked chambers at King's Manor. It hadn't taken her long to find the bloodied satchel Grizel had spoken of, and Anne marvelled again at Thomas's naivety, in that he had trusted to the old lock on his door to keep the contents of his rooms safe. She set her candle on his desk and laid out on it the plans she had found in the satchel. There had been no locking mechanism on the satchel itself — it had simply been a question of unfastening the buckles. There had been no special folding of the document inside, either. Anne wondered whether it was worth spending any time on it at all. But then there was the question of the blood. There would surely be some interest in that. She had already spent a short time looking over the official papers that were filed or left piled on Sir Thomas's clerk's desk in the outer room of his chambers and all appeared to relate to his present public duties in advance of the Duke of Buckingham's arrival. In his personal apartments, few of his own belongings, other than his clothing and some plate with the Faithly family crest, had yet been unpacked, but the satchel had taken her attention as soon as she'd entered the room. Unfolding the documents inside and laying them out on the surface of Sir Thomas's desk, Anne began to study them.

At first glance, even to the trained eye, they might have appeared to be nothing more than the plans for a substantial town house, of two storeys with attic and two short wings coming out from the central range. A second more careful glance might draw the attention to a greater than usual number of stairways in a house of that size. A third even closer survey would begin to suggest, to the trained eye at least, a number of features that really ought not to be there. Anne felt a little prickle of excitement. This was certainly something she would have to lay before Grizel, that she might see what those sharp eyes made of it.

From the pocket in her cloak, Anne removed two of the sheets of blank paper she kept there, along with a draughtsman's pencil. Quickly, she copied the broad outlines of the plan, not worrying too much about exact scale or dimensions or technicalities with more obvious purposes. It was the unusual features of these plans that most intrigued her, and to these that she gave most especial care. That task completed, she folded the originals away again and returned them to the satchel, the buckles of which she made sure to refasten, exactly as they had been. Then she turned her attention to Sir Thomas's small library of books.

She wasn't greatly surprised to find that his reading matter was almost equally divided between manuals on military tactics and on arboriculture and animal husbandry. Only the military manuals appeared to have been much read. There was no politics, very little history, a volume comprising gathered sheets, in differing hands, of poems. She recognised one or two in Andrew Marvell's hand amongst them. She had not realised that he and Faithly were acquainted. A pamphlet on arboriculture had been annotated and signed to Sir Thomas by John Evelyn and dated at around the time L'Estrange wished her to look into his movements – the autumn and early winter of 1656, shortly after Sir Thomas had been released from the Tower. This was the period during which L'Estrange suspected Faithly of having been in the pay of Damian Seeker. It was difficult to imagine now that the cerebral Royalist Evelyn and the blunt Republican Damian Seeker had once existed in the same place, at the same time, circling each other's worlds, and quite intriguing to think that those worlds might have overlapped in the person of Thomas Faithly. The curious thing for Anne was that she knew them all, and she could imagine Faithly more at ease in Seeker's company than he would be in the sanctimonious Evelyn's. That was hardly enough to condemn him, though, even now.

But there might be something here, in this room, that would be. Anne didn't like the thought – but why should she treat Thomas Faithly any differently from any other traitor, if she found evidence that he had betrayed the King as others had done? She told herself that she might just as easily find proof of his innocence. With that reflection, she set about her business once more.

Faithly's letters, which looked to have been stuffed, haphazard, in a trunk with old belts, boots and a fine set of prints of Flemish towns that he had not yet got framed, were of no great age. It seemed that his practice was to keep his private correspondence no longer than it might be relevant to whatever business or news he might have on hand. A large pile of correspondence, more carefully stored, related entirely to Sir Thomas's legal travails. She looked over them long enough to see that they were mainly concerned with his efforts to gain access to the small estate of Langton, left to him by his grandmother and sold by Cromwell's regime whilst Thomas had been in exile. In light of her own experience of such matters she concluded that Lawrence Ingolby was nothing if not thorough, and that there might be worse men to have on your side in a battle through Chancery. Nevertheless, these papers told her nothing of what she wanted to know.

Anne lifted her candle a little so that she might see the clock on the wall. She felt her stomach tighten. Surely it could not be long until Grizel came to warn her of Thomas Faithly's return? The strange house plan she had found in the bloodied satchel was of interest, but aside from that she could see nothing that might conceivably have any bearing on her own investigation, save the pamphlet gifted and dated to Thomas by John Evelyn at his house at Deptford, showing he had indeed been in London over the period that L'Estrange suspected him to have been colluding with Seeker.

Anne closed her eyes and sat down on the bed for a moment. She was tired and feared she would miss something. Thomas Faithly might trust too much and in too many, but he would not be such a fool as to leave lying around anything which might condemn him to a traitor's death. If there was any such thing here, it would be very well concealed. She dared not light another candle, but holding the one she had up a little, she saw that every wall of Thomas's bedchamber was panelled in light oak. There might be a loose panel amongst the rest. Weary, she made to get to her feet again, but as she did, she felt her hand press hard on something beneath her. With care, she pulled back the bed coverings and sheets then pressed down on the mattress. It was goose down, but not very thick. There! An object of some form beneath the mattress offered definite resistance.

Anne got down on her knees and with one hand lifted the mattress a little above its frame whilst sliding the other hand underneath. Her fingers closed on the boards of a book. She pulled it out and sat back against the bed, bringing her candle closer. The binding was rough, and there was no tooling on the cover. She opened it, and then she understood: it was a sketchbook. Most of the sketches were of things across the sea — palaces, houses, towns, bridges, towers — that might have been made as a record of Charles Stuart's wanderings around Europe. There was the palace at St Germains, there the mighty cathedral of Cologne, there some small castle clinging perilously to a cliff above the Rhine, there a windmill on the polder. There were scenes of life too, characters that had caught Sir Thomas's eye. He had a good eye, and some of the figures he had sketched made her laugh. She could see the life in them. Each drawing was dated. Anne would have liked to take more time over the book, but time pressed and she flicked through the pages looking for any dated 1656. Suddenly she lighted on an image that caught her breath — it was of herself, in the Flemish town of Damme, in August of 1658. The legend beside it read, 'Unknown woman'. Anne felt a curious jab of pain at the description. Thomas Faithly had known very well, certainly by the time they'd encountered one another in Damme, who she was. Methodically, she began to work back through two years of sketches and soon she came to what she was looking for — a drawing dated September 1656.

Faithly had made a sketch of the garden and building works at John Evelyn's home of Sayes Court, by Deptford. Anne had since visited the place and could see how much had been achieved in the six years since he had been there. The next drawing was of a clockmaker's workshop in Clerkenwell, with an affectionate sketch of a strange old man bent over the bench. Finally, there was a drawing of a young woman, surrounded by curiosities — shells, stuffed animals, even an old pair of boots. Unlike herself, this woman was given her own name, or part of it, by Thomas Faithly — Maria. Anne could supply the rest. Ellingworth, Maria Ellingworth, who was long gone from London, from England. Gone across the Atlantic Ocean, to make a new life in the Americas, along with her brother and his young family. Maria Ellingworth, sister of a lawyer who had fallen foul of Damian Seeker almost as often as Anne herself had and in whose chambers at Clifford's Inn Lawrence Ingolby had trained. Maria Ellingworth, with whom Damian Seeker had reputedly once been in love.

Anne felt her pulse quicken. Not only did this picture tie Thomas Faithly to London and to Lawrence Ingolby at the precise time L'Estrange wished to know of his movements, it was a link, faint and frayed but a link all the same, to Damian Seeker. Anne didn't know yet how this might help her in her task of establishing the treachery or innocence of Thomas Faithly, but it was unlikely to hinder it. Carefully, she loosened the picture from its binding, tearing out also the blank page further on through the book to which it was attached, then she closed the sketchbook and slipped it back carefully under the mattress where she had found it.

She had got back to her feet and was dusting down her skirts when there was a sudden thump at the window which almost made her jump from her skin. Quickly lowering her candle to the floor, she went to the window and peeked out through the heavy drapes which had already been drawn when she'd arrived. There, out on the lawn, was Grizel, gesticulating to her then pointing in the direction of the door. Anne understood.

She glanced quickly around the room to check that she had left everything as it should be, then patted the inside pocket of her cloak, where she had secreted the sketch of Maria Ellingworth along with her own rough copy of the house plan she had found in the bloodied satchel. She snuffed out her light and retraced her steps through the darkness to Thomas's clerk's anteroom and back out into the corridor. She had just stepped out into the generously lit corridor when she heard the sound of a man whistling, accompanied by footsteps coming up the stair. She slipped around the corner and pressed herself against the wall.

The whistling grew louder and the footsteps closer before coming to a halt outside the door to Sir Thomas's apartments. The handle turned and Thomas entered the anteroom. She took her chance and sped back round the corner and along the corridor until she reached the stairs. She had almost descended one flight when she heard Sir Thomas exclaim. 'What the Devil?' She was down another flight by the time she heard Sir Thomas stride out onto the corridor and knock at another door further along. Whom he was rousing she could not tell, because she had reached the ground floor where she was hailed by a low whistle that she knew to be Grizel's. Following the sound along a dark and narrow corridor, she felt a rush of cold air hit her from a side door that opened onto the gardens. She went through it and was a moment later greeted by her maid who manifested from behind a pillar. She let out a long breath of relief. 'My word, Griz, but that was close.'

Safely back in their own small house, Grizel busied herself with bringing the stove back to life and preparing warm drinks while Anne laid out on the table what she had found. She lit extra candles to illuminate the drawing of Maria Ellingworth as well as her rough copy of the plan she had found in the bloodied satchel.

'The sketchbook was hidden away, but the satchel had been left sitting out on a chair. As I said, too trusting, Thomas Faithly.'

They studied the house plans first, and it took Grizel little time to come to the same conclusion Anne had arrived at when she'd looked over them earlier. 'A spy house,' she said. Vents, where none were needed, unless to carry sounds; small, strangely placed windows that let in little light, but gave overview of other rooms; passageways behind rooms already more obviously connected by main corridors.

'Do you recognise the house?' asked Anne.

Grizel frowned. 'I think it is a template, illustrating ideas that might be put into practice rather than a plan of an existing house.'

Anne nodded in agreement. 'Which raises the question: who were these plans drawn for? Was it at the behest of Sir Thomas or someone else?'

'Hmm,' said Grizel. 'Well, whoever they were for, it was that murdered surveyor that drew them. The bag you found them in, the one that Sir Thomas and the lawyer Ingolby were so keen to get from the churchman, belonged to him.' Then she turned to the sketch. 'And what about this woman. Who is she?'

Anne told her.

'So, she is connected, through her brother, to Lawrence Ingolby and herself to Damian Seeker. And Sir Thomas was in love with her.'

'That would appear to be the suggestion of the sketch,' agreed Anne. 'Certainly, it suggests Sir Thomas was in Damian Seeker's orbit in London six years ago.'

'Things are indeed swirling,' said Grizel. 'How shall we begin to pin them down?'

'Given what I have found, I think we must certainly invite them to supper.'

Grizel looked up from her perusal of the sketches. 'Invite who?'

'The Ingolbys.'

TWELVE

A Supper

'Do we have to?'

'Yes, Lawrence. She is my friend.'

Lawrence grunted as he exchanged his favourite brown jerkin for a claret-coloured velvet one onto which Manon had sewn silver buttons engraved with oak leaves and acorns. The jerkin, which she had had made for him last Christmas, pleased Lawrence very well, but he didn't think a supper at the house of Anne Winter warranted the wearing of it.

'Your father warned me about her, you know,' he said, fastening the buttons. 'He said you couldn't take your eye off her for a minute. Not one minute.'

Manon smiled as she came to help him arrange his collar. 'Then surely it is all the more important that we accept this invitation to take supper with her tonight. We can have our eyes on her the entire evening.'

'Hmm.' As Lawrence reached for his boots he tried another tack. 'And I don't like to leave Lizzie, either.'

'You know Lizzie likes nothing better than to go with

Madge to Aunt Flo's. She will be fed and spoiled and made a great fuss of until she falls fast asleep. It will do her the world of good. Besides, it's only on Colliergate, and Jed will go with them.'

'Serve him right,' said Lawrence, taking some consolation from knowing that his clerk would have to spend the evening in the company of not only his grandmother, but also her sister who was, as Lawrence and Jed fervently agreed, 'even worse'.

Lawrence was a long way from forgiving Jed for his carelessness around Lizzie and was pleasantly preoccupied in imagining the impending dreadfulness of Jed's evening when he caught sight of Manon, seated once more at her dressing table, pushing back her hair a little to tie the clasp of a delicate gold necklace. Sometimes he was taken like this, caught for a moment in doubt that she had truly married him, that he had not dreamed it. Sometimes he was taken with a fear that should he close his eyes then open them again, she would be gone. The necklace glinted in the candlelight. He had gifted it to her on the day of their marriage. He went over to help her to tie the clasp, and kissed her on the neck.

'My God, but you're beautiful.'

She lifted a hand and ran her fingers over his hair. There was a small sapphire, entwined amongst tiny pearls at the heart of the pendant, that always seemed to him to be the exact colour of her eyes. He could never himself have afforded such a gift three years ago on their marriage – he could hardly have afforded it now – but his patron Matthew Pullan, who had always treated him as a foster-brother, had gifted him the money and insisted he buy something fitting for his bride. Tonight, Lawrence wished that Damian Seeker could see his daughter right now, see the woman she had grown into, and the life that she had.

Manon saw his face in the glass. 'What's wrong?' she asked.

'What? Oh, nothing.' As he said it, he wasn't sure there hadn't been a sudden pulse in the blue velvet of her gown, where it lay in soft folds over her stomach. He watched a moment longer, but there was no further kick from the baby.

Despite Manon's protests that she could walk perfectly well between here and Oglethorpe, and that she liked the snow, Anne Winter had insisted on sending down the carriage from the Fairfax stables at the Treasurer's House, and for all his mistrust of her Lawrence had taken Lady Anne's part. For the short distance between their home on Fossgate and Madge's sister's house on Colliergate, Lawrence ceded his seat beside his wife to the elderly housekeeper, who on sighting the carriage had begun to complain loudly of the rheumaticks. Lizzie was bundled up warmly with her mother, and Jed instructed to jog alongside.

'Do I have to go?' pleaded Jed. 'I mean, wouldn't it be better if I stayed and watched the house?'

'No, it would not. You'll take your medicine and like it. Besides, I need you keeping an eye on Lizzie. A *close* eye.

Anyone appears at your aunt Flo's door before we come back for you, they don't get in. Understood?'

Jed put his hand to where he'd stashed the dagger Lawrence had provided him with a little earlier. 'Understood,' he said.

Up on Colliergate, where Madge's sister Flo ran a small lacemaking establishment, there was a tremendous fuss and bother as the housekeeper alighted from the carriage, it soon becoming clear that the whole point of the exercise was that her sister should see her do so.

Flo, as Lawrence noted to his satisfaction, was briefly flummoxed as to how to do down her sister's elevation. 'You've grown too fat, Madge. You were ever prone to it. Mother always said it: one day you would grow too fat, and then you would stick!'

'Stick!' countered the outraged Madge, pulling her best shawl about her with great dignity. 'Well, if anyone should know a stick, I daresay it would be you, Florence Booth! Little wonder you've never . . .' and the bickering followed them under the lintel of Flo's neat abode.

Lawrence grinned broadly as he handed Lizzie and her wrappings to a disconsolate Jed with an, 'Enjoy your evening.' A moment later he'd taken his place beside Manon and told the coachman to get on.

He pulled Manon closer and arranged the fur rugs round her as the carriage bumped its way up cobbled streets. Icicles had begun to form on the overhanging storeys of houses on either side, their jetties reaching out to each other, almost touching to form a sparkling canopy over their heads. Few people were out on the streets. It was as if they had York to themselves. 'You know,' he said, 'we could always send word that you're over-tired, or that I've been taken ill, or that a wheel came off the carriage or . . .'

'Lawrence!' she scolded.

'We could travel round York all evening, just you and me under this fur blanket. We could get him to stop at the Golden Slipper, fetch us some nice warmed possets and some of that rabbit pie they do . . .'

'We are going to Lady Anne's house, Lawrence, and you will dazzle her with your wit and charm.'

Lawrence sat back, pulling the furs up to his own chin. 'Bet I don't,' he muttered, as the clopping of the horses' hooves on the frosting cobbles carried them relentlessly towards the house on Ogleforth.

The boy from the Golden Slipper had brought the last of the food, and it was all keeping warm in chafing dishes on the sideboard. 'More than a body could eat in a week,' remarked Grizel.

'It will be worth our while,' said Anne. 'And I will see that whatever is left is passed to the parish at Holy Trinity. The more at ease our guests are, the better our prospects of learning something worthwhile.'

'Mmm. That fellow doesn't have the look of one who is often at his ease,' said the housemaid. As she finished lighting the candelabra in the middle of the dining table

there came the sounds of a carriage drawing up outside
and she hurried downstairs. Lawrence Ingolby, evidently
surprised to have the door opened so quickly, was instantly
on his guard.

'You must have been standing there waiting for us. You'd
freeze to death waiting on any of my servants getting to
the door,' he grumbled.

'You had perhaps better employ more servants then,'
she answered, keeping her smile for when Manon Ingolby
appeared behind her husband. 'Come away in, Mistress
Ingolby. No doubt your husband will be ready to move
from the doorstep soon.'

Manon bit her lip to hide her amusement and before
Ingolby could make any retort Anne Winter had appeared
at the top of the stairs. 'Manon, Mister Ingolby, I am so
glad you are here.'

With a glower, Ingolby handed Grizel his hat and then
his wife's cloak. Finally, he took off his own and stepped
back to allow his wife up the stairs in front of him.

Grizel hung up the guests' outer garments. The narrow-
ness of the hall had allowed her fingers to dart quickly
into the pocket of Ingolby's coat without his noticing. She
wasn't greatly surprised to find nothing there of interest.
She hurried upstairs after them.

Anne had already got the Ingolbys seated on either side
of the fire. She herself was standing at the sideboard, a
silver jug in her hand, ready to pour out some of the dean's
best wine. As Grizel would have suspected, whilst Manon

Ingolby's eyes surveyed the room ready to be delighted, her husband's declared he would be less easily impressed. Grizel had to admit, the room looked well. They had lit up every candlestick in the place, Lady Anne being concerned not to miss anything in her guests' expressions. The plate and glass provided with the house had been augmented by silver and crystal lent from the Treasurer's House, again on account of Anne's friendship with Lady Fairfax. The table carpet, a deep blue edged with silverwork, perfectly set off the finely engraved cutlery and serving spoons.

'Shall I see to the wine, your ladyship?' Grizel enquired, nodding towards the claret jug.

'No, Grizel, thank you, I think we will manage quite well.' Anne smiled now at Manon Ingolby then turned back to the maid. 'Mistress Ingolby and I are old friends. We have no need to stand on ceremony. You will no doubt have plenty to be getting on with.'

'I generally do, your ladyship,' said Grizel, giving the sullen curtsy that always brought a sparkle of amusement to Anne's eye.

Once Grizel left them, Anne was pleased to see Lawrence Ingolby a little less on edge. The aromas coming from a dish of hashed mutton seemed to be distracting him from his examination of the room. Looking at her husband, Manon stretched a hand out beneath the table to Anne's hand and squeezed it. All would be well.

Anne had heard that the lawyer was a person of some

intelligence, and knew that Damian Seeker's trust in him bespoke a wariness in his character, but his evident suspicion of herself suggested that Seeker had told his son-in-law more about their past battles than she had first suspected. Manon, of course, was all brightness and openness and light, as if there could be no badness in the world. She lit the room as surely as did the candles Grizel had set everywhere.

Grizel had scarcely left when Manon had got to her feet, ready to take the maidservant's place. Anne put out a hand to stay her. 'No, my dear, you are no servant here, but a guest.'

Lawrence Ingolby leaned forwards. 'That's what I keep telling her. She's no servant any more, at home or anywhere else.'

Anne nodded. 'You are mistress of your own home now, Manon, with your own servants to command.'

'Exactly,' said Lawrence, and Anne saw that she had unwittingly found a way to ease herself into his trust. He turned to his wife. 'See? Even Lady Anne says it.'

'Oh, I know it,' said Manon, 'but there is a great deal to be done in a household such as ours, with you gaining clients by the day, and our family growing. Jed helps where he can, but Madge cannot be left to do the rest herself.'

'No,' said Lawrence, leaning towards his wife, 'but she will not be told, and you're too close to your time to be doing it for her.'

The young woman, clearly having heard this line of argument before, was not swayed. 'But if you were not grown so grand, Lawrence, and we back at Faithly, no one would raise an eyebrow at me doing it. I have worked all my life.'

'But we're not at Faithly, are we? With half the village ready to step in without a by your leave. We're in York, and like it or not, the world looks on you as a lady.'

'But Madge will not have anyone—'

'Grizel,' said Anne.

Lawrence Ingolby's head whipped towards the door, but it was still shut and no one had entered.

'Grizel,' Anne repeated. 'Mistress Penmore would accept her, for a time, would she not?'

Lawrence frowned at her over the top of his goblet. 'Your maid? That Scotswoman?'

'Yes,' said Anne. 'She is really very efficient, and not quite as . . . prickly as she might at first appear. She works hard, although she's no cook, I'm afraid,' she said, indicating the dishes that had come from the Golden Slipper, 'but I think she made a favourable impression upon your housekeeper, did she not?'

'Aye,' said Lawrence, putting down his goblet, clearly coming over to what Lady Anne was suggesting, 'she did. And it's not often that happens. Would you part with her for a while?'

'Lawrence!' exclaimed Manon. 'We cannot take Lady Anne's maidservant from her.'

'Why not?' he said. 'She's offering.'

Anne managed to hide her amusement at the lawyer's blunt-speaking.

Manon looked at her, almost distressed. 'But how would you manage?'

Now Anne did laugh. 'Oh, my dear, if you but knew of some of my adventures these last few years. In the days when your— in the days of the Protectorate, after I fell foul of Cromwell's authorities, I had to learn a great deal in how to tend to myself. And there were times, particularly during my exile, that I was forced to manage this on very little.' Manon's eyes were brimming with sympathy, and Anne felt a desire to be as honest with her as her situation allowed. 'But in truth, Grizel suits me very well because she understands I am often better on my own.'

Manon seemed to understand.

'But would she come?' It was Ingolby himself who was leaning forwards now, anxious for the answer.

'Oh yes,' Anne assured him, 'she will go where I tell her to go.'

Manon, however, had another worry. 'But how will we talk Madge round?'

'We won't,' said Lawrence. 'We'll just present her with the information, and if she doesn't like it, she can—'

'She won't argue if Grizel's already there,' interjected Anne. 'I saw how she was yesterday – a little dumbfounded. Grizel often has that effect on people.'

'I can imagine,' said Lawrence. 'I suppose we could send Madge out for an hour or so on some errand in the morning, then your maid could—' he began.

Again, Anne interrupted. 'Take her home with you tonight,' she said.

Eventually, she persuaded them to it. From being a thing unthought of to a thing decided took less time than it did for Lawrence Ingolby to eat two dishes of poached pears. As she dispensed a fine sack posset that Grizel had seen fit, herself, to prepare, Anne dismissed any question of referring the matter to her maid's approval, saying there would be time enough to tell her once they had finished their evening. The thing settled, they might enjoy their meal.

They finished with sweetmeats of Anne's own preparation, and nuts and cheeses bought that morning at market. Lawrence Ingolby seemed particularly to enjoy the wine – all the more for knowing it came from the dean's own cellar – and they began to speak of London and their old familiar places. Anne was careful not to go straight to the subject of Thomas Faithly. She sought instead for mutual friends and amongst those found Andrew Marvell, for whom she had always had a great fondness, and Dorcas Wells, landlady of the Black Fox tavern with whom Manon had made her London home. They spoke of William Faithorne who made maps and of Sam Pepys who had always made Manon blush.

All was going well until Anne began her approach to the matter of the Ellingworths – the lawyer Elias, and his sister, Maria, whose portrait Thomas Faithly had drawn. She apologised that on such a cold night she could not offer a drink of chocolate to the Ingolbys, to warm them for their journey home. Grizel, she said, had never got the knack of making it and they were a little too far from the coffee house off Stonegate to send for any in such dreadful weather. Even at this, Anne noticed a slight change in Lawrence Ingolby's demeanour. She pressed on nonetheless, telling them of the first time she herself had tasted chocolate, at Kent's Coffee House in the city. 'What happened to the family that had it, I wonder? That kind old soldier and his niece, Grace.' Grace had once shown her kindness, and unbeknownst to more than a very few people, Anne had repaid that kindness a hundredfold. 'They were very good people. I think I heard that she married the lawyer, Elias Ellingworth, and that they left for the Americas. The lawyer had a sister too, I remember, who I think was friends for a time with Sir Thomas. I must ask him if he has heard from them.'

There could be no doubting the look of alarm that passed now between Manon and her husband. In an instant, Lawrence Ingolby was on his feet. 'I doubt Sir Thomas keeps much in touch with such casual acquaintances, if he even remembers them. But we'd better be off, your ladyship, if you wouldn't mind sending for the carriage. It's late and my wife is tiring.'

In fact, Manon Ingolby had now grown quite pale, and when she tried to stand up, as her husband had done, she swayed a little on her feet, and had to sit back down again. Anne went instantly to the top of the stairs and called for Grizel who was there in moments, out of breath and red in the face from her hurry.

'Mistress Ingolby is tired and a little dizzy, Grizel. Will you bring her some of my tonic, please?'

As the housemaid hurried once more downstairs, a flushed Manon said, 'It's nothing. I'm just a little giddy from sitting so long in the warmth.'

'I will have Grizel make you up a bed for tonight.'

'No,' insisted Manon, beginning to stand again. 'I must go home. Lizzie will need me.'

Lawrence was now white with concern. 'Lizzie'll be fine with Madge. You stay here and . . .'

But Manon was adamant – she drank down Grizel's tonic and insisted she had suffered nothing more than a dizzy spell and would not be parted any longer from her daughter.

'You will come, won't you? Tonight?' said Lawrence.

Grizel, to whom his appeal had been addressed, looked from him to Lady Anne.

'I have offered your help to Mistress Ingolby for a short time, Grizel. You will go tonight, and assist Mistress Penmore in Master Ingolby's household, until such time as other suitable help is found.'

'Indeed?' said Grizel, with a good show of looking surprised at this development. 'Well, I daresay I'm better employed there than here, at any rate, and I noticed yesterday there was plenty needing doing. I'll be there presently, Master Ingolby.'

By the time the carriage had arrived to collect Lawrence and his wife, Grizel had gathered up in a bundle what she needed of her belongings, and, Bible beneath her arm, was preparing to set out into the night.

'No,' said Lawrence, shaking his head. 'No. You ride up with myself and my wife. It's not fit that any woman should walk down these streets at this hour and in this weather.'

Anne noticed with amusement Grizel's unaccustomed flush of pleasure, and was glad to see her companion did not seem to have caught Ingolby mutter under his breath, 'not even a Scotswoman'.

As the bells of the minster rang out for eight, Manon and her new maid were wrapped up beneath the furs while Lawrence Ingolby took up his seat across from them in the carriage. Anne watched until they had disappeared around the bottom of the street onto Goodramgate before turning back into her own house and bolting the door behind her. She stood with her back to the door, the chill air that had snaked in from outside helping her marshal her thoughts. What was very clear to her was that if there was one thing Lawrence and Manon Ingolby did not wish to discuss, it was the departure from London for Massachusetts of Maria Ellingworth in the company of her brother Elias and others of their friends. This suggested to Anne that the rumours of some attachment between the woman Ellingworth and Damian Seeker were true. Moreover, the overreaction on Lawrence Ingolby's part to the suggestion of a connection between Thomas Faithly and the same woman only had the effect of making Anne Winter more certain that there was one. Thomas Faithly and Damian Seeker were connected through Thomas's friendship with Lawrence Ingolby, and they were also connected through some sort of mutual attachment to the same woman. And yet such links were a long way from being proof that Thomas had betrayed the King. Sighing, Anne set off up the stairs to the task of clearing up that she must do for herself tonight. She consoled herself with the knowledge that before the clock struck another hour, Grizel would be ensconced in the Ingolbys' home, and there she would discover whatever was there to be found out.

THIRTEEN

A Break-in

As the carriage trundled away from her sister Flo's door, Madge considered that never had she had such a triumph! Her initial shock at seeing the Scots housemaid sitting up in the carriage with her dear Manon, and the master holding open the door like a footman, had been swiftly dealt with. This Griselda Duncan, lately maid to *Lady* Anne Winter, had been put under her, Madge's, charge, and would, Lawrence assured her, take her guidance from Madge herself. The look on Flo's face alone had been worth the trouble of having to squeeze into her place between the Scotswoman and her mistress. Madge would not, of course, consent that the newcomer should take charge of Lizzie for the journey home, but she did, with only a little reluctance, give the child up to her mother.

'Jedediah would have made a very fine footman, you know,' she said to Grizel, as her grandson jogged alongside the coach, 'but he was too bright, of course. The vicar said it – he should be trained to clerking, and now the master will have him at the law!' The look on the Scotswoman's face was gratifying. It was a pity that she was so much older – a good bit over thirty, Madge would calculate, to Jed's twenty. She'd soon have to turn her thoughts to finding him the right wife. The right wife would put an end to her worries.

Such pleasant musings on their short journey from Flo's were brought to an abrupt end when the carriage drew up outside the green door of the Ingolbys' house, and Madge saw, almost at the same moment as did Lawrence Ingolby, that the lock had been forced open, and the door was swinging on its hinges.

'Stay there!' shouted Lawrence to the women in the carriage. 'Jed, with me. Draw your knife.' Madge's hand flew to her mouth as her grandson followed the master into the darkness of the house. She was about to call out a warning when, to her astonishment, Griselda Duncan jumped from the carriage to disappear through the door after them.

The blackness of the night, so often a help to Grizel in her work, was here a hindrance, and it took time for candles to be lit by spills from the hearth coals. The men had gone first to Ingolby's closet, where chairs had been turned over and drawers pulled from the desk. Briefs and ledgers littered the floor, and bound notebooks had been swept from their shelf. The lock on a chest had been split, but to Grizel's surprise, Ingolby didn't even bother to look inside. Instead, he took the lamp she had just lit and strode from the room to bound up the stairs. Jedediah was soon at his heels. Grizel had instantly to decide between examining the workroom alone whilst she had the chance, or following them. She followed them.

The clash and clatter of the men's feet as they stormed through the house meant there was no possibility that any intruder should be surprised. On the first floor, rather than go to the parlour, where Grizel supposed the best plate and other valuables were like to be kept, Ingolby pushed open the door to his bedchamber. An exclamation from Jed Penmore told her she had run right into the clerk's back, for she saw too late that he had stopped in the doorway, almost filling it. Perhaps he didn't like to enter somewhere so private in his master's life. For all that his grandmother's praise was no doubt overblown, the clerk's slight air of sullenness seemed to overlay a quick enough intelligence. She squeezed in front of him, just inside the room. Ingolby had set his candle down on the mantelpiece, and appeared to be smoothing his hand over a piece of wood panelling in the far wall. His hand went to his neck and he drew out a chain on which Grizel briefly glimpsed a key. At that moment, Ingolby seemed to become aware of his clerk's presence. He turned around. 'It's all right, Jed. There's no one in here. You get up to the attic and check there's nothing amiss there.' He caught sight then of Grizel. 'I told you to stay in the carriage. Get yourself back outside and wait with the women till I say it's safe. Make sure to shut that door behind you.'

She mumbled an apology. She'd learned over the years that shamefacedness worked much better in such circumstances than attempts at self-justification or defiance.

'Straight back outside, now,' he went on, 'until we tell you it's safe.'

Grizel did as she was bid. She had learned as much as she needed to, for now.

It was not a great deal of time later that Lawrence and Jed emerged back onto the street, where Grizel had had to relay every detail of what they had come upon in the house. Jed was given instructions to go for a constable and then to knock up a locksmith. Lawrence was determined that the house should be secured again well before daybreak. Grizel was instructed to set and light fires in Lawrence's closet and in his and Manon's bedchamber, whilst Madge set about the preparation of spiced caudles to warm them all. The family huddled in the kitchen while Lawrence told his wife what he had come upon.

'There's no one in the house now, and nothing has been disturbed anywhere but my office.'

'What! Not even the good plate in the parlour, or the mistress's jewels!' exclaimed Madge.

'The plate's safe enough, Madge, and,' here Ingolby gave a small smile in his wife's direction, 'the mistress is wearing her jewels.'

Grizel's eyes went to the simple gold pendant at Manon Ingolby's neck and felt an unexpected rush of warmth for the lawyer and his wife.

'You have searched the rest of the house?' asked Manon, real anxiety in her eyes. 'Everywhere?'

'Everywhere,' her husband assured her.

Some of the apprehension seemed to go out of Manon Ingolby when he said this, and she bent over her sleeping child and kissed her softly on the forehead.

'You need to be in your bed, pet, you and babby,' said Madge who herself looked exhausted, the earlier delight of her evening gone from her face.

'And you too, Mistress Penmore,' said Grizel. She waved a hand around the kitchen, where their unexpected late-night supper had left a deal of clearing up to be done. 'I will see to all of this. You go to your bed and rest. All will be well in the morning.'

To Grizel's surprise, it was not Madge but Lawrence Ingolby who said, 'No.'

'No?' she asked.

His face was set. 'No. This'll keep. Jed and me'll have to stay downstairs while the locksmith does his work, and then we'll have to set my closet to rights, see if anything's been taken.'

Grizel opened her mouth to protest that she might see to what had to be done in the kitchen without in any way disturbing them, but Lawrence Ingolby spoke again to forestall her.

'In here'll keep to the morning. I want you upstairs, in our bedchamber with Manon and Lizzie. You shout for me if anything untoward should happen. Understand?'

Sometime later she found herself lying down, still fully attired, on a pallet on the floor of the Ingolbys' bedchamber. She had watched Manon put her daughter into the cot by her bedside, and then helped Manon undress and get into the bed in which she'd already placed a warming pan. She'd closed the drapes around the bed, leaving the small gap Manon had insisted upon so that she could see her little girl, and she'd placed the brass *couvre feu* over the coals in the hearth to prevent sparks flying out in the night. Mother and child were both already asleep by the time Lawrence Ingolby came up to bid goodnight to them. Grizel made to leave.

'No,' said Ingolby, standing over his daughter's cot, as if mesmerised by her every breath. 'I need you to stop the night up here. I'm going to be hours yet going through the mess they've made of my papers.'

'But who might have done such a thing?' she asked.

He shook his head. 'I've no idea. But I will have, once I see what's missing.'

'Do you think,' she said, choosing her words as carefully as she could, 'it would have anything to do with the luring away of the wee one?'

Lawrence's face was grim, and in his eyes she saw tears and anger contend for control. Anger won. 'Aye, I do. I'll tell you what, though, they'll rue the day they ever set their sights on this family.' He put his hand to his side and drew a dagger much like the one she had seen Jed Penmore carrying into the house and which she herself often carried. She waited, and he took a step closer to her.

'You're in Lady Anne's service,' he said, watching her.

'Yes.'

'So I don't think you're any ordinary housemaid.'

She opened her mouth to speak but he held up a hand. 'Now, I'm not going to say I know all about Lady Anne and her business, because I don't, but I know enough to know that she doesn't spend her time doing embroidery and playing the lute.'

For all of her experience, and all the difficult situations Grizel had found herself in in the past, she felt herself flush at this and was glad of the meagre light of the fire and the one candle lit in the room.

'But what I do know,' he said, 'is that someone *I* trust trusted *her* with the safety of my wife. My wife considers her a friend, and I believe – and I hope to God that I'm not wrong – that Lady Anne wishes my wife well.'

Grizel felt she could speak now. 'Oh, she does. She wishes her well with all her heart.'

Ingolby gave a brisk nod. 'Good. Right.' He handed her the knife. 'I daresay you know your way round one of these. Tonight, I'm trusting you to watch over my wife and child for as long as it takes me to sort out what has happened downstairs. I've got Jed at the front door and Madge's benighted dog guarding the back. I want you here, in this room, with them, until I'm ready to come up. '

The tolling of a nearby church bell told Grizel that almost an hour had passed since she had returned to the Ingolbys' chamber with the small bundle of clothing and other things she had brought with her. She had left the bedchamber door a little ajar, the better to hear what passed below. The sounds coming from Lawrence Ingolby's office hadn't changed – a regular shifting and pausing of feet and papers, fragments of the occasional murmured exchange between Ingolby and his clerk. The one lit candle on the mantelshelf continued to burn down. When it was nearly done, Grizel set another candle in a holder and lit it from the first.

She had thought it might take her considerably longer to get the chance to explore the most private corners of Lawrence Ingolby's house. Here she was, though, in his bedchamber by the panel where he had already inadvertently shown her he kept that which he most feared being discovered.

Moving as silently as she could, in her nightgown and cap and her stocking soles, she ran a hand over the panelling where she thought Ingolby had touched it. It would not be the first time that she had come upon panelling with a secret door that would open inwards when pressed in the correct place. But after a few moments, having gone further along the wall than where Ingolby had stood, nothing had given. Then she remembered the glint of candlelight off the chain he had pulled from beneath his shirt. A key. She held her candle closer to the wall and began again her examination of the square framed panels. And there it was, in the top left-hand corner of a panel a little higher than her shoulder – a small keyhole. Looking towards the bed for any signs that Manon Ingolby might be stirring, Grizel quickly unclipped the pin that held her shawl together. On more than one occasion she had been complimented upon it, the delicacy of the pin, the intricacy of the work. What craftsman had made it? people asked.

'Oh,' she would say with a wistful smile, 'it was a gift from my father.'

But Grizel's father had been no silversmith, rather a cordiner in a small town on the southern shore of the Moray Firth, and this lovely item had been made for her in Germany, by a very skilled Hanau locksmith. It would have been of no use against a great lock such as that on the Ingolbys' front door – for that she would have required a key like the one possessed by Anne Winter – but it had given Grizel access to many small cases and cabinets. It took her very little time to turn it in the lock, and as the mechanism gave, the panel swung inwards on unseen hinges. Grizel's candle revealed a square compartment behind this door, and in it a box which she lifted out. Her heart beat a little faster. This surely contained whatever had had Lawrence Ingolby rush up earlier from his wrecked office, where he had not taken the time even to right a chair or close a cabinet drawer, instead stepping over papers fallen to the floor and taking the stairs two at a time to his bedchamber.

The box was of polished walnut, the size of a small travelling escritoire. Hardly daring to breathe as she checked once more for sounds coming from downstairs, Grizel applied her intricately wrought pin to the lock. The click, when it came, almost made her jump, and elicited a squeak from Lizzie. Grizel watched anxiously as the small pursed lips worked themselves until they found the comforting thumb. She lifted the walnut lid and inside found what the weight and feel of the box had suggested she would find: letters.

There appeared to be eight in all, folded neatly in two distinct piles and tied in blue silk ribbon. The top letter of one pile had 'Manon' written on it, and on the other, 'Ingolby'. Grizel wondered at first if they might be old love-letters between the couple, but even a cursory examination suggested the names had been written in the same hand. She undid the ribbon on the pile marked 'Ingolby' first.

She could see that the letters had originally been folded with a locking pattern, which must have been broken when they had first been opened. Whoever had sent these had been keen that any interference with them should not go undetected. Grizel's hands were growing white and numb with the cold. As she continued to listen for sounds of Manon waking or for Ingolby's foot on the stair, her fingers fumbled at the paper but eventually she managed to open the letter on top and set to examining it. It was written over three sides of two sheets of paper. The writing was small and precise, and, aside from the date written at the top – xv. Jul. MDCLXII – the fifteenth day of July, sixteen hundred and sixty-two – Grizel could not make sense of a word of it. The letter was written either in a foreign lan-guage, or in some cypher that she had never seen before. The fact that the pages had been so intricately folded and locked argued for the latter – a cypher. Grizel, moreover, was not ignorant of foreign tongues and did not recognise in it any language that she knew. Her fingers, surer of their work now, went to the top letter on the other pile, the one marked 'Manon': here was the same hand, the same folding pattern, the same date, and more incomprehensible words. She looked at the words, presumably valedictory, at the end of each letter. They were different. The person sending the letters signed themselves off in a different way depending on whether they were writing to Manon Ingolby or to her husband. But the handwriting was the same, and Grizel was sure the letters had been written by the same person. She was not completely without skill in deciphering, but she was much, much slower at it than was Anne Winter. She couldn't risk taking the letters either, for she might have no chance of replacing them, and if the theft were discovered, as it must surely be, Lawrence Ingolby would have no difficulty in lighting on her as the culprit.

The night was passing and she must work quickly. Grizel went again to the bundle she had brought with her from Anne Winter's house and brought out a package, wrapped in two pairs of woollen stockings. Inside were a bottle of ink, a quill pen and a half-dozen sheets of paper, cut to size octavo. Reasoning that the letters on top of each bundle would be the most recent, she chose the one at the top of Lawrence Ingolby's bundle first and began to copy it.

Her candle was spluttered far down by the time Grizel lifted her head from the careful copying of the two most recent letters – one to Ingolby and one to his wife. She had just finished refolding the latter and was reaching for the next most recent one in Ingolby's pile when she heard a voice from downstairs. 'That'll do us for tonight, Jed. Let's get an hour or so's sleep and we can finish the last of it in the morning.'

Grizel's heart thumped as she hastily retied the two bundles of letters and returned them to the wooden box. She was inserting her pin-key back into the lock when she heard Ingolby's study door below click shut. Her hand shook as she tried to relock the escritoire with the sound of the men's feet already on the stairs. Only as Jed Penmore bid his master goodnight on the landing outside the door did she manage to lock the casket and slide it in to the cavity behind the wall panel. To her horror, she realised the only means of properly closing the panel was to pull it shut with the key inserted in the lock and then turn it.

'Here, Jed, you take the candle or you'll break your neck on them attic stairs.' The handle of the bedchamber door was turning as Grizel snuffed out her candle. She had thrust her pin back into the lock and was pulling the panel door to as Ingolby came through the door.

'Ouch! What the . . . ?' Lawrence cursed as he hit his shin on the corner of an iron-bound coffer on coming into his chamber. In steadying himself he managed to knock over a small footstool and the sound reverberated round the room. Lizzie cried out in her sleep and he heard Manon's sleepy voice through the darkness.

'Lawrence, what is it?'

'That, that Scotswoman of Anne Winter's,' he spluttered. 'Where is she?'

From somewhere on the other side of the room, by the wall where she'd presumably laid down to sleep, came the affronted tones of the Scotswoman. 'I am here, Mr Ingolby, keeping guard on your wife and child, as you requested.'

'I didn't request that you did it in the pitch dark!' he muttered. 'Why is there no candle lit?'

'Well, sir, I thought it was a waste, for Mistress Ingolby and little Lizzie are sleeping, and what would I be needing light for? Candles do not pay for themselves.'

'No,' he said. 'I pay for them. So that I can see where I'm going! Now, get one lit and take your things down to the kitchen. You can sleep there the rest of the night and let me get to my bed.'

FOURTEEN

Papers and Letters

Thomas felt a shiver overtake him that was nothing to do with the cold of his bedchamber in King's Manor. 'My papers?'

Lawrence nodded. 'Jed and I were up half the night putting things right. The only things taken were the papers relating to your claim to Langton.'

'You're sure?'

'Certain. I keep a tidy office and a note of every last scrap of paper in it.'

Thomas was looking out of the window over the abbey grounds. 'This on top of the incident with my clerk and page the other night . . .'

'What incident?'

'Oh,' said Thomas, 'some prank amongst the clerks, or so I thought, until you brought me this news.'

'What incident?' repeated Lawrence, with greater firmness this time.

'Two nights ago, when we had just got hold of William's satchel from the churchmen. I took it here before going over to Peasholme Green to meet my friend Ogilvie at the Black Swan. Not long after I left, a message came for my clerk, Frank, purporting to have been written by me. It instructed him to take Will, my page, down to the castle, where they were to attend me in my old apartments. If I was not there, they were to wait.'

'And you never wrote any such note?'

'No, I did not. When I returned here after having my supper with Ogilvie, I found my rooms in darkness and the boys gone.'

'And this note?'

Thomas pulled a sheet of paper from a drawer and handed it to Lawrence. 'Look at it — I would almost swear myself that that is my hand, and that my signature, but I know they are not.'

Lawrence frowned at the piece of paper. 'You sure you didn't write this?'

'Absolutely certain.'

'And it definitely wasn't a prank?'

'I thought so, until now.'

'Clearly, someone wanted them out of here while you were out.'

Thomas nodded.

'Were there signs of your rooms being searched? Did they take anything?'

'Nothing,' said Thomas, 'they didn't even open William's satchel.'

'And have you?'

'Yes, that very night. Nothing in it but plans for a town house. You may study them yourself.' Thomas fetched the satchel and opened it, laying the plans out on the table. Lawrence planted his hands on the table's edge and leaned over it. He scanned it for a short while then straightened up, shaking his head. 'Like you say, house plans. Don't know what William's problem with the job can have been – perhaps he didn't much like the client.'

Thomas grimaced and went to check that his chamber door was properly closed. 'His *client*, as I have been able to establish from his appointment book, was the Duke of Buckingham.'

'Ah well,' said Lawrence, straightening up and waving a hand about the room. 'Buckingham's the *client* of everyone at King's Manor, isn't he? I mean, he's lord lieutenant so everything done here . . .'

Thomas gave a brief shake of the head. 'This appears to have been a private commission.'

Lawrence looked down again at the plans. 'A bit modest for George Villiers, that. Maybe he's setting up a mistress here, for when he's in York.'

Thomas sighed. 'No doubt.'

'I don't blame William for not being happy about it then,' said Lawrence. 'Having to do Buckingham's grubby work.'

'But hardly something to get killed for.'

'No. And besides, whoever killed him wasn't interested in the contents of his satchel, or they wouldn't have left it with him.'

'No,' said Thomas, despondent. 'But some unknown person summoned him by note and then murdered him, some unknown person forged a note from me, in order to make sure they might search my premises undisturbed, and they took nothing, and then the next night, someone broke into your home and stole nothing but my papers. You're certain they took nothing else of mine?'

Lawrence frowned, perplexed. 'There was nothing else of yours in there, Thomas.'

Thomas turned back from looking out over the abbey gardens towards the icy river 'There was nothing pertaining to . . .'

'To what?'

'Our work for *the captain.*'

It was Lawrence's turn to lower his voice. 'No, there was not. I keep nothing of that sort in there. Jed's privy to every paper I have in that office. The lad can't hold his drink and his grandmother can't hold her tongue. There's no chance I'd let him near those *other things.* Half of York would be talking about them before he'd left the Three Tuns.'

'Of course, of course,' said Thomas. 'So your wife's letters from her father . . .'

'Safe,' said Lawrence. 'Nothing was taken but your Langton papers.'

Thomas sank his chin into his hands, deflated. 'So my case is back to where it began. All those months on end of arguing, and waiting, all for nothing?' He kicked at a log that had rolled off the hearth. 'It will take us years just to get back to where we were. I might well be dead.'

'You might be dead by dinnertime,' said Lawrence, pulling round a wooden chair and sitting astride it. 'But never worry. The stolen papers were copies I'd had Jed do. I lodged the originals with the clerks down at Westminster Hall, and I've got other copies safe here at the Guildhall should I need to look at them, which I may have to do soon enough, because your case is almost done.'

Thomas's head shot up. 'What? I have lost?'

'No. It looks as if things might fall out well for you after all.'

'But why didn't you tell me?'

Lawrence brushed at a mark on his jacket sleeve. 'Because I didn't want to get your hopes up. Besides, I'm telling you now. You might just be in possession of your grandmother's estate come Whitsun.'

Thomas Faithly closed his eyes. All the months, the years, of wandering and rootlessness seemed themselves to disintegrate in front of him and to dissolve into the sharp air of the morning. He heard a movement and felt Lawrence's hand on his shoulder.

'You're nearly there, Thomas. Whoever broke into my office and stole your papers is going to find themselves disappointed. There's nothing of use to anyone but you and me in them. You keep yourself out of trouble a while longer, and you'll be there.'

★

Ingolby gone, Thomas locked the door behind him and went to his desk. It really shouldn't be too much to ask, that he might hold his manor of Langton at last and live his life in peace. He feared that just as Lawrence Ingolby had almost unravelled the entanglements of the law that had kept him from his inheritance, new entanglements were preparing themselves to lie in wait for him. With reluctance, he opened the drawer of his desk and took out the letter that had arrived only moments before his clerk had announced Ingolby.

The letter was from the Duke of Buckingham and detailed events that had lately unfolded in London which, the duke wrote, offered some useful lessons for his coming rule in York. There was a risk, under the benevolent reign of the King, that the people might forget the threat posed by fanatics and malcontents risen far above their station in the dismal days of Cromwell's rule.

It was necessary for the security of the state that they be reminded that the ordering of their affairs was better left to those born to it.

Thomas was somewhat unsettled at this opening and unsure what it portended, but he had no choice but to read on. The lessons of the Protectorate had not been lost on the intelligence operatives of the restored Stuart crown: listening to the lower orders as they went about their lives in the streets, taverns, coffee houses and churchyards of the capital could reveal things of great use to their masters. Some discontents had lately been come upon in London – men who had had a taste of power or influence that they had not been born to and, since the King's coming in, had lost it once again; men who had made the mistake of bemoaning their lot when the wrong ears were listening. The one thought to be their ringleader had been brought in, and given a choice: he might spend the rest of his days in a stinking cell in one of London's finer repositories of forgotten souls, or he might turn trepanner. His task had been to draw others of a like mind to himself to the point that they might talk sedition and have the full weight of the King's authority fall upon them, for the sake of the public peace. Careless talk had become a plot that was hardly a plot and then been whipped up to the wild heights of plans to take Windsor, to march on London, to kill the King. The 'plotters' had been informed upon, taken, imprisoned, tried and executed.

Thomas set down the letter. He had heard already of some such ludicrous plot, the 'Tong' plot, though not of the agents who had promoted it. He had heard, too, of the executions. Why was Buckingham bothering to tell him of something he might read of in any common news-sheet?

He poured himself a goblet of wine and read on, and as he did so, he grew cold, finally understanding what it was that Buckingham was really saying to him. The duke was of the view that it would do no harm at all should a similar threat be encouraged to show itself in the north, in order that he, Buckingham, might happily crush it, all to the approbation of the people and the further advancement of the duke.

The wine tasted sour on Thomas's tongue. The duke informed him that he was to encourage, not suppress, any small signs of discontent, any grumbles that might come to his ears. Former members – officers and common men – of Oliver's New Model Army that might once have made a noise in the world but were now forced to return to their humble trades and labours were to be listened to in workshops and alehouses, spied upon as they went to their churches. They were to be cajoled, threatened into enticing others into agitating to the point where their movement would be brutally crushed, all so that such as Buckingham might jostle for position at the King's court.

Thomas stood up and walked over to his fireplace, leaning a moment on the mantelpiece before consigning Buckingham's letter to the flames. 'Dear God, Ingolby. Bring my case to an end that I might pass up this poisoned chalice.'

FIFTEEN

Women in York

Anne Winter had been surprised by the urgent rapping on the door and more surprised to find Grizel standing on the street.

'Griz! Don't tell me Lawrence Ingolby has thrown you out already?'

The housemaid sniffed as she moved past Anne into the hallway. 'Let me into the warmth and I'll tell you.'

Anne listened as she hung Grizel's cloak over the back of a chair and added wood and coals to still-glowing ashes to bring the kitchen fire back to life. She knelt to help Grizel off with her snow-sodden boots, and heard the tale of the break-in at the Ingolbys' house, what the family had found when they'd returned to the house, and what had happened next – the evidence of a break-in, the disordering of Ingolby's business room, but most of all, the lawyer's main concern having been for whatever was hidden behind a panel of his bedchamber wall.

'What did he have there?' asked Anne. 'Money? Manon's jewels?'

Grizel shook her head and undid the knot on the linen kerchief she wore about her hair. As she slipped the garment off with one hand, with the other she removed a small packet, wrapped in a white handkerchief, from beneath it. Despite what Anne knew of Grizel's deftness, she had not expected her to come upon anything of value quite so soon. It was a letter.

Anne took it as if it might crumble to dust in her hands. 'You stole this? But he will know.'

Grizel shook her head. 'The original is still there. That is a copy.'

'Are there others?'

Grizel's look became defensive. 'Yes, but I had not the time to copy them all. That one was on the top of the pile and I thought it would be the most recent.'

'Very likely,' said Anne, unfolding the pages then looking up. '"Manon"?'

'That was what was written on the outside of the original. I took it that it was addressed to her. Other than the date inside, I couldn't make out any more of it. It is in code, as you will see.'

At first glance, it was not in any code Anne recognised, but a few minutes' study would tell whether it was a simple question of transposition of characters, of substitution, or of something more complex. 'And you managed to return the box to its place? You won't be suspected of tampering with it?'

Grizel sniffed, ready to be offended at the very idea of

her proficiency being questioned. But then she gave way to a smile and the laugh she sometimes fell into that always made Anne imagine her as the girl she must have been. 'It was a close-run thing, but Lawrence Ingolby was too busy cursing me over a bashed shin to wonder what I was doing in the darkness, on the other side of his bedchamber.'

Anne laughed. The world thought Grizel severe, critical, humourless. Even amongst her own people, she would not let her guard slip. For a time, even with Anne, she had not let that guard slip.

'And what of Ingolby's business papers? What was taken from amongst them?'

But Grizel was up on her feet again, making ready to leave. 'I must not be away too long. I told Mistress Penmore I had just to come up to fetch some stockings and a clean shift that I had forgot in the hurry last night.' She took a pair of stockings from a pulley above their heads. 'As to the lawyer's papers, it seems nothing was taken but documents and letters relating to Thomas Faithly's claim on his dead grandmother's estate. Dry as dust, Madge Penmore said.'

'But surely the housekeeper cannot have read them!'

'Well, she can certainly read,' said Grizel. 'She keeps a pile of news-sheets and pamphlets on a shelf in the kitchen, which she has said I may borrow should I ever be at leisure.'

Anne was surprised. 'And she has read the papers relating to Thomas Faithly that Ingolby keeps in his office?'

Grizel folded a clean shift and bundled it up with the stockings. 'Yes. She is an uncommonly nosy woman, but her main end in life seems to be the advancement of her grandson. I believe she is in hopes of seeing Jedediah steward of Langton estate, somewhere out on the northern moors, if Lawrence Ingolby can get it back for Sir Thomas. She is very keen to get him away from "low types and undesirables" – I think she means his tavern friends.'

'But I thought Ingolby was sending him down to the Inns of Court?'

'There is some talk of that. There was some preparation made when they were lately at London, but for "a touch and a polish only", Madge says. She thinks less of the Inns than she does of the lowest York tavern, it would seem.'

Anne laughed, remembering her scrapes with some of the more august habitués of those Inns in Cromwell's time. 'She may well have a point. But is Sir Thomas keen?'

'Pah, I doubt Sir Thomas has been consulted. Madge means to have all in readiness and Jed will be in his employ and off up to Langton before the ink is dry on the deeds.'

'And herself no doubt with him, to be installed as housekeeper.'

Grizel shook her head. 'Madge is devoted to Manon Ingolby, and to the little one. I don't think she would leave them for anything.'

And then Grizel, her boots and cloak still sodden, was out again into the streets of York leaving Anne to breakfast late and alone, before settling herself to the task of decoding this new letter.

★

As the door to the little house on Oglethorpe closed behind her, Grizel felt the sensation of guilt begin to creep over her like a parade of caterpillars. She and Anne had their secrets from one another but she had never before actually deceived her friend, yet she had no choice. Anne had seemed content enough to be handed one coded letter copied from the Ingolbys' secret cache. When Grizel had told her she hadn't had time to copy them all, Anne had not pressed her, and Grizel had allowed her to believe that she had only managed to copy one letter, that addressed to Manon Ingolby. The second letter, addressed by the same writer to Manon's husband, remained secreted in an inner pocket of her skirts. Anne might be the expert cryptographer, but Grizel had not travelled with her for the last four years without observing, and learning. After Lawrence Ingolby, swearing about his barked shin, had sent her down to the kitchen to sleep, Grizel had not slept, but instead had lit a candle and set to work. She had not managed to establish the entire cypher, but she had got enough to tell her who the letters were from and to get some little sense of their content. The letter to Manon had been signed 'Your loving father', that to Ingolby, 'Damian Seeker'. Grizel had felt a thrill of excitement. Manon's letter, as far as she could make out, seemed to be of family and domestic detail and of little possible interest to anyone else, but in Ingolby's there had been two recurring words of which she had had no doubt: 'Thomas' and 'Faithly'. Ordinarily, Grizel would have rushed to Anne with such a discovery. But this was no ordinary time.

Grizel put these reflections away for the moment, to be taken up again when she should next have the opportunity to decipher more of the letter whose copy she had kept. A slight relenting of the winter frost had encouraged people back out on the street. Grizel remained alert and was glad to reach the Ingolbys' house without incident.

Manon was anxious to get out to the haberdashers' for some ribbons she wanted for the little dress she was sewing for Lizzie's favourite doll, but she knew Lawrence would not countenance her going into town alone, and she didn't like to take Madge away from her household tasks. She was glad when the new maid arrived back from her visit to Lady Anne's house on Oglethorpe. Madge had also been waiting for the return of Griselda Duncan, ready with a barrage of pointed remarks about the length of time she had been away, and how they were not yet caught up with the work occasioned by the previous night's 'outrages'. Hastily tying on her kitchen apron, Griselda had apologised, confiding that her mistress was the most shocking slattern, and she really had not liked to leave the kitchen in Oglethorpe in the way she had found it – with half the dishes from last night still needing to be scrubbed. She added, throwing Manon a conspiratorial smile, that she was glad to have come to such a well-ordered household as was under the rule of Mistress Penmore.

As they walked up the street, Manon said, 'It is truly very good of you to have come to help us, Mistress Duncan.'

'It was Lady Anne that wanted it. She has a great fondness for you, and there aren't many people she's fond of. Besides, it'll no' do her any harm to see to herself for a few days and get an idea of all the work I do. But you must call me "Grizel", mistress.'

'And you must call me "Manon".'

The Scotswoman gave a brief shake of her head. 'No, mistress, I must not.'

The maid's response had not been unfriendly, but in it she had made their positions clear, and Manon hadn't argued further. They had got what she wanted at the haberdasher's, though Grizel had expressed shock and had shared her views on parting with such an amount of money 'for the sake of a bairn's poppet' all along Coney Street and much of Coppergate too, until suddenly she had stopped, her attention taken by something across the street. Manon had followed the line of her gaze and felt a sudden chill.

'Do you know that man?' she asked.

'No,' the maid replied, taking Manon's arm. 'I don't. We had better be getting on. Mistress Penmore will be needing me.'

Manon didn't argue, but she did glance back and saw that the man was watching them. 'I've seen him before,' she said. 'He looked at me strangely then, too.'

Grizel's response was to grip her arm the more firmly and to hurry her along the street. All the way back along Coppergate and the rest of the way home, the Scotswoman kept looking behind her, and they were hardly through the door before Grizel was demanding of Jed to know if the master was home.

'Black hair, grey at the temples. Older than yourself – maybe forty – and about your own height. Has the bearing of a soldier. Clothes of good quality and hardwearing – greys and blacks.'

Lawrence was wearing a path back and forth in front of the fire in his office. 'And this man was watching my wife, you say?'

'Aye, sir. As we came back down Coppergate today. And she thought she had seen him watching her before, too.'

'Would you know him again?'

The maid's face had set like stone. 'Oh, I would know him again. And I would counsel you never to let him over the door, should he ever come here.'

'Never concern yourself over that. No stranger will be allowed into this house until I say otherwise. You did right to tell me of it, Mistress Duncan.'

Once the Scotswoman had gone back to her duties in the kitchen, Lawrence had ascended the stairs where he'd found Manon and Lizzie in the parlour.

'This man you saw when you were out with Anne Winter's maid today – she says he was watching you and that you said you'd seen him before. Tell me again about it.'

Manon wrinkled her brow. 'It was the day Lizzie went missing, and that put everything else from my head. Besides, that time he just looked at me in passing, as I was about to come out onto the street from the top of Baker's Lane. I think I surprised him. He looked as if he might know me, but then he just went on his way without saying anything.'

'And this was definitely the man you saw watching you today?'

Manon nodded. 'I wouldn't have noticed him, but Grizel was almost turned to stone at the very sight of him.'

Lawrence went over to kneel down in front of her, taking her hands. 'Thank God she was with you. For all your father mistrusted Anne Winter, he trusted her to look after you, and this Scotswoman clearly knows her business.'

'You still think Lady Anne to be an intelligencer?'

'Down to her bones,' said Lawrence. 'I do believe that she would never do anything to harm you, though, or Lizzie. No doubt she's in York to see Buckingham about some skulduggery or other. Good luck to them. But,' he took a deep breath, 'whatever *she* might be up to, *I* couldn't do without you, you know that, don't you?'

Manon nodded and Lawrence continued. 'If this man Griselda Duncan saw is the man Andrew Marvell warned us was looking for your father, we can't take any more risks, at all. These regicide-hunters are ruthless, they're brigands, assassins. For all the Stuarts make a show of trials and executions under the law, the folk entrusted with hunting regicides make their own laws, and they wouldn't scruple to use a pregnant woman or a child to get to their quarry. Now, I don't know who this man is, and I don't know if William Briar's murder was anything to do with the hunt for your father, but until we have the answer to both those questions, I don't want you leaving this house unless you're with me. Do you understand?'

Manon lifted a hand and ran it gently through his hair. 'Yes, Lawrence,' she said. 'I understand.'

As Grizel finally laid herself down to sleep on the bed in the kitchen of the Ingolbys' house, her mind whirled, exhausted though she was. She had been unsettled enough before the episode out in town with Manon Ingolby, but at least until then she had thought she understood the nature of the danger she had to face. Now she was not certain of anything, other than that it would be to risk too much for her to tell Lawrence Ingolby that she knew the identity of the man who was watching his wife. Perhaps Manon Ingolby had been mistaken. Perhaps David Ogilvie had not been watching her at all. Perhaps Ogilvie would leave York soon. Perhaps her fears were groundless and all would be well, but for now she had made certain that Lawrence Ingolby would never allow him into the house. Trying to make herself believe this, Grizel had eventually passed into a restless sleep.

SIXTEEN

An Invitation

Anne had spent an afternoon at work on the copy of the letter Grizel had brought to her from the Ingolbys' house. Using the sample cypher keys she carried with her in her travelling escritoire, she had seen straight away that the code in which the letter was written was not complex and guessed that its relative simplicity had probably been chosen with the recipient in mind. Anne knew Manon Ingolby was no simpleton, but she was not, or at least should not have been, one whose life required the skills of the life Anne had chosen to live.

Anne wished she might have seen the original letter, for sometimes the formation of the letters or numbers told her things, the curl of the pen, the slant of the hand. She worried too that Grizel, in her haste, might have made some error of transcription, but she had had to put away such thoughts because she must work with what she had in her hands.

The code, one of transposition of characters and substitution by number and symbol, had hardly challenged her.

The letter itself, a page and a half long, had not taken her a great deal of time to decipher, but for Anne it had opened up a whole world. She had read in it a domestic tale, an affectionate passing of news from father to daughter, the usual anxious enquiries as to a daughter and a granddaughter's welfare from a father many, many miles away. Anne had not read very far down when she'd suddenly sat back, realising what it was she was reading in this copy of a letter that had travelled across an ocean. She was assailed by an ill-assorted procession of emotions – shock, warmth, affection, relief and, finally, apprehension. What would Roger L'Estrange not give for the information she now held in her hands? Damian Seeker, whose whereabouts and welfare she periodically wondered about, was not only still alive, but settled in Massachusetts and, if his letters to his daughter were to be believed, making a new life as a village carpenter on which to raise a new family. 'What will you do, Damian Seeker?' she had once asked him. 'What will you do, Anne Winter?' she'd asked herself when she'd been sent to York. Not this.

Anne got up from her desk to put more coals on the fire. She was about to call for Grizel to bring up some of Madge Penmore's bread pudding that she had brought that morning, but then remembered that Grizel had already gone back down to the Ingolbys' so went and fetched it herself. She poured herself a good glass of claret from the jug on the dresser, and took it to her armchair by the fire where she read over her transcription of the letter once more. Massachusetts.

A family. A new life, and he was living it. Her old adversary, who had always played her fair, in as far as fair play might be possible in their great game. The contentment she felt was tinged with a little sadness. She missed him sometimes. Thurloe had said it to her – John Thurloe of all people! – when she had gone to visit him in the Tower after the King's restoration, 'You were worthy of one another.'

The light came in the window from the north-east and penetrated to her little sitting room in grains of grey. The greater height of the Treasurer's House backing on to the stable yard over which her window looked, and the looming city walls about Monkgate Bar both cast shadows where on clearer days there might have been sun. Anne lit another candle and considered what she had read. She could not help but smile, laugh a little even. But did Manon Ingolby really believe it all? Probably. The child – Anne could not think of her as anything else – believed everything she was told, for she could not conceive that others were not as open-hearted as she herself was. But she surely knew her father well enough to wonder whether he would really be content to pass his days on the edge of a forest in the New World, a farmer and carpenter? Oh no. Anne could not see it. How long had he managed it, she wondered, before the inadequacies and misjudged familiarities of his neighbours had become too much for him? A year perhaps, or maybe six months? Would he have managed six months? And as to Maria Ellingworth that Thomas Faithly had somehow made a sketch of, how long might she have managed the life of a contented housewife? Not even six months, surely not even three. With what regularity, Lady Anne wondered, would Seeker have to extricate the ink-stained hands of his wife from trouble she had managed to scribble herself into?

And a child there was, too, a boy. Anne could picture him – a wild thing, strong and troublesome, surely. In such a happy reverie about her old opponent, Anne fell asleep. When she woke, her candle was far burned down and the coals in the fire near to ashes. Had Grizel come in she would have tutted that the shutters were not closed and the night outside black. If any watched Anne from that blackness, they were well hidden. She closed the shutters and made ready for bed. She lay in the darkness, picturing that homestead in Massachusetts, hearing the rumble of that old familiar voice as finally she fell asleep.

It would be another two days before Anne answered the door of the little house on Oglethorpe to find Grizel standing there again.

'Griz! I thought you had forgotten me!'

'It's not as easy for some of us to come and go as the fancy takes us as it is for others,' muttered Grizel, stepping briskly past her to make a point of surveying the condition of the kitchen. Anne could not help but smile; left to her own devices, she kept almost as tidy a house as Grizel did, so many years of having to move on swiftly and with little warning having taught her the virtues of neatness and good order.

'Mmm,' said Grizel, disappointed of any fit object for her disapproval. She sat down. 'You'll have been out and about, I suppose?'

Anne had. She had made a point, for a start, of visiting her horse both morning and evening at the King's Manor stables, and in the course of doing so had learned much about Thomas Faithly's habits. He rode out of town at every possible opportunity and his most frequent conversation was on the matter of his plans for his own stables at Langton. There did not appear to be a woman of especial importance in his life, although it was known all around York that should he wish, Sir Thomas might have his pick of whoever took his eye, from kitchen maid to countess.

'I was sure to look suitably shocked at this disclosure, of course,' said Anne.

'Aye, no doubt,' said Grizel.

If Sir Thomas rode out for pleasure rather than on official duties, he most often went alone, but if he should take anyone with him, it was most often the lawyer, Lawrence Ingolby. More than one groom had expressed the view that they would rather have Sir Thomas as lord lieutenant than the one that was coming. Anne had casually tried a few names out around the stables, of men in Yorkshire who were suspected of being less loyal to the King than they should be, but none were taken up as having been seen or heard of in company with Thomas Faithly. In sum, there was not a single word to be heard against him.

'It's a wonder they don't just paint wings on him and set

him on a plinth in the minster,' said Grizel, lifting the lid
from a pot over the fire to inspect its contents.

Anne handed her a spoon, which she dipped into the pot,
before murmuring, 'More salt,' and then, 'And did they say
anything about that Scotsman that has lately turned up in
Sir Thomas's company?' It was as if the question had only
just occurred to her and was already halfway out of her
head again.

'Ogilvie?' said Anne.

'Aye, him. Sir Thomas's friend.'

Anne shook her head. 'Nothing at all. I fear if we are to
dig down to the matter of Sir Thomas, we must find some
different witnesses.'

Grizel made her voice light. 'So there was nothing useful
in that letter I gave you?'

Anne had dreaded this moment. She did not like to keep
anything from Grizel, but to tell her would be to betray
that long-ago promise to Damian Seeker. Besides, this was
not something her friend needed to know.

Anne touched a hand to the pocket of her apron. 'Oh
no. Not at all. In fact, there is very little in it.'

'Oh.' Grizel was a little crestfallen. 'I had hoped it might
be of use.'

'It might well have been, for all we knew. I would rather
spend a hundred evenings working on letters of no consequence than miss one that is significant through indifference.'

'But if the letter is of no consequence, why was it written
in code?' persisted Grizel.

Anne looked away and busied herself with folding linens that had been drying by the fire. She would lie no more than she had to. 'Because it is from someone who does not wish their business and whereabouts to be known.'

Grizel was watching her closely. 'And who is that person?'

Anne took a deep breath. 'I cannot tell you, Griz. It is someone I made a promise to, a long time ago. The promise is older, though not stronger, than the bond I have with you. I hope that in keeping the one, I do not risk breaking the other.'

Grizel pursed her lips and brushed at her skirt and a speck of dust that was not there. She didn't look up but said, 'You may have no fears for our friendship, and I would hope for nothing else than you would keep your old promise. You may be sure of me.'

Anne let out a deep breath and embraced her friend. 'Thank you.'

'But,' said the Scotswoman, extracting herself, 'your time and mine will not be wasted if at least I might see how you have deciphered it so that I can practise myself. It may be that there are other things in Ingolby's house using that code, that may be of more use to our investigation into Thomas Faithly.'

Anne could hardly deny the sense of this. She tore off the beginning and the end of the letter, the only parts by which Seeker could be identified and the closest details of his situation revealed, dropped them into the fire and handed Grizel the body of the letter that was left. Then she went upstairs to fetch her own notes on the cypher. As she was coming back down, there was an eager rapping on the front door.

'Buckingham!'

The boy who had brought the message to the door looked none abashed at Lady Anne's open astonishment. No doubt, thought Grizel, he was well-used to this reaction to the news that his master was near at hand.

'Indeed, your ladyship,' said the page, bowing for the third time since the opening of the door. The practice didn't seem to annoy Anne, but Grizel was on the point of telling him that three times was a great deal more than enough, when she caught the warning look in Anne's eye, and held her tongue. 'His Grace made land at King's Staith a little after dinner, and is already in residence close by, in the Treasurer's House.'

If Anne Winter had been perturbed by the news that George Villiers, Duke of Buckingham, was in York, she was even more so at discovering he was now her very near neighbour, the Fairfaxes' town residence lowering over the small back garden of her house, which itself formed an adjunct to the Fairfaxes' stable yard.

'Lady Fairfax had not told me that I might expect . . . so exalted a near neighbour.' Anne's mind was whirring. She knew that Lady Fairfax loathed her son-in-law, Buckingham, for that he treated her daughter with contempt and made the young woman's life a public misery. She was almost certain that Lady Fairfax could not know he had commandeered their town house, or she would never have suggested Anne make use of one so very close by.

'His Grace finds the Treasurer's House answers to his dignity a good deal better than King's Manor, where he would get no peace. His Grace made the decision on the sudden, your ladyship, and it is possible her ladyship does not know.'

'Too many ladyships,' murmured Grizel, to another sharp look from Anne.

The boy now stood dumb, still tendering the letter towards Grizel, as the evident servant who might pass it to her mistress.

'Well, this is good news indeed,' said Anne, marshalling her forces and nodding to Grizel to take the ominous note. 'If you would wait down here, you will have a reply momentarily.'

'Oh no,' said the boy, come back to life. 'His lordship said he would not need a reply.' He then gave a fourth bow, and waited to be dismissed. Anne motioned to Grizel who, with something of a bad grace, showed him to the door.

'A' that bowin' an' scrapin'. Ah canna thole it,' she muttered, lapsing into her native Scots as she followed Anne up to the parlour.

'This is not good.'

'Nothing to do with Buckingham ever is. What does he say?' asked Grizel.

'That he is delighted to find me in town – "an unlooked

for amelioration to the prospect of a stay in York," he says — and he takes great pleasure in expecting me to join him as his guest . . .'

Grizel was instantly indignant. 'Well, you can't go there on your own!' Buckingham's reputation was known far beyond London, and for all Anne's wit, it would not defend her against real power such as that man wielded.

'I have not finished,' said Anne. 'His Grace expects me to join him as his guest at the dinner to be given in his honour, at the Merchant Adventurers' Hall, tomorrow evening.'

'Well, I never heard of any such dinner,' said Grizel, 'and Ingolby's house is only yards up the road from the place, and Madge Penmore has not said one word of it.'

'I suspect the Merchant Adventurers are not long in hearing the news themselves. If you hurry, you may find you have stolen a march on Mistress Penmore with the revelation.'

Grizel shook her head. 'Wouldn't be worth the offence she'd take.'

Anne continued to read. 'I am furthermore invited to join the duke at King's Manor beforehand, that I might take a glass of wine with him and his friends, before proceeding down to the Merchant Adventurers' Hall.'

'You're to arrive on his arm like a bauble, then?'

'So it would seem.'

'Hmmph. And who are these friends?'

Anne glanced again at the letter. 'Sir Thomas Faithly, and his Scottish friend, David Ogilvie. Good. If anyone can get Thomas Faithly in his cups and loose of tongue, it's George Villiers, our most estimable Duke of Buckingham.'

Grizel had not waited long with Anne after their discussion of Buckingham's invitation before going out with Anne's cypher notes tucked into her skirt's hidden pocket. Even had she not already known of Buckingham's arrival in York, she would quickly have guessed that something was afoot. There was a new sense of hurry on the streets and of urgency in the air. As she turned onto Colliergate, she could almost feel the hubbub arising from the Shambles and by the time she reached the top of Fossgate, scurrying delivery boys and kitchen maids left her in no doubt that the cause of all the bustle was the hastily arranged feast in honour of the Duke of Buckingham.

When she finally stepped into the kitchen of the Ingolbys' house, Madge Penmore's cheeks, where they were not white from the flour of the pastry she was thumping, were almost purple with the effort of having to hold in her news so long. 'Mistress Duncan! I had begun to think you were surely dead or run back to Scotland. Make haste, make haste. Jed will be back from the Shambles soon with the poultry and game, and there are a thousand things to be done.'

'But whatever is happening, Mistress Penmore?'

'Why, the Duke of Buckingham himself is come to York, and will dine tomorrow night at the Merchant Adventurers', and Master and Mistress are to be in attendance, and I am to make pies!'

And there was not time, in the flurry of Madge's kitchen and in dashing up and down the stairs to measure for adjustments to Manon Ingolby's dress, for Grizel to think much on the fact that her mistress, Anne Winter, would be spending the following evening in the company not just of Buckingham and Thomas Faithly, but of David Ogilvie too. Later that night, though, as she sat by the light of many candles, cutting and stitching and tying on new tapes to Manon's dress, there was plenty of time for Grizel to worry about what might happen when those four met, and how far her old world and her new would collide.

SEVENTEEN

The Duke of Buckingham

The day had been long and silent and Anne had been glad to see darkness fall. Today, more than any other since Grizel had gone to the Ingolbys, she felt her friend's absence. Their different stations in the world allowed them access to almost every conceivable place – where one could not decently or properly go the other might. And yet, within the confines of their own home, wherever in their peripatetic existence that might be, they had been as close to equals as their respective pasts would allow.

Anne was sorry that Grizel was not here now to help her dress her hair. It was at those times that they were closest. Grizel would warm the tongs in the brazier before winding long tendrils of Anne's hair around them, and they would speculate fantastically upon the lives that might have been theirs, the great loves, had not the war come. Neither asked the other much about the marriages they had actually had – one each – or the husbands who had left them widows. When Anne had confided to Grizel once that her marriage to John Winter had come about because 'there was little else she could safely do,' Grizel had said her own marriage had come about for much the same reason, and so they had left things at that.

Tonight, as she considered which jewels she would wear, Anne first selected the case containing her amber beads, but quickly closed it again, for Grizel had told her the beads were the exact match of the flecks in the dark of her eyes, and would entice any man she had a fancy for. Buckingham was not a man to wait on encouragement and she would have to have her wits about her as it was. Had she been here, Grizel would have warned her thoroughly about him, regardless that no warning was needed. Grizel would have pulled the brush through Anne's hair with more than the usual vigour, in her determination to emphasise her point. As Anne finished the brushing and tonging and pinning and surveyed the result, she missed the tingle of pain there should have been in her scalp. Her one true friend.

Setting the amber aside, she opened instead the case gifted to her on her husband John Winter's death by Lady Cromwell. She had always wondered if Oliver's wife had guessed at her lack of love for John Winter – she need not have guessed, for it had, by the time of his death, been an open secret. The unexpected gift-giving had come after the burial. The Lady Protectress had asked her to her own rooms, and there gifted her an old, plain leather case with, inside, an old, plain gold chain from which was suspended one small pearl. 'John Winter was a good man,' Lady Cromwell had said, 'a plain man. May you remember him by this, for the pearl was made by grit, and the gold is pure. I pray you might find such another.'

Anne had never worn it, but tonight, for the first time, she placed it round her neck and tied the clasp. Plain and pure. It went better than anything else her jewel case might offer with the russet silk gown Grizel had advised her to wear in such circumstances. 'Fine enough to give no offence, but it'll not look like you were bothering too much on their behalf either.' To finish, as she looked to the bottles of her toilet, Anne was careful to select the rosewater of which Grizel occasionally approved and not the jasmine, of which she certainly did not.

The last thing Anne put on before her gloves was her long, brown velvet mantel with its hood, tied at the neck with an oak-leaf clasp given to her by the King himself. Now she was ready. She stepped out into the night. Whatever excitement might be building down around the Merchant Adventurers' Hall, all was still along Chapter House Street, frost glittering off the stones in the moonlight while suggestions of candlelight glowed through tiny window panes. Far above, the stars arched over the minster, as if daring it to greater feats in its attempts to pierce the heavens.

Within a few minutes she had reached the front gates of the Treasurer's House, which stood open. The path across the gardens had been lit with torches as if for a ball, and more torches flamed from sconces at either side of the heavy panelled doors which opened before her as she ascended the steps to reach them. The footmen waiting there were decked out in the duke's livery and clearly knew who she was.

At the moment of passing through the main door, she caught a voice that stopped her in her tracks. It could not be, surely, it was not possible that the King himself was in York. She looked to the footmen, who having closed the outer doors were staring rigidly at the wall beyond her shoulders and offered no help.

Unlike the garden and entrance way, the great hall of the Treasurer's House was only dimly illuminated, with just the fire and one candelabra lit and tiny dots of light lining one wall of the room. No alternative presenting itself, Anne stepped further into the hall and stopped again. The King's voice came from the darkened, far end of the room, where he appeared to be giving vent to a litany of the most scurrilous complaints about the Duke of Buckingham. To Anne's astonishment, the recitation of these outrages was being accompanied by gales of helpless laughter from Thomas Faithly and his Scottish friend, Major Ogilvie, seated opposite each other by the fire. Of the duke himself she could see no sign. In a state of utter perplexity, Anne prepared for the deepest of curtsies, but as her name was announced the figure declaiming at the other end of the hall turned around, his arm raised as if to launch an irrevocable decree. He stopped, then held out his arms and strode towards her. Buckingham.

'Lady Anne, well, bless my soul, you're a vision to light up a room.' As he spoke, candles all around flared into life, courtesy of the pages who'd been waiting beneath the sconces with their tapers.

Anne was speechless, but Buckingham, delighted with his trick, was not. 'Thank God you are truly here! I thought to find nothing in York but mooning Cavaliers in threadbare shirts and miserable Scottish lairds. Come, come, we have been dull without you.'

Almost dazzled now by the light, Anne rose from the profound curtsy she had made, and took the long, slim hand being extended to her. 'Dull, Your Grace? The room can never be dull that has Buckingham in it.'

From the settles, David Ogilvie and Thomas Faithly watched with amusement still sparkling in their eyes. How was it she could have forgotten that George Villiers, second Duke of Buckingham, was the best mimic in England, that he could pick out every last small mannerism of voice and person, and amplify them so that often even the victim of his humour was reduced to helpless tears of mirth? And how was it she had never before heard Thomas Faithly truly laugh?

Buckingham led her to the armchair closest to the hearth as a king might lead his consort to the floor. Oh, what grace he had, George Villiers; how difficult it was for man or woman to take their eyes from him as he extended his arm to encompass the two men already there.

Before she took her seat, Buckingham said, 'You are acquainted with Sir Thomas, of course, Lady Anne?'

'Of course. Sir Thomas and I have encountered one another on several occasions, while on His Majesty's affairs.'

Buckingham gave a filthy leer. 'Fair subject for a ditty, were not the lady so fair.'

'You surely mean, "were not the lady a lady", sir, which I assure you, I am.'

He lifted her hand to his lips. 'As is well known, madam. You must forgive my oafishness – I have grown too used to the manners of the court. Besides, we must mind our behaviour when in the company of a man of such uprightness as my Presbyterian friend Major Ogilvie here.' He indicated David Ogilvie who made little more than a nod, to which she returned an equally brisk curtsy.

'You must pardon Ogilvie his brusqueness, Lady Anne. He is Scots and quite unaccustomed to polite company, although,' and here he made a show of frowning, 'tonight we must rejoice that he has at least managed to borrow an almost serviceable suit of clothing from the corpse of a recently expired cleric. We should otherwise be treated to his preferred garb of sackcloth. And ashes.'

Anne saw that Major Ogilvie was dressed in a black suit of good quality but little ostentation. She imagined it would be the finest he possessed. She was lost for a response, but was saved by the low and unexpected rumble of Ogilvie's laugh. 'Indeed, George, I hope these merchants of York have put on a good dinner for you, or otherwise it will hardly have been worth my while to strip the poor fellow. But Lady Anne and I were introduced by Sir Thomas here, a few days ago, on my first arriving in York.'

'I was not certain you would have remembered me from

that occasion,' said Anne, recalling his sullen, almost surly responses to her at the time.

'What?' Buckingham broke in, the conversation having been in danger of turning away from him. 'Under all that black and drab and those fearsome looks, even Ogilvie is not such a miserable wretch that he would not notice a beautiful woman. But come, Lady Anne, let us take a glass of wine and a bite of something then get us to this tiresome banquet, for I see if we do not, one or other of these fellows is of a mind to eat you.'

The burgundy was predictably fine, and despite the vicissitudes of travel and the weather, Buckingham had managed to procure fresh Humber oysters. 'Twelve pence a peck,' he said, as if it were the easiest thing in the world to be got. The company was in good cheer and Buckingham mercurial. The awkward subject of Mary Fairfax, Buckingham's wife and daughter of the great parliamentary general, was politely and quickly got over. The plain, intelligent girl who had been educated on her father's Yorkshire estate by Andrew Marvell had made a poor choice in her husband. But then, what young woman might have resisted the ardent wooing of George Villiers? The astonishment on all sides when Buckingham had left the King's presence in exile and skulked back to England, to present himself as suitor to Mary Fairfax, whose father had been granted half his escheated lands, could only have been brazened out by one as bare-faced as Buckingham. A spell in the Tower at the instance of an outraged Cromwell had barely dented his bravado. That bravado had been to the fore again when the King, still unforgiving and cold towards the companion of his childhood and youth, had first set foot back in England. When Charles's carriage had left Dover bearing himself and his royal brothers away towards London, Buckingham had leapt onto the back of it and stayed there. If ever there was a man not to be thrown off, it was George Villiers. Now, over two years later, he no longer had to cling, he might stride about, secure in his growing power, setting up his pawns in the shadows while the world was distracted by his brilliance.

When Anne enquired of Ogilvie what had brought him to York, so far from home in so ill a season, Buckingham, none abashed, volunteered the response that the Scotsman had been constrained to chase him here over the payment of a debt. From the easy manner between the two men it was clear that the debt had now been paid.

'You will be hoping for a swift improvement in the weather, I think, Major Ogilvie, that you might soon get away from York and home to Scotland,' said Anne.

'Not so soon,' he replied. 'There is someone I am anxious to find before I leave.'

'Oh?' she said, her voice as light as she could keep it. 'A friend?'

Ogilvie wiped his mouth with his napkin then pushed aside the dish of oysters and stood up. 'I doubt they will think so,' he said, before turning to Buckingham. 'Your Grace will excuse me, I hope, but I have little appetite for feasts in merchants' halls, nor for dancing either, as you know.'

Buckingham sighed. 'Ah, David, will you not play yet?'

'There is a time to play, Your Grace, but by your leave I have letters to write and,' here he smiled, 'my account book to make up.'

'See that you mark me down as "paid" in good thick ink then, and we shall make shift somehow to get along tonight without your stony looks and leaden wit.'

Ogilvie laughed and bowed to the duke. 'Goodnight, George. Good luck, Thomas. See you do not engage yourself in your usual entanglements. There are ladies in York who would lead you the merriest of dances.' It was almost as an afterthought that he turned and inclined his head to Anne. 'Your ladyship.' And then was gone.

After the doors were closed behind Ogilvie, Buckingham and Thomas Faithly exchanged a look of mutual regret.

'You have been friends with the major a long time, I think,' said Anne.

'Twelve years,' replied Sir Thomas.

'And what years,' said Buckingham. 'Will ever men, and indeed women too, live through years the like of those to which we gave our youth?'

'We are not old yet, George,' said Thomas.

'No, but I wonder that anyone was ever so young as we three. You ought to have seen us, Lady Anne. Thomas and I were the most elegant, the most spirited of Cavaliers in attendance upon the King. David was a serious young Scots officer who had come to Breda in the escort of those grave covenanters who crossed the sea to treat with His Majesty. We formed a bond then, we three, young men upon the world, as we danced in the orbit of our exiled King, vying to shape the world about him.'

While Sir Thomas and Buckingham reminisced, Anne considered the fates of those three young men. The duke was still in the King's orbit, and Thomas Faithly clinging on, but she could not fathom how the dour Scottish soldier might have any place in it now. It was clear to her, nonetheless, that despite their contrasting characters and the vicissitudes of the intervening years, those early bonds between these three men had not been broken.

'Were you ever in Scotland, Lady Anne?'

Anne considered how she might answer, her only visit to that country having been on the business of Roger L'Estrange, but as she had often found to be the case with powerful men, Buckingham had no actual interest in what her answer might be, only that the question might afford him further opportunity for observations of his own. 'Never think of going. Miserable as death and twice as cold. Do you remember, Faithly? How their Covenant was forced upon His Majesty twelve years ago in exchange for the Scottish crown?' He shook his head in a convincing semblance of horror. 'Dear God! He was not long in learning that if Paris was worth a mass, Scotland was not worth the Covenant.'

Thomas Faithly was morose in his sympathy. 'Sermonised, lectured and prayed at, morning, noon and night.

Never a morsel of warm food in his belly by the time those nigh-interminable graces were finished. He was forced to do penance for the "sins of his family", that was dead and murdered and living lives of penury and exile. Little wonder he tried to flee them.'

Buckingham was eager to take up the tale. 'When he heard Cromwell had defeated the Scots army at Dunbar, he hardly knew whether to groan for his country or leap for joy for himself. And after Worcester . . . no power on earth could have forced him to set foot in that country again, and I would counsel you never to do so, either, Lady Anne.'

'I have a Scots maid, and that is quite enough to persuade me of the wisdom of remaining on this side of the border,' she assured them.

'Keep your eye on her, Lady Anne, they would betray their own mothers.' Then Buckingham leaned in. 'We are all friends here, I hope?'

As Thomas nodded vigorously, Anne said, 'I know when to speak, Your Grace, and when to keep silent.'

And for the next half-hour Anne did keep silent, as did Thomas Faithly, while Buckingham relayed to them things he should not have told them, that he had brought from London. Secretary Bennet was proving himself to be an able student of the methods of John Thurloe, and turning skills learned from the former Republican intelligence network against those very Republicans. Old enemies of the King were being tracked down and caught by means dogged and ingenious, and most of all, underhand. 'It's not just the regicides,' confided Buckingham, pouring himself some more wine. 'Any who have ever betrayed the King should sleep with one eye open.'

'Oh?' said Thomas Faithly. Even by candlelight, Anne thought he appeared a little paler.

'Yes,' continued the duke, going on to tell them of the plans afoot to take the Scottish covenanter, Johnston of Wariston, who had made too close an accommodation with Cromwell and was now fled abroad. A relative imprisoned over another matter had been persuaded to bargain betrayal of his cousin in return for his own freedom. 'The cousin will keep the King's agents informed of his whereabouts and Wariston will be trapped. He will be returned to these shores to face justice in the form of a trial and hung from the highest gibbet. This is the genius of the thing – using those close to a target, and they don't even know.' Then he laughed and clapped Thomas Faithly on the shoulder. 'You might think yourself lucky that you have no wife yet and no family left, Thomas, for there is no relative, be they ever so close, that cannot be used to ruin a man.'

And then it was time for the duke's carriage to be brought round and for their small party to progress to the feast at the Merchant Adventurers'. For the duration of their journey down through the town, Buckingham told witty and increasingly scandalous stories of life at court and Anne watched Thomas Faithly. Sir Thomas laughed at the right moments but all the time she could see his mind was at work, his senses alive, like a hind alert to the presence of the hunter. Oh, Thomas, she thought, if you but knew who was the hunter.

Grizel saw the front door shut behind the Ingolbys and let out a long sigh of relief. When she turned around, she caught the end of a similar sigh from Jedediah Penmore.

'I thought the master would never be done with his instructions,' the clerk said, by way of explanation.

'As I thought your grandmother would never be done with hers,' she wanted to say in response. She held her tongue, though, for the old woman was kind to her, and she had no wish to demean Madge in the eyes of her grandson. Despite Lawrence Ingolby's best efforts, Madge had somehow inveigled her way into the cohort of cooks and servers called upon by the Merchant Adventurers to cater the feast. She had spoken of nothing else since word of it had first travelled from across the street and Grizel imagined she would speak of nothing else for weeks to come.

Grizel had helped Manon Ingolby dress. 'I am like a great green ship at sail,' the young woman had lamented.

'Nonsense,' Grizel had chided. 'You are a goddess of the forest. No man will have more cause for pride tonight than Master Ingolby.' And it was true, she thought. Manon was dressed in greens and golds and reds, in velvets and in silks embroidered with leafy tendrils, winter fruits and song-birds. Threaded through her hair where a richer, plainer woman might have worn lace and pearls were the most delicate ribbons of silken foliage and winter berries, fashioned over two nights by the expert fingers of Madge's sister Flo. Panels and pins and hooks and eyes and ribbons had done their work of letting out gown and bodice to accommodate the eight-month swell of the child she was carrying, but the fecundity of this young couple was there for all to see. Lawrence Ingolby, the foundling bred of the moors, and his woodland goddess.

Now, Grizel was left to mind Lizzie, whilst Jedediah was to guard the house. 'You do not mind,' she said, after the others had gone, 'that you will miss so grand an occasion?'

The young man snorted. 'Drunken merchants making long speeches while the Duke of Buckingham ogles their fat wives? I'm glad to stay here.'

Grizel was unconvinced by his nonchalance. She thought the young man, in his way, was as ambitious for himself as his grandmother was on his behalf. She noticed him glance up the stair over her shoulder. 'You'll have plenty to do in the kitchen, I suppose?' he said.

'Not so much.' Grizel was determined to make the most of the Ingolbys' absence, and keen not to have to waste the time on domestic tasks. 'I shall put Lizzie to bed soon, and spend the evening upstairs, lest she wakes,' she said.

'I can do that,' Jedediah offered. 'She knows me better.'

'She knows me well enough,' Grizel said. 'Besides, you are to remain down here, keeping watch, are you not?'

'Aye,' said Jedediah, with more bad grace than she thought warranted. He was clearly finding tiresome the constant state of vigilance in which the house was now to be held, and bridling at his own role of watchman. She wondered whether, were she not here to report back to his master, the clerk would have remained in the house at all.

Upstairs, assured that her kitten was safely curled up in her mother's wool basket by the hearth, Lizzie settled quickly in her cot. Grizel slipped across to the parlour, where she gathered pen, ink and paper from Manon Ingolby's writing desk, before coming back and locking the bedchamber door. She sat herself at Manon's dressing table, close by the sleeping child. Lighting an extra candle, she then drew her copy of Anne Winter's cypher key from the pocket of her apron, along with the copy of the letter she had *not* shown to Anne, that written by Damian Seeker to Lawrence Ingolby, in which she had discerned the name of Thomas Faithly.

Before dipping her quill pen into the ink, Grizel again smoothed her hand over the two sheets of paper in front of her. With the aid of Anne's transcription, she began to understand which numbers and symbols had been substituted for which letters, the order in which words had been transposed. By the time the bells of York had marked another hour of the night, Grizel had in front of her the full, deciphered text of the second letter, the one she had singularly failed to give to Anne Winter.

The opening was a brusque, 'Ingolby,' with no further civility or greeting. Neither was there any of the domestic news that had formed the body of the letter to Ingolby's wife. Instead the writer went straight to the matter of Thomas Faithly.

No doubt you will find a way through the mire of Thomas Faithly's affairs and wrest his grandmother's property at Langton from the hands of whoever paid their money for it. See to it, before you pass the deeds into his hand, that you have his fee in yours. For all his fine looks and talk, I never knew him to have more than a shilling in his pouch, and I doubt the turning in the world's fortunes will make him any the better with money. Do not be the loser.

Faithly is not the worst, or anything near it, of those who rise now in the service of Charles Stuart, but a man may do many things to save his own neck. Word reaches even to here of the lengths to which Charles Stuart's cabal will go to hunt down those who brought his tyrant father to justice. You will know better than I how right was the cause, and with what propriety the case put by John Cooke. I trust should you ever have such a brief in your hands, you would execute it with as much honour.

Here, the letter almost fell from Grizel's hands, as if she had been burned by it. For Ingolby to keep hold of such a letter, even in its original cypher, was surely madness in these days when the net to snare any involved in the late King's death, even those who had spoken in favour of it, was cast wider and wider. John Cooke, who had drawn up the charges for that notorious trial, had himself been amongst the first to die a traitor's dreadful death on the Stuarts' return. Grizel could scarcely believe that anyone, whoever they might be, would encourage Lawrence Ingolby to present himself for the same fate. Checking around her that she was not observed, even here, she read on.

Word has come to Massachusetts, from the mouths of those who have cause to know the truth of it, of the lengths men such as George Downing go to, to ensnare those once loyal to Oliver or who worked for the cause of the Commonwealth. Thomas Faithly, as you know better than any, performed some small services for the Protectorate under my direction, and at the behest of John Thurloe. He had been turned to our service, but was turned again, by none other than Rupert of the Rhine, who had a leading hand in the business I was then set to investigate.

Again, Grizel could almost feel the skin on her fingers, the soft hairs on them, singe just from proximity to such a letter.

What you must not forget is that a man once turned can be turned again, and again. Be assured that the Stuarts have learned from John Thurloe's methods and that those imprisoned under them will be offered some modicum of mercy only if they will inform on their former comrades. There is nothing Thomas Faithly values higher than his liberty as an Englishman, and in all your dealings with him, as lawyer and client or as friends, you must never forget that. Should you ever suspect that he, to save his own liberty or neck, is tempted to betray those with whom he worked at my behest, I give you this letter as your personal insurance and my certification that he worked for me.

Take care of those so dear to me whom I and God have entrusted to your protection and know, however far away I might be, that my eye is ever on you,
Damian Seeker.

Grizel laid down her pen, her heart thumping. This letter was indeed what she had thought it might be – the proof that Anne sought, the point of their mission: Thomas Faithly had betrayed the King at the behest of Damian Seeker. She sat back, relief coursing through her, then looked again at the remnant of the letter, that had been written in the same hand, to Manon Ingolby. The secret that Anne Winter kept from her was her knowledge that Manon Ingolby was Damian Seeker's daughter.

Only now did Grizel become aware of the sounds of the contented breathing of Lizzie Ingolby, all innocent and ignorant in her cot, and of the snatches of laughter and strains of music drifting out into the night from the Merchant Adventurers' Hall. Was David Ogilvie there amongst them? Was one of those Thomas Faithly's laugh? Perhaps, even at this moment, he was leading Damian Seeker's daughter to the floor to dance, before the eyes of all the world. Perhaps, she reflected as she spilled a little sand over her transcription and blew on it, waiting for it to dry that she might fold it and put it away again in her bundle, Anne had been right not to fully trust her after all.

EIGHTEEN

Strangers and Adventurers

Growing up at her father's house near Oxford, Anne Winter had known many feasts and balls, but all that had come to an end when the black pall of civil war had settled itself over England. She had feasted since, danced since – on the continent and, once or twice, here and in Scotland in the course of her work for L'Estrange. Always, though, there had been a falseness, a whiff of desperation in the exaggerated opulence and hectic joy, as if the feast or the dance might nullify what had gone before, or give proof that such madness and horror could never take hold in England again. Anne had seen men and women at their worst and most desperate, and was not fooled.

Nonetheless, as she stepped into the Great Hall of the Merchant Adventurers of York on Buckingham's arm, she saw an England that she recognised of old. Her years in the Low Countries and about the towns of England had shown her no man would hold his nerve as well as the successful merchant. She saw it in their faces – the men decked out in their finery here, the sumptuously dressed women on their arms, had held their nerve and would again if need be. Protector or king: each must rise or fall on his ability to persuade the merchants of England to part with their coin. Buckingham thought these people welcomed him with such a show in order to win the favour of the new lord lieutenant. Anne understood rather that they were demonstrating to him their own power.

The place, dim in the daytime with the light from narrow, high mullion windows, was ablaze with light, candelabra hanging from the massive oak cross-beams of the double-vaulted nave, and dispersed every few feet down the long tables set all along the hall and upon the dais to which Buckingham was leading her, Thomas Faithly just behind them. The side-tables gleamed with salvers and goblets of pewter and of Venetian glass, the table at the top with silverware and crystal. Anne could scarcely believe the amount of food that had been gathered and prepared in so short a time. As well as endless trays of tarts and pies and countless custards, there appeared to be roasted fowl of almost every conceivable sort – fat chickens and geese, huge turkeys, and in pride of place at the centre of the top table, a swan. Little wonder Grizel had not had the time to come to see her since news of Buckingham's feast had first broken. Anne glanced about her, but saw no sign of her friend, while Ingolby's cook had got herself closer to the table of honour than any other servant there had managed.

Anne had hoped she might be seated next to Thomas Faithly, but Sir Thomas was seated several places away from her, charming the elderly wife of a senior guild brother. Her position on the dais nonetheless gave Anne the perfect vantage point from which to survey the room as she listened and responded to the conversation of Buckingham to her left and the governor of the company to her right. She cast her eyes down the tables. There, halfway down the long table, was Lawrence Ingolby, satisfied, complacent, and beside him, Manon. All others around her might have fallen away. She glowed. Again, Anne wished Seeker might have seen what his daughter had grown to. It would surely not be many years before the lawyer and his wife were seated where she was now.

'That is a remarkably pretty girl.'

Anne was startled out of her own thoughts by Buckingham's comment. 'Which one, Your Grace? I can see many even from here.'

'Yes,' he said, 'but none quite so enchanting as that woodland nymph — you see her there in the green velvet, with the long, pale hair, sat beside that fox-faced fellow in brown?'

Anne was discomfited to find the duke's gaze was resting on the same couple as her own. 'Ah, I believe that is the lawyer, Ingolby, and his wife. I understand he is a good friend of Sir Thomas's.'

'Ah, is he, by Jove? I shall have to have Sir Thomas effect an introduction. He must be a damnably good lawyer, to land a wife like that.'

'He is indeed fortunate,' replied Anne. 'And I understand she is very soon to provide him with a second child.'

'Child?' Buckingham looked again down towards Ingolby's seated wife.

'A good eight months gone,' said Anne, lifting her goblet and taking a long draught of wine before setting it down with finality.

Buckingham gave a sour pout before casting his eye elsewhere. Anne decided nonetheless to keep a close watch over Manon Ingolby tonight, diverting herself a while in private speculation as to what Damian Seeker might do to George Villiers, should he ever learn that the duke had as much as looked his daughter's way.

Once Buckingham himself had eaten a sufficient quantity of meats and sampled an adequate number of custards, he began to talk of dancing, and at this the governor's wife raised a hand that instantly summoned a legion of servers from the shadows to clear the remnants of the banquet.

With a short respite for rest, a turn outside in the night air and the necessary recourse to jakes and privy, tables and benches were pushed against the walls and the duke's pleasure enquired after by the musicians. Of course, Buckingham would have a pavane to start, that everyone might watch him, stately, dignified, so graceful, and Anne, of course, must partner him. As they stepped carefully around each other in time to the music, Anne accepted that any privacy she had hoped for during the time of her investigations in York had died the moment Grizel had opened the door to Buckingham's page.

It was good, nonetheless, to be dancing, and it was not

long before Thomas Faithly made his bow to her and offered her his hand. Thomas danced with a little less practised grace than did Buckingham, less awareness of himself and more of her. She found herself breathing in the scent of him – horses, and leather, and some last-minute effort at whatever pomade he might have had to hand. It was the smell of a man, without posturing. Anne felt suddenly that she was sixteen once more, with one of her older brother's friends taking her up to dance. She almost missed her step in her new confusion. Thomas Faithly looked down at her, his blue eyes suddenly very dark. He might have said something but a movement near the bottom of the hall caught her eye and she let slip an 'Oh,' before dropping her arms and curtsying to him. 'I am sorry, Sir Thomas, but I have just seen someone I must talk to.' Then as Thomas Faithly stood there bewildered, she began to push her way through the hall.

How could it be *him* that she had seen? But Anne was certain, he was not a person she would mistake. The hall seemed to be crammed full of people, not only dancers but merchants and lawyers in varying states of inebriation, army officers, matrons and excitable young women, servants bustling and threading through all. She lost sight of him but then, as a new tune began and men and women took their places for the next dance, Anne saw, to her disbelief, that he was taking his place in a set. There could be no doubt now. The dancing began, and she saw a swish of green velvet. Manon Ingolby. But not Lawrence. Lawrence was far at the other end, near the dais, talking with the governor, while turning his head from time to time to keep an eye on his wife. The musicians played faster and the dancers moved down their lines. Anne tried to push between two overweight men, but succeeded only in receiving a lascivious squeeze from one of them before he finally stepped aside, letting her pass. But it was too late. The person she had been watching had caught up to Manon Ingolby and was whispering urgently in her ear. The next moment, Manon was turning around in a panic, clearly looking for her husband. The man leaned towards her again and put a hand on her arm. And Manon went. Anne tried to shout to her, but her voice was lost amongst the music and hubbub.

Anne made to go after them but almost instantly came up against the substantial frame of Madge Penmore. 'Lady Anne! Good gracious, whatever is wrong?'

'Your master. You must get your master this minute. And Sir Thomas. Someone is taking Mistress Ingolby.'

The woman opened her mouth, drawing in a great breath of outrage, but did not give vent to it, instead shoving aside all and sundry, and cursing profusely at any who voiced their objection, she forged a path towards Lawrence Ingolby. Leaving the housekeeper to her task, Anne pushed through the crowd with a renewed determination. At last she gained the passageway leading to the top of the steps out of the hall. Two footmen opened the huge double doors at her approach and she flew down the steps and along the passageway until she was finally out in the street. Manon was up ahead, crossing over as if headed for her own home, and the man was still at her elbow.

A sudden noise from the top of the street alerted Anne to the horse and cart that were clattering down towards the pair. The man lifted his arm and Anne realised that his intention was to bundle Manon into the cart and carry her off. 'Manon!' she shouted. 'No!'

Manon seemed dazed for a moment then, looking at the oncoming cart, shook off the man's arm and began to run towards her own home. As neighbours appeared at windows and doors in response to Anne's cry, Manon Ingolby's would-be abductor jumped alone onto the cart and shouted up to the driver to make haste away. The green door of the Ingolbys' house opened just as the cart sped by, revealing Grizel, surprised, and the shadow of someone, Ingolby's clerk, Anne imagined, behind her. Anne heard a clatter of boots and turned to see Lawrence Ingolby and Thomas Faithly thundering out onto the street, a red-faced Madge puffing some way along the passageway behind them.

Ingolby continued running, across the street to his wife, but Thomas Faithly came to a halt behind Anne, beneath the lamp at the end of the passageway. 'What happened?'

'Someone tried to abduct Manon Ingolby. Almost in plain sight.'

Lawrence was aware he was shouting but he could not stop himself. 'You're absolutely sure, the pair of you? Neither sent that message over to the hall?'

Jed appeared speechless, but the Scottish housemaid was not. 'Absolutely certain, Master Ingolby. If the bairn had been ill, we'd one of us have come over and fetched you both. But she was sleeping sound, and we've neither of us set foot outside this house tonight, nor sent any message either.'

Lawrence leaned against the back of Manon's chair, his knuckles white. 'You're sure that's what he said, love?'

Manon looked up from where she'd been bent over Lizzie, gripping her tight and kissing her head. 'He said she was ill, that word had come from the house and that I was to come straight away. I looked for you but there was such a press of people and he was so insistent.'

'Have you ever seen this man before, Manon?' asked Thomas Faithly.

'Never.'

'What was he like?'

She shook her head, sniffing. 'Dark. Slight. Reddish hair, I think. He had his hood up.' She rubbed her wrist. 'His grip was strong.'

'Thank God for Lady Anne,' said Sir Thomas.

'Aye, thank God,' echoed Ingolby. 'But how did she know, Thomas? Did she say anything to you before she went off in the duke's carriage? How did she know that man was a threat to Manon?'

Faithly shrugged. After the incident, Anne Winter had not wanted to go into the Ingolbys' house and had been in a hurry to get back to her own. All she had said was that she'd had a feeling as soon as she'd seen the man that something was not right. He'd had his hood up. He'd moved in the shadows. He had been out of place amongst the feast-goers and then, the way he had gripped Manon's arm . . .

The duke's first reaction to the news that Thomas Faithly would not be returning to the hall but instead would remain to watch the night at the home of his lawyer friend had been irritation, but then he had checked himself. 'You must forgive me, Lady Anne. I am sorry the young woman got such a scare, and I hope it will not be repeated. Of course, Faithly will want to go to the aid of his friend, but it is an inconvenience to me all the same.'

'Oh?' she asked.

'Ah, it is nothing for you to concern yourself with, only some papers I am eager to have found. Drawings, in fact, that I had made by that surveyor fellow – Briar, his name was – that got himself murdered in some tryst in the minster. I asked at the draughtsman's office and the best they could tell me was that Thomas might have them. I had thought to ask him about it tonight, as we travelled home.'

'Are they very important?' she asked, thinking of the sketch lying in her own house of the drawings she had found in the bloodied satchel in her search of Sir Thomas's rooms.

Buckingham appeared to ruminate. 'Not so very important, I suppose. But a man likes to have irons in the fire, you know, and Briar's death is already an irritation. I would rather not be put to the further inconvenience of having to find another to do them. I shall have to ask Faithly about them tomorrow, is all.' At another time, Anne might have given more thought to the unfortunate surveyor whose death appeared to be at most an inconvenience, but tonight she had more pressing matters on her mind, and was glad when the duke's carriage drew up at her front door. Buckingham raised an enquiring eyebrow even as he kissed her hand when handing her down from the carriage, but Lady Anne simply shook her head, according him a rueful smile.

'Ah well, you will succumb to my charms one day, your ladyship, I am quite determined upon it. But for tonight,' he made her a delightful bow, removing his ostrich feather hat with a most perfect flourish as he did so. Despite her protests that she would be perfectly fine from there, Buckingham insisted that a footman alight and see her safely into her house.

Anne did not argue further. 'Goodnight, Your Grace.'

'Goodnight, Lady Anne,' he said, before hopping back up into his place and knocking with his stick to tell the driver to continue

When the footman departed, having lit candles in the hallway and up the stairway, Lady Anne remained downstairs and listened. It was now not far off midnight, when tolling bells would echo through the crisp and emptied streets of York. She stepped into the kitchen and found a lamp. She could see nothing out in the darkness of the back yard through the ice that had crept up window panes. Above, she could hear the gutters start to creak with frozen drops of water. But she could hear more than that. Hear

or sense it, another presence in the house. She lit her lamp
and began to ascend the stairs.

'I hope I have not startled you, Lady Anne.'

'A little,' she said, moving further into the parlour and
setting down her lamp on the table, so that its pool of light
illuminated some of the room, casting the man's shadow
against the wall behind him.

'You will excuse me that I was forced to break the lock
on the back door, in order to gain entrance here.'

'Had I known I was to expect you, here in York, you
might have come by the front, Mr L'Estrange.'

'I had not thought to be here, but there comes a point
where a man must see to things for himself.' Roger L'Estrange stood up and went to lean on the mantelshelf. Then
he realised his mistake: he was not an especially tall man
and Anne, in her heeled silk evening shoes, matched him.

'We might have a fire, I think, your ladyship,' he said.

Anne looked at the cold grate. 'I have been out all evening
and had not expected to have company on my return,' she
said. 'My maid is engaged elsewhere tonight.'

To her relief, L'Estrange did not enquire where that might
be. She was as confident as she could be that this man, in
whose employ she had spent over two years, had never
guessed at Grizel's involvement in their business.

'A pity,' he said before nodding towards the log basket.
'But no doubt you have picked up some skills of self-
preservation on your travels. We all did.'

Anne took a breath and with as much dignity as she could, went to the hearth and knelt in front of it, setting the fire. She noted the position of the poker. She took care to keep herself as clean as possible, but was glad nonetheless that she was not wearing one of her finer evening gowns. The fire lit, she sat not in her seat at the table, but in the chair on the other side of the hearth from where L'Estrange stood, making sure the poker was now only inches from her hand. She did not like this man and nor did she trust him. 'There is brandy on the sideboard,' she said. 'Please – you must wish to restore yourself, arriving in York at so late an hour.'

He went over to the sideboard and poured himself a glass, without offering one to her. 'I have been in town several hours. I had some business this evening at the Merchant Adventurers' Hall. You were there too, of course.'

Anne knew herself to be in dangerous territory now. She was glad that while she could see his face – his long Roman nose sharp in the candlelight, the colour in his cheeks high, as usual – hers would be more obscured in the darkness.

'I was,' she said. 'I was of the party attending His Grace the Duke of Buckingham. I wonder that I did not recognise you amongst it.' This was a gamble. She had recognised L'Estrange, despite the hood he'd worn, and seen him move through the hall towards Manon Ingolby, but she didn't think L'Estrange had been aware she observed him, other than possibly at the end, when she had called out her warning to Manon on the street. Anne was gambling that his natural arrogance would make him believe himself so adept at disguise and clandestine activity as to be beyond discovery.

L'Estrange smiled. 'My business was not with the duke, but with the woman you shouted to out on the street. What was that about, Lady Anne? Why did you call out to her?'

'Manon Ingolby is a friend of mine. I encountered her in York many years ago and have renewed my acquaintance with her since finding she lives in York now.'

'It might have been useful if you had told me this before.'

'You hadn't informed me she was of interest to you. Besides, I had not seen her since she was a girl, long before her marriage. It so happens that her husband is a friend of Thomas Faithly's and I have been careful to cultivate our connection as a means of my investigation into him.' Anne bristled a little. 'I'm sorry if the slowness of my investigation into Sir Thomas has caused you to take matters into your own hands.'

L'Estrange gave a short laugh and Anne's imagination was taken by a sudden vision of a spark flying out of the fire she had just lit, to set his long, rust-coloured frizz of hair ablaze. His voice pulled her back to reality. 'You need not be offended, Lady Anne, I am content to wait until you have satisfied yourself as to the facts, one way or the other, in the case of Sir Thomas. My interest in Mistress Ingolby relates to another matter entirely, but your intervention tonight prevented me questioning her as I had intended to do.'

'My intervention? I merely wished to warn her to look

out for that speeding cart as she was crossing the road. I had no idea that you . . .'

He gave her a look of feigned pity. 'Oh, come now, Lady Anne. Would you really so insult me? You are no fool and neither am I. The purpose of that cart was that I might lift the woman from the street, and take her for questioning.'

Anne knew this very well, but still felt the anger rising up in her to hear him say it. 'Lift her from the street? She is eight months gone with child! It might have been the death of them both.'

He shrugged. 'She looks a healthy enough specimen. I would have had no interest in keeping her longer than was necessary to get the information I wanted, or to bring her husband to heel.'

A realisation flashed into Anne's mind. 'It was you who broke into the Ingolbys' house several nights ago.'

L'Estrange gave a short burst of contemptuous laughter. 'Me? A common housebreaker? I fear you misunderstand our relative situations, Lady Anne. If I need a house broken into, I employ someone like you.'

Anne bit down the insult. 'And have you?' she asked.

The sneer on L'Estrange's face was replaced by a glint of anger. 'You make very bold, your ladyship, to think that you might question me.'

'Not so bold, Mr L'Estrange,' she said. 'Do you forget that I spent this evening in the company of the Duke of Buckingham, whose ear I have and who is higher in His Majesty's favour than you can ever conceive of rising? If you will let me know where in York you are staying, I will shortly send my report on Sir Thomas to you there and then I will regard my service to you as finished.' She stood. 'Now I would like you to leave my house.'

L'Estrange took a step towards her. His face was white with anger, two red spots the only colour on the usually florid cheeks. 'I leave York for London at dawn. You will send your report to me via the safe house, as usual. And *I* will decide when your service for me is finished. Would you wish it to become known what you have been employed in doing over the last two and a half years?'

'No more than you would wish it to be known on whose account I have been doing it. But my actions at least have been motivated by an honourable desire to root out those who once betrayed the King. Yours are less clear, are they not? To me, they have the whiff of a man who wishes to distract attention from suspicions about his own past behaviour. It would not suit you should anyone enquire too closely into just why Cromwell let you back to England to live in peace in the days of the Protectorate. Suspicions of you had some heat amongst the King's courtiers in exile, I assure you, and I could rekindle them with as little difficulty as I rekindled that fire.'

L'Estrange took another step towards her looking as though he might strike her. Anne held her ground and he stopped a few inches from her face. 'Write me your report on Thomas Faithly and then let you be damned, Anne Winter.'

Not daring to move, Anne listened as he went down the stairs then she watched as he went out at the street door without bothering to close it behind him. Taking hold of the poker, she followed him down the stairs and closed the door on the cold night air and all the evils it held. Having turned the key in the lock and set the bolts, she went to the back door, with its broken lock, and made sure she shot the higher and lower bolts that she had previously neglected. She stood with her back against the door, her eyes closed, still gripping onto the poker until the thumping of her chest subsided. Then she went upstairs, opened a chest and took out her heaviest furs.

NINETEEN

Churches

Observing the discussion between her present master and mistress, Grizel found herself, not for the first time, in agreement with Lawrence Ingolby. The troubled evening of Buckingham's feast, with the attempt to lure Manon away on the false report that Lizzie had been taken ill, had been followed early the next morning by the arrival of Anne Winter. Lady Anne had come to warn Ingolby of good intelligence that the incident of the previous evening had been a definite attempt to abduct his wife, and had urged him to guard her very closely. Ingolby had immediately declared that Manon should no longer leave the house at all. Anne had arrived swathed in furs and had then informed Grizel, privately, of the role played by Roger L'Estrange. Reluctant to take the man at his word, she had traversed the frozen city long before dawn, to assure herself that L'Estrange was indeed leaving York. She had not had to distribute many coins amongst the bargemen on the dock to learn that someone answering his description had indeed not long before boarded a boat bound for London. The boat was to cast off at first light, so long as the river did not freeze over. Anne had watched from beside the burning brazier of a riverman's shelter until daylight had begun to edge its way over York and the boat had made ready to depart. Only after she had seen L'Estrange himself emerge from below to take a turn around the deck, and then the boat at last cast off and commence its journey downriver, did she leave her post to hurry with her warning to the house on Fossgate. Grizel had chided her roundly when she appeared, for that, despite her furs, she was clearly 'frozen half to death', and Madge Penmore had not consented that the master be woken to speak with her until Lady Anne had taken two good mugs of the caudle she already had warming.

That had been three days ago and miraculously, Anne had not taken as much as a chill. Lawrence Ingolby had succeeded in keeping his wife at home, and in conducting all his business from there himself, but now it was Sunday and Manon was intransigent.

'Not on your life, Manon.'

'But just that, Lawrence, on my life and my soul and Lizzie's and this baby's. We have had two deliverances and instances of God's grace in as many weeks. It is the Lord's Day and we must worship and give thanks.'

They had argued back and forth nearly half an hour, with Lawrence calling on Grizel, Jed and even Madge for support, but Manon would not be swayed. She would go to church and be edified by the preaching, and give thanks to

God for preserving her and Lizzie in the face of their late dangers, and ask for His protection in her trials to come.

'I suppose we could go to All Saints with Madge and Jed,' he conceded at last.

'No, Lawrence. We will go to our own church.'

'But St Michael's is so far away, my pet,' said Madge. 'Will you not come up to All Saints with Jed and me?'

Manon began to tie on her own cloak. 'St Michael's is hardly three streets away and I am as well as can be, Madge, and only think, if I were to let my husband walk about the town in his Sunday finery without me? Any wandering jade might think to replace me.'

Madge's ire rose. 'I should like to see the jade that would get over *my* threshold to meddle here. She would rue the day and the mother that bore her!'

Manon gave her a squeeze. 'She would indeed. Come. We mustn't be late.'

Grizel had intended to attend Lady Anne to service at the minster, but acceded to Lawrence's request to accompany him and his wife to St Michael's. 'Should anything untoward happen, I'll need you to look after the bairn. I wouldn't put Madge into any danger, and Jed has no way with her at all.' Seeing the sense of it, Grizel had agreed, making sure she had her knife secreted below her jacket.

The snow and the wind had stopped, and streams and straggles of neighbours, wrapped and cheerful in the welcome respite of bright winter sunshine, made their way by the sound of bells to their chosen churches. Lawrence, in truth, had not an especial preference for St Michael's. He didn't pay much heed to the matter of religion or what was said in such places, and would have been hard put, if asked afterwards, to say what the sermon had been about. He was unmoved by the service of the Book of Common Prayer, the bells, the surplices, the endless, unthinking repetitions. The organ, though, that was different. The power of God. In boyhood, he had taken on the views instilled in him by Bess Pullan, the Puritan woman who had brought him up. The rest, he thought, was flummery.

In St Michael's, Lawrence found a place of quiet in his week. And there was space there for God, too, should God have wanted to find him. He'd told Manon that, when she'd worried about his lack of faith. 'I've faith enough. I know where to find God when I need him. And I go to St Michael's on a Sunday so he knows where to find me.'

They left Madge and an aggrieved-looking Jed amongst the crowd waiting to get in the door of All Saints, then made their way down towards their own church on Spur-riergate, Lawrence nodding to acquaintances as they went.

'Poor Jed,' said Manon.

'Well, she's his grandmother, and it's only right. Besides, he just needs to show her in, then he can stand playing cards with the other young lads at the back till it's time for the last hymn, same as usual.'

'Lawrence!'

'What?'

'You mustn't say such things, you might get him into trouble.'

'Who from? The only one that ever gives him trouble is me. And it's true, anyway. I heard from one of the other lawyers down the Guildhall. Jed cleans the other clerks out every Sunday. Good luck to him. Besides, if I'd asked him to come with us today, he'd want to do it every week. I like it on a Sunday, down at St Michael's, just you, me, Lizzie.' He looked down and patted his wife's stomach. 'And the one to come.' As they approached the church, Lizzie, squirming in his arms, squealed with laughter and pointed up to her favourite gargoyle. 'Yes,' he murmured out of Manon's earshot, 'there's Granddad.'

At the minster, Thomas Faithly took his place beside Buckingham and relaxed into the magnificence of it all. He had never been much of one for the church as a boy, unless instructed to attend his parents and brother to the small church in Faithly village. The sermons, regardless of how short his father had persuaded the vicar to make them, had seemed to drag on for hours that would have been better spent on horseback, or with a fishing rod by some hidden beck.

Degraded in the days of the Protectorate, fouled by the New Model Army, the minster's magnificent windows saved only by the intervention of the Lords Fairfax, it glittered again, resplendent. Every candlestick, every swinging censer, surplice and chasuble, every Madonna and child, every stone-faced king crowned in gold that looked out from the quire screen, told him that England was his England once more and that the Protectorate had been consigned to Hell where it belonged.

Buckingham, usually so magnificent on any occasion for public display, was already in his travelling clothes, his knee bouncing. He was in a hurry to get on, away from York, his business done and back to better pleasures. George Villiers had absolutely no intention of spending his Christmas at York and an amelioration in the weather suggested that now might be his best opportunity of avoiding that fate. He had left Thomas with ample instructions as to what was to be done in his absence.

Their discussion about the death of William Briar had been brief, Buckingham's main concern having related to William's papers, which Thomas had been able to furnish him with – the house plans Thomas had found in William's bloodied satchel. When he had queried their importance, Buckingham had smiled. 'Think on it, Thomas, for I have already as good as told you what I need them for. It does a man no harm to have irons, or should I say "Tongs", in the fire.' He had laughed at his own private joke before pushing aside his trencher and announcing, 'Well, I suppose we must show face at the minster.'

They had gone in at the west door, as was fitting for the King's lord lieutenant, and Thomas had, as ever, felt himself almost overwhelmed by the power and scale of the magnificent cathedral. Throughout the week, townsmen might meet and wander and talk in the great nave, but today it was given over to the glory of God. Buckingham strode up through the nave towards the quire. Keeping pace with him, Thomas glanced to his right and the steps that led down to the crypt. He felt a wave of coldness go over him, as if the spirit of William Briar, murdered there, remained, accusing, calling out to him for justice.

As they'd taken their seats, Thomas had turned his head to look down the aisle and eventually found Anne Winter. There was no sign, however, of David Ogilvie. His eyes scanned further down the minster, but even had he been able to see behind every one of the columns or into every chapel, he knew he would not find his friend there. David would be somewhere else, attending to his austere God, still fighting a battle that was lost. Despite their friendship and Ogilvie's adherence to the King, the Scotsman had never wavered in his aversion to the Anglican form of worship, with its robes and its prayer book and its 'ceremonies'. Ogilvie would have found out the most desolate, Puritan-looking, clandestine scrap of a meeting house York had to offer, and be making his devotions there.

It would not surprise him, Thomas thought, should Anne Winter's forbidding maid have found her way to the same Presbyterian gathering as Ogilvie, for she gave off that same resolutely Calvinist air. And so there was Anne Winter, alone. She was surrounded by people, and yet it was as if there was some unseeable wall between her and everyone near her — ice, perhaps, or glass, transparent but not quite as fragile as it looked.

The introit began, and Thomas's gaze was forced to the glistening parade of churchmen heralded by the music as the triumph of the Anglican Church reverberated through and around these ancient walls. Thomas could feel Buckingham's impatience rise as the clerical procession made its slow way up the aisle.

'Perhaps the service will not be too long,' he offered, as Buckingham's knee continued to bounce in impatience.

'You might wager your skin on it, Faithly – I've left very clear instructions with the dean that it should not do. I'll be away out of here on his tail. The weather may worsen and it is not my intention to be caught in York a night longer than necessary. God's teeth, I might be here all winter. Thank Heaven you are in post that I don't have to be. But here – I almost forgot.' He turned to his page who was standing behind him. 'Where is that other package for Sir Thomas – the one that had come loose from the others?'

'I have it here, Your Grace.'

The lad held out a small package, which looked to be letters, bound in green ribbon, then handed them to Thomas in response to Buckingham's nod.

'What are these, Your Grace?' asked Thomas.

'Damned if I know. Letters, I suppose. They were lying around in my offices at Whitehall and were directed to you up here. My secretary had put them in a different bag from the official papers I had prepared for you, and only came upon them again last night.' He raised a smile that had in

273

it some of his usual wit. 'I dare say they can't all be from disappointed women or angry husbands.'

Thomas caught sight of the writing on the letter at the top of the packet and smiled. 'I think the top one at least may be the other way around. I'm almost prepared to swear that is Samuel Pepys's hand.'

Buckingham frowned a moment and then laughed. 'Ah yes, the navy fellow that's always hanging around my lord Montagu. No doubt it is. A sound fellow. Well, you must tell me the next time I come what gossip he might have about me.'

'You'll not even wait on your dinner?'

Buckingham shook his head. 'I'll be off the minute the last warble has left the throat of the youngest choirboy. A boat awaits me at King's Staith and I mean to be on it and away long before dark. You need not attend me further, Thomas, but get on down the aisle after Anne Winter before the masses swallow her. I saw the look on your face just now. She will have none of me, of that she has left me in no doubt, but I think those deadly eyes of hers smoulder somewhat when they light upon you. Trust me, a woman like that should not be left alone too long.'

'He wasn't hanging about then. Good riddance is what I say,' said Lawrence, lifting the jug of claret and pouring some into Thomas's proffered glass. 'You know, you'd make a better lord lieutenant than him any day. They've been saying it down the Guildhall and everywhere else.'

Thomas laughed. 'His Majesty is not going to hand oversight of the north to the landless younger son of a long-dead knight.'

Lawrence swallowed a mouthful from his own glass and shook his head. 'He would if he had any sense.'

'I'm glad if he has not, in that case,' said Thomas. 'All I wish is for you to win me back Langton, that I might retire from public life to run my estates.'

'Course you do,' said Madge, beaming at Sir Thomas, and then at her grandson, behind whose chair she was standing.

Lawrence looked down the table then opened his mouth, alert to injustice. 'How comes he gets all that crackling?'

Madge paused in her distribution of the prized, crisped skin of the recently butchered and roasted pig.

She was unmoved. 'Jedediah is a growing lad, and you've already eaten half of yours.'

'Haven't,' said Lawrence, returning to his trencher after giving Lizzie in her high chair beside him a gentle nudge with his elbow. 'Jed's going to get a fat belly.'

Thomas smiled as he surveyed his friend's family: Lawrence, Manon, Lizzie and Lawrence's clerk seated about the oak table whilst his cook and Anne Winter's Scottish housemaid flurried and fussed around them, laying out food, passing plates, avoiding stepping on terrier or kitten. He moved slightly to the side that the housemaid might deposit a ladleful of steaming apple sauce on his plate at the side of the pork, the smell of which was tantalising. 'I noticed your mistress at worship in the minster today. It made me wonder how it was that you came into her service?

Your voice puts me in mind of my friend Ogilvie, your countryman, who hails from far in the north . . .'

He had made the mistake of addressing her before she had let go the sauce, with the result that it was dropped to his plate from a height that assured a splash on the sleeve of his best suit.

'Told you you shouldn't wear your best finery round here,' said Lawrence. 'That one's worse than Madge.'

Thomas rubbed at the mark with his napkin. 'I had little choice. I had to attend George to the minster, I could hardly go dressed like,' he looked Lawrence up and down, 'a lawyer.'

Lawrence grinned and speared a piece of crackling from Thomas's plate.

Once dinner was over and Manon and Lizzie gone for a rest while Jed was released for the afternoon, Thomas and Lawrence went to Lawrence's office.

'So,' said Lawrence, 'what did Buckingham have to say about William's death? Have you got any further along with it?'

Thomas shook his head. 'I've been at the duke's beck and call the entire time he was here. His only concern about William was for those drawings he'd had him make up for him, the ones that were in that satchel.' He pointed to the leather bag Lawrence only now noticed lying on the chair behind his own desk.

'You're not serious? Buckingham's been looking for the

plans we found in that bag William was carrying when he was killed and you've brought it here, to *my* house?'

Thomas raised his hands in a placatory manner. 'Calm yourself, Lawrence. The duke has seen the papers. I gave them to him as soon as I knew he was looking for them. He was somewhat nice, however, in the matter of the bloodstains on the bag, and asked that I find a discreet draughtsman to have a less . . . contaminated copy made for him. Which I did. The copy is locked away in his rooms at King's Manor. The papers in that bag are the originals.'

Lawrence still looked at the bag with deep suspicion. 'And why have you brought them here?'

To Thomas it was obvious. 'I thought we should have another look. See if they might help us in trying to get to the bottom of why William was killed.'

'Hmm,' said Lawrence. 'What did Buckingham have to say about them, then?'

Irritation crept over Thomas's face. 'He claimed he'd all but told me what he wanted them for. Seemed to think it funny that I hadn't worked it out.'

'We'd best have another look at them, then.'

Thomas took out the plans and opened them out on Lawrence's desk, weighing the edges down with pewter candlesticks and Lawrence's prized bust of Cicero. 'We'll need more light,' he said. Fossgate was a wide enough street compared to many in York, and the ground floor of Ingolby's house wasn't overhung by the upper storey, yet this late on a winter afternoon the light coming in at the windows was poor.

Lawrence went to the door and called for Jed, but it was Griselda Duncan who appeared. 'Is Jed still about?'

'Away with ice skates over his shoulder, to some fish pool that's frozen over.'

Lawrence tutted. 'Sounds likely enough. He'll be up at King's Pool, showing off. Right, well, fetch us some more candles, will you.'

She'd been back in no time and had had the sense to bring extra candlesticks too, which she placed carefully around the edges of the plan, where they could do most good. Lawrence went to light the candles from one already lit, but chastising him for risking wax on his papers, she took a taper from the pocket of her apron, put it to a flame then went round methodically lighting each candle. 'Will there be anything else?'

Grizel had known what it was that Thomas Faithly and Lawrence Ingolby were looking at before she'd finished lighting the candles. It was the original of the plans Anne Winter had copied while searching Thomas Faithly's rooms several nights beforehand and which she and Anne had pored over together. The spy house.

As she left, she took care to not quite close the door behind her.

Once out into the hall she stopped. Madge could already be heard, snoring from the kitchen, and Manon and Lizzie were safely upstairs, also taking their afternoon rest. Quietly, Grizel stepped close to the gap she had left between Ingolby's office door and the jamb, and she listened.

'You really have no idea what this is for?' said Ingolby.

'Some nefarious purpose, I fear. If you would look at it with fresh eyes first and tell me what strikes you about it.'

There was silence from the study for a few moments, and then Lawrence Ingolby said, 'You know Coffee Yard?'

'I've been into the coffee house now and then. Never given much thought to the courtyard and the building in it, though. It's an old religious hostel, broken up into smaller lodgings, is it not?'

'Mmm, that's what it was,' said Lawrence, 'but I've heard rumours it's been used as some sort of meeting house of late. Puritans probably.'

'Oh? A great risk to take, in the heart of the city,' said Thomas. Successive Acts of Parliament since his restoration had thoroughly eroded the King's desire for greater religious tolerance and any joining in a religious meeting not held according to the principles of the Anglican Church risked loss of office, fines and imprisonment.

'But this looks like plans to turn it back into a grand house. Or something.'

'Or something?'

Grizel felt her heartbeat quicken; now they were getting to it.

'See there?' said Ingolby. 'Well, that looks like the window of an upper chamber, doesn't it? But look at this.'

'What am I looking at?'

'It says hall, doesn't it?'

'Yes,' said Faithly. 'William's handwriting is small but perfectly clear.'

'Maybe so, but the dimensions aren't right.'

'What do you mean?'

'Well,' said Ingolby, 'if the alterations are made according to what William's got down here, the window from that bedchamber won't be overlooking the roof of the hall, it'll be looking right into it.'

'Are you certain?' asked Faithly.

'Certain. And look here, at these two storerooms, the pipes that carry into them.'

'I see them.'

'Well?'

'Well what?'

'What are they carrying,' prompted Ingolby, 'and from where? It's not water from the gutterings or from a source outside or in – there are no pumps.'

Grizel heard Thomas sigh. 'This is beyond me, Lawrence. I can't think what they might be. They are simply pipes.'

'Aye,' said Lawrence, clearly becoming animated. 'Small, narrow pipes, set high up in the wall almost so's you wouldn't see them, each end open in a different room.'

'Some form of ventilation?' suggested Thomas.

Lawrence shook his head. 'They're taking air from the one room to the other all right, but it's what's in the air that's important. They're taking *voices*.'

'Voices?'

'Words. Speech. Sounds. Anyone watching from this window up here, seeing persons of interest in the hall down here, would take no time coming down these back stairs here and taking up a position in one or other of these storerooms.'

It seemed Thomas Faithly at last understood. 'And from there,' he said, a hint of excitement in his voice, 'he'd hear whatever was being said in the hall without having to go in or being seen.'

'Exactly.'

Grizel smiled. It had taken the pair a good deal longer than it had taken Anne and herself to understand that what they were looking upon was a spy house, one where George Villiers, Duke of Buckingham – or more probably some agent – might settle himself, that he might overhear and take note of everything said within its walls.

'But why's he doing this somewhere he's clearly not going to be living? Why not just have alterations made at King's Manor, or even at the Treasurer's House, where the real power will lie?'

Faithly let out a long breath. 'That I don't know. All he had to say about it was it was good to have irons in the fire.'

'Irons in the fire?'

'Yes. Well, actually, he specified "tongs" which he appeared to find very amusing.' And then Grizel heard the sound of a hand slapping off a forehead. 'Idiot!' said Faithly. 'I've been an idiot. The Tong plot. Of course.'

For the next half-hour Grizel listened as Thomas Faithly

outlined for Lawrence details of events that had lately unfolded in the murkier corners of Westminster. The Tong plot, named for one of the initially unwitting conspirators, had been fabricated so that the authorities might be seen to have cause to eliminate any rumblings of dissent.

'Buckingham has taken a lesson from it that he seeks to apply in his rule as lord lieutenant. He believes the north is ripe for rebellion, that there are some old Republicans here who might not be finished yet.'

'He may be right,' said Lawrence. The last true opposition to the restoration, disordered and fractured and ultimately hopeless as it had been, had been in the north. 'And that's to say nothing of all the sects. Most of them came from the north. The Commonwealth may be over, but I doubt all of those emboldened by it have been crushed.'

'Which is exactly what Buckingham thinks,' said Thomas. 'He believes it would be of benefit to the peace of the realm should any such elements still in the north be flushed out, that they might be dealt with, once and for all.'

'It would be of benefit of Buckingham, you mean,' said Lawrence.

Thomas nodded. 'I am to keep my eyes and ears open for signs of dissent. But the thing is, what he has learned from the Tong plot is that rather than warn or crush individuals now, means should be found to quietly encourage them, to such an extent that they commit themselves to some outrage, the plans of which might be brought to light before they actually come to fruition. He says it would just be a question of bringing likely types together, then finding proof.'

'Likely types,' said Lawrence. 'By which he means the disaffected — labourers, old soldiers, folk that have come down in the world since the King came in. Exactly the sort that might gather together at a Puritan meeting house, or even find themselves employed in carrying out the work to set it right. Carpenters. Stonemasons. Not hard to see what it was about the work that William didn't like, is it?'

'No,' agreed Thomas. 'And while I'm heart sorry for William's fate, I own to being relieved that, as seems clear from this, his murder was nothing to do with any agent of L'Estrange's looking into our business with Damian Seeker, but instead the result of Buckingham's machinations.'

'You think the duke had him killed?'

Thomas Faithly made a dismissive sound. 'Not George. He'd have made sure he had hold of the plans first.'

'We're no further on then, are we?'

'No,' agreed Faithly, 'we're not.'

There was a puffing sound and then the faint whiff of smoke from extinguished candles. Grizel slipped back to the kitchen and the seat opposite the sleeping Madge, and picked up her knitting needles and wool, considering how best she might put this information to use.

As Lawrence went around the room, snuffing out the candles, Thomas Faithly said, 'I'll lodge these plans safely back in King's Manor. For now, though, all I wish is to forget about it all for a while. Is that offer of a bed for the night still available?'

'Course it is,' said Lawrence. 'It's already made up in the parlour.'

'Thank you. God willing, we'll soon be done with this sort of thing.'

Lawrence didn't need to ask him what sort of thing he meant. Dark things they did not understand. Secrets they had to unravel. Mysteries that had to be locked away out of sight. The sort of thing they had had to do for Damian Seeker.

They left his study and Lawrence turned the key in the lock. He glanced towards the kitchen, from where he could hear Madge's regular snores and the click of the Scotswoman's needles. 'Sometimes I wonder,' he said, as he and Thomas ascended the stairs to the parlour, 'if we can ever be done with that sort of thing.'

It was many hours later, long after darkness and silence had enveloped York for the night, that Grizel was awoken by a sudden cry from upstairs. She leapt from her box bed, taking the knife from under her pillow, and ran up the stairs and into the Ingolbys' bedchamber. Manon, still sitting up in bed, had her hand over her mouth but Lawrence Ingolby, his face a picture of shock, was standing in front of the opened panel in front of the secret recess in the wall. In his hand was the travelling escritoire from which Grizel had copied the letters only a few days before. Even from the other side of the room she could see that the lock was smashed, the lid splintered, and the case empty. Thomas Faithly went past her into the room.

'Lawrence, what is it?'

Ingolby's face, even by candlelight, was ashen. 'We've had another break-in.'

It wasn't long until they were all assembled down in the kitchen. Madge was standing over a pot of steaming caudle, keeping up a constant stream of woe and worry. Manon was seated by the kitchen fire, wrapped in blankets and sipping the brandy Lawrence had insisted she take. Her hands shook and her face was desolate. Grizel sat on the floor at her feet, a sleeping Lizzie in her arms. At the table, Jed watched nervously as Thomas Faithly sought to calm his master.

'You are certain it must have been this morning?'

Ingolby, white with anger, nodded. 'Absolutely certain. I checked in there today before we went off to church, and all was well with the writing case.'

'And when you came back?'

Lawrence shook his head. 'Didn't think to look.' He hit his hand off his own forehead. 'Stupid, stupid.' Sitting accusingly, in the middle of the kitchen table, was the smashed writing box.

'It's my fault,' said Manon, her voice deadened. 'I should never have made you keep them.'

'It is *not* your fault. It is the fault of this Roger L'Estrange and whoever—'

'L'Estrange?' said Sir Thomas, colour draining from his face. 'Oh no.' He looked now to Manon. 'You mean that was where you kept your father's letters.'

TWENTY

Plans for Leaving York

Anne Winter was jolted from her sleep by a loud knocking at the door. Throwing on a warm robe, she ran barefoot down the stairs, not bothering about a candle as a dim hint of dawn light allowed her to see in front of her.

It was Grizel.

'Whatever is wrong?' said Anne, hastily letting her friend in and closing the door behind her.

Grizel went directly to the embers of the kitchen fire and worked to rekindle them. 'Roger L'Estrange,' she said as she applied the bellows.

'What?'

'Are you sure he has left York?'

'Certain,' said Anne. 'I saw him leave and I paid two porters down at King's Staith to send word to me should there be any sighting of him returning. Why?'

'Because there was another break-in at the Ingolbys' yesterday, which Lawrence Ingolby only discovered late last night, and when he was talking with Thomas Faithly he uttered the name of Roger L'Estrange. Surely you did not actually tell him who tried to abduct his wife? L'Estrange would come after you himself should he find out.'

Anne shook her head. 'Upon my oath, Grizel, I never mentioned that man's name to Lawrence Ingolby.'

Grizel nodded her approval. 'It would not be a good idea to make an enemy of L'Estrange.'

'No, but Ingolby isn't the type to fear even Roger L'Estrange, and should he know that he was the man who attempted the abduction of his wife, I doubt he would go about his response with discretion.'

'I meant it would not be a good idea for *you* to make an enemy of Roger L'Estrange.'

'I fear we may be too late for that . . .'

'I know you have never liked him, and he treats you with little respect, but—'

'I need to tell you, Griz. There wasn't time to say it when I came to the Ingolbys' house the other morning, but I have broken with L'Estrange. I have had enough. Enough of being in league with a man who would hound a young woman in that way. Enough of spying on decent men like Thomas Faithly. When L'Estrange was here, after his attempt on Manon Ingolby, I told him I would make my report on Sir Thomas and that then we would be done.' She gave a tight smile. 'I fear I have already made a dangerous enemy of Roger L'Estrange. I boasted of my influence with the Duke of Buckingham, but in truth I'm not certain that Buckingham would lift a finger to help me should it not suit him.' Anne stopped, confused by Grizel's sudden smile. 'What is it, Griz?'

'Oh, let us just say that last night I learned of something that I do not doubt would suit the Duke of Buckingham to have us keep to ourselves. You may be assured that you'll have no problem in gaining the protection of the Duke of Buckingham, should you need it.'

'Indeed? I am intrigued, Griz. But tell me first of this new break-in at the Ingolbys' house. What happened?'

Grizel told her. 'The secret panel in the Ingolbys' bed-chamber had been opened without any damage to it, so he didn't notice until he was putting some papers in there late at night. And that was when he found that his letter case had been broken into, the lock smashed and the letters stolen. He blamed Roger L'Estrange.'

'But . . . you left the case as you found it, did you not? I mean, you have your special pick-lock and you didn't take the letters. If this is true . . .'

'Oh, it's true,' said Grizel, 'I saw it with my own eyes — the lock was destroyed and the box empty.'

'Then L'Estrange has some other agent working in York. He as much as suggested it to me himself, when he said that the time had come to take things into his own hands. I cannot think it's good for us that he did not think fit to tell me who it is.'

Grizel considered this. 'You think this person is also hunting into Thomas Faithly's past?'

Anne shrugged. 'Good luck to them if they are. I have not found a soul with a bad word to say about the man, and not the slightest suggestion of suspicion about his past doings. I have learned very little in York that I did not know before. All he thinks of is to get back his estate and to get away. And the fact that he and Ingolby are still so close is to do with their place of birth and a common upbringing at Faithly Moor. As regards past work for Damian Seeker — I can find nothing but their shared misfortune in having met him.'

'And what of Thomas Faithly's other friend, David Ogilvie?' Grizel's question was posed with some hesitation.

'Your countryman?'

'Yes, him that is so lately arrived in York.'

Anne frowned. 'He came here to see Buckingham, to get back some money the duke owed him. You suspect he is here for another reason?'

Grizel was turned away from her, arranging her cloak closer to the fire, that it might dry a little more before she had to go out again. 'Both the incidents at Lawrence Ingolby's house have happened while he, Ogilvie, has been in York. Buckingham has been and gone — did he not pay his debt? Why should Ogilvie still be in York if that was all that brought him here?'

Anne was surprised by the maid's vehemence on the matter. 'Well, because he is also Sir Thomas's friend. They fought together for the King at Worcester, and I think they have seen little of each other since. But . . . oh.' She put her hand to her mouth, remembering something that the drama of L'Estrange's attempt on Manon Ingolby had put from her mind.

'What?'

'It was the night of the feast, when we were the duke's guests at the Treasurer's House. He told me he was still in York because he was looking for someone. And he didn't think they would be happy when he found them.'

Thomas had waited at Fossgate until Lawrence returned from the Guildhall with two of the town's officers in tow. He'd set up such a stink there that the commander of the watch had offered to come himself, but then Lawrence had calmed down and said two sturdy constables would be enough. Once the men were posted, one at the front door, one by the back gate, and Lawrence had assured him he would send word to King's Manor if he needed him, Thomas left to traverse the cold sodden streets of the early morning, back to his offices. Once there, he told his clerk he was not to be disturbed.

His door locked, he collapsed into the fireside chair and screwed shut his eyes. Lawrence had tried to persuade him that all might be well, for the stolen letters from Seeker had been written in code. Thomas had been hard put not to laugh in his face. Code? From the minute they could be got to Whitehall, it would be a matter of hours until the cypher office had broken that code.

There was nothing Thomas could do about it. The letters might have little bearing on himself, although the look in Ingolby's eye had suggested otherwise. What he did know was that he was in danger of losing his mind if he kept thinking about it. He considered instead his own case – his grandmother's estate of Langton that Lawrence was working to win back for him. At least Ingolby had been able to offer him some hope in that direction. For now, though, he would have to concentrate instead on his duties as a deputy to the lord lieutenant.

With the events at Ingolby's, he had not as much as looked at the rest of the papers Buckingham had left with him yesterday. Wearily, he pulled them out now. The first three papers related to everyday aspects of the administration of the North Riding that Buckingham wished Thomas to make arrangements for – to identify the appropriate functionaries, apportion them their duties. Thomas set to the planning with a purpose – there was a rhythm to the tedium of the task that was calming, reassuring against the background of the unsettling events of the last few days. Next came a list of Buckingham's personal requirements regarding his own establishment and residence in York. Thomas attached a paper with directions of his own over the top and marked it with the instruction to his clerk to make six copies, which were to be distributed amongst the appropriate household staff.

All that remained, aside from the packet, bound in green ribbon, of assorted personal letters to himself, was the set of plans drawn by William Briar that he and Ingolby had looked over the previous afternoon. The very sight of them sent a pain shooting through his already strained eyes, and for a moment he thought of consigning them to the fire and having done with it. But no, while Buckingham had a clean copy, he might at some point demand the original. And it was not Thomas's right, moreover, to destroy something that might ultimately help to track down William's murderer.

Had William Briar understood the full import of the scheme for which Buckingham had required these drawings? Had he perhaps been no more than a pawn, chosen to play his part without ever knowing what he did? Thomas had also secured the commonplace book in which William had noted his appointments. He had looked at it before, but then having found William had put no appointments down in his journal for the day of his murder, no doubt not knowing when exactly he might be returned to York from London, had laid it aside. Now he began to look through it again. Things that he had thought nothing of when first he had gone through it read differently to him now. There, the final one amongst all the appointments for his recent trip to London, was 'His Grace the Duke of Buckingham'. Thomas realised that William had seen Buckingham at Whitehall on the day before he had returned to York. It might have been nothing – what could be more natural than for a surveyor of the King's properties in York to give his report to the incoming lord lieutenant? On the other hand, perhaps during that meeting William had queried or been informed of the true purpose of the plans for the spy house. But would this have been enough to upset William in the manner he had appeared in at the Ingolbys' door all those mornings ago, and why should it have been to Lawrence Ingolby and not himself that William had tried to take the information?

When she got back to the Ingolbys' from her early visit to Anne Winter, Grizel was sorry to find the family still in a state of disarray. Lawrence was pacing about the kitchen, his hands run through his hair so much that it was almost standing on end. In the rocking chair closest to the hearth, Manon sat silent, tears brimming over her lower lids to tumble onto white cheeks. At her feet, Lizzie clutched her kitten and glowered across the room at Madge's terrier, which avoided her gaze from its place of refuge behind Jed's legs.

Madge herself was seated on a three-legged stool, all the usual pomp and flourish gone out of her. She looked bewildered and bereft, so that any onlooker might have thought the world had just come tumbling down around her. She grasped at Grizel's arrival as a drowning man would at a rope. 'Ah, my dear! Thank goodness you are come back, for we are all disordered and nothing I can do will set things right.'

Grizel surveyed the room again, but no one other than Madge appeared to be paying any attention to her arrival. She went over to the old woman. 'Is nothing any the better?'

Madge shook her head. 'Master is half-distracted and threatening all sorts on goodness-knows-who. Mistress will not say what is taken or why it grieves her so. My little Lizzie gives nothing but dark looks and has hid her sunshine right away.'

Grizel looked at the child, whom she would never have called a harbinger of sunshine, but saw that she was indeed more serious-looking than ever. It was hardly a thing to be surprised at, given that only a few days ago she had been locked in a coal shed, and that now all the people around her were descended into despondence. Lawrence's clerk sat, his hands gripping one another, his knuckles white, wondering, no doubt, how the blame for this latest catastrophe might land upon him.

'And another thing,' the lawyer was saying, 'I was to set out for Hull tomorrow, to fetch back documents relating to fishings that Sir Thomas's grandmother left to him along with Langton. I can't go now.'

'But, do they not have to be lodged before—' ventured Jed.

'I *know* when they have to be lodged,' said Lawrence, spinning round on him, 'but I can hardly leave here now, can I? A client murdered and the house twice broken into and my papers ransacked twice.'

'But Jedediah can look after us while you're gone, can't you, my love?' implored Madge.

Jed looked a little thrown by his grandmother's offer on his behalf. Grizel was surprised – she would not have thought him a coward. But then he spoke, and she felt guilty that she had maligned him. 'I could go.'

'What!' said Madge, alarmed.

'I could go. I know my way to Hull well enough.'

'But to go on your own – to such a town with folk coming in from all over the world and you not much more than a lad.'

But Lawrence Ingolby was interested. 'No, Madge, he's right. He did all right in London without me having to hold his hand every hour of the day. He'd manage Hull no bother. You would, wouldn't you, Jed?'

The young man nodded.

'And John Walker's as good a skipper as you'll find.' Lawrence directed himself to Madge now. 'He'll see Jed to Hull safe and sound, and direct him to where he needs to be. He'll have my room for the night in the inn – all to himself, mind – and they'll treat him as well as if it were me. He'll be back in no time.'

Still the old woman looked uncertain, then Lawrence played his trump card. 'And think how grateful Sir Thomas will be. If those papers don't get lodged in time, he could lose his claim on those fishings. But if he should keep them, and owe it all to Jed . . .'

Grizel could see light dawn in the housekeeper's eyes. She saw the prospects of the young man's bright future as Sir Thomas's steward contend there with her fears about him setting out alone, in such foul weather, for a strange town. She nodded, and Lawrence turned, his face eager, to Jed.

'Are you certain now, Jed? I won't force you.'

But Jed was certain. He would set out the next morning for Hull, in place of the master. Still voicing her fears, Madge bustled him out of the kitchen and up to their attic chamber, to see what he might need to take with him upon such a grand adventure, 'in the very maw of winter'.

Once they were gone, the terrier betook himself to his

basket and Lizzie released the kitten to roam free once more. The silence in the room was as heavy as the great clouds of snow Grizel had noticed on her walk down through town, waiting to void themselves on York. Manon, who had seemed to pay little attention to the matter of Jed and Hull, now spoke for the first time since Grizel's return.

'It is not Hull we need to send to, but Massachusetts.'

Ingolby's eyes swept over to where Grizel was. Grizel bent herself over a tub of vegetables and began to sort through them, making a grand show of not listening. 'Hush, love,' she heard him say.

But Manon Ingolby did not hush. 'Griselda doesn't know. How would she know? But we must warn him. We—'

Lawrence tried to hush his wife again. 'I will write, right now.'

'A letter takes so long.'

'A letter will take not a minute longer to get there than a man. Whoever took those letters and thinks to avail himself of what's in them will not reach your fa— will not reach *him* any quicker than the letter that I send, and may be longer.' He squeezed her hands. 'We can do no more, Manon. But there is one thing in the midst of all of this for which we can be grateful.'

His wife cast doubtful eyes at him, and he looked directly into them, to be certain that she understood. 'Whoever has been doing all this has what they want now. They won't bother us any more.'

TWENTY-ONE

Encounters

The morning and afternoon spent locked in the confines of his room at King's Manor had left every muscle in Thomas's body feeling as if it might snap. Should even one tendon give way, all the rest would follow, and he might collapse there, on the floor of his office, and never get up. His eyes stinging with smoke from pipe and fire and the strain of reading all day long, he put away William Briar's papers and Buckingham's instructions and heaved himself to his feet.

The sky outside was black now, and the stars glinting in it as if they were there one moment and gone the next. He longed for the fresh night air and an evening of forgetting, a good brandy and the sound of other men's voices. The clock on his wall told him it was eight o'clock. He snuffed out his candles, locked his door and went down through an eerie King's Manor. He had not got halfway across to Bootham Bar when he cursed himself, realising he had not brought his purse.

Spinning on his heel, Thomas strode back towards King's Manor. He was soon inside and in sight of the stairs when he glimpsed a figure emerging from a side passageway that led direct from the old abbey grounds. A fresh draught of air told him the night visitor had not closed the outer door behind them. Some feeling of unease prompted him to put his hand to his knife. At that moment, the figure turned around, just as startled as was Thomas, and then broke into an easy laugh.

'Why, my friend, I would not advise taking out that knife. I have wrestled you to the ground more often than I remember, and would surely do so again.'

Thomas responded with a derisive laugh of his own. 'Ogilvie! You might have your throat cut, creeping about here at this hour.'

'So it would seem,' said David Ogilvie. 'I will think twice before I call on you unannounced again.'

Thomas relaxed his shoulders. 'I'm sorry, David. The murder of the King's surveyor and other recent . . . *incidents* have put me on my guard. If you wait a moment until I fetch my purse, I'll stand you a drink and your supper. And we will go out the back way that you have just come in, so I can show you the windows of my rooms. You might look up another time and see by the light if I am in or not.'

'That hadn't occurred to me,' said Ogilvie.

'No? You wouldn't make a very good spy then, my friend. As well you have your lands to win a living from.'

'Is espionage the only alternative then?' said Ogilvie with his half-smile.

'In these times, for a gentleman without means, there are few other. But come.'

A few minutes later, Thomas's purse secured, they were leaving King's Manor by the back way, as Ogilvie had come in. The ruins of St Mary's were like spectres in the night, and Thomas remarked that it would not take much to imagine a gathering of long-departed souls come to life there. They quickened their pace and were soon crossing into the town, by way of the gate in the walls by St Leonard's.

'I'm glad you came to find me,' said Thomas as they went down Coney Street. 'I've hardly seen you since that evening with Buckingham and Lady Winter. I almost thought you had left York but I have been so much taken up with . . .'

Ogilvie put an arm loosely around his shoulder. 'Never worry about me, Thomas. I knew the duke would have you dancing attendance all the time he was here. Besides, I have not wanted for occupation.'

'Oh?'

'In truth, part of my reason for seeking you out tonight was to ask for your help. But let's get us in somewhere and something warm in our bellies and then we can talk. You look all done in. I think George asks too much of you.'

Thomas led Ogilvie up Stonegate and they soon found themselves at the Punch Bowl.

Their eyes smarted a little as they went in, the smoke from fire, pipes and guttering candles assailing them after the cold clarity of the streets, but they soon accustomed themselves to the miasma of the tavern. Men played cards or dice at tables, with no fear for their liberty or their mortal souls as they might have done in Cromwell's day.

Only once they had eaten, and warmed themselves on brandy, were they ready to discuss the business Ogilvie had sought him out for. Ogilvie looked about him as if to make sure they could not be overheard then leaned in across the bench. 'What I would ask of you concerns a woman named Griselda Duncan.'

Grizel sat late, darning a pair of Lawrence Ingolby's stockings, as she waited for the household to fall asleep. After the events of recent days, an air of bustle and a hint of cheer, forced though it was, had returned to the Ingolby household. Grizel found that most of the ordinary household tasks fell to her, as Madge spun in anxious circles, fretting over Jed's imminent departure and what he would need for his journey and his time away.

Jed, for his part, found himself pulled as if in a tug o' war between his anxious grandmother and Lawrence, who drilled into him what he was and was not to do, where he was to go and whom he was to see whilst in Hull. Most of all, he was to take care to get all of the papers relating to the fishings that were Sir Thomas's due and then return as quickly as possible with them to York.

Only Manon seemed untouched by the activity. Since the discovery that her letters – the letters, Grizel knew, that had come from Damian Seeker and pointed to where he was to be found – had been stolen, she had been as a woman shut off from the world. Only Lizzie, who would not leave her side, nor go to Madge, nor Jed, nor Grizel, nor to anyone but her mother and father, was in any way able to reach her. Lawrence tried, time and again, to reassure her that all would be well, but it was as if she didn't hear him.

Around mid-morning, Lawrence had persuaded Manon to go and rest in their bedchamber, then closeted himself in his office, forbidding anyone from entering. After a time he had emerged, a sheet of paper in his hand, and gone upstairs. Quickly, Grizel, who had been warming an infusion of honey and ginger, had poured it into a small mug for Manon and carried it upstairs after him. At the Ingolbys' bedchamber door she had stopped and listened.

The sounds from inside were at first indistinct, but then she began to make out the lawyer's words. 'I've *told* you, love – I'll go to the post myself directly I leave here. This letter will be with your father's agent in Liverpool as soon as can be, and he'll have it on the first ship out.'

'But whoever took the letters will be gone already . . .'

'No,' Ingolby soothed, 'it'll take them long enough to decipher it, and even then they won't be able to tell exactly where he is. By the time they do, he'll have had my letter of warning and you'll likely have written him another to tell him he's a granddad again. And Maria, God help us, will send over more of her knitting . . .'

At this, unexpected laughter had burst through the sound of Manon's sobs, and Grizel could sense her husband's relief through the door. Whatever else was said between husband and wife, though, she had not heard, because Madge had been coming fussing down the stairs from the attic, waving a ridiculous muffler knitted in the most lurid hues. 'Ah, Mistress Duncan, I was up half the night, but it is finished.'

Grizel had stepped back from the door, the mug with the infusion still warm in her hands. 'But what is it, Mistress Penmore?'

'What is it?' Madge had repeated, astonished. 'Why, it is the muffler I had been making for Jedediah for his Christmas box, but he shall have it now, or Lord alone knows what colds and draughts and ill humours he will be subjected to, out on the water all the way to Hull in this weather, and then on the coast there and all the gales that come in from the sea.'

She had held the item up in front of Grizel's face, but Grizel was spared having to respond when the bedchamber door opened and Lawrence Ingolby came out, some of the weight he had lately been carrying evidently having been lifted from his shoulders. 'Have you two nothing better to do than stand gossiping on the landing?' he'd said, making to move past Grizel.

'I was just bringing this tincture for the mistress.'

'Aye, all right. Very good.' Ingolby had been about to turn down the stair when he'd caught sight of the muffler. He'd stopped, staring at it. 'What in the name of all that's holy is that?'

Madge had drawn in her breath to explain, but Grizel had not been able to restrain herself. 'It's a muffler that Mistress Penmore has made for her grandson. He is to wear it to Hull!'

A hint of the spark that had been gone of late from
Lawrence Ingolby's eyes had flickered. 'That?' he'd said,
his face twisted as he inspected the item that Madge was
now brandishing before him.

'There is such a chill wind on the river, and Jedediah's
father—'

'—"of sainted memory",' Lawrence had murmured.

'—of sainted memory,' continued Madge, 'was as hale
and hearty as Jedediah, before he went on the river and
caught a chill and that was the end of him.'

'Fell drunk into the water's what I heard,' Lawrence had
retorted, provoking a howl of indignation. He'd pointed to
the muffler then turned down the stairs. 'I don't care what
he does on the boat, but no clerk of mine is walking the
streets of Hull wearing that.'

Grizel had awaited the retaliatory outburst from Madge,
but none had come. Instead, the old woman was beaming,
her spirits restored by the resumption of hostilities with her
employer. Their great struggle, so overshadowed by events
she didn't understand, had been revived and the household
might soon revert to its usual assured rhythm. As the housekeeper had descended the stairs, eager to present her gift
to her grandson, Grizel had knocked gently on the door
to Manon Ingolby's bedchamber and gone in.

It had been after dinnertime, with Jed departed to the dock
on the arm of his tearful grandmother and her sister Flo,
who'd both insisted on seeing him off, that Grizel had left

the Ingolby household. Lawrence had made all the right noises about seeing his clerk down to King's Staith from where he would get the boat to Hull, but Jed had been keen to assert his independence. 'Besides,' he'd said, lowering his voice 'you've the mistress and little Lizzie to mind.'

The mistress had come downstairs to see him off, eyes brimming with gratitude and full of pleas that he would look after himself. His instructions from Lawrence checked and checked again, Jed had departed on his great adventure. Flo's delight in the muffler that Madge had forced around the young man's neck had been unrestrained. The two women had still been going at it hammer and tongs when Grizel had opened the door to them on their return, but the look on the lacemaker's face as she'd watched the sobbing housekeeper retreat to the depths of the house had been kindly. 'Don't judge her badly for her folly, Mistress Duncan. Our Madge has vexed herself over that lad his whole life.'

Grizel knew, as soon as she set foot back in the house on Ogleforth later that afternoon, that something had changed. The place was spotless, not a thing out of place. The fire was not lit and the air was cold and still, as if they had left it already. She didn't remove her cloak or bonnet, didn't call out but, her boots leaving wet marks on the scrubbed pine of the steps, she ascended the stairs. On the landing were their travelling chests – Anne's two large ones and her own small one, each almost fully packed. The door to Anne's bedchamber was a little ajar and Grizel pushed through it. She looked at Anne and immediately she understood. Anne had laid out the red velvet gown in which she liked to travel. Laid out beside it was the matching coat, its brocade of black silk and buttons of jet glinting in the chill air. A black mink hat, gifted to Anne some time ago by a Russian ambassador in Berlin, sat atop it.

'It is finished?'

'Everything is done but the posting of the letter to L'Estrange, exonerating Thomas Faithly. You can take it with you on your way back down to the Ingolbys and leave it at the safe house of All Saints Pavement. I've made provision to fill your place in the Ingolby household, and we may be off and away from York tomorrow.'

Grizel had felt a mix of relief and unease at hearing this, and it must have been the latter that had shown on her face.

'What's wrong, Griz? I thought you would be happy to be going from here.'

'I am,' she'd responded, 'but there's something I must do first.'

'What?'

'I cannot tell you, Anne. I ask you simply to trust me, just as you asked me to trust you over the matter of who it was that wrote the letter to Manon Ingolby.'

'All right,' Anne had said. 'How long will it take, this thing you require to do?'

'A night, that is all. Give me a night, and then you may post the letter exonerating Thomas Faithly tomorrow, and that done, we will depart from York.'

'What has it to do with Sir Thomas?'

Grizel had given a tight smile then said, 'Very little, really, like almost everything else the man seems to land himself in the middle of. But it matters very much, for me, that you do not post that letter to L'Estrange tonight.'

And now, as the Ingolby household finally slept, she lay down her darning, pulled on her boots and tied on her cloak. Checking she had with her what she needed, Grizel slipped out into the darkness.

TWENTY-TWO

Old Shadows

In the Punch Bowl, Thomas waited while the serving boy cleared away their plates before saying, 'Griselda Duncan? What is your interest in this woman?'

Ogilvie shook his head. 'I cannot tell you.'

'Then I cannot help you, David,' he replied.

'But you can,' said David, leaning closer. 'I saw her out on the street some days ago, with a woman whom I only tonight learned is the wife of a lawyer, your friend Lawrence Ingolby.'

Thomas stood up. 'I'm sorry, David. I cannot talk to you about Lawrence Ingolby's business.'

Ogilvie looked taken aback. 'I have no interest in Ingolby other than his connection with Griselda Duncan. All I thought was that you might ask him where she is to be found. I will go and ask myself if you will give me his address.'

Thomas shook his head. 'No, David. I will not. And I will ask you to stay away from Ingolby's home. At most I am prepared to try to ascertain whether the woman will see you, and even that I can't promise.'

This time it was for Ogilvie to say 'No'. 'If she hears I am looking for her, that will be the end of my chances of finding her. You must trust me, Faithly.'

'I'm sorry,' repeated Thomas, putting on his hat, 'but at this moment I trust nobody. I'll bid you goodnight.'

As he left the Punch Bowl, Thomas considered going down to Lawrence's house and asking him what he knew of the maid he had been lent by Anne Winter, but it was almost ten o'clock; the family would be abed and after the upheavals of the last few days it would do them no good to be disturbed at this hour of the night.

When he reached his apartments, it was a relief to close his bedchamber door behind him, and with it to try to shut out the mounting concerns that beset him. He had never once doubted David Ogilvie, never had cause to, but that his recently appeared friend was taking an interest in the Ingolby household at this very time, disguised or not as interest in their newly acquired housemaid, sat very ill with him.

For all he wanted to banish thoughts of the evening just passed, the music of the players came back to him. As he had been leaving the Punch Bowl, the fiddler had taken up his bow to accompany his companions in a spirited rendition of 'Have you e'er seen the morning sun?' Thomas was assailed by a sharp pang of nostalgia, recalling an early morning meander homewards with Sam Pepys when Sam had sung that song as they'd watched the sun rise over the new dock at Deptford. A wistfulness overcame him for

some of the friends and fun of his London times. At that
moment, Thomas remembered the letters Buckingham's
page had handed him in the minster and that he hadn't had
the leisure even to open.

Lighting a candle, he pulled the packet out from where
he'd stored it and undid its green ribbon. There were three
letters in all, all from Sam by the look of the handwriting.
Thomas prised open each in turn and quickly checked their
dates. He would start furthest back. Soon he found himself
chuckling, picturing his friend caught in the tempest of his
marriage or the aftermath of too much wine and song, as
he had often seen him. It was a delight to Thomas, and a
relief, for Sam never put anything of the affairs of state into
his letters, instead filling them with gossip of acquaintances,
the plays he had seen and who he had seen at them, and
the latest fashions of town.

By the end of the second letter, Thomas was longing to
be back in London, on the roof tiles of Sam's house, singing
along to Sam's lute and telling stories. His chamber had
grown cold and he rekindled his fire and poured a good
measure of brandy which he took with Pepys's letters to
the armchair by the hearth. Above the mantelshelf was a
pair of paintings – landscapes by some minor English artist
that could not begin to compare with the treasures of the
late King that Cromwell had sold off, or the Titians gifted
to the restored King by the Dutch, by way of apology
for their heinous treatment of him in his exile. Thomas
smiled. For all the tales Sam told of London, Thomas would

have chosen these two over anything that hung now at Whitehall or Hampton Court. One painting was of his childhood home of Faithly Manor, now irrevocably in the hands of Lawrence's patron, Matthew Pullan, and the other of Langton Manor, of which he was now allowing himself to have hopes.

Thomas had only been to Langton a handful of times in his boyhood, to visit his grandmother. The paintings he was looking on now, inferior works though they might be, told their own story. There was Faithly Manor, high on the moors and bleak as the stone it was made of, and yet he loved it with all his heart. Langton Manor, on the other hand, was smaller and had the appearance of being a good deal better-tended and more comfortable.

His thoughts slipped into pleasant visions of future days at Langton, where he and some as-yet-nebulous beauty would raise a brood of strong boys and spirited girls. He would teach them all to ride, and to hunt and to fish — if Ingolby's lad would only bring the papers safe back from Hull. Another brandy down and all concerns about William Briar, David Ogilvie, even his past with Damian Seeker had evanesced entirely from Thomas's mind. He was soon asleep and for the first time in many weeks, dreaming happy dreams.

It was either the knock on the door that woke him, or his consequent dropping of the empty brandy glass to shatter on the slate hearth. He stood up with a jolt, mildly confused by the crunch of crystal under his boot as his bleary-eyed clerk came into the room.

'Sorry, Sir Thomas, but there's a woman here wants to see you. Insisted I wake you.'

'At this hour?' Thomas stood up, suddenly aware of the undone buttons of his doublet and how disordered his hair must be. 'What woman?'

'This woman,' said a voice.

Thomas stared, all concerns for his unkempt hair gone, as Anne Winter's Scottish maidservant stepped firmly past Frank to stand in the middle of the room.

'You!' he said.

'Me,' she acknowledged.

Frank, now showing signs of being fully awake and interested, lifted his lantern the better to illuminate the Scotswoman.

'You may leave us now, Francis,' Thomas said.

The boy looked disappointed. 'Should I bring—'

'No,' interjected Thomas. 'Bring nothing. Go back to bed. I will show the . . . lady out when the time comes.'

The boy went, and only once the door had been firmly closed behind him did Thomas turn his attention back to Grizel Duncan. 'What do you want?'

'I have come to make a proposition to you.'

'Do you say so? And the nature of your proposition?'

The woman took off her gloves and her cloak. He saw now that in her hand was a folded document. He was suddenly aware of his own heart thumping.

'You are friends, as I understand, with a man called Ogilvie. Major David Ogilvie.'

Thomas felt his breathing deepen. What had he been thinking of, only a few hours ago, to not hear Ogilvie out about this woman?

'And what's that to you? What's your interest in David Ogilvie?'

'My *interest* in David Ogilvie is to remain as far from him as possible, but I think the major has other plans for me. What has he said to you about me?'

Thomas might not have been certain of his friend's motivations, but he did not trust this woman one inch, and he would be telling her nothing. 'Why should he mention you to me at all? Why should he even know your name or expect that I would? You are a housemaid, in the employ of Lady Anne Winter, and your services loaned by her to Lawrence Ingolby.'

'Oh, that's all very true, Sir Thomas, but I have been other things too, and given your friendship with the major, and your position here in York, I think it not unlikely that he might have made certain accusations against me, and sought your help in pursuing them.'

Thomas watched her. Her face gave away nothing. 'What accusations?'

She tilted her head as if amused, but he didn't think she was really amused. 'Well, if you don't know, I am hardly going to accuse myself.'

'Are you telling me you intend harm to the Ingolby family? That you have done them harm?'

At this, Griselda Duncan looked genuinely shocked.

Some of the mask, supercilious, superior, with which she seemed perpetually to go about her business, slipped and he could see another person beneath. 'No,' she said, shaking her head. 'I would never do that. Lady Anne would never have put me there for that and I would never do it.'

'And does Lady Anne know of the accusations you fear Ogilvie has made against you?'

Her voice became smaller as she answered him. 'No.'

'Then why are you here? Are you afraid I will tell her what Ogilvie says of you?'

'More than that, Sir Thomas,' she said, exhibiting some of her former confidence. 'I am afraid you will tell anyone at all.'

Thomas leaned towards her. 'I act in York on behalf of the lord lieutenant. It is my job to see that firm governance and good order are held throughout the territory under his oversight. If you think I can be persuaded to silence any accusation the major might have against you, whatever it is you think you know of me, Mistress Duncan, you have been sadly deceived.'

Now the glimmer of superiority had returned to her eye. 'What I know of you, Sir Thomas? Oh, I feel quite certain my information is good. But perhaps it would be better to consider again the question of what you know of me.'

Thomas was confused. 'I have no wish to offend, Mistress Duncan, but I am not in the habit of acquiring knowledge about ladies' maids. It is late, and I have better things to do than to listen to you, or to engage in whatever game you and Ogilvie may have on hand.'

The Scotswoman smiled, as if he had just walked into a snare she had set for him. 'Because you are so far engaged in your own?'

'What?' said Thomas.

Grizel Duncan took a breath, as if at the beginning of a story. 'You will have heard, I think, of a person in White-hall by the name of Roger L'Estrange?'

Thomas's stomach lurched. He swallowed against the wave of nausea threatening him. 'What have you to do with L'Estrange?' Surely this woman couldn't be the spy Andrew Marvell had come from Holland to warn Lawrence Ingolby about. 'Are you in his employ?'

She appeared to consider. 'Not exactly, Sir Thomas. But Lady Anne is.'

He was winded for a moment, but quickly reasserted himself. 'I don't believe you,' he said.

'Do you not, though? Only think a while. Reflect, in fact.'

Thomas didn't flinch under the gaze of the steady, dark eyes. But he did think, and he did reflect. Bruges, Damme – had he not learned in Flanders that Anne Winter was very much more than just another Royalist widow abroad, waiting out her days in hopes of a restoration of the Stuarts?

'But she's done with all that business, surely? The King is on his throne.'

'Indeed,' said Griselda Duncan. 'And there are such around him now, and in his royal service, who grew weary of waiting for that glorious day. There were such as sold their loyalties, sold their souls, and live out their days now in plain sight, in the hope that their past crimes will never see the light of day. Are there not, Sir Thomas?'

Thomas felt the heat rising in him. 'I know nothing of such people.'

'Do you not, Sir Thomas?'

He felt her eyes drilling into him. The time for pretence and prevarication was over. 'What do you want?' he said.

'I've told you. Whatever David Ogilvie might have to say about me, you are not to act upon it, other than to counsel him to silence. Lady Anne and I will be away from York soon, and should he come looking for me after that, so be it, I will meet the threat as I must.'

'David Ogilvie is an old and trusted friend. You, on the other hand, have brought me nothing but your own speculation.' Even as he said it, though, Thomas's eyes travelled to the folded document that she now played about her fingers.

The woman was watching him. 'As I think you have surmised, Sir Thomas, that is not true.'

'What is it?' he said, openly indicating the document.

She handed it to him. 'This is a copy. The original is also in my possession. I removed it from Lawrence Ingolby's house.'

Understanding dawned on Thomas. 'It was you who broke in, who took my papers from his study and then whatever he had in his bedchamber.'

Griselda shook her head and Thomas's understanding crumbled into so much dust. 'No. I copied this and another document between the times of the first break-in and the second. Initially, I returned the original of this document to its place. It took me some time to decipher the contents of it. It's addressed to the lawyer, Lawrence Ingolby.'

'Decipher?' Thomas now felt sick. 'A letter to Lawrence Ingolby?' but she was not to be interrupted.

'As I say, I had initially returned the original of this to Lawrence Ingolby's hiding place after I'd copied it, but after I'd managed to decipher it and read what it said, I thought it prudent to have the original in my possession, as well as the copy.'

Even in the midst of his fear, Thomas felt a sensation of disgust. 'You say this so coolly.'

'Indeed, and you might take it with a better grace, Sir Thomas, for had I not had the foresight to remove this document when I did, it would have fallen into the hands of whoever ransacked the secret compartment behind Lawrence Ingolby's bedchamber wall two nights ago.'

Thomas swallowed. 'And what does the document you have deciphered say, Mistress Duncan?'

'It says a good deal. What is pertinent to yourself is that it is from Captain Damian Seeker – the *former* Captain Seeker, that is, of whom everyone appears to have an opinion – to his son-in-law, Lawrence Ingolby.

'And what the former captain writes to his son-in-law is a confirmation of your own involvement in spying on your Royalist comrades on behalf of the captain's Republican masters, in the year of God sixteen hundred and fifty-six.'

'But—'

The woman waved her hand in a dismissive gesture. 'It's late, Sir Thomas, and we do not have the time. I have kept knowledge of this document from her ladyship, with the result that this very day she has written a letter to Roger L'Estrange in Whitehall, informing him that she has found no evidence that you were ever a traitor to His Majesty in the days of the Protectorate.'

Thomas sank back in his chair, closing his eyes and letting out a long sigh of relief. But the woman had not finished talking.

'Her ladyship wrote the letter today, but I have persuaded her not to send it yet.'

Thomas's eyes flashed open.

'I have persuaded her to wait until tomorrow to post the letter that exonerates you to L'Estrange. If you agree to what I have asked, Lady Anne will never know of your treachery to the King all those years ago. We will come here tomorrow to bid you farewell and she will post her letter to L'Estrange and you will be forever after free of suspicion in the matter. I will pass you the original of this letter then.'

'And if I don't agree?'

'Then this letter will be in her hands before the bells of the minster have struck ten tomorrow morning, and with the commander of the garrison of York Castle as soon thereafter as she can carry it there. And,' here Grizel Duncan gave an affectionate smile, 'Lady Anne can move very quickly indeed.'

She stood up now, and began to tie her cloak and look round for her gloves. Thomas also stood up. 'What exactly is it that binds you and David Ogilvie?' he asked.

She looked to him as if surprised at his impertinence. 'That is none of your concern.'

'But my life—'

'Is in your own hands. Do what I ask and it will remain so. Neglect to do what I ask and we will see how long it is before L'Estrange has you painted as black as the most guilty of regicides.'

Thomas could envisage the consequence. 'And so I should end my days on the scaffold, alongside Damian Seeker.'

The Scotswoman paused in picking up her gloves. 'Damian Seeker? I hardly think it. He is very safe away, I believe. Lady Anne's work for L'Estrange concerns itself with those of your own side who betrayed the King in his days of greatest peril, and have now slunk back to his side to reap the benefits of his restoration. Cromwell's people, that were openly officers of the Protectorate, are of no interest to her.'

Again, Thomas was thrown into confusion. 'But, were you – was she – not sent here by L'Estrange to find out where he is?'

'Where Captain Seeker is? No. We were not.'

He leaned towards her, angry almost. 'I was *told*, though, warned, through a source that is beyond suspicion, that L'Estrange had an agent in York engaged in hunting down the whereabouts of Damian Seeker.'

Grizel Duncan finished putting on her gloves and started towards the door. 'That may well be, Sir Thomas, but I can assure you that whoever Roger L'Estrange might have sent to York on the trail of Damian Seeker, it was not Lady Anne, and it was not me.'

TWENTY-THREE

The Posts

Anne ate a solitary breakfast – the last she would have in this house, and she was glad of it. She wanted to be away from York and its collection of people whom she had it in her power to allow to be happy or to destroy. Anywhere else, she had made her peace with this, but York was different: she felt a strong affection for Manon Ingolby, and a reluctant liking for her husband. And for all that they had not seen each other often, there was something about Thomas Faithly that she felt she knew to her marrow. They had been the same, once, she and he, imagining the same futures, he in Yorkshire, she in the West Country. Then the war had come, and he had ridden to the King's standard, and on to defeat and exile. Her father had also ridden to the King's cause, and death, and Parliament's soldiers had come to her house and killed her brother and burned the place to the ground, and marriage to John Winter had saved her. Thereafter, she and Thomas Faithly had not been the same. He had continued to believe that the old England was possible again, that the life he had looked to might be at last attained, and he grasp it, unchanged. She thought he probably was unchanged, but she knew she was not. She didn't even know what the England they had now attained really was, or what she might be in it, because she could not be this forever. In all her work on her list for L'Estrange over the past two years, she had never been so relieved to find no evidence for a suspect's guilt as she had been in the case of Sir Thomas Faithly. She could feel the weight of the guilt she had carried in her work for L'Estrange begin to slip from her shoulders. A few hours more and it would be gone.

It was a little after nine, later than Anne had hoped for, when Grizel, all duties at the Ingolbys' house completed, hopped down from the cart Lawrence Ingolby had insisted on sending her by.

'I told him I could walk, and it isn't as if I had very much to take with me,' she said, depositing her bundle, 'but he insisted upon it. I daresay he was keen to see the back of me.'

'I doubt it, Grizel. He is very grateful, you know, for the burden you took from his wife in going there to assist Mistress Penmore. And I think poor Manon will miss you. I hope the new arrangements will answer their needs.'

'There is much kerfuffle about them, which I think is good in that it takes their minds away from their greater worries.' Grizel took off her outer things and began to clear the remnants of Anne's breakfast from the table. 'I think your suggestion that Madge's sister, Flo, should send down one of her girls to help suits them both, for Flo does not like the girl, and Madge is of the view that she can prove herself a better mistress than her sister.'

'And you, Griz?'

'Me?'

'The thing you had to do, is it done?'

Grizel bit her lower lip and nodded. 'It is done. You may bid Sir Thomas farewell with a clear conscience, and post your letter to L'Estrange.'

'Good,' said Anne. 'I am glad of it. I feel certain Sir Thomas is at bottom a good man who has already paid a great price for his choices over the years. I would not have liked to see him pay a greater one.'

Grizel's nose wrinkled in a familiar gesture of disapproval and Anne teased her. 'You are sorry to be deprived of your prey, Griz?'

'Not a bit of it. It is just that I do not like to see you sentimental. It troubles my stomach.'

'Which Heaven forfend. But tell me, how were they at the Ingolbys' this morning, really?'

'They were well, all-in-all. Manon Ingolby still frets over the stolen letters, but a little of the colour has returned to her cheeks. As to the lawyer himself, though none would claim he is cheerful, he at least displays something of his accustomed humour. Poor Madge Penmore indulges herself by turns in fretting over her grandson and in revelling in his advancement. She is certain that Jed only has to return with the last of Sir Thomas's papers and his position as steward at Langton Manor is sealed. Ingolby encourages her mercilessly in this idea, never missing the opportunity to suggest Sir Thomas will also be needing a housekeeper.'

Anne smiled at the picture of the household on Fossgate. 'And the child?'

'A strange little imp, but fortunately she seems none the worse for her stay in that coal shed Sir Thomas and I found her in. Indeed, she had a slightly less suspicious cast to her mien this morning than she has had of late. There will be trouble to come from that one, mark me.'

Anne laughed. 'I can believe that most heartily. But I'm glad the family is more itself.' Then she became serious again. 'Nonetheless, I would be happier if I knew who it was that had enticed the child away, and broken into their house.'

Grizel was by now busy scrubbing at Anne's dish and beaker. 'Sir Thomas is of the view that it was some agent of Roger L'Estrange who did those things.' Suddenly she stopped, then recommenced scrubbing with greater vigour, but Anne was taken aback.

'Sir Thomas? When did Sir Thomas say that?'

'Oh.' Grizel was colouring and seemed uncharacteristically confused. 'It was last night,' she said at last. 'He came by the Ingolbys after supper. I heard him say it as he and Ingolby were going into the lawyer's closet. Before they closed the door.'

Anne looked at her a moment, wondering at Grizel's fluster, but her friend never looked up from her scrubbing. Tentative, Anne tried another question. 'And did they say who they thought this person might be?'

Grizel shook her head, more composed now. 'No, they did not. But we have not been given the task of finding that out, Anne. Whatever business L'Estrange has set this other agent upon, it is none of ours. All that remains is for you to make arrangements for the horses, bid your farewell to Sir Thomas and post your letter exonerating him to Roger L'Estrange.' She dried her hands very briskly now on her apron. 'And then we can go home.'

'You are in a great hurry to be away from York. You do not like the place, I think?'

Grizel now took hold of the broom and gave her attention to the kitchen floor. 'A person is not obliged to like every place she sets foot in. Now, you might finish dressing while I do this. You know how long a fouter you have tying all those buttons on that red coat of yours.'

Anne smiled to herself. Grizel's pronouncements in Scots often signalled that she had said all she intended saying on a matter. She moved the conversation on.

'Are you going to accompany me to King's Manor, Griz? I don't mind if you'd rather rest a while before our journey.'

Grizel set the broom aside and straightened up. 'I'll be coming to King's Manor all right. I've seen the looks Thomas Faithly casts your way, and I won't deny the man is somewhat pleasing to the eye. I wouldn't trust you not to forget yourself. Besides, there's little left for me to do here, and the Devil makes work for idle hands.'

Anne laughed. 'The Devil would turn on his tail and run should he ever encounter you, Grizel.'

'The Devil is not so easy to shake off,' said the Scots-woman. 'But as to idle hands, I have a great curiosity to know how you think we shall live now you are to sever your employment with Roger L'Estrange.'

'Well,' began Anne, 'I don't need the money. Much of the revenue of my father's estate has been restored to me, and you and I have spent little of what we have been paid over these last years. It's not as if I intend going to London, or to the court. We will go back to Northumberland where we might live quietly and at little expense.'

It was all Anne could do not to burst into laughter at the expression on Grizel's face.

'Indeed!' said Grizel, clearly indignant. 'And what are we to do there, living quietly in Northumberland, save I to do all the work and you to gaze out at the window? Raise sheep, I suppose?'

Anne smiled. 'Well, we can certainly keep sheep if you wish. But I thought we might try our hands at a school, for women and young girls.'

The indignation remained in place. 'What? Teach young ladies to embroider and play the spinet? I will not do it.'

Now Anne did laugh. 'I know you will not. And that is not the type of school I had in mind. We will teach them to sew, yes, for a woman will hardly manage without that, but also to read and write and cast accounts and all the rest. I do not wish them to be educated as I was, but as you were.'

Grizel sat down and stared at her. 'As in Lady Rothie-may's school?'

'Why not? What is it you are always telling me – girls were to be taught "to write and sew and . . ."'

'". . . any other art or science whereof they can be capable",' finished Grizel. At length she said, 'Do you mean it?'

Anne went to her and pushed back a strand of Grizel's hair that had come loose. 'Of course I mean it. Who knows better than we two what it is that a woman can be capable of? Who is better fitted to teach young women than we who have travelled so far, done so much, at times without a penny and all on our wits? Of *course* I mean it.'

It was not yet ten when they at last set out together from the house on Ogleforth, lady and lady's maid, into the precincts of the minster. Anne glanced upwards. 'What a glory it is, though.'

Grizel didn't trouble herself to look. 'To God or man?'

'To both. Surely even you must concede that there is wonder in what man created here.'

Her companion's face had taken on the pinched look it often had when she was confronted by what she considered the extravagances of the Anglican Church. '"God that made the world and all things therein, seeing he is Lord of heaven and earth, dwelleth not in temples made with hands."'

'You are harsh, Grizel.'

'I am honest.'

Anne waved her hand at the minster. 'But look. *Look* at it. Centuries of human endeavour, centuries of faith have gone into this church. You cannot think that all those thousands of souls who worshipped here did so in vain?'

Grizel sniffed. 'No, of course I do not. But their faith is in the air between the stones, beneath the roof, not in coloured glass and chiselled pillars.'

'And you do not think those too tell a story?'

'They tell the stories the people who made them wanted them to tell. They do not tell the story of the people who worshipped there. And they don't tell the story of that poor fellow that was murdered there, either.'

Anne was about to ask what she was talking about but then she remembered: the surveyor William Briar, who had been killed in the crypt of that cathedral almost at the same time she had also been there, being warned off by Thomas Faithly's friend, David Ogilvie, lest she meddle with Sir Thomas's affections. She was ashamed that she had all but forgotten about him. 'I wonder if they will ever find out his killer?'

Grizel shook her head. 'I heard at the Ingolbys' that it's been put about that he was murdered by a vagrant.'

'I would wager my life that he wasn't.'

Grizel walked on briskly. 'You would do well not to wager your life on a thing that cannot be known. You would do well not to wager it at all.'

Anne ignored the admonishment. 'But it *should* be known. Look at this city – castle, soldiers, guards, walls, sentries, sheriff, constables, King's Manor stuffed full with officials of the lord lieutenant – how is it they cannot find out the murderer of one man?'

Grizel stopped and Anne stopped too. 'Because it doesn't matter, or they don't want to. Either way, it must be nothing to us, either, Anne. We cannot let it detain us.'

'But if it should touch on the question of Roger L'Estrange's other agent in York . . .'

'All the more reason that it cannot be our concern. That our path may from time to time have crossed that of one of his other agents is not to be wondered at. An hour more and we will have done everything that has been asked of us and be away, and free of York and free of Roger L'Estrange. You cannot make everything right, Anne, but meddling where you should not might make a great deal wrong.'

Anne Winter looked away from her friend, ahead to the minster, beyond it the walls which contained so many things unexplained. She knew that Grizel was right and that they must just finish their own business and get away from York. She picked up her pace through the dean's park in the direction of Bootham Bar and thereafter King's Manor.

Thomas had been five times already through to his clerk's room to check whether Anne Winter and her maidservant had arrived. Francis was beginning to exhibit signs of concern for him.

'Will you not lie down, Sir Thomas? You have slept very little of late and it will be a wonder if you don't make yourself ill.'

Francis seldom noticed anything, and Thomas wondered what kind of sight he must present to the boy to provoke such concern. He glanced in the glass that hung in the anteroom and saw that his eyes were red-rimmed and his skin grey and grown stubbled. For the first time, he saw his own father looking back at him. Thomas splashed water from the washstand onto his face. 'A little time yet, Frank, and all will be well, but have you really not seen anything of these women yet?'

Frank bit his lip and shook his head. 'At least go and sit, sir, and take a little of the breakfast I have brought you, and I will not delay a minute in bringing them to you whenever they appear.'

Thomas did as he was bid, but the bread tasted like chalk in his mouth and the ale sour. He had not slept since the moment last night that Griselda Duncan had left his room. He had not as much as changed an article of the clothing he had worn at that interview, and the clothes he now stood up in were those he had put on yesterday morning. His stomach churned almost as much as his eyes burned. Bells that seemed to surround him on all sides had already sounded ten and he doubted they would sound eleven before he fled York or threw himself into the custody of the captain of the castle garrison and confessed all. Whichever it was, he could not survive like this an hour longer.

But before the clapper had struck the inside of the last bell Francis was at his door. 'They are here!'

Thomas jumped up from his seat, brushing at his doublet as if somehow a clean doublet would mask the extent of his dishevelment. 'Show them in. And bring cake. And some of that Canary wine that was got in for His Grace.' He glanced again in the looking glass and lunged for a comb that might do something for the long blond curls that he now saw were knotted. He cursed his vanity that he had never yet indulged in a wig. He was still in the process of attempting to make himself presentable when the door again swung open and Frank, in the midst of announcing Lady Anne, was superseded by the entrance of the women themselves.

Thomas dropped the comb and found himself unable to offer even the most perfunctory of greetings. It didn't matter. Anne Winter was smiling as a friend might smile who has caught a fellow in a misdemeanour.

'I thought His Grace had left York three days since, but it appears you have not yet got over a night in his company, Sir Thomas.'

He struggled for an answer, but then saw that it was not necessary, because her face had become serious. She had come to do business. Behind her, like a hooded crow, watched Griselda Duncan.

Thomas gave one last smooth to his hair then extended his hand. 'Please, your ladyship, take a seat. Francis, bring in some refreshment.' To the Scotswoman he said nothing.

Anne Winter sat down on the seat across the desk from his own. 'I have come to say goodbye, Sir Thomas. I am leaving York today.'

'Oh,' he said, 'I am sorry to hear it. You will not stay here for the winter, after all?'

'No,' she said. 'I was not in a position to be entirely open about my reasons for coming here, which I hope you will excuse, but my business in York is done now.'

Thomas could not help but glance at Griselda Duncan who remained standing, and looking straight ahead.

'I . . . I understand that it is not always possible, or politic to reveal one's business, but I hope whatever brought you to York has reached a,' he searched for the right words, 'satisfactory conclusion.'

'It has, Sir Thomas. And I am confident there will be nothing further to come from that business, for me or for anyone else.'

Anne Winter was not a woman who was easy to read, but in that moment Thomas was certain she was telling him more than she was openly saying.

'Then I am pleased about that,' he said.

Now she smiled again. 'As am I. But I am come to beg a favour.'

This was more his territory. 'Anything, your ladyship, anything.'

'I wonder if you would continue to stable my horse, and Grizel here's too, until such time as the way is more suited for them to be ridden back to Northumberland.' She placed a bag of coins on the desk. 'I will pay, of course, for their stabling and for lads to ride them back. Grizel and I leave by water today.'

'Of course,' he said. 'But really, the money is not—'

'Take the money, Sir Thomas. When you come into your

estate at Langton you will need it for your own stables, no doubt.'

Thomas felt a mix of discomfort and relief. Whether Anne Winter knew it or not, he had only just the means of stabling his own horse as his affairs currently stood.

'Langton is a very pretty estate, I think,' she said.

'Not as wild as Faithly,' he conceded, 'and a tidy enough place.'

'And a good halfway between here and my house in Northumberland, too.' She stood up. 'I hope you will think to visit us, should you ever be up on the coast.'

'I, yes,' he blustered, 'of course.'

'Good.' She stood, just as Frank returned with the cake and Canary wine Thomas had sent him for. 'Oh, I'm afraid we have not the time to wait. We must get to the posts and then make ready for our journey. Come, Grizel. Time and the day move on.'

Thomas felt a panic begin to rise in him as the women made to leave. The maidservant had not moved from where she stood since they'd arrived in the room. She could not possibly have laid down the letter she had promised him without him having seen. 'Wait,' he said. 'You have taken no refreshment. A long journey in this weather – let me send for some hot food at least.'

'We will find somewhere to eat before we board, Sir Thomas. Grizel and I are seasoned travellers.'

He was walking towards the door, as if he might stop them leaving. 'But surely . . .'

Anne finished putting back on her gloves, Griselda Duncan turned around with a sharp, 'We must be gone, Sir Thomas.'

Thomas watched, helpless, as the Scotswoman followed her mistress out into the anteroom where Frank, paying attention for once, was ready to escort them down the stairs.

'Don't put yourself to the bother,' he heard the maidservant say to the boy. 'We know the way.' And she left, taking with her the evidence that might seal Thomas's fate.

'I hope Sir Thomas will find that sketch of Maria Ellingworth down by his chair where I dropped it,' said Anne. 'And I hope he will get his estate back. He is not a man at ease behind a desk.'

'Hmm,' said Grizel, casting her a suspicious glance. 'If he gets his estate back, it will be because God wills it. But . . .'

'What?'

'I am sure even the Lord does not will that I set out on our journey without my black muffler.'

'I thought you had it with you when we left Thomas Faithly's chamber,' said Anne.

'If I had it then, I do not have it now.' Grizel held out her empty hands.

Anne sighed. 'I suppose we had better go back up.'

'No, I will go back up. He has done enough gazing at you with those blue eyes for one day.'

Grizel was back up the various flights of stairs leading to Sir Thomas's offices in very little time. She had long perfected the demeanour of someone who knew where she was going and was not to be interrupted.

Thomas Faithly's clerk, his mouth full of cake, was clearly surprised to see her back so soon, and he said so, showering his waistcoat with crumbs.

'I have left my muffler,' she said, brushing past him and back into Thomas's room unannounced. The boy called after her and came running through the door behind her. Thomas Faithly, looking even more dishevelled than earlier, stood up, knocking a goblet of wine over the papers scattered on his desk.

'I'm sorry, Sir Thomas, she just . . .'

'That's all right, Frank,' he said. 'I think Lady Anne must have sent Mistress Duncan back for something. You may close the door.'

He did not invite her to sit after the boy had gone, and himself remained standing, facing her. 'You have brought it? The letter you said you would bring?'

She slipped her hand inside her cloak, and brought out a letter, its seal broken, and laid it on his desk.

He felt almost afraid to touch it. 'That's the one from Seeker? To Lawrence Ingolby?'

She nodded. 'The original, that confirms your role in spying for him on behalf of the usurper Cromwell's government. He sent it as a protection for Lawrence Ingolby should you ever chose to betray Ingolby.'

Sir Thomas shook his head. 'Lawrence is my friend. I would never betray him. Besides, he never claimed to be a Royalist. He has always just wanted to get on with his own life, regardless who might be in power.'

'Well, we must envy him in that, you and I, Sir Thomas.'

Thomas reached out a hand and touched the paper. 'And you have really not shown this to Lady Anne, nor told her of it?'

'Your interview with her this morning would have been of quite a different nature had she known of this letter's existence, I can assure you, Sir Thomas. And now, you must keep your bargain.'

He nodded. 'I am to give no credence to whatever David Ogilvie might tell me of you, and impede him from acting on it while he is in the territory of the lord lieutenancy.'

'Precisely.' Grizel Duncan turned to leave, but then turned back to him. 'Mind, if you do not, I will hear of it. I may not have the letter any more, but I know every word that it says, code or not. Should you go back on our bargain, I will tell Lady Anne what I know, and she will inform L'Estrange, and you may be assured he requires no proof but her word, and she requires no proof but mine.'

'I have given you my promise. I think I must count this nameless grievance between yourself and David Ogilvie to be my good fortune, I suppose.'

'Hmmph. You might add my affection for Anne Winter to the debit side of your account also. I kept Seeker's letter about you from her to protect her almost as much as to use on my own behalf.'

'How so?' he asked. 'Is she taken up in this thing with Ogilvie too?'

Grizel shook her head. 'She never heard his name until the day you introduced them, and knows him only as your friend. Ogilvie is nothing to her. But if I had passed that letter to her, you may be in no doubt that she *would* have passed it on to L'Estrange, and you would even now be in a dungeon in York Castle or on your way back to the Tower. She has a powerful sense of duty, and of honour too. But she also holds you in a strange regard, perhaps even affection, and I think it would have been like a canker in her to know she had sent you to the executioner's block. I kept the letter from her not just for my own sake, and certainly not for yours, but for hers, Sir Thomas.' She put her hand on the door, then paused. 'See that you do visit her in Northumberland. She has never invited a single soul there before.'

Back out at the gates to King's Manor, Anne was waiting for her. 'You have got it?'

'I have got it,' answered Grizel, holding up her muffler.

'Good. Then all that remains is for us to go to All Saints and put the letter exonerating Sir Thomas into L'Estrange's posts, and all will be well.'

Grizel gave a brisk nod of her head and walked on.

Madge was in her element, observing the work of the new maid lately taken off the hands of her sister Flo, to fill the place of Grizel Duncan. Madge had liked the Scotswoman –

she kept a trim house and waste was anathema to her – but there had been perhaps a little too much presumption on her part. There was only room for one mistress in the kitchen of the house on Fossgate, and her name was Madge Penmore.

This new young woman showed promise, and Madge was confident that under her guidance the deficiencies in the girl's training would quickly be made up. For now, though, she was content to remark in loud asides to Manon Ingolby that 'the lass has been got out from under Flo just in time.'

Manon watched all from the firm, high-backed chair that Lawrence had carried down from the parlour. It was one that her father had made for himself and that used to sit by the hearth of his room on Knight Ryder Street. Cushions had been added, that Manon had embroidered, with acorns and birds and brambles, and it soothed her to sit on the chair, with Lizzie nearby. Lawrence was fearful that she might trip going up and down to the parlour without him. It had been the same when she'd been carrying Lizzie, although she had not been so vast with Lizzie, she was certain of it. 'A lad,' Lawrence had pronounced of this second child. 'A big strong lad that'll probably carry you one day.' Manon liked to be in the kitchen in any case, even when she could do little to help, other than nod at Madge's pronouncements or give encouraging smiles to the new housemaid, attempting to communicate to the girl that all would be well.

And all might be well, or so Lawrence was determined on persuading her, and sometimes she felt herself almost convinced of it. Lawrence had written to her father that an agent of this Roger L'Estrange, the man so determined to have his revenge upon him, was on his trail and like sometime soon to track him to Massachusetts. The letter would be in her father's hands before L'Estrange had managed to decipher and follow up on those that had been stolen from their home, her husband had assured her. It might be many months before hired assassins such as Marvell had told them were hunting down the regicides on the continent found their way across the Atlantic.

The baby in her womb kicked, and she smiled to see the rounded outline of a sturdy heel pulse through the layers of her clothing. Lawrence was certainly right – despite all their concerns of the past few weeks, this was a strong and healthy child. She looked over to Lizzie, who had been following Madge and the new housemaid all morning around the kitchen and into the larder and out to the yard. She was almost like her old self, happier by the day, and the memory of being locked away in that shed three streets away perhaps fading a little, though she was still seldom to be persuaded to relinquish hold of her kitten.

Madge was explaining the rhythm of their day to her new acolyte. 'Master's in midday, regular as the bells of St Saviour's, and he's not one to wait on his dinner. Good wholesome English food he likes too – won't touch that French muck Flo preens herself on.'

Manon's heart swelled towards the old woman. Madge's sister Flo had been apprenticed to a French lacemaker in her youth, and although she was a very fine lacemaker, she had picked up the culinary tastes of the land of her apprenticeship, but sadly not the attendant kitchen skills. Madge had told her that poor Jed had had to spend half their recent evening at Flo's out at the privy, on account of the badly dressed crab Flo had pressed upon him at the start. 'Frozen, he was, out there all that time, poor lad,' she had said. Suddenly, at Manon's feet, Prince Hal's ears pricked up. She glanced to the clock on the kitchen dresser. It still wanted a half-hour of midday — too early for Lawrence to be coming back from the Merchant Adventurers' down the street, where he had said he would have business all morning. The clock had also been her father's, one of the few ornaments in those sparse lodgings of his. Manon felt a bleak surge of longing for those days when she had sat at his feet by the fire, his great shaggy hound, Dog, nuzzled into her, and he'd told her tales of his itinerant northern childhood. Perhaps it would not be so hard a thing for him, in Massachusetts, to be forced to move again . . .

She jumped as Prince Hal stood up on his stubby legs and set to a furious yapping, almost before the sound of rapping came from the knocker on the front door. Lizzie hid behind Madge's skirts and the housekeeper directed the maid to answer the door. 'Tell them Master's not in, and they'll have to come back after dinnertime. 'less it's Sir Thomas. You can let him in.'

When the girl went to the door, Manon said, 'But what if it should be business for Lawrence, Madge?'

The housekeeper shook her head, implacable. 'Business or

not, I'm not to let anyone in when Master's not here, not with Jedediah being away an' all. Them's Master's instructions.' As she said this, she patted her apron, and Manon realised that what she had thought to be some utensil Madge had put in there for handiness was in fact Lawrence's pistol.

'Come to me, Lizzie,' she said to her daughter.

Whatever was being said at the street door could not be heard properly from the kitchen, but the maid's voice was raised before there came the sounds of a mild scuffle, then a firm closing of the door as the girl ran back into the kitchen. 'I said no one was to be let in, missus, but . . .'

Manon looked beyond the girl to the figure standing behind her in the doorway and a chill went right through her as she saw standing there the man she had seen watching her on the street, that Griselda Duncan had hurried her away from, and that Lawrence had given orders should never be allowed into their house.

TWENTY-FOUR

Extraordinary Things

As the papers in the grate began to yellow, then to brown and smoke until at last the flame took hold and set about destroying the proof Damian Seeker had penned against him, Thomas sat back and closed his eyes. He hadn't known an hour's peace, hardly a minute's, since the day Lawrence Ingolby had told him of Andrew Marvell's clandestine visit and his warning of the spy sent by Roger L'Estrange. But now, with Anne Winter and Griselda Duncan gone, and Damian Seeker's letter against him burned to ashes, he felt the tension and anxiety leave him. Examining again the condition of his clothing, his hair, he could scarcely believe that he had allowed himself to fall into such a state. He called Will and told him to ask for hot water to be brought up. 'And a tub. I am of a mind for a good wash. And have a barber sent for, too.'

The barber arrived before the tub and made short work of trimming Sir Thomas's moustache and banishing the stubble from his jaw. With a ruinously expensive pomade, he worked a comb expertly through the knots in Thomas's hair. The pleasurable scents of orange and bergamot had almost lulled Thomas to sleep by the time the tub and buckets of hot water had been set ready for him in front of the fire. He tipped the barber handsomely and told Will to bring him a glass of sack and to fetch his satchel.

'The one with my personal correspondence. Set it down on the chair there, and put the wine on the side table. I have the leisure to read my letters at last and to consider what will be my responses.'

The boy raised his eyebrows. 'Surely the letters risk getting wet, Sir Thomas.'

'Don't concern yourself, Will. I don't intend to throw the water over them. Now, put some more coals on the fire, and then you and Frank may go to your dinner. And for God's sake, tell Frank to lock the outer door lest any more women find their way to this chamber!'

When the boys had gone, Thomas stripped and stepped into the tub. He took a cake of soap of Castille and, filling a jug with warm water from one of the buckets, he poured it over his shoulders and began to scrub. He breathed deep as the steam from the water rose to mingle with the oils in his hair, infusing the air with scents that took him back to places he would likely never see again. He did not care. His travelling days were over. Give him the scent of God's own Yorkshire earth and nothing else and he would be happy. Perhaps he might ride up to Northumberland from time to time, to the coast. The buckets emptied of warm water and his skin rubbed pink, Thomas cast about for the clean hose and stockings his page had looked out for him and slipped on the pale blue, long-sleeved silk vest that had been a gift from the King himself. Wrapping himself in his best, fur-lined dressing gown, he sank into his favourite chair. He felt as if he had rid himself of the dirt of years.

Outside, the snow was falling lightly, but Thomas was content. He rummaged in his satchel and brought out first a letter from a fellow he had known abroad who now hung constantly about the King's court in the hope of a preferment that was never going to come. He returned it to the bag. He was not in the humour for the pettiness and backbiting that such communications invariably contained.

Next, he came upon the letters from Samuel Pepys that Buckingham had brought up with him and that he'd begun to read the other night. He passed over the first two, that he'd already read, and unfolded the most recent of the three, that he had not yet begun. 'Ah, Sam, Sam,' he said, grinning to himself, 'come, tell me of your nights and your music and your lovely wife.' And as the fire in the hearth flared and crackled, and the wine in his glass went down, his friend did not disappoint him. The plays he had seen, the tribulations of life with so pretty yet unreasonable a wife, the mutual friends he had recently met with.

The glass was almost empty as Thomas came to the last page of Pepys's most recent letter.

I have been delighted to see Ingolby a time or two whilst he has been down here on your business, and am much pleased to hear from him that he has your case proceeding tolerably well, and is in hopes of seeing you settled at Langton come Easter. Then only this morning, I encountered another of our mutual acquaintance, William Briar, also down from the north, on the business of the surveyor's office in York. I stood him his dinner at the Dog on King Street that I might hear more of his news and yours . . . I forbore to ask after any of your entanglements of a – ahem – more delicate nature, as I did not wish to introduce a froideur, it being clear to me he was still much grieved by his own jilting by some pretty wench. The awkward subject largely avoided, we were merry enough, and just on the point of parting in good spirits when there occurred the most curious incident.

We were near to Scotland Yard and I on my way for a meeting with my Lord when William observed a person coming out of the little house that Roger L'Estrange has somehow got his hands on. You will recall L'Estrange no doubt – a vicious, cheerless type, who is death on any associated with the late Protectorate. I am half-persuaded he would hang even me if he could, and I take great pains to avoid him. At any rate, William was certain he recognised the fellow coming out of L'Estrange's house and raised an arm to hail him, calling him by name. The fellow faltered in his pace and glanced round, for the merest moment, but I'd lay a pound to the penny that he had heard William call him, and that he knew William as well as William did him. William called his name once more but the man increased his pace and did not turn again.

Thomas could feel his heart thumping and the paper begin to quiver in his hand so that he almost dropped the sheet.

William was in a state of the greatest perplexity, not to say offended, and would have gone after the other man, I think, had not one of my acquaintance from the navy office who had been coming along a little behind us intervened.

'I am sorry, sir,' he said, 'but I think you must be mistaken, for that man's name is certainly Godric Purvis.'

William was adamant that he knew the fellow and that that was not his name — he was determined that the fellow went by the name he had called out, and he would not have it that he might be mistaken. He seemed greatly troubled by the incident, and for myself, I cannot blame him, for I should be greatly troubled to think that any acquaintance of mine should associate with Roger L'Estrange. I trust he got to the bottom of the matter once he had returned to York and quizzed this . . .

As Thomas read the name of the man known about Whitehall as Godric Purvis, he was almost sick. 'Oh God. Oh no.'

He leapt from his chair, knocking into the tub and splashing his satchel and its remaining contents with tepid, dirty water. He stripped off his dressing gown and began to throw on his clothes, never heeding if it was today's fresh laid-out shirt or the morning's discarded, filthy item that he pulled on over the King's silk vest. Not pausing to put on a collar, he roared for Will to fetch his boots, then cursed himself as he remembered he'd sent the boy away for an early dinner.

By the time the water in his bath was fully cold, he was running through the snow falling on the streets of York, his hair crisping in the cold, his lungs burning as if they might take fire.

Lawrence burst through the door, the maid who had run to fetch him from the Merchant Adventurers' trailing behind him, Lizzie bundled in her arms. 'Where are they?' he shouted to her.

'In your study. Mistress Penmore . . .'

But Lawrence didn't pause to hear the rest. He wrenched open his office door and went into the room to be confronted by the sight of Manon sitting at his desk, in his chair, Madge Penmore in position behind her, her hand in her apron pocket, and seated opposite them, a man whose back was to him but who had turned around at his entrance. Lawrence looked from Manon to Madge and back again.

'What's going on?'

'This is Major Ogilvie, Lawrence. He claims to be a friend of Sir Thomas's. He is looking for Grizel Duncan. I have not been able to help him, and he insists on speaking to you.'

The man stood up and Lawrence Ingolby found himself appraised by a pair of hard grey eyes.

'I'd thank you to sit back down, Major,' said Lawrence, and Ogilvie did. Lawrence then walked slowly around his desk and placed a hand on the back of his wife's chair. 'You get on back through to the kitchen, love. Lizzie'll be wanting you. You too, Madge. See that new lass isn't burning my dinner.'

Madge nodded towards the new arrival, whose insolence had clearly aggrieved her. 'I told him you'd see no one till after your dinner.'

'You did right, Madge. You go and see to the dinner, though.'

As the old woman followed Manon out of his office, Lawrence went to close the door behind them, and stopped Madge. A finger to his lips, he pointed to her apron. Understanding, she slipped her hand inside and handed him the pistol, which he thrust into the belt beneath his jacket. 'Scotch collops today, is it, Madge?'

'Aye, Master.'

'I look forward to them,' he said, closing the door behind her. Then he went across the room and took up his accustomed seat behind his desk.

'Right, Major Ogilvie. State your business.'

As their belongings were loaded onto a cart to be carried to King's Staith, Anne Winter and Grizel walked down through the town. Having left their horses at King's Manor to avoid the difficulties of travelling over the snowy moors, they would return to Northumberland by water. First, though, they must perform their last duty in York, and then their obligations to L'Estrange would be over.

They walked towards Colliergate. Grizel would deposit Anne's letter to L'Estrange, exonerating Thomas Faithly of all suspicion, at the safe postal drop in the church of All Saints Pavement.

The snow continued to fall. Anne watched from across the street as Grizel rapped on the door of the church. As she'd passed down this same street yesterday, something had taken her attention that she had meant to tell Grizel because she was sure that it would have amused her. She couldn't now for the life of her recall what it had been, but it would come to her.

The verger had taken his own good time in coming to answer to Grizel's peremptory knocking, and Anne smiled as she heard the maid's chastisement of his tardiness.

'What you want?' he asked when he at last appeared, the very picture of disgruntlement.

Anne mouthed the words as Grizel spoke them. She had heard them so often, in so many places as they'd travelled around on L'Estrange's business, that she fancied she could render Grizel's very voice. 'I have a blackbird I would have you take care of.' A blackbird that would sing its song from Anne's pen to L'Estrange's ears. Nothing of the verger's disgruntlement went, but he did at least open the door and step aside to accord Grizel admittance. Grizel was not long in the church, but Anne found herself grow colder and colder as she waited. The tips of her fingers were always the worst. She was sorry she had sent down her hand muffler with the blankets and other things for use on the barge from King's Staith. That was it! She remembered, smiling as Grizel finally emerged from the church and crossed the road towards her.

'Did all go well?' she asked.

'Of course,' said Grizel. 'You surely do not need to ask.' She started to walk on. 'Anyway, what is amusing you?'

'Oh, I just remembered something I saw here yesterday that I had meant to tell you of and had forgotten in all the business of packing to leave, but it did bother me and I could not get to the nub of it.'

'What was it?'

'There was a young man coming out of All Saints there as I passed yesterday, with the bad-tempered verger closing the door on him just as he just did with you. There was something familiar about him, but I could not quite get it because I was so distracted by the ridiculous muffler he wore – the most violent-coloured thing. Oh, Griz, I know you would have to have seen it for yourself to appreciate just how— Grizel, what is the matter?' The housemaid's face had turned as grey as a headstone.

'When was this, Anne?'

'Yesterday. Late morning, I think. While you were still with the Ingolbys.'

'Tell me about the muffler.'

Anne was confused. 'The muffler? It was the *man* I couldn't place.' But the look on Grizel's face admitted of no mistake. 'All right then. Well, it was knitted as if of yarn leftover from a jester's outfit that had been thrown out by a band of travelling players. And the work of it appeared very lumpy and ill-done.'

Grizel swallowed, her face even paler. 'And the young man, what did he look like?'

Anne tried to summon a clearer memory of the man, of his face and his shape, and as she did so she felt herself grow colder. 'He was . . . a little above medium height. Broad shoulders. Fair, straight hair coming to just below his ears. A farmer's face. And . . . the peach.'

'What?' said Grizel, her face screwed up in incomprehension. 'I don't know where you think he would have found a peach, at this time of year, but the man you describe is Madge Penmore's grandson, Jedediah, and he should have been off on a barge to Hull by that time.'

Anne felt a jolt of shock. Suddenly, she knew where she had seen the man before, and it had not been in York. 'A peach,' she repeated, her words coming slowly. 'Over two years ago. In London, I sold him a peach and I watched him bite into it.' Even as she said it, she knew that she was right and that Grizel was also right. 'Lawrence Ingolby's clerk.' She looked back at the church that had been their postal safehouse for mail to and from Roger L'Estrange. 'Lawrence Ingolby's clerk that has been living with them for . . . what?'

'Two years,' said Grizel, her voice almost a whisper.

'He was at All Saints yesterday. Sending a blackbird to Roger L'Estrange.'

Mindless of the people around them and almost heedless of the state of the streets, Anne Winter and Grizel Duncan began to run, slipping past carters and hawkers and merchants going home to their dinner, forcing startled townsfolk to step quickly aside, out of their way. As they turned the corner onto Fossgate, Grizel slipped and would have fallen under the hooves of the shire horse pulling a fast-approaching brewer's cart had not Anne caught hold of her arm and pulled her clear. They stopped, shaken, and began again, taking more care with their steps. They were hardly past the second door on the street when they realised Thomas Faithly was there ahead of them, banging on the door and shouting Ingolby's name.

'All right, all right.' Lawrence Ingolby pulled open the door with one hand and readied his pistol with the other. 'What in God's name, Thomas?' He lowered his pistol and pulled his friend inside, about to shut the door again when he saw Grizel Duncan and Anne Winter a few yards behind him. He waited till the women were also into the house before closing the door.

'What . . .' he began.

'Where's your housekeeper, Ingolby?'

'My housekeeper? Thomas, are you—'

But Grizel Duncan had come past him and was heading for the kitchen. Ingolby stopped her. 'No, Mistress Duncan. You must go to my study. There is someone there you must see.'

The woman's face went the colour of curdled milk and

he thought she might attempt to run, but instead she said, 'I will, but first we must find your housekeeper.'

'Madge? What on earth do you want Madge for?' But Thomas Faithly, ignoring him, was already in the kitchen with Anne Winter having run in after him.

Madge was standing at the door to the back yard, her hands balled into fists where they gripped her apron, a look of terror on her face. Manon was on her feet and about to go to the old woman.

'Stay where you are, Manon,' said Thomas Faithly, holding up a hand to stop her.

'But . . . Lawrence?'

Her husband could only shake his head, no more idea what was going on than had his wife. Anne Winter was now standing in front of the housekeeper.

'Where is your grandson, Mistress Penmore?'

'What do you mean, where's her grandson? Jed's gone to Hull,' said Lawrence, becoming irritated.

'I don't think he has, Lawrence,' said Thomas softly.

Tears had formed in Madge Penmore's eyes and were beginning to roll down her reddened cheeks. She slumped down the door and came to rest on the floor, her chest heaving with sobs.

'Madge!' cried Manon, trying again to go to her, but again Thomas stayed her.

'Where is he, Mistress Penmore?'

'I tried to stop him,' she protested. 'He's a good boy. He was always a good boy, he just got in with the wrong sort.' She stopped for a huge blow of her nose. 'It was his mother's fault, taking him away to London when my Henry died. That's where all the trouble began.'

Lawrence felt a terrible dread take hold of him. 'What are you saying, Madge?'

She looked up at him, her small, red-rimmed eyes pleading. 'That's why I come here, to keep an eye on him, and to look after you all, make sure no harm come to you. Soon as I knew he'd come back to York, I knew it couldn't be for anything good. But he's been such a good lad ever since I been here, I thought he'd put all that other stuff behind him.'

'What other stuff?' said Lawrence.

Madge shook her head, her plump cheeks sodden. 'He got in with the wrong sort. Bad lads, thieving, gambling, catching folk out at night. Got caught with the rest of them and put in Newgate – my Jedediah in Newgate! All because that wicked daughter-in-law of mine took him away from me, to London.' She sniffed as if to recover some of her old dignity.

'And what happened in Newgate?'

'Well,' said Madge, getting into her tale, 'there was a man came round, a gentleman, looking, he said, for likely lads to save from their certain doom. Saw straight away that our Jedediah was a cut above the others, a bright lad, just like our vicar had always said when he was a boy. He took Jedediah out of there and set him to work for him, and very well Jedediah did for him too, before he came to York.'

'What was this man's business?' asked Sir Thomas.

Madge shook her head again. 'I don't know. Jedediah never told me, only that he was a very important man that knew the King and all sorts, and that his work was not to be spoken about. When I saw him back in York, he wouldn't speak about his old master and said I was never to mention his name again, so I was sure the fellow had thrown him off and feared Jed might go back to his old ways.' She looked from Lawrence to Manon. 'That's why I come here, to make sure he didn't fall in with thieves and gamblers again. And he's been a good lad, has he not, Master? Never a minute's trouble since and there's him away to Hull for Sir Thomas's papers and he'll be back and all will be . . .'

As Madge dissolved again into tears, Anne Winter asked. 'This man's name, that was his master in London, it was Roger L'Estrange, was it not?'

Lizzie Ingolby, watching all with her kitten gripped close to her chest, turned her head and stared at Thomas Faithly as at someone hard of understanding. She spoke one word, very deliberately, to him. 'Shed,' he thought she said, at first, just as he'd thought weeks ago when he'd asked her who had enticed her away after the kitten. Then she said it again, 'Jed.'

Manon Ingolby dropped the cup she'd been holding and Thomas stared, appalled, from Lizzie to Lawrence. In that moment, Lawrence saw it all – William Briar's shouting at Jed when he'd come to this house on the morning of his death, Jed's supposed failure to find him that day, the clerk coming home late to dinner, his clothes apparently ruined with dirt stains that must have been blood. Then there had been the attempt to cast suspicion on the stonemason Ralph Plowman – who else would have thought of that but the person who'd helped Lawrence draw up William Briar's case against Juliet Venn? And there had been the ploy to mislead them over the causes of the break-in, by taking only Sir Thomas's papers . . . it went on and on. Lawrence found himself gripped by an impotent fury, so that he hardly heard when Anne Winter put the question to the distraught old woman. 'Your grandson's name isn't Jedediah Penmore at all, is it?'

While the questioning of Madge Penmore had gone on in the kitchen, Grizel had slowly stepped away, back from the huddle around the housekeeper. Her first thought on hearing what Ingolby said when she arrived had been to get out by the back and into the maze of vennels that spidered through York. But Madge Penmore herself was blocking the back exit from the kitchen, so Grizel decided there was nothing for it but to quietly go out by the front.

She had backed into the hall without anyone in the kitchen having noticed, and now turned around, ready to make for the front door. She froze.

David Ogilvie stood there, watching her. 'No, Griselda,' he said, 'I think you have run far enough, do you not?'

Grizel turned back to look at the group in the kitchen,

wondering if she might somehow force her way through them, to freedom, but Ogilvie had his hand on her arm. She moved her other hand to the knife she kept in a pocket beneath her cloak but before she could reach it, he had hold of her wrist.

'No,' she said, glaring now at Ogilvie. 'I will not burn for him.'

Ogilvie heaved a great sigh. 'Mistress Duncan, you are the most unconscionably stubborn woman I have ever encountered. You will give me a quarter-hour of your time and then may the Devil take me if you ever hear from me again.'

With no option, Grizel allowed herself to be led into Lawrence Ingolby's study. As she took a seat by the unlit fire, she heard the click of the lock turning in the door. The man came and stood across the hearth from her, his elbow resting on the mantelshelf, on which he had placed the knife he'd removed from her pocket, along with the key he had taken from the door.

'My name is David Ogilvie,' he began.

'I know who you are,' she said. 'You are kin to the Ogilvies of Boyne.'

'That's right, on whose lands your husband, William Ogilvie, grew up. I was also his commanding officer in the late wars.'

'I will not burn for him,' she repeated. 'I will kill myself first, but I will not burn for that man.'

'You will do neither,' he said, exasperated. 'That is what

I have been trailing round York these last few days trying to tell you, since first I caught sight of you here.'

Grizel felt a frown forming, almost indignant at the unexpected turn in the conversation. 'I don't understand,' she said.

'As has been evident, so now you will hear me out. I was your husband's commanding officer. He was a ruthless soldier who kept good discipline in the camp and in the field, but it was also evident to me and others that he took too great a pleasure in . . .' He paused, searching for the right phrase.

'The brutality?' she offered.

He looked at her a moment and then looked away. 'Yes. In the brutality, the inflicting of pain, in the killing and in the aftermath.'

Grizel made to get up. 'You have wasted your time, Major, if you have sought me out expecting this to be news to me.'

He took a step forward to stay her. 'I know full well that it isn't news to you. I also know that seven years ago, in a house near the cliffs at Findlater, you killed him.'

Grizel sat down again. It had always been going to come to this, eventually. She could see it all as if it were being played out in front of her. She could smell the sea, hear it over the sounds of the sheep outside, the shrieks and cries of the seabirds. She could smell her husband too, sweat, tobacco and ale, and she could see his arm raised, fist clenched and the familiar smile on his face. She had kept a knife with her then too, beneath the straw of the mattress, and as he had raised his fist to the full extent of his arm, opening up his chest, she had taken that knife from beneath her and plunged it, up to the hilt, into his heart. Then she had taken every penny she could find and fled, dousing herself in water from burns to wash the blood from her, until she had found a boat to take her far, far from Scotland, where the law decreed that a woman deemed guilty of murdering her husband should burn at the stake. She closed her eyes and said nothing.

'A neighbour saw you fleeing,' continued David Ogilvie. 'A woman who knew what manner of man your husband was. She fetched her husband and he fetched me, and together we took William Ogilvie and we threw him off those cliffs.'

Grizel opened her eyes, but Ogilvie carried on speaking.

'And then we got hold of an old ewe and threw her in after him. By the time they washed up at Burghead a few weeks later, you would have been hard put to tell the one from the other. Other than yourself, me, that neighbour and her husband, no one on earth knows anything other than that William Ogilvie went over the cliffs at Findlater, trying to save one of his sheep. The neighbour swore to anyone who asked that you had left him weeks before, to return to your own people in Buchan. There is not a soul who mourns him.'

Grizel was staring at David Ogilvie, her hands over her mouth, fearful that she would say something to break the spell, that this man would disappear and this encounter never have happened. He took another step towards her and crouched down in front of her. 'I don't know how it is that you have survived these last few years, Mistress Duncan, I don't know how you came to fetch up in the company of Anne Winter, and I have no wish to know what you have done since then, but I am here to tell you that wherever you have been, however far you have run, you need not run, nor hide, any longer.'

EPILOGUE

Massachusetts, New England

February 1663

The deciphering of the letters he had managed to find, at last, at the Ingolbys had taken little time, once he had managed to get back down to London, having got a place on a boat down from Hull. L'Estrange had been pleased, for once, his brief visit to York having been filled with threats as to what would happen if Godric did not fulfil that part of his mission soon. With the money in his pocket, a full half now of what he had been promised for the completion of his task, Godric had considered melting away, beginning a new life of his own. He had, after all, lived with a second name for long enough, why not a third? Purvis to his mother's people in London, Penmore to his father's in York. Madge had never liked his given name of Godric, and had been overjoyed when he'd said he'd rather be called for her father, Jed. What name might he go by now, that he could make himself anew without any of them?

He'd been excited, for a while at least, at the prospect of

his voyage to this new country, and the possibilities it might offer him, but what excitement had survived the rigours of the voyage and the sermonising of his fellow-travellers had died away to nothing after a day or two ashore. There was a deal too much emphasis on work and on God in Boston, and Godric was not sure it would be the place for a young man like himself to make his money and his mark. There would be opportunities elsewhere, further south.

It would not be so cold further south either, thank God. He was sick of the cold. Winter had yet to take itself off from New England, although everyone assured him the snows and frosts had not been near so bad this year as they often were. Some claimed even that there had lately been tremors in the earth, and looked to God's displeasure for the cause. This further determined Godric on getting his business here done and being off as soon as possible – he had heard more than enough of God's displeasure from his grandmother. He was done with God's displeasure.

Nonetheless, it was necessary here that Godric should make some attempt to blend in. He had heard, in secret corners aboard ship and more openly in the taverns and ordinaries of Boston, murmurings about the trackers sent from across the ocean, assassins come to hunt down those who had stood high in Oliver's service or to bring them to public trial and execution at home. It was clear from the tenor of these conversations that such trackers would not be made welcome in Massachusetts. Godric must certainly blend in. And so he had put on a mien of piety, and spent a little more of L'Estrange's

money than he might have wished, to bolster his claim to be
a young man of means, thinking to marry and bring his bride
to the godly city state, but first he would find a business to
invest in, and had a mind to do so in logging.

Logging! Tobacco, more like, and Virginia, that's where
he would go when this business was done. A man might
rise in the world there as he might never do at home, forever kept in his place by the matter of his birth. Godric
had always thought he might have done well in Cromwell's
time, but he had been just too young, just coming into
manhood as the Protector had breathed his last. 'Bide your
time,' his mother had told him. 'See which way the wind
blows.' And so Godric had, and before too long, the wind
had blown him in the direction of Roger L'Estrange.

Godric had liked the work from the start – listening in
taverns, cookshops and alehouses for mutterings of sedition,
mixing with the apprentices of printers, booksellers and
any other L'Estrange held suspect, reporting back what he
found. Break-ins and raids upon printers' shops had been
his favourite pastime, as other young men wasted theirs
hanging around the Spital Fields or the Spring Garden,
or the theatres that his foolish grandmother had been so
enamoured of. 'I have other fish to fry,' he'd told her.

There had been difficulties, along the way, and he had had
to spend much longer in York than either he or L'Estrange
had expected. To make matters worse, he had scarcely got
his feet under the clerk's desk in Ingolby's office than his
grandmother had appeared at the door, like a horsefly that

would not be shifted. Or perhaps a hawk, for she had watched him like a hawk, but eventually he had managed to convince her that he was reformed in his ways, had thrown off his old associates and employment, and aspired to a settled life. There had been times in these near-two years in York that he had almost come to believe it himself, and to be frank, life in the house on Fossgate had really not been so bad.

And then Ingolby had taken it into his head that he, or 'Jed', should be sent back down to London to be trained for a time at an Inn of Chancery, and the worlds of Godric Purvis and Jedediah Penmore had collided. L'Estrange had demanded to see him and told him in no uncertain terms that he must redouble his efforts to find out the connection between the Ingolbys and Damian Seeker, and then find out Seeker's whereabouts. To make matters worse, William Briar, one of Ingolby's own clients, had recognised him as he'd been leaving L'Estrange's house. Shaking off Briar in London had been one thing, but shaking him off back in York had been quite another. Briar's arrival at Ingolby's door early on the morning of his return from the capital had put paid to any hopes Godric had had that the surveyor might have persuaded himself he'd been mistaken. So William Briar had died that day, and alongside him had died the fantasy, so cherished by Godric's grandmother, that his life as a clerk to the humourless lawyer might soon be replaced by that of steward to a tattered Cavalier, whose glory days were disappearing into the mists behind him.

And now, three months later, Godric was in Boston, a news-sheet with the title *New England Clarion* in his hand. The news-sheet bore the unmistakable marks of Elias Ellingworth's pen. Ellingworth, as L'Estrange had lately informed him, was the brother of the woman believed to be Damian Seeker's wife. Some discreet enquiries into the newspaper man had soon elicited references to his sister, married to a carpenter, in a settlement some miles from town. When Godric relayed his story of being a man with a view to investing in logging, and declared that the carpenter might be the very man for him to approach for advice, he found little encouragement, but was told that if he was intent upon travelling further up the Jones river, he should not think of doing so without the aid of a guide.

The finding and selection of the guide had been another matter. Godric had been directed to the docks, where a succession of desperate men who would have robbed him and cut his throat the moment his back was turned claimed that they, and none other, were capable of seeing him safely to his destination. Godric knew their type – each and every one of them reminded him in some way of his father, a worthless drunk and useless thief. To go instead by established carriers as he was urged to do would have been to announce himself from miles and hours in advance, and too many mistakes of that sort had been made by the regicide-hunters in Europe for Godric to fall into the same error here. He said he had not the time to wait, for he had much to do before he left Boston on the next stage of his travels in New England. He had been on the point of engaging the least dissolute-looking of the proffered guides when a local pork merchant had intervened. 'That man is not to be trusted, sir. If you are intent on going alone into the interior, you must take with you a native guide.'

'A native?' Godric's alarm must have shown on his face.

'They know the forests and the beasts within them. They know the pathways that are safe, and the territories best avoided. If you are indeed in the hurry you claim to be, you must have a native guide. Go to the chandlery and tell them I sent you. They will find you one who is to be trusted.'

Godric had no option but to go along with what he was told, although at first he suspected he had been sent to the chandler only that he might be persuaded to buy items for his journey – shearling gauntlets, hide leggings, a beaver hat. It was as he was haggling over the price of the hat that a shadow fell across the floor in front of him, cast by someone who had stopped in the chandler's doorway. Godric felt eyes upon himself, and the hairs on the back of his neck prickle. The man he saw standing there when he turned might have been made of burnished wood. Long, black hair was pulled back tight above the shaved sides of his head and held by a broad headband of black and white shells. His cheekbones were high and his lips long, thin and unsmiling beneath a strong nose. He was dressed in what appeared to be hose and tunic of some animal hide, and had a cloak of pelts about his shoulders. From his belt hung a knife and an axe, and in his hand was a long spear, tipped with a sheer metal head. He regarded Godric without moving, and with an air of mild displeasure.

'Ninigret,' said the chandler. 'This man is looking for a guide.'

The native sniffed and lifted his chin slightly as if asking a question.

'Not long arrived from England. Wants to go to John Carpenter's. You take him?'

The man called Ninigret looked at Godric with even greater displeasure then gave a short nod.

'You best pay him now,' said the chandler.

'With what?' asked Godric. 'Beads or such?'

'Shillings,' replied the chandler. 'You pay him in shillings.'

Godric opened his pouch and began to lay out Massachusetts shillings until such time as the chandler said, 'Aye, that'll do him,' and took one for himself before handing the others to the native guide.

Godric drew closer to the shopkeeper. 'He speaks English?'

'If he feels like it,' said the chandler. 'Sometimes a bit of French too. Narragansett, mainly.' Then the shopkeeper raised his eyebrows and nodded towards the door. 'You'd best be off. He keeps a good pace.'

Godric was forced to break into a short jog to catch up with the guide who merely glanced at him and continued on his way. Soon, by means of small ferries and paths around the feet of the hills that seemed to constitute the town, they had left Boston behind them, and were headed south-westwards. They traced the banks of a river and as they went, they passed the occasional English settlement, with signs of agriculture and animal husbandry. On the opposite bank, Godric now and again glimpsed what he guessed must be native settlements. Only a few yards back from the river, on either side, were woods of oak and chestnut and hickory. From time to time the guide's head would move to the right or the left and he would remain utterly still. Godric quickly understood that he must also remain still, and silent.

By the time they had been going half a day, Godric, whose great love was a city, had come to the conclusion that the wilds of Massachusetts were even worse than the North York Moors, to which his grandmother had thought to banish him. At least on the moors, you knew what you might encounter. Here, Godric's imagination ran amok with tales he'd heard of wild beasts – bears that were not the poor, drunk, lumbering things that he had seen as a child at the Bear Garden, cats ten times the size of the worst, most feral creature that might screech the night away amongst London's alleyways. And as to the people – he looked ahead at his guide, the glints of metal from the blade of his axe, the point of his spear, and he thought of massacres that Madge had read of in the news-sheets and relished telling him of.

The trees seemed to become closer and the woods darker the further from the town Godric got, the ice floes in the river to rush by with more determination. He recalled now foolish childhood tales his father had told him, of dark powers and green men who resided deep in the forest, awaiting the wicked or unwary. He chided himself, who could traverse the darkest snickets of York or dankest London alleys without fear, that he should grow nervous here. He imagined the place might be pleasant enough in spring or summer, if not bedevilled by mosquitoes and the like. But while fish and forest fruits would no doubt be plentiful in their season, for now it was cold as a Puritan's heart and almost as bleak. They did not stop for food or drink and suddenly, when Godric's stomach had been growling a good while, the native spoke his first word in his hearing. 'Here,' he said, pointing to a path into the woods which he swiftly turned onto. They walked through the thicket, the guide's steps so silent that all Godric could hear were his own footsteps and the occasional creak or squawk from creatures in the thicket. They cannot have been going through the wood for more than half a mile when Ninigret stopped again. Ahead of him, the path opened into a clearing. 'Carpenter's,' he said, before turning and beginning to lope through the wood, back the way they had come.

Godric wasn't worried. He would need no hired guide to see him back safe to Boston. He was good at remembering his way, and his business being done as he intended it should be, the authorities could hardly detain him, an agent of the crown.

Just after his guide had disappeared, a bird darting suddenly from a bush sent Godric's hand to the hilt of his pistol he had tucked under his jacket, and he cursed the creature thoroughly. But then, amongst the scents of earth and pine and unseen animals, Godric detected a whiff of woodsmoke, and his irrational fears began to calm. He paused a moment and took some long, deep breaths until he felt his heartbeat slow. Any nerves he had would be required for the work of the next hour, the culmination of two and a half years of his life and labours on behalf of Roger L'Estrange.

The smell of smoke became stronger and the forest track started to dapple with light as he approached the clearing. He stepped off the path and went a few feet to the left instead, in order to survey the homestead from the cover of the forest.

The house was sturdy, built of wood and roofed with turf, larger and better-made than many he had seen. The smoke he could smell was curling from a central stone chimney into the clear-blue February sky. Some of the windows looked to be glazed, some covered in beaten horn or stretched hide. A porch ran along the front of the house, steps leading down into a well-kept yard, where hens pecked and a turkey strutted. Stretching behind the house was what looked to be a garden.

To the river side of the house was a barn, in which Godric could see a fat and contented cow munching on hay. A small horse and a child's pony were also in evidence, but no animal comparable to what he would expect a man of Seeker's reputed dimensions to ride. To the left of the house was what must be the carpenter's workshop, but there were no signs of life or sounds of occupation. It had not occurred to Godric that his quarry might be away from home. No matter – the business might take longer, but the results would be all the surer.

Godric took one step forward and was stopped in his tracks by a low and threatening growl. His eyes darted to the right and his heart almost leapt from his chest. Not six feet from him, at the entrance to the clearing, stood what he at first took to be a wolf. The animal was huge and grey and bared its teeth as if he were a morsel some butcher was taking his own good time in handing over. Godric swallowed and raised his hand in an attempt at pacification. The brute only growled again and bared its teeth the further. Old though it evidently was, Godric was in no doubt that the creature might rip out his throat, should it have a mind to. Godric was wondering how he might slip his hand into his jacket to withdraw his pistol without further provoking the beast when he heard a child's voice calling, 'Dog! Dog! Where are you?'

The animal's ears pricked up but he did not shift his glance an inch from Godric.

The voice came again, and Godric saw a boy emerge from the workshop and begin to cross the clearing. The boy was dark-haired, sturdy and had the look of one big for his age, at least three years old, Godric would have said. He was about halfway towards the edge of the clearing near where Godric stood rooted to the spot by what he now realised was not a wolf, but a hunting dog of indeterminate breed, when the door to the house opened and a woman with long, unruly dark hair stepped onto the porch. She carried a child of perhaps six months at her hip.

'Sam,' she called, 'what is it?'

'Dog has gone off, but I hear him growling. He's in the wood.'

The woman's look flicked straight to the wood and, Godric felt, directly to where he stood. It was a chance he must take. He called out, 'Mistress! Mistress, I beg of you. Call off your dog!'

The woman peered towards him, but he was frightened to move and show himself.

'State your business,' she said, still peering and showing no sign of doing as he'd asked.

He looked to the dog again before calling back, 'I am not long arrived from England. I am of a mind to settle here and to invest in a logging business. I was advised that your husband . . .'

The woman disappeared suddenly, then reappeared without the baby, but holding a musket. 'Sam,' she said, 'go back into the house.'

'But, Mam, Dog is—'

'This very minute, Sam, or I will tan your hide till next Tuesday. House!'

The child, whose dark, defiant eyes looked as if they might fill with tears, gave one last look towards the forest and ran back to the house. His mother pushed him through the door behind her and closed it, then stepped down from the porch and began to walk towards where Godric still stood. The musket was raised and as she drew closer he saw it was cocked and the fingers that held it stained with ink.

She stopped at last about ten yards from his hiding place

and called the dog to her. To his immense relief, with one last snarl, the creature went to take up its position at the woman's side. 'All right,' she said, not lowering her musket, 'come out.'

Slowly, trying not to look at the dog, Godric did. 'Mistress Carpenter—' he began, but with a quick shake of her head, she silenced him. 'In the workshop.'

All the better, thought Godric, preceding her across the clearing, the dog mercifully at her heels, not his.

They reached the workshop and his eyes quickly took in its structure, its nooks and crannies. Boxes of apples stuffed in straw were stacked in a corner. Along a shelf opposite him were jars of plums and of peaches, preserved in syrups. He came to a halt on one side of the workbench, thus providing himself with a buffer, however temporary, between himself and the hound. An overhanging shelf, with tools suspended from it, would create obstacles for the woman's view, and little space in which she might raise her musket. He felt the pistol he had stashed against his chest – that for the dog, first, then the knife would do for her. Godric had not practised at the butts with Lawrence Ingolby every week for nothing. He was ready.

'Now,' said the woman again, lowering her musket. 'State your business.'

Carefully, he slid his hand inside the breast of his coat, his fingers touching the reassuring steel.

'My name is Godric Purvis,' he said, beginning to slide the pistol from its place, 'and—'

But Godric Purvis got to say no more before the arm

of the hand that held the pistol was pulled back, the sleeve of its jacket being pinioned to the wall behind him by the blade of the axe which had just hurtled through the air. He hardly had time to make sense of this before his other arm was whipped back just as tightly by the blade of a long, Indian hunting knife. Godric's eyes darted to the doorway at the far end of the workshop, a doorway that had been closed when he'd come in. Standing there, observing him with his arms folded, was his Narragansett guide. Godric's mouth was moving to form a question when the blur of an arm passing in front of him was followed by a fist crashing into his cheek, and then another into his stomach, so that only the native's weapons pinioning him to the wall stopped him from collapsing to the floor.

Again, the colossal fist crashed into the other side of his face, sending teeth and blood spurting to land amongst the sawdust.

The next Godric knew, the axe and knife were being wrenched from the wall. His fingers spasmed and the pistol he'd still been holding clattered to the wooden floor. A shove in the back soon sent him after it. Tasting blood and sawdust, he reached out to grab the weapon only for a boot to come down so hard on his fingers that he heard the bones break before the searing shock of the pain went through him. Without knowing what he did, he clenched shut his eyes and screamed. When he opened them again, he saw the woman's fingers close round the handle of the pistol as she picked it up and pointed it at him.

The boot that had crushed his hand now lifted from it, only to connect with his side, forcing him from his front to his back. This being done, the heavy foot of his assailant came to rest on his chest. Godric found himself looking up into the face of the man he had spent two and a half years searching for, and in that moment, all of the dreams of the life Roger L'Estrange had offered him crumbled to dust. The man, he knew, must be fifty, but he had all the appearance of one in his prime. He shook his head as if somehow disappointed in the quality of his opponent. Then he lifted one hand and threw the axe over one shoulder, before lifting the other and throwing the knife over that. 'Here, Ninigret, you'll be wanting these back.' With astonishing dexterity, the native caught each by its handle. He grinned and then, giving a low laugh, backed out of the doorway.

Seeker now brought his face down closer to Godric's, and Godric felt himself riveted by a gaze so contemptuous it took him back to a lawyer's house in York and the eyes of a sixteen-month-old child. Seeker's voice was broad York-shire, and the calmness in it terrified him.

'Godric Purvis?' A brief snort of contempt and a paper, a letter in fact, written in a hand very familiar to Godric, was held up in front of his face before being tossed aside to lie amongst the blood and sawdust all around him. 'Well, lad, that's not what my benighted son-in-law says here. So, let's you and me start again, shall we?'

374

ACKNOWLEDGEMENTS

Much of the work, and much of the joy in writing historical novels is in the physical research, the visiting of sites and locations to be used. This book, like one of its predecessors, was inspired by my love for the city of York – I have never quite got over my astonishment at what I saw the first time I walked out of York railway station, to kill an hour or so between trains. Subsequent visits have increased that sense of wonder. The main research trip for this novel was carried out in February of 2022, as snow fell on the city and the flood waters rose, as they have done so many times before. I'd like to record my admiration for the resilience of the city's inhabitants, now and in times past, in protecting and preserving their incredible inheritance.

As always, my husband and children have supported me throughout the writing of this book, and cheerfully tolerated all the usual gloom and grumbles. Support from the team at Quercus – Flo Hare, Ella Patel and Lipfon Tang, but most especially my editor, Jane Wood – has been patient and encouraging as ever. This is the eleventh book Jane has somehow disciplined and cajoled, from whatever horror I have first presented her with, into a work of historical crime fiction, and I am grateful to her for every one of them.